Tainted Love

Sunday Times #1 bestselling author Kimberley Chambers lives in Romford and has been, at various times, a disc jockey and a street trader. She is now a full-time writer and is the author of eleven novels.

Join Kimberley's legion of legendary fans on
facebook.com/kimberleychambersofficial
and @kimbochambers on Twitter

Also by Kimberley Chambers

Tainted Love
Kimberley CHAMBERS

HarperCollins*Publishers*

HarperCollins*Publishers* Ltd
1 London Bridge Street
London SE1 9GF

www.harpercollins.co.uk

HarperCollins*Publishers*
Macken House, 39/40 Mayor Street Upper,
Dublin 1, D01 C9W8, Ireland

This paperback edition 2016

First published in Great Britain by
HarperCollins*Publishers* 2016

ISBN: 978-0-00-752179-1

Set in Sabon LT Std by Palimpsest Book Production Limited,
Falkirk, Stirlingshire

Printed and bound in the UK using 100% Renewable
Electricity at CPI Group (UK) Ltd

In memory of my dear friend David's father.
Frank Fraser
1923–2014

ACKNOWLEDGEMENTS

The more I learn about the publishing world, the more I realise how very lucky I am. I could not wish to be in a better place right now, so many thanks to the loyal readers, retailers and the amazing team at HarperCollins who made this happen.

A special mention to my blinding agent, Tim Bates, and my totally brilliant/brutal editor, Kimberley Young. Laura Meyer and Charlie Redmayne, your support has been so much appreciated. Same goes for the lovely Sue Cox, Rosie de Courcy, Mandasue Heller and Pat Fletcher who have all been part of my journey from the early days. Also Cait Davies and Emily Priestnall for helping me with computer technology.

God bless you all,

KC xx

Sometimes I feel I've got to
Run away, I've got to
Get away
From the pain you drive into the heart of me
The love we share
Seems to go nowhere
And I've lost my light
For I toss and turn I can't sleep at night

Ed Cobb

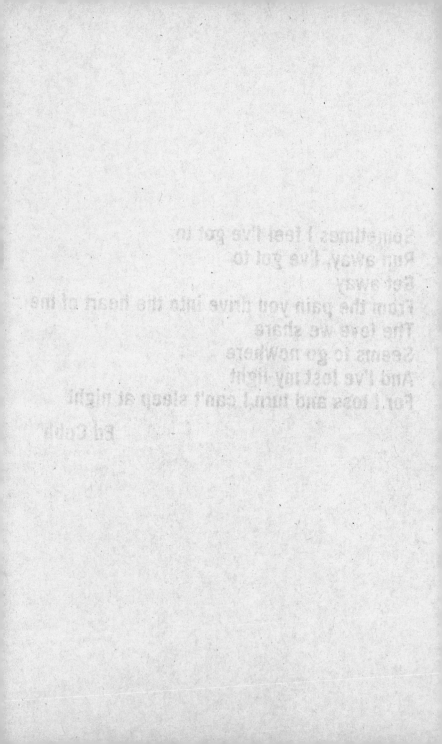

PROLOGUE

Autumn 2001

Queenie Butler slung another of her ornaments in the box marked 'RUBBISH' and momentarily felt comforted by the sound of it shattering into tiny pieces. That's how her heart felt right now: broken and beyond repair.

Delving into a bag, tears stung Queenie's eyes as she came across the first suits she'd ever bought her beloved boys. Vinny had been about nine, Roy seven and Michael a mere toddler. So smart they'd looked at their nan's funeral. Everybody had commented on how fine they were turned out, but what was the point of keeping the bloody things? Wouldn't be needing them now, would they?

Huffing and puffing, Big Stan ambled down the stairs with yet another heavy load in his arms. 'That's the last of it, Queen. The loft's empty, love.'

'Thanks, Stan. Only remembered I had stuff up there this morning and didn't know who else to bloody ask. Thanks for always being there for me and mine over the years. I was never the perfect neighbour, I know that. Too wrapped up with me own, I suppose.'

'Don't be daft! You've always been the Queen of this

street and always bleedin' will be in my eyes. Ain't gonna be the same without you and Vivvy, that's for sure,' Big Stan replied, his voice tinged with genuine sadness.

Queenie handed her neighbour a photograph. 'Remember that night?'

Big Stan stared at it solemnly. Queenie and Vivian, so happy and vibrant-looking, done up to the nines in their expensive furs. Vinny and Roy, fresh-faced teenagers, suited and booted with a menacing edge even back then. Michael and Brenda, innocent schoolchildren with their whole lives ahead of them – or so you would've thought. And young Lenny Harris, poking his tongue out for the camera. 'Course I remember it. Early sixties, was taken at the opening of the Butlers' club. Brilliant night that was, the joint packed to the rafters. Teddy Drake the comedian and Dickie doobry – what was his name? The singer.'

'Parker. Dickie Parker. Those were the days, eh, Stan? The good ol' days. Look how happy we were. Breaks my heart to think the majority of us in that photo are now dead. None died from natural causes either. Murder and bleeding mayhem killed 'em all. What did my family ever do to deserve such tragedy, Stan? Perhaps we were wicked bastards in a past life, eh?'

Big Stan's eyes welled up. 'Bless your heart, Queen. Gonna miss you, ya know. Me and the missus moved 'ere in 1944 and you were the first neighbour we ever spoke to. You were pregnant with your Vinny and I offered to carry your shopping bags. Where have all those years gone?'

'In a puff of misery, that's where.'

Awkwardly hugging the distraught woman, Big Stan mumbled, 'I wish there was something I could say or do to make things right for you, lovey. I'm truly sorry for your loss and for what happened at the wedding. Me and the missus will be attending the funeral of course and . . . Well, you've got our number if you need us for anything else in the meantime.'

'You're a diamond, Stan. What's the fucking racket outside? Because if it's that scum over the road again, mood I'm in, I'll march over there and take an 'ammer to 'em.'

Big Stan looked out the window. 'Yeah, it's them. I'll have a word. When did our wonderful Whitechapel go so downhill, Queen?'

Telling Stan to pour them both a large brandy, Queenie settled herself in her armchair and waited for him to take a seat on the sofa. 'I'll tell you exactly when things went from bad to bloody worse, shall I? Now cast your mind back to the spring of 1986 . . .'

PART ONE

Love me or hate me,
Both are in my favour.
If you love me,
I'll always be in your heart.
If you hate me,
I'll always be in your mind . . .

Anon

CHAPTER ONE

Spring 1986

'Sit yourselves down, boys,' Queenie Butler ordered. Vinny was forty now, Michael thirty-six, but both obeyed their mother as though they were still small children. Respect went a long way in their world.

'I'll make us a cuppa. I don't know what this bleedin' world's coming to, I really don't,' Vivian mumbled miserably.

Vinny and Michael glanced at one another. Their mother rarely summoned them to her house at such short notice these days, and it was obvious that both she and Aunt Viv had their serious heads on.

'What's up?' Vinny asked.

'Mr Arthur, that's what. Poor old sod had his medals stolen. Inconsolable, he is. Wasn't that long ago he was mugged, was it? That old bag Sylvie Stanley's son was involved, by all accounts.'

'Delhi Duncan or Ginger Kevin?' Michael asked. All Sylvie Stanley's kids looked very different.

'Duncan. It was him and that loudmouth with the shaved head. The one who wears the gold chains and walks about with them two Alsatians.'

'What loudmouth?' Vinny asked.

'I know who Mum means. He's only appeared round 'ere in the last few months. I'm sure someone told me Duncan is knocking out drugs for him. The pair of 'em are hanging around the betting shop most days.'

'And the Grave Maurice. That's where they nicked the medals. Both were drunk and taking the piss out of Mr Arthur, asking him questions about the war. He didn't realize they were taking the mick. Knocking on now, ain't he? Bless him. And he's gone deaf in one ear. Anyway, they sits with him and asks to see his medals, so he took them off his jacket to show 'em. They gave him back four and pocketed the other two, the no-good bastards. Big Stan was stood at the bar, saw what was going on and confronted them. Obviously, they denied taking 'em, said Mr Arthur was senile and he'd only shown 'em four. When Stan demanded they empty their pockets, the big thug threatened him. Said he knew where Stan and his wife lived and unless he wanted a petrol-bomb through his window, he was to mind his own business.'

'He said fucking what!' Vinny exclaimed.

Vivian put the tray of teas on the table. 'Getting worse round 'ere by the day, it is. Something needs to be done about it.'

'And this family owes Mr Arthur big time. If it wasn't for him getting on that bus and following Jamie Preston home, we might never have got justice for Molly. Well, we haven't exactly got our justice yet, but you know what I mean.'

'Don't worry, Mum. We'll sort it,' Vinny promised.

'I want it sorted immediately. I think because neither of you live round 'ere any more, people have forgotten how to behave. They need reminding, and Mr Arthur needs those medals back, so yous two better get cracking.'

Michael took a gulp of his tea, then stood up. 'Come on, bruv. Let's go and teach some manners.'

Mr Arthur froze as he heard the hammering on his front door. Helen, his kind neighbour who often cooked him dinners and popped in for a chat would always phone him first, and he rarely had any other visitors these days.

Creeping into the hallway, Mr Arthur yelled, 'Who is it?' Since the mugging, he never answered the door without first knowing who it was.

'It's Vinny and Michael Butler. We heard what happened yesterday and wanna help ya get your medals back,' Vinny shouted.

Vinny's deep, gruff voice was unmistakable, so Mr Arthur twisted the key. 'Sorry, lads. I don't answer the door any more unless I know who it is. Been asking the council for ages to put one of them spyholes in my door, but they haven't got round to it yet.'

'Forget the council, they're useless. I'll sort the spyhole for you, Mr Arthur. You'll have it fitted by tomorrow at the latest,' promised Vinny. 'Now, in your own time, tell me and Michael exactly what happened yesterday in the Grave Maurice . . .'

When Vinny and Michael were growing up, a man would dress to impress of a Sunday. While the wives stayed at home to knock up the only decent meal most could afford all week, the men would gather in their local, all suited and booted.

Vinny and Michael were never seen in public in anything but a suave suit and expensive shoes. 'If you want to be taken seriously in life, you need to dress like you mean business. First impressions really do count,' their mother had drummed into them from a young age. So Vinny was unimpressed by the sight that greeted them as they stepped out of Queenie's front door.

'State of those shitbags over the road. No self-respect whatsoever. Gotta be in their thirties. Don't they realize how ridiculous they look in those shell-suits?'

'Obviously not, bruv. And what is it with all that gobbing over the pavement with the other mob? Is it part of their religion or something?'

'Scum, Michael. I wish Mum and Auntie Viv would move. Worries me sick, them living round 'ere now – and I certainly want better for Ava. I've offered to buy 'em gaffs wherever they want, but neither will budge. See if you can talk some sense into 'em, will ya?'

'Hello, lads. Where you off to?' Nosy Hilda asked.

'Church.' Vinny grinned.

'I take it you heard what happened to Mr Arthur yesterday? Is that where you're going, the Maurice? They're in there, you know. Just popped in for my Guinness and saw 'em. Terrible state of affairs, isn't it?'

'You toddle off home, Hilda. There's a good girl,' Michael said, checking out his reflection in a shop window.

'Nosy old bat. No wonder Mum hates her,' Vinny remarked, when Hilda did a U-turn and walked back in the direction of the pub.

Michael handed his brother a cigarette. 'Right, how we gonna play this?'

Delhi Duncan wasn't actually from Delhi, but had been given the nickname at school because of his dark skin. He had no idea where his father was from or who he was. His mother was an old lush and a whore.

'What's up?' Russ Collins asked his latest gofer. Duncan had gone white.

'The Butler brothers have just walked in. I told you to give those fucking medals back, didn't I?'

'Chill, you prick. I'll deal with this.' Russ was from Luton, had only moved to Whitechapel recently and even though he'd heard some rumours about the Butler brothers, he wasn't scared of anybody.

Vinny Butler sneered at the big old lump with the shaved head and silly gold chains. He was also covered in tattoos. Vinny hated tattoos with a passion.

Not clocking the petrified expression on his pal's face or the smirks on the regulars', Russ decided to give it the big 'un as Vinny and Michael approached. 'Fuck me, Dunc, it's the Brylcreem Boys!' he chuckled. Vinny's thick jet-black hair was Brylcreemed backwards, Michael's parted and smoothed to the side.

'Shut it, will ya?' Duncan pleaded, before nervously holding out his right hand. 'Excuse my pal. He's new to the area. How you doing, lads? Long time no see.'

The locals were in their element as Vinny went to shake Duncan's hand, then twisted it so violently, the man screamed in agony. They were all aware of what had happened to Mr Arthur and thought it was disgusting.

When Russ threw a punch at Vinny, Michael kicked him so hard in the groin the big lump fell straight to the floor. Vinny then grabbed the massive chains around the idiot's neck and twisted them tightly. 'Walk,' he ordered.

Holding his throbbing groin and going purple in the face, Russ spluttered, 'Can't walk,' in a voice that bore a striking resemblance to a Dalek's.

'Fucking crawl then,' Michael spat, before grabbing hold of Duncan and marching him into the men's toilets.

'It wasn't my idea, I swear. I told him not to take the medals. Honest, I did,' Duncan begged.

Still clutching the man's gold chains, Vinny led him into

13

the toilet like a dog on all fours. Once inside, Vinny placed his foot on the back of Russ's head so his face was actually in the urinals. 'Where's the fucking medals?'

'I dunno what you're talking about. What medals?' Russ stammered.

Vinny stamped repeatedly on the liar's right hand.

'Me fingers – you've broken me fucking fingers!' Russ screamed. He was well out of his depth for once, and he knew it. What a shame he didn't have his Alsatians with him. Vicious bastards, were Ronnie and Reggie.

'The medals you stole off an old war hero . . .' Vinny lifted him off the floor by his neck chains in one swift movement, half choking him to death.

'In my flat. They're in my flat! It wasn't my fault. I swear on my life. He wanted to pawn 'em tomorrow,' Duncan cried, no longer in awe of Russ. Russ was a pussycat compared to the Butlers and Duncan could not believe how Michael had changed. They'd been in the same year at senior school and back then Michael had been a bit of a Jack-the-lad, and popular with the girls, but he wasn't violent. Now, however, his piercing green eyes were shining pure evil. Both he and his brother had the glare of murderers and Duncan had a nipper to think about, which was why he'd been working with Russ in the first place: to provide for his son.

'You go with him and I'll wait 'ere with this prick,' Vinny urged Michael. 'And I'm telling ya now, if I don't get those medals back, you're both dead,' he vowed, treating Russ to a sharp kick in the side of his head.

When Michael marched out the pub with the visibly trembling Duncan, the guvnor and all the customers pretended not to notice anything amiss. Even Nosy Hilda looked the other way. Whatever happened to Duncan and his loudmouth pal, nobody would dare grass. The Butlers would always stick up for one of their own, and that's why they were legends.

Mr Arthur could not hide his delight when the Victoria Cross was placed in the palm of his hand. It had been one of the proudest moments of his life when he'd been awarded that, and the other stolen medal meant just as much to him, as it had belonged to his brother who had never returned from the war.

'I dunno what to say. I can't thank you enough, lads.' Mr Arthur's eyes welled up with tears. 'I really didn't think I was going to see these again. The VC's worth a lot of money, I think.'

'A word of advice, Mr Arthur. It's up to you, but Whitechapel isn't the area it once was and if I was you I wouldn't wear the VC when you go out in future. Too many chancers about these days, unfortunately. If you want, I can lock it in my safe at the club for you?' Vinny offered.

'No. I might be wary answering my front door, but I'll never let the bastards get the better of me, Vinny. If I stop wearing it, they've won the battle. I won't let them defeat me.'

Michael and Vinny glanced at one another, full of admiration for the elderly gentleman.

'I've had a word with the carpenter pal of mine,' said Vinny. 'He'll be popping round tomorrow afternoon to sort that door out for you, Mr Arthur. I told him to leave it until after half three as I know you like your lunchtime pint.'

'Thank you so much. You really are kind. As for them other so-and-sos, they better not be in the pub when I get there tomorrow, else they'll get some of this,' Mr Arthur said, lifting up his walking stick.

Michael chuckled. 'You won't be getting any more grief

off them, trust me. They've both been sent packing with their little tails between their legs.'

Mr Arthur smiled. 'Good boys, yous two. Last of a dying breed.'

Vinny winked. 'You know our motto, Mr Arthur. Same as yours in the war: An eye for an eye and a tooth for a tooth.'

'Well? How did it go? Where's Michael?' Queenie Butler asked.

Vinny grinned. 'Pour us a Scotch and I'll tell you all about it.'

Queenie Butler clapped her hands with glee as Vinny related the day's events. 'That's my boys! Was the Maurice banged out?' she enquired.

'Fairly busy. Not like the old days though. About forty-odd in there, I'd say. Nosy Hilda was there though, so you can guarantee the whole of the East End will know by now.' Vinny laughed.

'Well, that'll give the tale-bearers something to dine out on for a while, eh? I am so chuffed you got Mr Arthur's medals back. I bet he was over the moon. What did he say to you?'

Vinny repeated the conversation. 'Touched me and Michael right 'ere, it did,' he said, patting the skin covering his heart. 'To think men like him and his brother laid their lives on the line and fought tooth and nail for this country, and for what? To be disrespected and end his days living in the dump Whitechapel has now become? Seriously, Mum, you have to move. Me and Michael walked along that High Road earlier and thought we were in a different fucking country. And this ain't just about the foreigners. The newer breed of English round 'ere now are scum. State of 'em – pure shitbags.'

'Don't start all that again, Vinny. Me and Vivvy are quite happy living 'ere, thank you very much.'

Vinny held his hands up. 'OK, I rest my case. But when it gets even worse in the next ten or twenty years and something bad happens, don't say I didn't warn you.'

When Queenie mocked her son and called him a 'worry-pot' she truly had no idea that one day his words would come back to haunt her, big time.

CHAPTER TWO

Michael Butler shot his load, kissed Katy Spencer on the forehead, then tumbled out of bed.

'Do you want me to leave now?' Katy asked awkwardly. She'd been working for Michael for the last twelve weeks, but it was only this past month they'd been a couple, so to speak.

'Yeah, you'd better make tracks. The lads are coming in early today, and we don't want them knowing jack-shit, do we?'

Katy put on the glittery mini-dress she'd worn the previous evening, then draped her arms around Michael's neck. She could never get enough kisses off her man. At thirty-six, Michael was fifteen years Katy's senior. But with his dark hair, piercing green puppy-dog eyes and cheeky schoolboy grin, he looked much younger. Katy wasn't bothered about the age gap. She'd been obsessed with Michael since the first day she'd laid eyes on him, and her friends couldn't believe how lucky she was to be waking up in his bed.

Michael gently released Katy's grip around his neck. Shagging his twenty-one-year-old housekeeper/nanny hadn't been the cleverest move he'd ever made, especially since she'd taken it upon herself to keep turning up at the club.

'Will I see you tonight?'

'Not tonight, babe. I've got a bit of business to attend to,' Michael lied.

Katy's expression changed from hopeful to crestfallen. 'OK. Do you want me to ring you after the boys have had their breakfast?'

'Yeah. That'll be cool. And remember, keep *us* to yourself. I don't want Lee and Daniel finding out. It's too soon after their mum.'

Katy smiled. Michael's words led her to believe that he was in it for the long haul. Apart from her friends, she'd told nobody. Her parents were both regular church-goers who would have a fit if they thought she was dating Michael Butler.

When Katy left, Michael sat down on the edge of the bed and put his weary head in his hands. Shagging Katy was all Bella's fault, and Vinny's. His brother had convinced him jumping back in the saddle would help mend his broken heart. It hadn't worked. Fucking Katy meant nothing to him. It was just sex and would never be anything else.

Bella D'Angelo packed the rest of hers and her son's belongings into the Gucci suitcases. She couldn't stay in Sicily any longer. It was doing her head in and, as much as she adored them, so were her parents.

'Mummy, will Michael be coming to see us when the plane lands?'

Bella stroked the hair of her pride and joy. Antonio would be five soon and he was a wonderful child. Polite and intelligent, her son had everybody he met eating out the palm of his hand. Apart from his dark hair and piercing green eyes, he was thankfully nothing like his father.

'Rupert's picking us up from the airport, darling. Mummy has lots of work to catch up on,' Bella explained, referring to her gay PA. Rupert had been running her modelling agency while she'd been skulking in Italy.

'Will Michael be waiting for us in Chelsea when we get home?' Antonio persisted.

Bella forced a smile. 'We'll see Michael soon. Now go and spend some time with Nonna and Nonno. They're going to miss you so very much.'

When Antonio skipped happily away, Bella felt that awful lurch in her stomach that she experienced so often these days. She loved Michael Butler with all her heart, but was dreading looking him in the eyes. Fate was a bastard at times, it really was.

'Morning, Mum. You OK?' Vinny Butler asked.

'Not bad, love. Ava's gonna play over at Susan's with Destiny while we're at the cemetery. We can pick her up before we go to lunch,' Queenie informed her son.

Sneering, Vinny shook his head. 'I ain't having her going in Stinky Susan's shithole. She'll catch lice or something worse. She can come with us.'

'She doesn't want to come because she can't bring Fred. You know what a little madam she is. Had the screaming abdabs earlier when I suggested the mutt stay at home.'

Vinny chuckled. Ava was a character all right, a real chip off the old block.

Hearing squeals of delight coming from the garden, Vinny looked out the window. Ava was running up and down the lawn and Fred was chasing her. The mutt had been a great addition to the family, the perfect distraction for the kid after her mother died. Ava rarely mentioned her mum at all these days. She was far too obsessed with Fred to miss Joanna.

'The dog can come with us an' all, Mum.'

'We can't take him over the cemetery, Vin. The little sod's dug massive holes in my lawn. He'll dig some poor bastard up over there.'

When Ava spotted her father watching her, she ran inside the house. Hands on hips, her Butler-green eyes sparking with anger, she announced, 'Nanny said Fred can't come with us, so I not going.'

Vinny picked his four-year old daughter up and tickled her until she begged him to stop. He hadn't even known of her existence until a couple of years ago, had found out while he was in prison. He knew he spoilt her, but why shouldn't he?

When Vinny told Ava the mutt could join them, Queenie scolded her son. 'Why do you always give into her? She knows she can play you and that's why she misbehaves. It's me that cares for her most of the time, boy, and you're making my job difficult. Sees you as the knight in shining armour and me as the wicked old witch.'

Vinny laughed. 'I've been seen as worse, Mum. Far worse. And so have you.'

Hormonal teenagers, Daniel and Lee Butler nudged one another and giggled as Katy bent over to get the hash browns out of the oven. Daniel especially had been peeved when their father had announced that he'd employed a housekeeper to pop round every day to help out with the chores. Daniel had guessed part of her job would be keeping an eye on him and Lee. However, as soon as the boys had laid eyes on Katy they'd changed their tune.

Katy Spencer had straight blonde hair that reached her bum, brown eyes, and the longest legs Daniel had ever seen. At five foot nine, she towered over him and Lee. Both boys were besotted with her and although neither would admit it, Katy had been the focus of their first ever wank.

'Who wanted sausage and who wanted bacon?' Katy asked.

Putting his hand over his mouth to control his laughter, thirteen-year-old Daniel whispered in his fourteen-year-old brother's ear. 'She can have my sausage any time.'

When both boys laughed uncontrollably, Katy smirked and stirred the baked beans. She was well aware of the effect she had on Daniel and Lee, and found it highly amusing. She could hardly wait to see the look on their little faces when they were told she was going to be their new mother.

Michael Butler laid the flowers on his son's grave. Adam was his youngest child, and had been such a loveable kid. He'd been killed last year, messing about with his brothers running across train tracks, got his foot caught. Adam's little body had been chopped into pieces by the oncoming train, God rest his soul.

Michael glanced at his watch, then lit a cigarette. He'd wanted to sell his house to rid himself of the constant reminders of Adam, but Daniel and Lee had begged him not to. Rather than put his sons through any more trauma, Michael had taken the property off the market for the time being.

Spotting his mother and Vinny in the distance, Michael walked towards them. Today would've been his brother Roy's thirty-ninth birthday, hence the meet.

Dressed in a long black coat, Queenie Butler linked arms with her strapping sons. Lots of people had stopped her in the street, praising her boys for getting Mr Arthur's medals back, and Queenie was extremely proud of them. Vinny, her first-born, owned a gentleman's club in Holborn, while the Whitechapel club that Vinny and Roy had purchased as teenagers now belonged solely to Michael.

'You all right, Mum?' Michael asked.

'I've had better days, boy. But what can ya do? No bringing back the dead, is there?'

The Enemy put the hood up on his sweatshirt before he got on the train. He'd been away so long, he doubted anybody would recognize him, but it was better to be safe than sorry. One of the conditions of his early release was that he didn't travel out of Dagenham. He was currently living in a hostel there, although the nice lady at the council had promised to try and find him a flat.

Happy memories of time spent with his dad and grandparents flooded his thoughts. He never allowed himself to think about his mother any more. She'd washed her hands of him when he'd done what he did, and the Enemy was glad. She was a slag and an embarrassment to him.

When the train stopped at Whitechapel station, he leapt off and walked towards the road where Queenie and Vivian lived. His nan had despised those pair and so did he, especially Queenie. It was she who'd raised the monsters who had ruined his life, and he would now repay her in full. See how she liked her nearest and dearest bumped off for no good fucking reason. Queenie Butler would suffer all right – he'd make damn sure of it.

As proud as a peacock, Queenie Butler strutted along Roman Road market with her sons either side of her. It was rare they accompanied her here, especially on a busy market day and she was aware of the dolly birds' admiring glances. So handsome her boys were. Stood out in a crowd wherever they went.

'Daddy, that nasty lady nearly stood on Fred,' Ava squealed.

'Carry the dog for her, Mum. Me and Michael can't

exactly walk about cuddling a lapdog, we have a reputation to uphold,' Vinny chuckled.

When her sons were suddenly surrounded by a group of people wanting to chat with them and shake their hands, Queenie could've burst with pride. She'd raised her boys to be somebodies in life and they'd exceeded all her expectations. Feared and respected in equal measure, Vinny and Michael were now seen as kings of the East End. The only family who could even hold a candle to her boys were the Mitchells out of Canning Town, and they were Vinny and Michael's friends.

'Nanny, I want a poo-poo,' Ava announced, tugging her grandmother's arm.

Telling her boys she would meet them in five minutes outside Woolworths, Queenie led Ava towards the nearest toilets.

'Is my daddy famous, Nan?' Ava enquired innocently.

Queenie couldn't help but smile. 'Yes, darlin'. Your daddy is a legend.'

After indulging in pie and mash for lunch, Vinny Butler suggested they leave behind the hustle and bustle of the market, and instead have a drink in the Palm Tree.

'Not been in this boozer since your loser of a father brought me 'ere when we were courting. It's not changed much. Got a good old days feel about it,' Queenie reminisced.

'Roy brought Colleen here as well. The day he proposed down the Roman, they came here to celebrate afterwards. You heard from that slag lately?'

'Don't call her that, Vin. Colleen is a decent girl, that's why your brother loved her. I know you think she moved on too fast, but it was Roy who ended things with her. She was brilliant, caring for him after the accident.'

Roy Butler had been shot in the head outside his club

in the early seventies – hit by a bullet that had been meant for Vinny. When he finally awoke from his coma, he'd been told that he'd never walk again. For a respected man who'd lived to walk the walk and talk the talk, it was a crushing blow. Unable to cope with his disabilities, Roy had ended his own life in 1976 – by shooting himself in the head. He left behind one child, Emily Mae, who lived in Ireland.

Michael raised his glass. 'To a top brother and a true legend.'

Vinny and Queenie chinked glasses. 'To Roy,' they said in unison.

Bella D'Angelo shut her eyes, thankful that Antonio was fast asleep at last. She badly needed some thinking time.

It had been nine years ago that she first set eyes on Michael Butler, back in the spring of 1977. She'd gone to the Carpenter's Arms with a pal, and her first memory of the immaculately turned out man she would fall in love with was how much he looked like the pop star David Essex.

Their affair had been short and sweet, but so very passionate. Michael had admitted to Bella early on in their relationship that he was in love with her, but he'd still chosen to end things. He'd been married to Nancy at the time and had called it a day for the sake of his young sons.

Shortly after Michael broke up with her, Bella moved to New York to start afresh. Back then she'd been a catwalk queen herself, so there'd been no shortage of male admirers. Bella had dated many, but none had matched up to Michael. It was on one of her trips back to London that Bella had met Antonio's father. She'd been in a club up town with a friend and had spotted a guy who had reminded her of Michael. He wasn't quite as good looking, but had the same colour hair, green eyes and that same gruff East End accent.

A steamy sex session had followed in a hotel. Bella had been rather tipsy, and had totally let her hair down. It had been her idea to indulge in a bit of dirty role play. How ashamed she felt about that now.

'You OK, Mummy?'

Bella opened her eyes and smiled at her beloved boy. She was anything but OK, had even toyed with staying in Italy for good. But she could not get Michael out of her mind. Nights were the worst. His handsome face would haunt her dreams and she'd wake up happy, until remembering the party and the smirking face of the bastard who'd fathered Antonio. No way could Michael ever find out what she'd done. It would totally destroy him.

Strolling confidently into the fishing-tackle shop, the Enemy headed straight for the counter. 'I need a decent filleting knife, mate.'

The owner asked his age, then showed him half a dozen. 'That one's your best bet, but it's expensive. Like most things in life, you pay for what you get.'

'I'll take it,' he replied, taking a wad of notes out of his tracksuit pocket. He wasn't short of dosh. He'd sold cannabis resin while inside, and was continuing to do so now he was out.

Fifteen minutes later, the Enemy was on a District Line train on his way back to Dagenham. He hoped his dad and granddad were looking down from heaven and were proud of him. That's if his granddad was even in heaven, of course. Rumour had it, Vinny had put him in a cement mixer and he was now propping up the flyover along the A13. That's what Billy Carver reckoned anyway.

Turning his thoughts to his purchase, the Enemy smirked. Fish were harmless and didn't deserve to be filleted. As for the Butlers . . .

CHAPTER THREE

'Morning, Queen. Silly-boy lemon's strutting up and down the garden again with his holster and cowboy hat on.'

Queenie chuckled. She and her sister Vivian lived next door but one to each other, and the neighbours in between them were a proper pair of notrights. They were harmless enough though and provided Queenie and Viv with hours of entertainment.

'Got a houseful today, Viv. Little Vinny's coming, Michael's bringing the boys, Vinny and Ava will be here – an' he's invited Jay Boy and Jilly.'

'The more the merrier,' Vivian replied. She actually wanted to add, bar one, but chose to hold her tongue. Her and Queenie had made a pact to stop dragging up the past and instead concentrate on the future.

'Answer that for me, Viv.'

Vivian picked up the phone, had a short conversation, then returned to the kitchen. 'It was Michael. Albie's had a fall. He's OK, but Michael didn't want to leave him today, so I said it would be all right for him to come for dinner an' all.'

Slamming her potato peeler on the kitchen counter, Queenie turned to her sister, eyes blazing with fury. 'I don't want that womanizing old tosspot round 'ere, thanks very much. You had no right to tell Michael he was welcome. It's my bloody house and it's gonna be overcrowded as it is.'

Vivian sighed with annoyance. Queenie and Albie had split up donkey's years ago, yet still her sister wouldn't let bygones be bygones. 'Make me laugh, you do. Ain't it about time you practised what you preach? If I can be adult enough to breathe the same air as that murdering bastard of a son of yours, why can't you at least be polite to poor Albie?'

Seething, Queenie turned her back on her sister and took her anger out on the saucepans, banging them about like drums.

'Well?' Vivian spat. Lenny had been her only child. A wonderful, loving lad who'd never let his learning difficulties hamper his life. Unfortunately, Lenny's life had been wiped out at the tender age of twenty thanks to Queenie's eldest son. Not only had Vinny Butler taken her innocent boy to a knocking shop, he'd driven them home while out of his nut on drink and drugs and smashed the bastard car to smithereens. Vinny being Vinny, he'd walked away without a scratch, but her beloved son hadn't been so lucky. Poor little sod had been virtually beheaded.

'Me, make you laugh! Well, let me tell you a few home truths: you make me laugh twice as bleedin' much. "Poor Albie" indeed! You hated the bastard when I was married to him. Called him every name under the sun. I've met some two-faced fuckers in my time, but you're top of that list, Vivian Harris. Molly would still be alive if that disgusting old toad hadn't stuck his John Thomas up Judy Preston's snatch. Now piss off back to your own house. How dare you put that vile excuse of a man before me! Me and you are finished. You're no sister of mine.'

*

Michael Butler had just got out the shower when he heard the front door slam.

'It's only me, Michael. I happened to be passing, so thought I'd pop in to see if you or the boys needed anything,' Katy shouted out.

Michael gritted his teeth in annoyance. Sunday was Katy's day off and he certainly hadn't entrusted her with a key so she could come and go as she pleased. He dressed hurriedly and bounded down the stairs. 'Pop up the shops for me, boys. I'm out of cigarettes. Tell Bob they're for me.'

'I'll go if you want?' Katy offered. She liked to make herself indispensable.

'Nah, they'll go,' Michael replied, handing Lee a fiver.

Waiting until the boys were out of earshot, Michael asked, 'So what you doing 'ere on a Sunday? It's meant to be your day off.'

Not prepared to admit she'd missed Michael so much that she'd driven past purposely in hope his car would be there, Katy pretended she was on her way to visit a friend. 'We're going out for lunch,' she added.

'Same 'ere. I'm taking the boys out. Was meant to be going round my mother's, until it all kicked off.'

'Oh my God! What's happened?' gasped Katy, putting her hand over her mouth for full dramatic effect.

'Oh, nothing major. My mum had a row with my aunt, that's all. You best get off then. As soon as the boys come back, I'm making tracks.'

Katy drank a mouthful of tea, then stood up. 'I might be popping to the club tonight with a friend. Please don't worry, she doesn't know about us.'

Wanting to yell 'There is no fucking us!' Michael instead nodded dumbly. Why was it men could separate love and sex yet women couldn't?

*

Vinny Butler laughed as his grandson tried to chase Fred around the garden. He'd mastered the art of walking, but not running yet.

'Oops-a-daisy,' Queenie said, picking the child up.

Oliver Butler held his great-granny's face in his tubby hands. 'Foo, Nana, foo.'

'He's only asking for grub again. No wonder he weighs a ton, the cheeky monkey,' Queenie chuckled. She was still livid about her sister's betrayal and harsh words, but was determined not to let the argument spoil her day.

'Give us him 'ere, Nan. I got a whiff of something nasty. It's either him or you've had the accident,' Little Vinny chuckled.

'I'll put arsenic in your dinner, you, if you carry on,' Queenie joked. She was genuinely proud of the way her grandson had turned out. He'd been a horror as a child and a teenager, causing her no end of grief, but meeting Sammi-Lou and becoming a father had been the making of him.

Vinny Butler sat next to Sammi-Lou. 'Not long until he makes an honest woman of you now, eh?'

As Sammi-Lou Allen excitedly chatted about her forthcoming wedding, Vinny listened with a wide grin on his face. His son had been an embarrassment to him as a youngster, especially when he'd gone through that skinhead stage and knocked about with that weirdo Ben Bloggs. Thankfully the lad had changed beyond recognition. He now worked with Vinny in the Holborn club and had proved himself to be an asset to the business, with an astute brain on him.

It was as well for Little Vinny that neither his father nor his grandmother had any idea that he'd done more than act up a bit and run wild during his teenage years. And there was no way Sammi-Lou would be happily making wedding plans if she knew she was marrying a child killer. And God help Little Vinny if his father ever found out that the three-year-old he'd throttled to death was his own little sister.

Michael and Albie Butler were in the Royal Oak.

'Why didn't the boys come with us?' Albie asked.

'I couldn't drag 'em away from the pool table, so I left 'em a tenner for a pizza. Keeps 'em out of trouble, that cabin I had built.'

Albie smiled. 'I'm so glad you ain't moving out of Barking, boy. I never said it when you put the house up for sale, but I wouldn't arf've missed ya.'

Michael squeezed his old man's hand. Unlike Vinny, he'd always been close to his father. Now sixty-six, Albie's once thick hair had thinned a bit over the years, but it was still jet black. He kept himself smart, always wearing a suit, and despite everything he'd been through he hadn't lost the cheeky twinkle in his eyes.

'How's Bella, son? You spoken to her lately?'

'No, I left her alone after she said she needed some space. She rung me last week, but I didn't call her back. Done me up like a kipper, she did. Vinny said she wouldn't return from Italy and he was right. I don't even believe her nan was dying. She obviously just got cold fucking feet.'

'You don't know that for sure and you shouldn't listen to your brother. You know what Vinny's like. When has he ever been in love, eh? Do what your heart tells you. Bella adored you; I could see that the night of the party. You need to call her back, see what she wanted.'

'Bit late now. Got meself in a right pickle, I have. The boys' nanny turned up at the club one night about a month back. I'd had a drink, she had virtually no clothes on, and . . . well, you know the rest.'

'Oh dear. Katy's a bit young for you, isn't she?'

'Twenty-one. Becoming a proper pest, she is. Keeps turning up at the club, staring at me with those puppy-dog eyes. She's got it bad, and I'm never gonna feel anything for her. After Bella, I doubt I'll ever feel anything for a bird again. More grief than they're fucking worth, women.'

'Mind she don't trap you like Judy Preston did me. Can't you tell her that I'm gonna help you out indoors and you don't need her any more?'

'Not that easy, Dad. The boys adore her. It's been good for them to have a woman pottering about the house again. I'm just going to have to let her down gently, and hope she still wants to work for me.' He shook his head ruefully. 'My mistake, I let me dick do the thinking instead of me brain.'

Albie chuckled. 'Like father, like son.'

Having given birth to three sons who'd made her so proud in life, Queenie was the first to admit her daughter was a terrible disappointment. Brenda had turned into an overweight lush and a crap mother, which was probably why Queenie had bonded so well with Jay Boy's girlfriend. In Queenie's eyes, Jilly was the daughter she'd never had.

'Jilly wants your mum to give her away when we get wed,' Jay Boy whispered in Vinny's ear as they watched the two women chatting nineteen to the dozen in front of the telly.

Vinny looked at his pal in amazement. They had first met in Pentonville prison. They'd bonded immediately, and the chirpy Liverpudlian was now Vinny's right-hand man at the club. 'You're kidding me. That will make my mum's year.'

'Straight up. Jilly's dad is dead and she doesn't get on with her own mum. She told me last night she wants your mum to do the honours.'

Vinny was about to tell his mum the good news when the doorbell rang and Queenie leapt up to answer it.

'Daddy, Fred's being rude. He's got his dingle-dangle out again,' Ava giggled, tugging her father's arm.

Hearing a commotion in the hallway, Vinny ignored his daughter and dashed to his mother's aid. 'What's up?'

'Tell Vinny what you told me,' Queenie ordered, ushering her daughter's tearful children into the house.

'Mum and Dave were drunk, and they were fighting. They smashed all the furniture up. Then Mum fell over when Dave hit her and we couldn't wake her up. We were scared she was dead, so we ran to the phone box and called an ambulance. Then we got on the train and came here,' eight-year-old Tommy explained.

'Mum's head was bleeding. We was worried the police would come and take us away,' Tara added.

Vinny glanced at his mother. Both were thinking the same thing. Neither had any time for Brenda, but she was family. Flesh and blood counted for everything and so did keeping up appearances.

Michael Butler poured another Scotch and pressed play, then rewind, then play again on his answerphone. It was the message Bella had left him last week, and he'd listened to it over and over again.

He was trying to make up his mind whether to take his father's advice and return the call when he was disturbed by a tap on his office door.

'Katy's here,' said Gerry the bouncer, sticking his head round the door. 'Said she needs to speak to you about Daniel and Lee.'

'OK, send her in.'

The club was booming to the sound of Page Three bird Samantha Fox's 'Touch Me (I Want Your Body)' as Katy walked in. Michael had no doubt that she wanted him to touch hers again. She was virtually fucking naked. 'Where's your mate?' he asked.

'She wasn't well, so I came alone,' Katy lied.

Well on his way to being slightly more than merry, Michael couldn't help but take note of Katy's pert breasts.

Aware of what the man of her dreams was staring at, Katy felt her confidence soar. 'Aren't you going to offer me a drink?' she asked, sitting on his lap and rubbing his thigh.

Michael sighed as his erection grew. What was a man to do?

Unaware that their father was currently in an extremely compromising position with Katy Spencer, Daniel and Lee Butler were currently discussing what they would like to do to certain parts of her anatomy.

'First thing I'd do is to take her bra off and suck them big titties,' Lee giggled.

Leaping off the chair, Daniel grabbed hold of his crotch making thrusting movements. 'I'd ram this straight up her, I would. Dad fancies her an' all, I think. I've clocked the way he looks at her.'

Lee shook his head repeatedly. 'No way. Dad's far too old for Katy. He still likes Bella. I honestly reckon Katy fancies me, ya know. Why else would she lean across the table like she did the other day? She even winked when she realized I'd seen her lils. That must mean something, eh?'

Daniel grabbed his brother in a playful headlock. 'You're making that up. I was sat at the table with ya, and I never saw her bazookas. If Katy fancies any of us, it's me. She well wants me to put my Hampton in her mouth.'

Laughing, Lee tussled with his brother. 'You wish. In ya dreams.'

*

Queenie Butler drank her sherry in one fell swoop. First the row with Viv, then Brenda getting seven bells knocked out of her. Today had been truly awful.

Not long after Tara and Tommy had arrived on her doorstep, the Old Bill had turned up. Brenda had been taken to hospital, was extremely drunk and also battered and bruised, they'd informed her.

Vinny had wanted to go straight to the hospital, then hunt down Brenda's bloke, 'Dagenham Dave' as the family called him. Queenie had known the first moment she'd ever laid eyes on the man that he was a drunken loser, just like Albie. Unable to stomach Brenda when she had booze inside her, and desperate to avoid her beloved son acting on impulse and landing himself in trouble, Queenie had insisted they visit Brenda tomorrow. It had taken some doing, but she'd managed to persuade Vinny to stay at hers tonight. He was upstairs now, settling Tommy, Tara and Ava down.

Queenie mumbled plenty of blasphemes as she poured herself another drink. On the advice of a neighbour, she'd had that drunken old priest round last Christmas. Fat Beryl was Catholic and had sworn Father Patrick could get rid of all evil spirits.

Well, the exorcism the silly old Irish bum had performed hadn't worked, had it? The Butlers were still cursed. Always had been and always fucking would be.

CHAPTER FOUR

The Enemy greeted his probation officer warmly. He'd learned how to play the system while banged up. Let the mugs think you were a reformed character and the world was your oyster.

'I've got the keys. The lady at the council said it's a decent-sized property. Near Dagenham fire station. Peverel House, to be precise.'

'Is that one of them tower blocks?'

'Yes, it is. Are you ready to view it?'

He grinned. Whatever the property was like, he'd snap the council's hands off for it. He had a plan, and once he had his own gaff, that plan would be far easier to put into action. He could almost smell the Butlers' blood.

Brenda was sitting up in bed, reading, when her mother and brother marched into the ward. She immediately threw her magazine down in annoyance. 'What do yous two want?'

Queenie stared at her once attractive daughter. She had a cut on her head, a swollen lip, a black eye and looked fatter than ever. 'What exactly happened, love? I didn't know that bastard knocked you about. Why didn't you tell us?'

37

'Because Dave isn't a bastard and he doesn't knock me about. This was all my fault, Mum. I goaded him until he snapped.'

'That's no excuse for hitting a woman. The geezer's scum,' Vinny spat, conveniently forgetting that he'd had the mothers of both of his children murdered. Karen, Little Vinny's mum, had popped her clogs thanks to a lethal dose of heroin being forced upon her. And Joanna, Ava's mother, had been killed when her car was rammed off the road by a speeding truck. On both occasions Vinny had got away with it. He knew how to stay one step ahead of the Old Bill and had made damn sure he had decent alibis while others were paid to do his dirty work for him.

'Don't start, Vin. I hit Dave first, about ten times. I bet his face looks far worse than mine. Anyway, there's no real harm done. The nurse reckons the doctor will let me go home soon.'

'You ain't going back to him, young lady. Petrified, Tara and Tommy were, poor little mites. You need to make a clean break. It's about time you sorted your life out once and for all. You need to stop drinking, lose some bloody weight and smarten yourself up a bit,' Queenie insisted.

'Where are Tara and Tommy now?' Brenda asked.

'At mine. Little Vinny's looking after 'em. Your brother is going to rent you a flat, so you can get away from Dave and start afresh.'

'Since when have yous two ever been bothered about me? I'm thirty-two, not ten, and no way are you dictating to me where I can or cannot live. I love Dave and he loves me. All couples argue, that's life. You and Dad never stopped fucking arguing, if I remember rightly.'

'That's why I chucked the old goat out. Can't see the wood for the trees, you,' Queenie hissed.

Brenda chuckled sarcastically. Ever since she was a teenager she'd had a difficult relationship with her family. Her mother especially, as she'd always favoured her precious boys over her. Even when she'd been young, Brenda had felt surplus to requirements, and that feeling had accompanied her into adulthood. It probably explained why her self-esteem was so low. 'And there was me thinking you'd slung my dad out because he'd got Judy Preston up the spout. Silly me.'

Snarling, Queenie tugged Vinny's arm. 'Come on, let's go. She's a waste of fucking space as well as an embarrassment to us. Let her go back to the tosspot and drink herself to death.'

'Hold your horses, Mum.' Vinny turned back to Brenda. 'How do you think Tara and Tommy will turn out, living in your current set-up? I know we haven't always seen eye to eye, Bren, but I wanna help you sort yourself out. Call it an olive branch. If you've got a brain, you'll take it.'

'I must be brainless then as I would rather eat dogshit than accept any help from you. Now fuck off and leave me alone, the pair of ya.'

'Come on,' Queenie ordered, tugging her son's arm again.

'You are one dumb cunt, Brenda,' Vinny said, shaking his head in despair.

'I'm not as dumb as you think, big bruv. I know you must've got rid of Karen and Joanna. Bit of a coincidence both mothers of your kids are brown bread, don't ya think? And I'm warning you now, if you lay one hand on my Dave, I will go to the police and tell them everything. And that includes Old Jack's lad, Terry Smart, Kenny Jackson and every other poor bastard in Whitechapel that disappeared off the face of this earth, thanks to you.'

When Vinny lunged at his sister, Queenie slapped him hard around the face to bring him to his senses. 'She ain't worth it, boy. Come on, we're going.'

'Bye bye. Thanks for the visit,' Brenda laughed.

Pushing Vinny towards the exit, Queenie turned towards Brenda and wagged her forefinger. 'If I had one wish, it would be I'd never given birth to you. You're dead in my eyes, girl. Dead!'

Madam Lydia's ability to see into the future was scarily accurate, and Bella D'Angelo felt her spirits soar when her spiritual guide predicted she would one day actually marry the love of her life. Bella totally believed in Madam Lydia. So many things she'd predicted over the years had come true. Including Vinny bloody Butler.

'Are you sure?' Bella mumbled.

'As sure as I can be, my love. The image is in the distance though, which suggests the wedding is too. In the forefront is this bad man. He is tall, dark and evil. But I feel you have a hold over him in some way and deep down he is scared of you. If you confront him, he will back away.'

'Are you sure?' Bella repeated.

Making a strange humming sound, Madam Lydia shut her eyes, then ten seconds later opened them again. 'Yes, he is disappearing into the distance. But you need to be the stronger person to make this happen. You need to frighten him off.'

Bella D'Angelo smiled. She had every faith in Madam Lydia, and for the first time in months knew exactly what to do. She would confront Vinny Butler, and call his bluff.

Over in Barking, Daniel Butler had the devil in him. 'Hurry up, you tortoise.'

'Where we going?' Lee asked, confused. They'd been in the middle of a game of pool when his brother had dragged him out of the cabin at the end of their garden.

'I thought we'd have a laugh. I heard Dad talking on the

phone earlier. Apparently, he bumped into dear Granddad Donald yesterday and the old git didn't even ask how we were. He crossed over the road and blanked Dad.'

'So what you gonna do?'

'*We* are gonna go in the café and wind the old bastard up. I fucking hate him now.'

'But Mary will probably be there, Dan, and she was always nice to us. Let's not start no agg. Dad might ground us if we do.'

Daniel grinned. 'Don't matter, does it? We spend all our spare time playing on the machines and pool table anyway. And if Dad grounds us, it means Katy Big Tits will visit more to keep an eye on us.'

Laughing, Lee playfully punched his brother on the arm. 'Katy Big Tits! That's well funny.'

'And so will winding up Donald be. Come on, let's run.'

Queenie Butler was well and truly on her soapbox. In Queenie's eyes, grasses were the epitome of all that was wrong with the world today. Absolute scum, and to say she was disgusted she'd given birth to one was an understatement.

'Calm down, for Christ's sake, Mum. You'll give yourself a bleedin' heart attack if you carry on like this. Don't get me wrong, Bren was bang out of order, but you know what she's like. All mouth and no action. She only said what she did to stop me giving Dave a good hiding. No way would she ever go to the Old Bill. She's trying to blackmail me, that's all.'

'Blackmail! I'll give her fucking blackmail if she ever darkens my doorstep again. Repulsed with her beyond words, I am.'

'What's up?' Little Vinny asked.

Ignoring his son, Vinny followed his mother into the

kitchen. 'Give Auntie Viv a knock. You need her and she needs you. Life's too short to fall out over silly arguments.'

'Nope. Don't want no more to do with her neither. And it wasn't a silly argument. Totally out of order, Viv was. Unless she apologizes and truly means it, that's us finished.'

Vinny led his son into the front room. 'I want you to sneak out and knock at Auntie Viv's. Tell her Brenda's been beaten up and your nan's in a right old state,' he whispered.

Little Vinny did as he was told and was back within a minute.

'Well?'

Little Vinny shook his head.

'What did she say?'

'Nan's problems have sod-all to do with her any more.'

'Didn't she even ask about Bren?'

'No. She only said what I told you, then slammed the door in my face.'

Donald Walker's face paled when he saw his unruly grandson walk in. He'd completely washed his hands of Daniel since the fiasco he'd caused at the service in honour of Nancy. 'Hold the fort a minute, Tina. I need to speak to Mary.'

Mary Walker was in the kitchen, flipping eggs. 'I know that look, Donald. What have you done wrong?'

'Daniel's just walked in with Lee. I have nothing to say to either of them. You go out front, love, and I'll take over the cooking.'

Mary sighed. She'd also washed her hands of Daniel after learning the truth surrounding Adam's death. It was Daniel who'd been taunting the ticket inspector and it had been his idea to run across those bloody rail tracks. An innocent, lovely boy Adam had been and had he not been so easily led by his older brother, he'd still be alive now.

'Go on then,' Donald urged.

Treating her husband to a withering look, Mary marched behind the counter.

'Hello, Nanny. How's you and that wonderful grand-daddy of mine?' Daniel sarcastically asked.

Determined not to rise to the bait, Mary smiled. 'We're fine, thank you. Now what can I get you?'

'Can I have a cheeseburger and chips please?' Lee asked politely. Mary and Donald weren't his real grandparents as he'd had a different mum to Daniel and Adam. His own mum had been killed in a car crash when he was young, and he'd lived with his dad ever since.

Annoyed by his brother's genuine politeness, Daniel gave Lee's ankle a sharp kick, then slouched across the counter, placing his chin on his hands. 'I'll have the same as Lee. I take it this is on the house, seeing as we're family?'

'Of course. Take a seat and I'll bring your food over,' Mary replied.

'Nah. We'll wait 'ere, eh, Lee? We wanna say hello to our beloved granddad, don't we?'

'Your granddad's out the back, cooking. Now move, Daniel, as I've got other customers to serve,' Mary ordered.

'Nah. I would rather chat to you. Any news on Mum's body? I thought the Old Bill might've found bits of her washed up on the beach by now,' Daniel said, nudging Lee with his right knee.

Mary looked at her smirking first-born grandchild in horror. Nancy's car had been found by the coastguard at the top of Beachy Head. She'd left suicide notes for them all, shortly after Adam had died. 'Get out and don't you ever come back. Go on! I never want to see you again,' Mary screamed.

Donald ran out from the kitchen. 'Do as your nan says – scarper,' he yelled.

43

Unable to stop herself, Mary burst into tears. As much as she disliked the way Daniel had turned out, part of her would always love him. How could she not when Nancy had given birth to him?

'Make me leave, you silly old cunt,' Daniel goaded, staring his grandfather in the eyes.

Lee didn't know what to do. He wasn't overly keen on Donald, but he'd always been fond of Mary. She was a very kind lady.

Aware of the dozen or so customers looking at him, a thoroughly embarrassed Donald lifted the hatch and grabbed hold of Daniel. 'Out now!' he yelled, dragging the lad along by his left elbow.

'Come on, Lee. Time to go. We only asked about me muvver and it's obvious the sharks ate her. Either that or she run off and she's still alive,' Daniel joked.

Hand over mouth, Mary Walker stood frozen to the spot.

Apologizing to his customers for the fracas, Donald led his wife into the kitchen. 'That boy is pure evil. Any reservations we had about our Christopher helping Nancy should be well and truly forgotten now.'

Mary nodded in agreement. 'Nancy did the right thing. That boy has a screw loose, and Michael would've driven her insane. She's better off without them.'

About to reply, Donald heard a shattering of glass and a loud scream. He immediately guessed the cause. A brick had been thrown through the window.

It was late afternoon by the time Vinny Butler finally made it to his club, having had a lousy morning. The gaff he owned was referred to as a 'Private Member's Gentleman's Club'. It was anything but. The premises were classy all right, but it was basically a lap-dancing joint with bunny girls as waitresses that catered for a clientele made up of just about every pervert who'd ever entered the legal profession. Judges, lawyers, magistrates and even the Old Bill visited the club regularly, along with a few politicians and yuppies. Thanks to these 'gentlemen' members, the club had made Vinny Butler a very rich man.

'Afternoon, boss,' said Paul the doorman. 'Jay Boy's popped out for a bit. He won't be long.'

'And Little Vinny hasn't turned up yet,' added his colleague, Pete. 'But it don't matter, as we're not that busy.'

Vinny Butler slapped his employees on the back, and explained he'd given Little Vinny the day off. He trusted Pete and Paul like family and treated them accordingly. Not only had they helped him dispose of the Turks last year, they'd worked for him since he and Roy had opened the Whitechapel club as teenagers.

'We heard a bit of news, Vin. Denny McCann kicked the bucket yesterday. Apparently it was a heart attack,' Paul informed his boss.

Vinny Butler raised his eyebrows. Denny McCann had once opened up a rival club and nicked a load of his customers. The bloke was only in his early fifties. 'Oh well, good riddance to bad rubbish,' Vinny said nonchalantly. 'Right, I'm off to the office. Got some phone calls to make.'

'Oh, that reminds me. A bird rung up earlier. Said it was urgent you contacted her, so I left her number on your desk,' Pete explained.

'What's her name?'

'Izzy.'

Momentarily lost for words, Vinny felt the hairs on the back of his neck stand up. She might be Bella to Michael, but she'd always be Izzy to him.

CHAPTER FIVE

Michael Butler leaned over Katy and grabbed the phone. 'Keep schtum,' he ordered. It wasn't even seven a.m. yet and whoever was ringing him at such an unearthly hour better have a damn good reason.

'Michael, it's Mary. You really need to keep those sons of yours on a tighter rein you know. Daniel is out of control and you're lucky Donald and I never called the police.'

Feeling dazed and slightly hungover, Michael sat upright. 'What you going on about, Mary?'

While Mary explained what had gone on at the café the previous day, Katy thought it would be a good idea to suck Michael's penis.

Instantly erect, Michael lay back on the pillow and allowed Katy to cheer him up while his one-time mother-in-law continued ranting. For one so young, Katy certainly knew how to give good head. He would have to jog her on soon though. The constant turning up at the club without being invited was borderline stalking.

Vinny Butler put on his black Armani suit and studied himself in the mirror. He looked mighty fine for forty and he knew it. Training regularly had bulked him up and the extra muscle suited his six-foot-two frame.

Touching his hair up with a bit more Brylcreem, Vinny thought about the phone call. She'd given nothing away, had just asked to meet up. 'We need to talk, in person,' had been her exact words.

Vinny wasn't stupid. He guessed this meet would be about Michael, yet that didn't stop his groin twitching as he thought back to that night he'd spent with her. The sex had been out of this world. She was a right raver, had made him come like a stream train. And truth be told, that was where the problem lay.

Bella D'Angelo was a dedicated follower of fashion. She had a luxury walk-in wardrobe filled with designer clothes, but today she'd decided to dress down. The thought of Vinny staring at her cleavage or buttocks made Bella nauseous, which was why she'd opted to wear a long baggy jumper, leggings and boots.

She'd tried to kill time by wandering around the local market, but had given up, unable to concentrate with the prospect of a meet with Vinny hanging over her. So Bella arrived at the bar forty-five minutes early and ordered herself a glass of wine. She'd chosen Covent Garden as it was often packed with tourists and there was less chance of anybody recognizing her or Vinny.

'Well, well, well. If it isn't the lovely Izzy. Can I get you a drink?'

Continuing to coolly flick through her *Vogue* magazine, Bella took her time looking up and replying. She was determined to have the upper hand. 'Get yourself a drink; I've already got one, thanks. And my name is Bella, so I would appreciate it if you'd address me as such.'

Slightly taken aback by Bella's cool demeanour, Vinny

ordered himself a large Scotch. He discreetly watched her from the bar. He'd put money on it she was only pretending to read that magazine. He also noted she'd purposely dressed down. Not that it mattered. She was that stunning; she'd look fuckable wearing a bin bag.

Vinny smirked as he sat opposite Bella. 'This is cosy, isn't it?'

'No, Vinny. It isn't. I do appreciate you agreeing to meet me though. We need to talk about Michael.'

'Whaddya wanna know?'

'How is he?'

'Yeah, Michael's good. Gets on with life, don't he?'

'What do you mean by that exactly?' Bella asked.

'That birds come and go, you included. Handsome man like Michael ain't ever gonna be short of female admirers.'

Bella's heart lurched. She hadn't officially ended her relationship with Michael, had just told him she needed some space. No way would he be unfaithful to her, Bella was sure of that. 'Don't fucking play games with me, Vinny. You're out your depth.'

Vinny chuckled. 'You didn't mind me playing games with you when we were holed up in that hotel. Begged me to tie you up, if I remember rightly. What's changed, Izzy? Sorry, I mean, Bella.'

Hating Vinny more than ever, Bella fleetingly worried if she should come clean to her father and let him sort the situation out. She quickly decided against it though. She could never risk anybody finding out Antonio was Vinny's child. That was her secret and hers alone.

'Want another drink?' Vinny asked cockily.

'No. I want you to listen to me carefully. I love your brother very much and I will not allow you to spoil our happiness. What happened between us was a stupid drunken one-night stand. Nothing more, nothing less. I was hoping you would've realized that by now, but you obviously haven't. So tomorrow, I am going to visit Michael and tell him everything. And believe me, Vinny, I will not leave one detail out. Michael needs to know the truth.'

Vivian Harris felt like a lost sheep. It was all right for Queenie when they had a row as she had all her kids and grandkids around her, but now that Lenny was dead, Viv had nobody.

'Where's your shadow?' Terry on the fruit-and-veg stall shouted out.

'We ain't joined at the bleedin' hip, you know,' Viv yelled back. Neither her nor Queenie ever discussed family business with outsiders. The nosy neighbours would have a field day if they even got a sniff of an argument.

'Hello, Viv. I thought you were gonna just walk past me then.'

'Sorry, Albie. In a world of me own today.'

'Where's Queenie?'

'Don't ask. We've fallen out good and proper this time.'

'Not over you telling Michael I was welcome to come for dinner, surely?'

Having had a rubbish day where she'd missed her poor dead son more than ever, Vivian couldn't help her eyes welling up. 'Take no notice of me, Albie. I'm going soft in me old age.'

'How about you let me buy you a drink or two? We can have a proper chat in the pub.'

Starved of company, Vivian smiled. 'Sod it. Why not?'

Vinny Butler was back-pedalling for all he was worth: 'Look, I'm sorry for calling you Izzy and mentioning the past. I was only winding you up. If you wanna be with Michael, then be with him. But don't be telling him anything about me and you. It'll crucify him and he'll hate the pair of us.'

Enjoying the sight of the colour draining from Vinny's face, Bella shook her head. 'I have to get everything out in the open; I've always been totally honest with Michael. If I don't come clean with him about you and he finds out in the future, he will never forgive me. But if I tell him I recognized you at the party, which explains me fleeing to Italy and my behaviour since, we might have a chance to make it work. It isn't as though I've cheated on him, is it? I was single when . . . you know.'

'I know my own brother, Bella, and he ain't gonna want you if he knows you slept with me. It will break his heart, trust. Is that what you want? Michael ain't no mug. Chances are he'll kill the pair of us.'

'Admitting the truth is better than spending the rest of my life looking over my shoulder waiting for you to make snide remarks or blackmail me.'

'Blackmail you! What do you take me for?'

'Well, you're hardly a gentleman are you, Vinny? When I fled that party and Michael went to get the car, you tried to kiss and fucking grope me. I wonder how your brother will react when I tell him that?'

Vinny had an overwhelming urge to remind the sanctimonious bitch that he'd done far more than grope her on the night they'd spent shagging one another's brains out, but somehow he managed to control his temper. Michael would never forgive him if he learned the truth. Their close brotherly bond would be ripped to shreds, for ever. 'Listen, I was out of order that night and I apologize. It was a shock seeing you and I was pissed.'

'Apology accepted, but it doesn't change anything, Vinny. Michael's family is everything to him, you know that. I can't avoid visiting your mother or family parties. Michael would know something was wrong if I didn't ever go with him, which is why I have to tell him the truth.'

'Seriously, Bella, you'll cause World War Three if you open your trap. My mum'll despise you, so will my aunt. And my brother will never forgive us. Why can't you just keep schtum?'

'Because you and I will have to socialize from time to time and you won't let go of what happened. It was meaningless sex, that's all.'

'Whaddya mean, I won't let go? Jesus, you must rate yourself, girl. I've had hundreds better than you in the sack, believe me,' Vinny lied. 'Look, let's be adult about this. You love Michael and he loves you. I want my brother to be happy in life. Let's not mention me and you ever again, and try to be civil to one another on the odd occasion our paths cross, for Michael's sake. The past is the past, we can't change that, but you can have a blinding future with my bro if you don't start blabbing your mouth off.'

'OK. But I'm warning you, Vinny, if you go back on your word, I swear I will tell Michael every single vulgar detail. Including that I only fucked you in the first place because you reminded me of him.'

Queenie Butler was feeling guilty. Vinny had given her a stern talking to yesterday. 'I feel sorry for Auntie Viv. You've got all us, but she must be stuck in her house on her Jack Jones. You're all she's got and I really feel you should be the bigger person. Give her a knock, an' tell her you wanna sort things out. That's the advice you gave me and Michael when we were at loggerheads,' her son had reminded her.

Determined to bite the bullet, Queenie picked her handbag up and marched next door but one. Deciding not to use her own key, Queenie rang the bell.

There was no answer.

*

Having not spoken to a soul for days, Vivian Harris was thoroughly enjoying a bit of company. She and Albie were in the Grave Maurice, reminiscing about years gone by.

'You are a funny one, Vivvy. Is that true?' Albie chuckled.

'Cross my heart, and hope to die. Pissed as farts, me father and the registrar were. Me mother couldn't spell. That's why my name's spelt like a man's. It was meant to have an i-e-n-n and e on the end. I thought you knew that story. Queenie must've told you, surely?'

'She probably did. But knowing me, I was bladdered at the time and don't bleedin' remember. You and Queen'll be as thick as thieves again soon, you know. Both as pig-headed as each other, ain't ya?'

'What will be will be. No way am I apologizing though, not this time. I've been a bloody good sister to her, Albie. Vinny kills my Lenny and she's got the cheek to throw a wobbler over a clash of words. I've even been polite to that murdering bastard of a son of hers since Christmas, purely to keep her happy.'

Aware of the twisted expression on Vivian's face and the unshed tears in her eyes, Albie leaned across the table, took her hands in his and did his best to comfort her.

In the far corner of the pub, Nosy Hilda very nearly dropped her Guinness in shock. She'd been glued to her chair watching Albie and Viv laughing and joking for the past half-hour. Now they were acting like lovesick teenagers.

Deciding to sneak out of the pub before either spotted her, Hilda grabbed her coat. She couldn't wait to tell Mouthy Maureen this bit of gossip. Albie Butler and Vivian Harris – whoever would have thought it?

Unsettled by his meeting with Bella, instead of going back to the club, Vinny Butler went on a pub crawl. To say he was seething was an understatement. Bella had come out on top today and he knew it. But he'd had no choice other than to agree with her in case she decided to carry out her threat and spill her guts to Michael. No way could his brother find out the truth. It would almost certainly tip him over the edge.

Strolling into the brothel, Vinny was met with a look of distaste by the old madam on the desk.

'Can I help you?' she asked curtly.

'Yeah. I want the tall dark-haired bird. Monica, I think her name is.'

Aware that the last time this man had visited these premises he'd been very heavy-handed towards Monica, the madam replied, 'Monica is currently otherwise engaged. Would you like to pick another girl?'

'Nah. How about you ask Monica if she can unengage herself for five hundred quid, eh? There's a oner on top of that for you, of course.'

Scuttling away from the reception desk, the old madam returned and held her hand out for payment. 'Monica is just freshening up. I'll take all the money up front, thank you.'

Fifteen minutes later, Vinny Butler had his rock-hard penis shoved as far up Monica's back passage as it would go. She was obviously in pain from the savage way he was banging her and Vinny liked that very much.

Losing himself in the moment, Vinny stroked Monica's long dark hair. The ugly slut looked nothing like Bella from the front, but from the back she did. 'You think you got one over on me, did you, eh? Well think again,' he hissed as he pounded away like a madman. 'Nobody messes with me, nobody,' he panted.

When he finally shot his load, Vinny yanked Monica's hair back with such force he was lucky he didn't break her neck. 'Oh, Bella,' he sighed in ecstasy.

CHAPTER SIX

'Gandar!' cried Oliver Butler joyfully.

Gary Allen picked his fifteen-month-old grandson up and lifted him in the air. He'd been so disappointed when his teenage daughter had first told him she was pregnant, but he couldn't imagine life without Oliver now.

'Whaddya think of his outfit?' Little Vinny asked.

Gary chuckled. Oliver, or Ollie as he was usually referred to, was dressed in brown corduroy trousers, leather boots, a chunky beige cardigan and a check cap. 'Looks like a little old man. Suits him though.'

Little Vinny beamed with pride. He and Sammi-Lou both loved shopping and dressing their son up to look the business. 'Once upon a time it was me and Sammi with wardrobes full of designer clothes, Gal. How times change, eh?' he joked.

Times had most certainly changed. The Beatles and the Rolling Stones had been all the rage when Gary was a teenager, but now groups like Duran Duran and Wham! topped the charts. Women no longer dressed like ladies. They wore ripped jeans and their hair messy. Grown men walked around thinking they looked cool in ridiculous bright-coloured shell-suits. But in Gary's eyes the most surprising change of all was Little Vinny. Gary had hated the lad with a passion when he'd first started dating Sammi-Lou, thought he was a total waste of space. Thankfully, the lad had proved him wrong. Considering he was still only nineteen, he'd turned out to be a top-drawer dad. He also made Sammi-Lou incredibly happy.

'My dad isn't meeting us now. He rung me this morning, said something had cropped up. He told me to pick the suits and he'll get measured up for his in the next day or two.'

Gary Allen was pleased. He'd never liked Vinny Butler. Michael was OK, but Vinny had a cocky arrogance about him. Having built up his construction business from nothing, gangsters didn't impress Gary Allen. He was a self-made millionaire through pure hard graft, so why would he be impressed by anything less?

Gary introduced his future son-in-law to his tailor, Maurice.

'I want all the main men at my wedding to be wearing the same suit as me. My fiancée has chosen crimson for her bridesmaid dresses, so I want a similar colour and style to this, but with a waistcoat underneath,' Little Vinny explained, showing Maurice the magazine.

'I have another suit in that colour. Would you like to try it on for size, sir?'

'You got one my son can try on first? I'm dying to see him in it.'

Oliver Butler's hair was now a strawberry-blond colour, which today was Brylcreemed with a side parting.

'Look at him, Gal. Cool dude or what?' Little Vinny gushed minutes later, grinning like a Cheshire cat.

'He most certainly is. Looks so grown up.'

Little Vinny crouched down and put some aviator-style dark glasses on his pride and joy. 'It'll be sunny in June.'

Gary Allen laughed. '*Miami Vice!*'

*

Vinny Butler was in a foul mood. He'd drunk a bottle of Scotch last night, had woken up with the headache of all headaches, missed his son's suit fitting, and was now running late for his meet with Eddie Mitchell.

Cursing as he stubbed his little toe, Vinny punched the door that had caused his pain. Trouble was, the door wasn't to blame. Bella was.

Vinny stepped in the shower and closed his eyes. Engulfed by hot water, he thought back to the past. Only one female had ever got under his skin in his lifetime: Yvonne Summers. When she'd broken his heart, Vinnie had vowed never to allow himself to be cast under a bird's spell again. He hadn't, but there was something about Bella that had an undesirable effect on him, and he was sure the bitch knew it.

The Enemy had learned a lot while banged up, including the art of deception.

Today, he was back in Whitechapel dressed like a geek. He'd purchased the duffel coat, woolly hat and satchel in a charity shop. Glancing at his reflection, he smirked. He looked like a student. To carry books under his arm had been an awesome idea.

Clutching the satchel close to his side, he walked towards Michael's club. Inside the satchel was the filleting knife and the first opportunity that arose to use it, the Enemy intended to take it. Seeing his father in that hospital, unable to talk or eat, had been a sight that would live with him for ever. No kid should ever have to go through what he had. That was why he'd been so messed up. Not any more, though. He was ready to get even.

'Sorry I'm late, Ed. The morning from hell,' Vinny Butler apologized, shaking his pal's hand. Eddie Mitchell was the youngest son of the legendary Harry Mitchell, and it was well known in the underworld that it was now Eddie who pulled most of the strings within the Mitchell firm.

Ordering the waiter to bring Vinny a drink, Eddie grinned. 'How's tricks? Seems like ages since we've had a proper catch-up.'

'All good my end, thanks. How's Jess and the kids?'

'Driving me mad and costing me a fortune, as per usual,' Eddie joked. 'How's Michael doing?'

'Plodding on. His club's been busy, so that keeps his mind off all the other shit. Still cut up over Adam, but he'll learn to live with it. I had to with Molly. Made of strong stuff, us Butlers.'

'Did Nancy's body ever show up?'

'Nah. Long washed out to sea, her. Never mind. At least she died the way she wanted to die, so that's a comfort,' Vinny replied, his voice laden with sarcasm. 'So, what's this business deal you've got for me? Fancy opening a club together, do ya?'

Eddie Mitchell chuckled. He liked Vinny Butler, but Vinny had a few skeletons in the closet. Ex drug baron, prostitute basher and suspected psychopath, to name just three. Perhaps one day Eddie would consider going into business with Vinny. But not until his pal had proved himself completely. Eddie was no man's fool and even though he trusted Vinny, loose cannons were a liability. Eddie only had to look at his own brother to realize that. 'Nah, I'm not ready to become a club owner yet, pal. However, I do have a container-load of booze up for grabs.'

Knowing that whatever Eddie had on offer must be kosher, Vinny rubbed his hands together in anticipation. 'Enlighten me.'

*

Having had no joy spotting Michael Butler, the Enemy could barely believe his luck when he saw Vivian Harris strolling along the street, arms weighed down with shopping bags. He quickened his pace and furtively glanced around. There were only two other people about, an elderly couple holding arms.

Sliding his right hand inside the satchel, he felt for his knife. He was a fast runner, had a change of clothes with him, and an alibi lined up.

He thought back to the last time he'd used a filleting knife. He'd felt no remorse on that occasion, none whatsoever. The incident had happened inside a packed carvery. He'd been a young lad at the time, happily tucking into a roast lamb dinner when he spotted a boy from school. Martin Mabbutt came from a big, loving family, and resentment and hatred had flooded the Enemy's thoughts as he'd lunged towards him. He'd ended up stabbing Martin twice and his interfering father once. Both had lived, but he'd revelled in the havoc he'd caused and how close he'd come to killing them.

Breaking into a jog, he felt pure adrenaline pump through his veins as he inched closer to his prey. He glanced around again. The coast was clear. This was it. The moment he'd been waiting for. He pulled out the knife and was about to plunge it in Vivian's back when he heard a voice shout 'Rex!'

The Enemy discreetly slid the knife back inside the satchel, before locking eyes with a bloke who asked, 'You seen a black-and-white dog?'

'Nah, mate. Sorry,' he replied, before crossing over the road. The geezer had got a very good look at him, and he wasn't stupid. Revenge would have to wait until another day.

*

58

Chuffed with the container-load of spirits he'd just shaken hands with Eddie Mitchell on, Vinny Butler was celebrating the deal with a spirit or two himself. 'I haven't seen you since the Deborah Preston drama, have I? Did you hear what happened, Ed?'

'No.'

'Deborah, the delightful mother of my ex-bird, Joanna. Well, she only went and made a home-made bomb with the intention of blowing up my club.'

'You what!' spluttered Eddie, spitting his Scotch back in the glass.

Vinny laughed. 'Honest to God. A nail bomb it was, the Old Bill told me. Her son tipped 'em off, apparently. Turned out she blamed me for Joanna and Johnny's deaths and had gone off her rocker. They've carted her off to the funny farm now, thank Christ. That's all I'm short of, some psycho bird lobbing bombs my way.'

Eddie Mitchell shook his head. 'I've never met the woman, but she sounds a proper nutjob. Speaking of the Prestons, how's your Ava doing?'

'Good, mate. Settled in well. Buying her that mutt helped. Took her mind off her mother's death, and she barely mentions Jo now.'

Eddie Mitchell studied his pal as he chirpily continued to chat about Ava. This wasn't the first time it had crossed his mind that Vinny'd had something to do with Joanna's death, but surely not? Even Vinny Butler would not stoop that low to get custody of a kid – would he?

'I'd never have hurt Jo. You know that, don't you, Ed?' Vinny lied. 'Me and her might not have always seen eye to eye, but she had a good heart and was a decent mother.'

It was now Eddie's turn to lie. 'I know you better than that, mate. It never even crossed my mind. How's your mum keeping? If Ava's living with her now, you really should consider getting your mum a gaff out my way. Whitechapel's had its day, like the rest of the East End. Unrecognizable from when we were kids. The schools are far better in Essex.'

Vinny explained he'd been badgering his mother to move, without success, then told Eddie about Brenda's latest escapade. 'I'm embarrassed to call her my sister, Ed. I goes to the hospital to try and help her and she threatens to grass me up to the Old Bill about things that happened years ago. Mum's insisted I leave her to get on with it. I wanted to give the geezer a right pasting, obviously – cheeky bastard. I mean, you don't hurt a woman, do ya? Even a nightmare like Brenda.'

'I feel your pain, Vin. My Ronny's more of a hindrance to me than a help. I cringe every time he starts opening his trap after a bevvy. Mouth starts running away with him and he's a fucking liability. However, if I had a sister and a bloke clumped her, I'd have to give him a dig. That geezer took a massive liberty. Bren's your flesh and blood.'

Vinny had no feelings for his sister whatsoever, but nodded in agreement. If Eddie Mitchell thought giving Dave a pasting was the right thing to do, then he would. He might not love Brenda, but he adored a bit of violence.

Having seen her sister arrive home, Queenie gave it half an hour, then strutted up her path and rang the bell.

'Oh, it's you. What do you want?' Vivian asked, pursing her lips.

'Us to get back to normal. Can I come in? Only if Nosy Hilda sees me standing on the doorstep, the whole of Whitechapel will know our bloody business.'

Secretly pleased that Queenie had made the first move, Vivian marched into the kitchen and put the kettle on.

'Spoke to me like shit you did, Queen. So hurtful, some of the things you said.'

'I feel exactly the same about the stuff you said to me. Why don't we just forget all about the row? We're both as bad as one another when we lose our rag. If Mum were still alive, she'd bang our bleedin' heads together.'

When Vivian and Queenie argued as kids, they'd always make up by linking their little fingers together and singing a rhyme. It was Viv who held hers out first.

Queenie chuckled as their fingers entwined. 'I've missed you, you miserable old cow.'

'Not as much as I've missed you, you cantankerous old bat.'

Talk about things coming in threes, Michael Butler pondered to himself. First, he'd had to sack two of his bar staff for thieving. Then his ice machine had broken. Now the toilet in the men's was blocked. It was the end to a perfect day – not.

Depending on the day and people involved, Michael would occasionally hire his club out privately. Today was one of those days when he wished he hadn't. Irish Danny had been a big old lump who'd probably killed himself due to his love of food. The club was packed with rowdy Irish relatives and there had already been two punch-ups.

Sighing as he heard yet another alcohol-fuelled rendition of 'Danny Boy' being belted out over the mike by some pisspot, Michael poured himself a Scotch, sank back in his leather chair and swung his legs on top of his office desk. He shut his eyes and was disturbed seconds later by a pounding on the door. 'What?' he yelled.

'You've got a visitor, boss.'

'Who?'

'A beautiful lady.'

Michael leapt up and kicked the leg of his desk with frustration. Katy had been stalking him via phone all day and he'd told her not to come here tonight. 'Send her in,' Michael spat. No way was he going to succumb to her charm. The only fuck she would get tonight would be him telling her to 'fuck off'.

He was pouring himself another drink when the door opened. He turned, ready to treat Katy to a barrage of abuse, then dropped his glass in shock.

'Bella!' he exclaimed.

CHAPTER SEVEN

As dawn broke the following day, Michael and Bella were still trying to sort out their differences. Michael wasn't happy with Bella's explanation as to why she'd disappeared for months. It had hurt him beyond belief when she'd told him she was staying away because she 'needed space'. Obviously, he was elated to see her, but he wasn't about to allow her to waltz back into his life as though she'd never been gone in the first place.

'Something don't add up to me, Bell. I can understand you shooting back to Italy to visit your sick nan, but not for all that time. You obviously got cold feet. I ain't no mug, so don't lie to me. We don't have a future unless you tell me the truth. Did you get cold feet? Or did you meet another geezer? There's definitely something you ain't telling me.'

Bella was sick of repeating herself. She'd guessed Michael would be peeved, but thought he would've been more pleased to see her. They'd not even kissed yet and he was as cold as ice. 'I am not lying to you, Michael. My nana was at death's door for a long while. Even the doctors were amazed she finally pulled through,' Bella lied. What else could she do – admit that she'd fucked his brother senseless?

'OK, so I believe your nan was ill. That still doesn't

explain you telling me you needed space. I thought we were a couple and I wanted to be there for you. That's what people that love one another do, Bella. No matter how awful the situation, we're meant to support each other. You were my rock when Adam died. I try to return the favour and you push me away like I'm some nuisance, a worthless piece of shit. I was still grieving an' all, you know. I didn't get over my son's death overnight. Still bloody haven't, and probably never will.'

Bella was a tough cookie, barely ever cried, but she finally broke down. She had been selfish, had not given Adam's death a thought when she'd first blanked Michael's calls, then ordered him to give her some space. How she hated herself for that now. But she'd been so consumed by guilt, she couldn't think about anything other than what she'd done.

'Well, say something then. Crocodile tears don't wash with me.'

'The truth is I was worried about the pace our relationship was developing. I love you with all my heart, Michael, always have done and always will. But to take on your two boys is a massive ask. Not so much from my point of view, but I have Antonio to think of – he is my world. Your sons are much older, and I'm not sure it would work out if we all lived together. No way will I risk my son's happiness by rushing into anything, especially marriage.'

'More lies, Bella? You were probably at it with some other geezer,' Michael spat accusingly. He had no idea why he was being so horrible to her. Was it guilt because he hadn't been able to keep his cock in his trousers?

When Bella began to sob and plead her innocence, he finally softened. Sitting next to her, he put his arms around her. 'I'm so sorry, babe, I know you'd never cheat on me really.'

'And I'm so sorry too.'

Michael held the woman he loved close to his chest. 'Everything will be all right, Bell. Please don't shut me out again though, that's all I ask. My life was like an empty shell without you, and believe me, I'm no soppy bastard that usually comes out with such crap. But it was. I only feel whole when we're together.'

Laughing and crying at the same time, Bella held Michael's handsome face in her hands. 'I swear to God, I will never shut you out again.'

'Things will work out, you know. Perhaps I came on too strong, mentioning marriage and stuff? I know it's not gonna be easy, us making a go of it with the three boys. So let's make a pact to take things more slowly. There's no rush for us to move in together. And even if we decide we want to, there's certainly no rush for us to get hitched. We'll make a fresh start. Go on some proper dates, and when the time feels right we'll introduce the boys properly. Sound OK to you?'

'I've missed you so much,' Bella murmured, in her sexy half-English half-Italian drawl.

Michael breathed deeply, lust taking over every part of him. 'I want you badly. I promise if you ravish me, I'll return the favour.'

Bella unzipped the man of her dream's trousers and took his penis in her mouth.

Michael Butler stared at Bella's beautiful face as she pleasured him. She truly was his soul-mate and he knew it.

Katy Spencer and her friend Lucy Tompkins were in high spirits as they joined the pharmacy queue in Boots.

'I'm so excited for you. When will you tell him – if you are?' Lucy giggled.

'As soon as I get him alone. I've never been a week late before, so I reckon I must be,' Katy convinced herself.

'I wonder if he'll ask you to move straight in with him?'

'Michael can be very romantic, so it wouldn't surprise me. You should see the faces and hear the noises he makes when we have sex. He's totally into me, Luce, I can tell. The only reason we're not already living together is because he thinks it's too soon for Lee and Daniel after Nancy. He loves me, I know it.'

'He is such a catch, Katy. You are one lucky girl. Which reminds me: while we're in Romford you must pop into Downtown and get that record. Every time I hear it, it makes me think of you and Michael.'

'What record?'

'The new one in the chart I told you about. It's so you and Mr Butler.'

When Lucy began singing the words to Atlantic Starr's 'Secret Lovers' Katy felt a warm glow inside. She put her hand on her stomach and as she neared the front of the queue, prayed silently to God that she was carrying Michael Butler's baby.

Ava Preston launched herself at her father's legs and nestled her head against them. 'Fred did naughties to Auntie Viv, Daddy.'

Vinny Butler knelt down to stroke Fred, who was also vying for his attention, then picked his daughter up and swung her in the air. Apart from Teddy (the mutt's toy) the only thing Fred ever wanted to shag was Viv's leg and Vinny found that highly amusing.

'You all right, boy? I was worried when I couldn't get hold of you last night. What's the point of having a mobile phone if you don't bleedin' answer it?' Queenie asked, hands on hips.

'Sorry, Mum. I had a business meeting with Eddie

Mitchell and we got on the Scotch. You know how it is,' Vinny winked.

Queenie batted her eyelids, then grinned. Both she and Viv lusted after Eddie Mitchell even more than they did that Dirty Den in *EastEnders*.

'I was thinking, it's about time we changed Ava's surname, legally. Best to get it done before she starts school. Whaddya reckon?'

'But I like my name being Ava,' the confused child mumbled, pouting.

Carrying Ava into the lounge, Vinny placed her on the sofa, and sat next to her. His mum had enrolled her in nursery school, but that hadn't turned out too well. Not only had Ava been devastated over leaving Fred at home, she'd also punched two of the other children in her first week and had left by mutual agreement. 'You'll still be called Ava, but instead of Ava Preston, you'll be Ava Butler,' Vinny explained gently.

'Why is my name Ava Preston?'

Queenie crouched down. 'Because when Mummy registered your birth, she forgot to put your father's name on the birth certificate. Fred's registered at the vet as Fred Butler, so you want to have the same surname as him, don't you?'

'Yes, but will Mummy be upset if the angels tell her?'

Queenie stroked the child's hair. 'No, love. Mummy's dead. She won't be able to speak to the angels where she is.'

Katy Spencer put the arm of the record player on repeat, lay down on her bed and daydreamed of her future. Lee and Daniel already adored her, she knew that much, and if her test came back positive, her and Michael would most definitely live happily ever after. Picturing what their baby would look like, Katy sang along with 'Secret Lovers'. Lucy had been right. This song was written for her and Michael.

Taking the test out of her handbag, Katy smiled as she read the instructions. The pharmacist had told her to do the test first thing in the morning before she'd had anything to eat or drink. Patience had never been Katy's virtue, so she ripped open the box.

The Enemy met his pal in the Eastbrook pub. Dale Grainger and himself had been best mates whilst locked up. In addition to being his drug supplier, he was also going to give him an alibi if and when needed. Dale had no idea what the alibi was for and that's the way the Enemy liked it. The Butlers were very well known, even in Dagenham, and the less anybody knew the better.

Two drinks and twenty minutes later, the teenager had attracted the attention of two extremely drunken, much older women. 'You're handsome, you, ain't ya?' the ginger woman slurred, nudging her equally awful mate.

Dale nudged his pal. 'Ignore them, otherwise we won't get rid. A nightmare they are, proper alkies. Been barred from the Keys, Bull and the Railway. The ginger one goes out with Brett Carpenter, the biggest knob-end in Dagenham. The other one's shacked up with Dave Green, another prick. You should see 'em perform down the Roundhouse of a weekend when the bands are on. It's hard to believe she's Vinny Butler's sister.'

'Who is?'

'The one with the frowsy blonde hair. That's Brenda Butler. Minging, ain't it?'

Nodding in agreement, the Enemy stared at Brenda and pictured her covered in blood.

*

'Michael! Stop it! I really do have to get home to Antonio. I promised my friends I would pick him up before noon, and it's nearly that now,' Bella explained.

Obligingly moving his finger away from Bella's clitoris, Michael propped an elbow on the pillow beside her and rested his head on his hand. 'When am I gonna see you again? And the little man? Missed him big time an' all.'

'I'm very busy the next couple of days. I have a lot of work to catch up on and meetings to attend. How about Saturday? I'd like to introduce you properly to my friends who run my favourite Italian restaurant. That's where Antonio stayed last night. Will you be able to take time away from the club?'

Michael grinned. 'You bet I can.'

'Fabulous. But you still haven't answered my earlier question,' Bella reminded him.

'What?'

'I asked you did you date anybody else while I was away?'

'Of course I didn't, you daft mare. Not unless you count my old mucker, Black Kevin. I took him out a couple of times to cheer him up. Split up with his old woman, poor sod. And I can assure you we're not gay.'

'I believe you, many wouldn't,' Bella chuckled.

Feeling edgy all of a sudden, Michael leapt out of bed. 'I'll put the kettle on, babe. You hungry?'

'No. A coffee will do just fine, thanks.'

Instead of the kitchen, Michael made a beeline for the sitting room. He'd switched his mobile off last night, then turned his landline and answer phone on to silent. Seeing the black machine flashing away like a good 'un, Michael sighed deeply. He would bet his club on who the calls were from and he had to get rid of her now, fast.

*

Vinny Butler was in a filthy mood. He'd been trying to get hold of Michael since early this morning, and had a vision of why his brother still wasn't answering his phone.

'I thought you were going to take Ava out for the whole day, boy?' Queenie questioned.

'Nah. Not today, Mum. I took her to the café and we've taken the mutt out for a run. Ava's happy here, playing in the garden.'

'It doesn't give me much of a break though, does it, Vinny? I'm going down the Roman all day on Saturday with Viv, so best you up your fatherly duties by then.'

'Glad you and Auntie Viv are OK. Who made the first move?'

'Don't change the bloody subject. I know you love Ava, but you can't put on me so much. I haven't had a chance to tidy upstairs properly and change the bedding since Tara and Tommy left. I'm no spring chicken now. I might look like one still, but me bones ache some days and I get tired in the afternoons.'

'When did Tara and Tommy leave?'

'The day Bren came out of hospital. I told you yesterday. Whatever's wrong with you lately? It's like talking to a silly boy, and you've got a face like a smacked arse.'

Rather than admitting to his mother that he'd spent most of the day visualizing his brother fucking Bella and wishing it was him, Vinny stood up, waving his hands. 'I'm going now. Can't be doing with you when you're in one of these moods. And you shouldn't be coming out with insults such as "silly boy". Champ wasn't exactly bright, was he? How would Auntie Viv feel, hearing you saying that?'

'Me and Viv both call him next door "silly-boy-got-none". Unlike you, Viv hasn't had a personality bypass,' she sniffed. 'Sod off then, and don't bother coming back until you're more cheerful. Or on Saturday, when you will be looking after your daughter for once.'

Without saying goodbye to Ava, who was in the garden with Fred, Vinny slammed the front door behind him.

Driving off like a maniac, he immediately regretted his actions and punched the steering wheel. Out of all the birds in the world, why did Michael have to fall in love with that cunt?

As soon as Bella left, Michael Butler listened to the messages on his answer machine. There were nine in total – six from Katy and three from Vinny.

Pacing up and down the room, Michael wondered what to do for the best. Katy was young, worked for him, so was it fair to sack her over the phone? It had to be wiser to do so in person. He should blame her dismissal on the boys' recent bad behaviour and pay her off with a wad of money. Surely that would keep her sweet? And quiet, regarding him and her.

Before he could pick up the phone and ask Katy to meet him, the buzzer disturbed Michael's pre-planned speech. Nobody else was at the club, so he answered it himself. It would be proper handy if it was Katy. Save him a journey.

'It's Vinny,' came the gruff voice over the speaker. 'Where the fuck you been and why aren't you answering your phone?'

Michael ran down the stairs and flung the door open. 'Sorry, bruv. I had a visitor last night – Bella. She's back from Italy and we're gonna give it another go.'

'How very romantic! And did it not occur to you that me and Mum might be worried if you wasn't answering your phone?'

A bit taken aback by Vinny's obvious anger, Michael shrugged. 'I'm a grown man, Vin, give me a break. I had to switch both phones off in case Katy rang. Good job I did: she's left tons of messages.'

'I'm not interested in your fucked-up love life, Michael. If you're silly enough to take a bird back who has already dumped you, that's your lookout. What I wanna talk about is Dagenham Dave. He needs to be taught a bit of a lesson. Brenda might be a pain in the arse, but she's still our sister.'

'But she threatened you with the Old Bill, Vin,' Michael reminded his brother.

'So what. It's a direct piss-take at us, him clumping Bren. We won't kill him, but he needs a stern warning. People will think we're mugs otherwise.'

'What people?' said Michael, wondering why Vinny was getting in a lather. 'Bren and Dave had a punch-up. Big fucking deal. They're back together now and everybody knows what a nightmare Brenda is.'

'I was out with Eddie Mitchell yesterday. Even he agreed that Dave needs a good hiding. I've done a bit of research and heard through the grapevine that he serves up in the Cross Keys at the weekends. Barred from there is our Bren, she's down the Roundhouse. So, we'll stalk the Keys at the weekend, take Carl with us to entice the cunt outside. There's a graveyard opposite. The perfect place for Dave to be taught who not to mess with in the future.'

'I can't make Saturday. I'm seeing Bella.'

'Business before pleasure, Michael. And family before whores. Always remember that, bruv.'

As Vinny turned his back and walked out the premises, Michael wanted to give him a slap; disrespecting him was one thing, but having a dig at Bella was another. Instead he punched the wall. Vinny was obviously in one of his Jekyll and Hyde moods and until he snapped out of it, he was best left alone.

CHAPTER EIGHT

Michael Butler put the boys' breakfast on the table.

'Ain't you having none, Dad?' Lee asked.

'Nah. And I need yous two to pop out for hour or so about half eleven. Someone's coming round and I need to talk business, in private.'

'Who's that then?' Daniel enquired.

'Nobody you know,' Michael lied. Today was the first chance he'd had to talk in private with Katy and he was absolutely dreading telling her that there'd be no more her and him, and he didn't need her taking care of the boys any longer. A thousand pounds he planned to give her as a pay-off, and he only hoped that would soften the blow.

'But I thought we were grounded?' Daniel questioned suspiciously.

'You were until today. Can't keep you locked indoors for ever, can I? Just learn to behave yourselves in future. And keep away from Donald and Mary's café. If I hear you've been within a hundred feet of that joint, I swear I'll send you both away to a bloody boarding school. Understand me?'

'If we're not grounded any more, does that mean Katy will be coming back to look after us?' Lee asked.

'No. Katy won't be coming round any more.'

Daniel pushed his plate away and leapt up. 'Why? What's she done wrong? We like Katy looking after us, don't we, Lee?'

'Yeah. We like Katy a lot,' Lee added.

'Tough shit. Anyway, you've only got yourselves to blame. I wouldn't have got rid of Katy if yous two had behaved. That was the whole point of her being here.'

Eyes blazing, Daniel punched the table then locked eyes with his father. 'Don't fucking lie! You've been shagging her, I bet.'

Grabbing hold of his brazen son by the throat, Michael pushed him up against the wall. 'Katy's nearer your age than mine. What do you take me for, eh? You ever spout such crap or speak to me like that again, you'll know all about it, for sure.'

Upset because he was probably never going to see the bird he'd had wet dreams over again, Daniel Butler burst into tears.

'Get off! I mean it! Leave me alone, you filthy little ratpig,' Vivian squealed, as Fred clung on to her leg and rubbed his little dingle-dangle against her brand-new nylons.

Queenie tried not to laugh, but couldn't help herself as she picked up Fred and put him in the back garden.

'Disgusting bastard creature. Look, it's laddered me bleedin' tights. New on today, these were,' Vivian complained.

'Go and change 'em, but hurry up. We're running late,' Queenie said. For years it had been a ritual that Saturdays were spent visiting their loved ones' graves, before getting glammed up to spend the rest of the day at the Roman. Roman Road market was the place to be seen on a Saturday these days and most of the women who came from far and wide to shop there got done up to the nines.

Spotting a bit of dust on the television, Queenie took the duster out the drawer. Both she and Vivian were the envy of their neighbours with their pristine homes and posh furniture. China and family photos were Queenie's pride and joy and her lounge was brimming with both.

Vinny had turned up early this morning to pick Ava up. He'd apologized for being short-tempered the other evening, explaining that he had something on his mind and he'd tell her what once he'd sorted it. 'Don't worry, Mum. It's nothing to worry about. Quite the opposite, in fact,' he'd assured her with a wink.

'Ready, Queen?' Vivian bellowed.

Queenie stared at herself in the mirror, flicked her dyed-blonde hair and sprayed on some more lacquer. Looking perfect down the Roman was a must, especially on a Saturday. 'Yep. Let's knock 'em dead, Viv.'

Katy Spencer was anxious, excited, scared yet buzzing, all at the same time. She hadn't seen Michael all week. Daniel and Lee were being punished for misbehaving, which was why Michael had given her a fully paid week off work. He'd also insisted she wasn't to visit him at the club, saying he'd had some business to attend to up north. Katy hadn't quite believed his story, so she'd driven past his house and club a few times and there'd been no sign of his car. She'd even got her mate to ring the club three times and the staff had said he wasn't there.

Pulling up outside Michael's house, Katy had the biggest butterflies ever as she turned off the ignition.

Peeping through the curtains and wishing this moment was already over, Michael Butler opened the front door before Katy had even got to it. He'd been a proper Lothario back in the day, had more birds than hot dinners, but even then he'd been as kind as he could when dumping them.

The stalkers he'd acquired along the way were few and far between. However, he had this awful feeling that Katy might turn out to be his biggest one yet. If Bella found out about his stupid fling, she'd probably chop his cock off. And the thought of losing her over something so meaningless did not bear thinking about.

'I've missed you so much,' Katy beamed, slinging her arms around Michael's neck as soon as the front door was shut.

When she tried to stick her tongue in his mouth, Michael swerved his head to the side, then gently prised her wrists away from his neck. 'We need to talk, babe,' he said, kissing her politely on the cheek.

Following Michael into the kitchen, Katy felt a feeling of dread in the pit of her stomach. She sensed from his coolness that he was going to dump her.

Having already prepared a story, Michael pulled a chair out for Katy, sat opposite her then squeezed both her hands in his. 'You know how much I think of you, don't you?' Michael began.

Tears in her eyes, Katy nodded. 'You're going to finish with me, aren't you?'

Wanting to tell the girl there was fuck-all to finish, Michael instead smiled politely. Treading on eggshells was a necessity at times, especially when it involved his beloved Bella, the love of his life. 'We've got a bit of a problem, Katy. The boys clocked there was something going on between us and were pretty upset about it. You know what teenagers are like. I actually think they have a bit of a schoolboy crush on you themselves. Anyway, as much as it pains me, I'm gonna have to let you go. You've been absolutely brilliant all round and I can't thank you enough, but I do feel it's best you don't turn up at the club any more either. A clean break would be best for both of us.'

'What do you mean, let me go?'

'I mean you can't work for me any more and neither can we see one another. It's too soon after Nancy's death for me to be dating again. I have to put the boys first, that's my duty as a father. You're young, Katy, and I'm far too old for you anyway. You're a beautiful girl who deserves far more in life than being stuck with some old git who has two unruly teenagers in tow. You can do so much better.'

Sobbing, Katy jumped up, darted around the other side of the table and flung her arms around Michael. She might be young, but she knew in her heart that she would love this man for the rest of her life. 'I think the world of Daniel and Lee. They're great kids. And I don't care about the age gap. I love you so much, Michael. Please don't finish with me. We can see one another in secret, if you want?'

Not knowing what else to do, Michael stood up and hugged the girl. He stroked her hair. 'I'm so sorry, Katy, but it's not just the boys. I'm not ready to move on from Nancy yet either,' he lied.

'But wouldn't you like to settle down again one day and have more children?' Katy wept.

'Not yet, babe. Not for a long while. It was only the back end of last year Adam died. It's far too raw for me to even think about having more kids. Perhaps one day? And who knows, one day when you're older our paths might cross again. You never know what the future might hold.' Michael wasn't trying to give Katy false hope. He only wanted to soften the blow.

Katy stopped crying and smiled. 'Can we still keep in touch via the phone?'

Michael shook his head. This was proving every bit as difficult as he'd expected, but it was his own fault for poking someone so young. 'Look Katy, I really like you and that is why I don't want you to contact me. If I didn't think a lot of you, I wouldn't care if you came to the club or rang me. I need some time on my own to sort my head out. It's been all over the place since Adam died and Nancy committed suicide. You do understand, don't you?'

Secretly thrilled that Michael was that obsessed with her he couldn't bear the thought of hearing her voice or seeing her, Katy nodded. 'I won't come to the club or phone you, I promise. I'll wait for you to contact me. Can I ask you a question?'

'Of course.'

'Do you love me, Michael?'

Hating giving her false hope, but knowing there was sod-all else he could do to get rid of her, Michael winked. 'You know I do. Now you'd better get going because the boys will be back soon.'

'How did they find out about us? What did they say?' Katy questioned.

'They're not stupid, probably clocked the way we were with one another. Daniel was more upset about it than Lee. Anyway, as I said, they'll be back soon, so best you make tracks. Look after yourself, sweetheart, and I wish you all the luck in the world for the future. This is for you,' Michael said, handing Katy an envelope.

'What is it?'

'A grand. Call it a month's wages. I thought you could treat yourself to a holiday. It'll do you good to get away, babe. Clear your head, and you might even meet the man of your dreams.'

Throwing her arms around Michael's neck, Katy savoured his touch and the smell of his aftershave. She knew what scent he wore and would buy a bottle tomorrow out of the money he'd given her. 'I love you, Michael. I will wait for you, I promise.'

*

The Enemy was munching on a sandwich outside Percy Ingle's when he spotted his prey. He'd heard the two old witches shopped at the Roman every Saturday, which was why he was donning his nerd disguise once again.

Watching the two women laughing and joking with a stallholder, he fought the urge to stab both there and then. He wasn't stupid though. He would only be able to get away with stabbing one of the women, and if he did so, it would have to be in the middle of the market where it was jam-packed. Queenie was the one he wanted to suffer the most, so perhaps he could knife Vivian in the back, then duck behind one of the stalls before anybody realized what had happened.

When Queenie and Vivian began to walk away from the stall, the Enemy pulled the woolly hat over his head and adjusted the glasses on his nose. He'd spotted a few old faces he recognized earlier, but no way would anybody recognize him. Firstly, they wouldn't have seen him since he was a child. And secondly, he was far too clever.

'Daddy, I don't like it here. It smells,' Ava sulked. Her father had brought her to some stupid farmyard in Essex to see the animals and Ava was extremely bored.

Vinny picked his daughter up. 'Look at those little piggies. They're playing,' he pointed out.

Ava turned her head in the opposite direction. 'No. Don't like 'em.'

'Shall we go to that boozer I told you about, Dad? They have a good play area for kids. Me and Sammi often take Ollie there. He loves it,' Little Vinny suggested.

Vinny nodded. Ava was a difficult child to please at times. Happy as a sandboy at home playing with Fred, but enjoyed very little outdoor activity. His mother had even tried her with Sunday school and that had ended in disaster. When the teacher had asked who Jesus was, Ava had replied 'A cunt.'

Half an hour later, Vinny was sitting next to his son in the boozer, relieved that Ava seemed to be enjoying herself in the play area. 'Look after Ollie,' he shouted.

'Yes, Daddy,' Ava beamed, holding her nephew's hand.

As proud as Vinny was at the way his son had turned out, he did currently have one issue with him. 'We need to have a chat.'

'About what?'

'The wedding suits. You might be happy to prance around looking like a pansy all day, but no way am I wearing that creation. I'll be the laughing stock of the East End.'

Little Vinny was slightly taken aback. 'The suits are smart and modern. What's wrong with 'em?'

'What's right with 'em would be an easier question to answer. For a start, they're bastard-well white! You ever seen me walking round looking like Whitechapel's answer to Larry Grayson?'

'Who's Larry Grayson? And the suits aren't white, they're cream.'

'It don't matter. I'm not wearing it.'

'For once this isn't about you, Dad. It's mine and Sammi-Lou's big day and we want it to be special. The bridesmaids are all wearing crimson and the males cream suits. You told me to choose what I wanted, so I did. Please don't ruin this for me. The photos will look ridiculous if you're the only one of us wearing a different suit.'

'It's got a fucking turtle neck an' all,' Vinny winced.

'If you hate the suit that much, you can change it before the reception. Please wear it, Dad, for the actual wedding. Michael said he liked his.'

'Michael's secretly gay,' Vinny replied sarcastically.

Oliver Butler toddling over stopped the discussion getting

any more heated. Vinny scooped the child up and sat him on his lap. Unlike the rest of the Butler males, Oliver was blond, but he'd inherited the trademark piercing green eyes. Vinny adored him, but still couldn't get his head around being called Granddad. He felt far too young to be addressed as such, so had taught Oliver to call him Vinny.

'Inny, Inny. Wha dat?' Oliver giggled, pressing his chubby finger against his grandfather's nose.

Little Vinny smirked. 'That's the nose of a man who won't do one small thing to please his son on his wedding day. Never mind, boy. When you're older and you get married, I'll do anything to make you happy. That's what being a dad is all about.'

'Bye, bye, Michael. I'm so excited now. See you tomorrow,' Antonio said, before handing the phone back to his mother and jumping up and down on the sofa with joy. He'd never had a daddy like his friends did, but whenever he was with Michael, he felt like he did. People always said they looked alike and Antonio loved that. It gave him a sense of belonging.

'Go and play in your bedroom if you're going to jump about, Antonio. Mummy is trying to talk to Michael.'

When her son skipped out of the room, Bella smiled. 'He is absolutely over the moon we are all going out tomorrow, Michael. He cried earlier, bless him, when I said you couldn't make today. He truly adores you as much as I do.'

'And I adore him too, babe. So sorry about today. I feel guilty now, but there was sod-all I could do about it. It's family shit that has to be sorted,' Michael explained. Vinny had sent Carl down to the Cross Keys yesterday evening, but unfortunately Brenda's loser of a bloke was nowhere to be seen. Michael could have defied Vinny by refusing to cancel his date with Bella in favour of waiting for a phone call, but to be honest, it wasn't worth the grief. Vinny seemed to have a real hang-up over his relationship with Bella and to put her in front of family business would only cause World War Three.

'How are your mum and aunt?' Bella asked.

'As mad as ever. I haven't had a chance to tell 'em you're back from Italy yet, but they're bound to want to see you when I do. Ava's living with my mum, so I thought perhaps Sunday week, I'll pick you and Antonio up and take you over my mum's for dinner? If I remember rightly, Ava and Antonio were inseparable at Vinny's fortieth, and Antonio adored the mutt. Fred lives there too,' Michael chuckled.

Bella's stomach churned. Ava was Antonio's half-sister and that thought alone made her feel physically sick. 'Let's not rush things, Michael. Don't tell your mum and aunt I'm back yet. Let me get settled again and then we'll surprise them together. I can't wait to see them again though. I thought they were lovely and so funny.'

'OK, babe. Whatever you want. I've gotta go now. There's a geezer here to see me. I'll bell you later.'

Bella said goodbye, replaced the receiver, rested the back of her head against the sofa and stared at the ceiling. Living a life littered with lies and deceit was awful, but what choice did she have? She'd tried to live without Michael and couldn't. She had to keep telling herself that she was the only one that knew the true identity of Antonio's father and there was no reason for anybody else to believe it wasn't Clint. Only Vinny, perhaps? And no way was Bella ever going to allow her son to be in his company. She was afraid if she did, Vinny would take one look at her beloved boy and, because of Antonio's age, black hair and piercing green eyes, put two and two together.

A sunny day always brought droves of shoppers to Roman Road market and the Enemy was pleased that the crowd started to thicken as he walked past Cardigan Road. He'd kept a good twenty feet or so behind Queenie and Vivian since he'd spotted them at Percy Ingle's and had stopped to browse at stalls whenever they had stopped. Queenie was wearing a floral dress accompanied by a bright-red jacket. Vivian's dress was bright green, and the silly old cow had some kind of fur draped around her neck. The Enemy liked animals – he'd recently bought a kitten – and in his eyes the fact some poor creature had been skinned alive so that old witch could drape it proudly over her shoulders was a good enough reason to kill her.

Spotting a gorgeous blonde, the Enemy began to smile at her before realizing there was no point as he was in this ridiculous disguise. Had he not been, he reckoned he could have been in with a chance. He'd always had all the girls at school after him and he hadn't done too bad while locked up. He'd lost his virginity to a twenty-five-year-old brunette called Dawn who was meant to be teaching him art. He'd been a hero amongst the other inmates when their affair had come to light. Dawn hadn't though. She was fired on the spot.

When Queenie and Viv did a detour into the arcade, the Enemy decided to wait outside and order himself a jacket potato. He wasn't hungry, but the less conspicuous he made himself look, the better. He was determined to carry out his plan today. Fucking hard-faced old slappers. They deserved everything coming their way.

Shirley Preston feared nobody. When her grandson Jamie had been falsely accused and then subsequently banged up for murdering Molly Butler, Shirley had dealt with the barrage of abuse and bricks aimed through her windows by chucking abuse back, along with the bloody bricks.

The police had strongly advised Shirley to take up their

offer of a safe house far away from Poplar, but Shirley was having none of it. Unlike her parents, she'd survived the war and Hitler's bombs, so could bloody survive anything. To run away would have been a sign of guilt and even though, at first, the evidence had been stacked against her grandson, Shirley had always known in her heart Jamie was innocent. A silly boy at the time for leading the police up the garden path, but no child killer.

Roman Road wasn't Shirley's usual stomping ground. She much preferred to shop at Chrisp Street market, but today was her friend Madge's sixtieth birthday, hence her visit to Bow. 'I like that top, Shirl. The glittery silver one,' Madge pointed out.

About to take a closer look, Shirley was struck in the side of the head by a fist. 'How dare you show your face around this neck of the woods! Scum like you and that grandson of yours should be hung from the rafters,' Queenie Butler screamed.

The Butler and Preston family had more bad blood and betrayal between them than your average soap on TV could produce in a whole year.

Shirley's lip curled up in fury. 'He's innocent, my Jamie, you senile old bat. You wanna look closer to home to find your granddaughter's killer. Jamie heard through the grapevine that Ben Bloggs killed himself on the day of Molly's funeral. I wonder why?' she bellowed.

Shoppers froze and looked on in amazement as all hell broke loose. 'Your son killed my Roy,' Queenie yelled, dragging Shirley to the floor by her hair.

'And your Vinny killed my Joanna and Johnny,' Shirley shouted. The driver of the red truck that had ploughed her granddaughter's car into a ditch had never been caught and Shirley knew in her heart that Vinny had organized

Joanna's death. Her son Johnny had been a broken man and had ended his own life shortly afterwards.

As Madge waded in, Vivian did the same. 'Get off my sister, you fat slut,' Vivian screamed, aiming blows at the over-sized woman. 'Your whore of a daughter ended my sister's marriage,' she bellowed, punching Shirley as well. Back in the sixties, Albie Butler had had an affair with Judy Preston, Shirley's daughter. Jamie was the child the Butlers had never known existed until he killed Molly.

When stallholders joined the fracas, the Enemy cursed his luck. Should he hang around? Or would his urge to murder a Butler have to wait until another day? In this crowd no one would see who struck the final blow . . .

CHAPTER NINE

'Put another ten kilo on for me, Jay,' Vinny ordered. He'd originally caught the training bug while serving time and now couldn't imagine life without his regular gym sessions.

'I spoke to Michael yesterday. You didn't tell me Bella was back on the scene, Vin.'

Grimacing as he lifted the overloaded bar above his head, Vinny hissed, 'She's a slapper and a messer. Don't you think I have better things to talk about than her?'

A bit taken aback by the look of hatred on Vinny's face, Jay Boy sensibly dropped the subject.

'I need to make a phone call. I won't be a tick,' Vinny said.

Vinny took his phone out of the locker and rang Michael. 'We're gonna sort out that little problem today. It's definitely a goer. I'll pick you up from your club at four.'

'No way can I make today, Vin. I had to blow Bella out yesterday 'cause you said it was definitely a goer then. I'm not cancelling my plans again.'

'You wuss! Can you hear your fucking self? Get a grip, Michael. Your bit of fluff sodded off for months on end with no real explanation, and now you wanna put her in front of family business. What are you? A man or a fucking mouse?'

When Michael slammed the phone down on him, Vinny smirked. His brother would blow Bella out in favour of giving Brenda's bloke a good hiding, and that was the plan.

Nosy Hilda and Mouthy Maureen loved a bit of gossip, and today's was far juicer than most. Neither woman particularly liked Queenie or Vivian, but they loved discussing their business.

'Start from the beginning and talk more slowly. You ramble when you're excited,' Maureen ordered her friend.

'I told you something was going on between Albie and Vivian when I saw them in the pub together, holding hands and gazing into one another's eyes. Well, Queenie's obviously cottoned on because it all kicked off down the Roman yesterday. Old Mother Taylor told me Jewish Harold on the clothes stall told her that Queenie yelled "You've stolen my husband!" Apparently, they were rolling about the pavement like a pair of fishwives, fighting.'

'Blimey! That's a turn up for the books. Let's go for a walk around Mr Patel's. Queenie usually gets her paper about nine-ish. Be good to hear what happened from the horse's mouth. The stuck-up old cow might even want to be friends with us now if her own sister's stabbed her in the back.'

'Can you imagine Viv and Albie humping? Makes me feel ill. I'll get me coat. Let's go.'

'Michael!' Antonio D'Angelo squealed with delight as he threw his arms around the man he hoped would one day marry his mum and become his daddy.

'It's so good to see you, Antonio. I've missed you and your mum so much. Open your presents, boy,' Michael urged.

'You really shouldn't have bought him gifts, Michael. He has everything a child could wish for as it is,' Bella chuckled.

Gesticulating for Bella to follow him into the kitchen, Michael took her in his arms and kissed her passionately. Even in a red velour tracksuit, she looked simply stunning. 'I'm so sorry I can't make the restaurant, babe. It's a long story but my sister's had some grief with her bloke. I'm gonna have to shoot off about three, if that's OK with you?'

Bella forced a smile. She knew exactly the way Vinny's evil mind ticked and what he was trying to do. 'That's fine, Michael. Family comes before pleasure.'

'Here she is! Say what you said you was gonna say,' Mouthy Maureen hissed.

As Queenie approached the newsagent's, the first thing Nosy Hilda noticed was her black eye. 'Oh dear! Are you OK, Queen? I heard what happened. You must be distraught. I mean, who'd have thought it? Your Albie and Vivvy. I was gonna tell you when I saw them holding hands in the pub, but you know me, I don't like to gossip about other people's business.'

Queenie looked at Hilda in astonishment. It wouldn't be the first time the ugly scarf-wearing old hag had got the wrong end of the stick. 'What the hell you going on about? I had a tear-up with Shirley Preston, not my Viv. Albie and Vivvy holding hands in the pub! When? And what fucking pub?'

'Sorry, Queen. We've obviously got the story arse-upwards.' Mouthy Maureen tugged her friend's arm. 'Come on, Hilda. Let's go.'

Vivian had offered to keep an eye on Ava and the horrid little mutt while her sister went out to get the newspapers and some eggs. 'Put the ratpig in the garden, Ava,' she ordered as the dog tried to hump her left leg.

'His name's Fred, not Ratpig! And he's got his dingle-dangle out again, Auntie Viv,' Ava giggled.

'Just do as I say, Ava, please. Now!'

'Ava, take Fred upstairs. I need to have a word with your Auntie Viv,' Queenie yelled, slamming the front door. She'd chased Hilda and Maureen down the road demanding answers when they'd tried to swerve their accusations.

'Whatever's wrong?' Vivian asked.

'You cosying up to Albie in the Grave Maurice, holding fucking hands, Viv, is what's wrong. A laughing stock, I am, thanks to you and that womanizing old wanker. How long you been seeing him behind my back?' Queenie yelled, her eyes blazing with fury.

Vivian leapt off the sofa. 'Don't talk so bleedin' daft. You've lost the plot, you have.'

'That nosy old trout Hilda told me exactly what she saw, and she'd be too scared to lie. I don't care about my feelings, what I care about is my sons'. Mouthy Maureen knows an' all. Can you imagine who else must know if them two old crows have been talking about it? My Vinny and Michael have worked bloody hard to secure their reputation and I am disgusted with you, Viv. Albie, of all people! I knew you'd warmed to the old goat, but truth be known, it was all your fault that our marriage failed. Did you always have designs on him for yourself? Well! Did ya?'

'I'm not listening to any more of this old bollocks. I had a quick drink in the Maurice with Albie when me and you fell out recently. He was trying to cheer me up – end of! And of course I wasn't holding his bastard hand. Nosy Hilda must want her eyes fucking tested. As for you blaming me for ending your marriage, look closer to home, sweetheart. That murdering monster of a son of yours lost you your husband. Not me. Just like he lost me my Lenny. Like it or lump it, your precious apron-string clinger is a complete and utter wrong 'un.'

'All right, bruv? The prick's deffo in the Keys today. Carl's already there,' Vinny explained.

Having spent a bit of quality time with Bella and Antonio, Michael decided not to moan. 'Sweet. At least we can get this done and dusted today. Don't go overboard on him though, Vin. I know what your temper's like, and Bren will know it's us if the tosser disappears off the face of the earth.'

'I won't. Just wanna give him a firm warning. You heard from Mum? She's in a right old state. Reckons Auntie Viv's been having it off with our wonderful father. I told her she must be wrong, but you know what Mum's like once she gets a bee in her bonnet. It better not be true, otherwise that old bastard will truly pay for his sins this time.'

'Of course it ain't true. And if you dare lay one finger on Dad, you'll have me to answer to, Vin. When you last duffed him up, I was only a nipper. Be warned. I'm not now.'

Vinny chuckled. Albie had spent weeks in hospital when Vinny had learned of his affair with Judy Preston, and it served him right. 'How's your stalker? You heard any more?'

Michael was absolutely relieved to have gotten rid of Katy. 'Not a peep, thank Christ. I think the grand did the trick.'

'You'll be lucky! She'll reappear as soon as she finds out you're seeing Bella. Nothing worse than a scorned young psycho,' Vinny taunted.

Michael glared at his elder brother. 'What is it that pisses you off so much about me being happy with a bird? Didn't you also try and split Roy and Colleen up in the past, if I remember rightly? Just because you can't find love, Vin, you shouldn't be bitter towards others.'

Wanting to yell that he too knew every part of Bella's body inch by inch, Vinny instead put his foot on the accelerator and said nothing.

Albie Butler had a Sunday routine. After finishing work at the club, he'd always pop into the Blind Beggar and have a catch-up with a few old pals before heading home to Barking.

'Does it still get busy with those strippers, Albie? I'm surprised your heart can take ogling all that young flesh at your age,' Big Stan joked.

About to reply, Albie was drenched by his own pint of Guinness. 'What the hell! Why d'ya do that?'

'Because you disgust me, you dirty old toad. And so does that so-called sister of mine. I know what the pair of you have been up to,' Queenie yelled, clouting Albie around the head with her umbrella.

Holding Fred's lead, Ava was standing behind her nan, giggling.

'You're deranged! Always bleedin' well have been. Me and Vivvy! Don't make me laugh. Ruined my suit now, you daft old bat.'

Queenie sneered, hands on hips. She loathed the thought of Nosy Hilda and Mouthy Maureen spreading gossip about how she'd been betrayed, which was why she'd decided to come to the pub and spread the word herself in true Queenie style. She'd give the bastards something to talk about, all right.

By the time he got to Dagenham, Vinny Butler was in a foul mood. He and Michael had been having a dig at one another throughout the journey and were now bickering over the wedding suits.

'We're gonna look a right pair of tossers, end of. You

should've backed me rather than telling my son you were happy to wear the bastard thing. Why tell him you liked it when you'd already told me you hated the poxy suit?' Vinny demanded to know.

'Does it matter? Jesus, Vin, we've only got to wear it for one day. Get a grip, will ya?'

'Gonna be a laughing stock, all thanks to you. You might be happy prancing around looking like a gay hairdresser, but I fucking well ain't.'

'Enough about the suits now, Vin. Can we discuss what we've planned for Dave? Only I know what you're like when you're in this type of mood, and the last thing I'm short of is you going overboard and snapping his neck.'

'I'm hardly gonna touch him. Well, not where bruises show anyway. Carl will get him out the boozer. He does most of his dealing in the car park, by all accounts. We'll drag him into the graveyard and give him a good warning about his future conduct. That's about it really.'

The men continued their journey in silence and five minutes later were parked up next to Carl. Carl got out of his motor and stepped into Vinny's Mercedes. 'He's still in there, but looks a bit pissed. I suggest I get him out now before he collapses,' said Carl.

'How do we know he's going to come outside and hand over drugs to a complete stranger?' Michael asked.

'He will. I got introduced to the prick the other night and bought him a beer.'

Michael glared accusingly at Vinny. 'But you said he weren't in the pub any of the other nights.'

Realizing he'd slipped up, Carl Tanner immediately covered his tracks. He had no idea why Vinny had sent him to the pub on three different days, yet still not acted on Carl being present. Vinny was his boss and Carl simply did as he was asked. 'Dave had too many hangers-on with him before, Michael. It wouldn't have been the right time. I told Vinny it was sensible to leave him be.'

Not overly convinced by Carl's explanation, Michael demanded, 'What we waiting for then?'

Dave Green was standing at the corner of the bar having a rant about the West Ham result when Carl approached him. Brenda had always been the one to advise him who he should and shouldn't trust, but she was barred from the Keys now so he had to make his own choices and happily followed Carl outside.

Vinny leapt out of the car and dragged Dave into the graveyard by his neck. 'Like knocking women about, do ya? Answer me, cunt,' he yelled, kneeing Dave ferociously in the groin.

Michael gave Dave a sharp dig in the ribs. 'Nobody hurts our sister and puts her in hospital. Understand what we're saying?'

Eyes like organ stops, Dave fell to the ground and covered his head with his hands. 'I'm sorry. Really sorry. I love Bren and it will never happen again,' he stammered.

Crouching next to the terrified waste of space, Vinny took a flick knife out of his pocket. 'Get your cock out.'

'No. Please God noooo! I really am sorry, Vinny. Truly I am,' Dave wept.

'Do as I say or I'll slit your throat,' Vinny demanded. He loved terrorizing the less fortunate, got off on it completely.

Hands shaking so much he could barely unzip his flies, Dave Green somehow managed to do as he was asked.

Vinny held the blade against the loser's manhood. 'I swear to you, you ever lay a hand on my sister or upset her kids again, I will dismember this little tinkler. And you're not going to mention to Brenda that you've been paid a visit. Comprende?'

'Yes. Y-you have my word I will never upset Bren or the kids again,' Dave gabbled. He'd never sobered up so quickly.

'Let's go,' Michael urged.

Unable to help himself, Vinny stood up and stamped on Dave's penis with all his might. He then did the same to the man's stomach.

Not for the first time, Michael had to witness his brother losing his rag completely and with the help of Carl managed to drag him away before they had another murder on their hands. Vinny was such a loose cannon on occasions, he really was.

Vivian Harris stared forlornly at the television. *Brookside*, *EastEnders*, *The Two Ronnies*, *This Is Your Life* and *Only Fools and Horses* were just some of the programmes she and Queenie always watched together, and viewing them alone was no fun at all.

Pouring herself another sherry, Vivian sighed with discontent. Her and Queenie had been inseparable since they were kids. Their father had been a drunken bully who'd beaten their lovely mum up regularly, therefore she and Queenie had always sought solace in each other. They'd had some fall-outs over the years, like all sisters do. None more so than when it turned out Vinny had killed her beloved Lenny in that car crash. But they'd always managed to put things right between themselves, until now.

When the phone rang, Vivian guessed who the caller would be. She and Queenie had never needed friends. They'd always been content with each other.

'How are you, love? Cheered up a bit today?'

'I'm not too bad, thanks, Albie. I rung Little Vinny about an hour ago. Told him no way can I face the wedding. She'll only go off on one again. Not worth the grief or spoiling that poor boy's big day.'

'Apparently, she's told Michael if either you or I attend, she ain't going. Ain't it ridiculous, Vivvy? A load of fuss over nothing. The woman's gone off her bleedin' head. Bonkers!'

When Albie stayed on the phone chatting for the next half an hour, he cheered Vivian up no end. Unbeknown to anyone, she'd always had a soft spot for him, and he was the only friend she had right now.

CHAPTER TEN

As spring turned into summer, the Butlers remained in turmoil. Queenie still hadn't spoken to Albie or Vivian and continued to insist that she wouldn't attend her grandson's wedding if either turncoat attended.

Today, Little Vinny had decided to visit his nan with Oliver in an effort to make her see sense. He was sick of all the childishness. It was spoiling what should be a happy time for him.

'Ain't he grown! Gonna be a tall 'un like you, your father and Michael. Give your nan another cuddle, Ollie. She's far more important than that scruffy mutt,' Queenie chuckled.

When Oliver tried to pull Fred's tail, Little Vinny gently scolded his son, then ordered him to go and play nicely in the garden. 'I bought you these, Nan,' Little Vinny said, handing Queenie a box of Milk Tray and a bottle of Baileys.

'Aww, bless you. But I've told you before to stop spending your bleedin' money on me,' Queenie said, secretly pleased with her gifts. Her grandson had been a selfish little sod in his youth, had never even bought her a card when he'd lived with her. He'd changed so much since meeting Sammi-Lou and having a child himself though. Turned into a real charming, generous, young man.

'Nan, we need to talk about my wedding. All this silliness going on is upsetting me and Sammi-Lou. I will be devastated if you don't attend. It will truly spoil my whole day.'

'I'm not sitting in church with them two traitors, boy. Either you uninvite them or I won't come. I would hate it to all kick off and your big day be ruined. What would Sammi's parents think? Be shameful.'

'You've got it all wrong about Granddad and Auntie Viv, Nan. They only popped in the boozer for a quick drink because Viv was upset about rowing with you and Granddad wanted to cheer her up. That's all that happened, honest.'

'How do you know? You weren't bleedin' there, were ya? Nosy Hilda swears blind they were holding hands and I for one believe her.'

'Use your loaf. As if they would be sitting in the Grave Maurice, of all places, if they were having some kind of secret affair. You're not thinking straight, Nan. As for Nosy Hilda, she's an interfering old bat, and obviously as blind as one. I cannot understand how you believe her explanation over your own sister's. Vivvy has been there for you through thick and thin. It's ridiculous – Granddad and Auntie Viv? Don't make me laugh.'

Queenie fiercely wiped away the tears. She knew she'd overreacted at the time, especially when she'd marched into the Blind Beggar, aired her dirty washing in public, and chucked a drink all over Albie. Whatever had she been thinking? However, it was a bit late to backtrack now. She knew in her heart that Vivvy would never fancy Albie, so why had she behaved so irrationally? Queenie had no fond feelings towards Albie whatsoever, bar him providing her with three wonderful sons. Shame about the daughter, but with Albie's sperm she'd been fortunate to be blessed with what she had. The only thing she could put it down to was Vivian's blossoming friendship with the man they'd both once despised. That grated on Queenie immensely.

Little Vinny sat next to his grandmother and put an arm around her shoulders. 'I'll speak to Granddad and Auntie Viv. I'm sure they'll forgive you, Nan.'

Her grandson's use of the word 'forgive' made Queenie see red again. '*Forgive* me! For what? They were the two cosying up in the pub whilst I was sat at home minding me own bleedin' business. I don't wanna upset you, lad, but this is how it is. If they go to the wedding, I bastard-well don't. The choice is yours.'

Another Butler having a meltdown was Vinny. Bella had sensibly stayed away from his neck of the woods, but every couple of weeks would invite his mum over for dinner at her gaff in Chelsea. Vinny would then have to endure his mother going on for hours on end about what a beautiful, classy girl she was. How wonderful her brat of a son was, and gloating over how fucking wealthy she must be because her apartment was straight out of the TV programme *Dallas*.

When Vinny failed to find a phone number he was looking for, and yanked the drawer out of his desk, emptying the contents all over the office, Jay Boy asked, 'Is something wrong, boss?'

'Yes. Fucking everything! Listen, I need to make a call. It's private, so leave me to it.'

On his hands and knees, Vinny searched through all the crap he'd hoarded. He'd gone to his mother's yesterday, looking forward to one of her legendary roasts, then hadn't wanted to eat sod-all when she'd driven him mad over her visit the previous day to that bitch's gaff. Even Daniel and Lee had met Bella now and spoke highly of the slapper.

Finding the number of her modelling agency, Vinny

poured himself a Scotch and downed it in one before dial-ling it. A camp-sounding bloke answered.

'Can you put me through to Bella, please? I've got an urgent message for her.'

'And may I ask who's calling?'

'Her boyfriend's brother, Vinny Butler.'

A moment later Bella came on the line, trying her hardest to sound composed. 'What can I do for you, Vinny?'

'To put it bluntly, I don't want you coming to my son's wedding. I don't care what you say to Michael, fake an illness if you have to, but I don't want you there.'

'To be honest there's nothing I would like better than to avoid your son's wedding, Vinny. But between me and you, Michael has started to get suspicious about my refusal to visit your mother's house. I intend to spend the rest of my life with your brother, and I cannot carry on avoiding such things. Not unless you want me to tell him the truth?'

'Of course I don't want you to tell him the fucking truth. He's my brother, it would break his heart.'

Unbeknown to Michael, Bella had no intention of attending the wedding. The thought of being in such close proximity to Vinny made her want to vomit, so she'd already hatched a plan to get herself out of it. 'Well, in that case, we need to come to a mature arrangement. I will avoid your son's wedding providing you agree to do the same for me on the odd occasion I visit your mother. There will obviously be other family events in the future, and we can liaise on which one of us will go. Do we have a deal?'

Vinny was seething. He wasn't used to being blackmailed, neither was he used to being spoken to like a child. Part of him wanted to call Bella's bluff, tell her he'd decided to tell Michael after all. That would wipe the patronizing tone straight out of her cocky gob. But much as he'd relish getting one over on her, it wasn't worth losing his brother for ever. His mother would probably disown him as well. Not over his fling with Bella, just the fact he'd kept schtum about it. She'd see that as treacherous and unforgiveable.

'I'm sorry to rush you, Vinny. But I'm very busy. I have a meeting with a client soon. Are you OK with what I suggested?'

'Ain't got a lot of choice, have I?' Vinny hissed. 'Just stay out my face, or else.'

Bella breathed a sigh of relief as Vinny cut her off. His idle threat at the end meant nothing. If he was going to tell Michael, he'd have done so long before now.

Vinny was absolutely furious. 'Cunt! Whore! Slag!' he screamed, throwing the phone at the wall. How dare the bitch say she'd let him know when she was visiting his mother, so he could stay away? That was the piss-takes of all piss-takes.

Katy Spencer took her linen jacket off to reveal the skin-tight white Lycra dress. 'Well? Can you see it?' she asked, turning to the side.

'Definitely. It's a big bump now,' Lucy Tompkins lied, knowing that's exactly what her friend wanted to hear. Katy was so tall and slim, even though she was now over four months pregnant, apart from a bit of a pot belly, there was no real sign.

'Come on. Let's start walking. I know we're early, but I don't want to miss them,' Katy said, linking arms with Lucy.

Having managed to keep her pregnancy secret from her parents, Katy now felt the time was right for Michael to learn the truth. She'd been very disappointed that he hadn't contacted her yet, but was sure once he knew about the baby they'd become an item once again. 'Are you sure Daniel and Lee will notice, Luce? Say they don't? I want you to hint or do something if they start to walk away without mentioning it.'

'Like what? You said you didn't want to blurt anything out,' Lucy reminded her friend.

'I can't do this on my own any more. My baby needs his daddy and so do I. Michael needs to know, and then we can tell my parents together, like a proper couple. If the boys don't cotton on, then point to my bloody bump and make a joke about me putting on weight and why. Obviously, don't mention their father. Michael will want to tell them himself. But Daniel and Lee are bound to tell him my news as soon as they get home. I bet he rings me tonight. Or first thing tomorrow at the latest. I can't wait to see him again,' Katy said dreamily.

'I don't want to burst your bubble, but you did say Michael didn't want any more kids yet. Say it's too soon after Adam and he isn't happy about it, Katy? He probably will be, but I don't want you to be upset if he isn't. I don't mind being there when you tell your parents if need be.'

'Michael will want to be there with me, Luce. He loves me, I know he does. Now he knows I'm pregnant, he won't even worry about the age gap. He only let me go because he thought I could do better than him. He told me that to my face.'

'Are you sure Daniel and Lee definitely walk this way?'

'Yes. I often walked with them. I think they fancied me and wanted to show me off to their school mates,' Katy chuckled. 'If we hang about on that corner over the road there, that's where they turn. They always go straight home to play on their pool table and gaming machines. They both thought I was so cool because I was good at Pac-Man. I know it's bound to be a shock for them at first, but once they get their head around me being with their dad, I reckon they'll love having me as their new mum.'

About to remind her friend that the reason Michael had finished with her was because Daniel and Lee had found out about her affair with their father and were unhappy about it, Lucy opened her mouth, then shut it again. Katy was in an extremely positive mood today, and all Lucy could do was be there for her if things didn't quite go to plan. 'The kids have started to come out now.'

Katy craned her neck and being tall had a great view. 'I can see them, I think. Hang on. Yep! That's definitely Daniel. Quick, let's go round the corner, then walk towards it again,' she said excitedly.

Daniel and Lee had just sparked up a cigarette when Lee spotted Katy. 'Shit, put the fags out. It's Katy. She might tell Dad,' he hissed.

Confident that Katy was far too cool to grass them up, Daniel strutted across the road like James Dean, fag in mouth. 'Long time no see. How you doing, darlin'?'

'Fine, thank you. I miss yous two though.'

'We miss you an' all, don't we, Dan?' Lee grinned.

'We're sorry we lost you your job. We'd never have bricked Donald and Mary's café if we knew Dad would sack you,' Daniel apologized.

Feeling the first stirrings of unrest, Katy enquired what exactly Daniel meant.

'Dad said it was our fault you couldn't work for him no more. He said if we'd have behaved ourselves you wouldn't have lost your job,' Lee explained.

Trying to hide her anguish because it was totally obvious the boys did not know about her affair with their father, and Michael had blatantly lied to her, Katy asked, 'How is your dad?'

'Yeah, OK. Loved up again with Bella, so we don't see him as much now. She's OK though, ain't she, Dan?' Lee said.

'Not as nice as you though,' Daniel added, putting an arm around Katy's back.

Lucy felt so sorry for her friend as she burst into uncontrollable tears. 'Come on, mate. Let's go,' she urged.

'Bastard! What a lying fucking bastard,' Katy sobbed.

'Have we said something wrong? Sorry, Katy,' Lee spluttered.

Horrified when a group of schoolchildren gathered around, Lucy was the one to dig her friend out of a hole. 'No, boys. You've said nothing wrong. But your dad told Katy she lost her job for another reason, that's why she's upset. Oh, and she's also pregnant which makes her emotional as well.'

'You got a boyfriend now, Katy?' Lee gawped.

Instead of answering, an inconsolable Katy fled the scene.

Vinny Butler was in a random boozer where nobody knew him, knocking back Scotch after Scotch. Jay Boy, Carl, Pete and Paul were all at the club and no way did he want them to know he was on one. Neither would he ever mug himself off in front of his wealthy clients.

Cocaine had been a problem to Vinny back in the day, which was why he'd given it the elbow. Today, however, he'd felt a strong urge to get off his face and had purchased a couple of grams. Ahmed had introduced him to the crap in the first place, and Vinny was reminiscing how he'd not only paid the Turk back for that, but also every other treacherous thing he'd ever done. Ahmed had died the most horrendous death. Credit where it was due, the Turk had acted like a man even though he knew his fate. But that had all changed when Vinny had sliced his cock off. Ahmed's screams were priceless, and every now and again Vinny would dream about that memorable night and wake up with a big smile on his face.

Clocking a bird staring his way, Vinny stared back. She was nowhere near as pretty facially as Bella, but there was something about her that was similar. Long dark hair, olive skin, tall, slim.

When the bird smiled, Vinny gestured for her to join him. 'What's your name?' he asked.

'Nadia. Yours?'

Vinny had no idea why he replied in such a way, but he grinned and said, 'Michael. My name is Michael, sweetheart.'

Daniel Butler was furious and ranting at Lee: 'Of course it must be Dad's baby, you div. Didn't you see the look on Katy's face when you told her he was with Bella? That's when she called Dad a "fucking bastard". Why would she say that if it weren't Dad's baby?'

'Nah. Dad wouldn't do that. He loved Mum and now he loves Bella. Katy is far too young for Dad to fancy.'

'You are so thick at times, Lee. Dad didn't love Mum, and she weren't your mum anyway. I think we should both call her Nancy from now on 'cause I never loved her neither.'

Lee was about to stick up for himself when he spotted their father's car pulling up outside. 'You gonna ask him, Dan?'

'Watch and learn. Leave this to me.'

Michael poked his head around the door of the lounge. 'All right, boys? You eaten yet?'

'No. Why? Gonna cook us a nice meal?' Daniel replied, his voice full of sarcasm. Apart from the odd fry-up at breakfast time, his father never bothered cooking for him and Lee. He bunged them regular money to get takeaways instead.

Michael slouched in the armchair. 'I ain't got time to

cook, need to get back to the club by eight. I thought we might have fish and chips. Wanna shoot out and get it?'

'Nah. Don't fancy it. Me and Lee bumped into Katy today and we told her how much we missed her cooking, didn't we, Lee?' Daniel replied, studying his father's face.

Michael immediately felt edgy, but tried not to show or sound it. 'How's Katy doing? She got another job yet?'

'Nah. She can't work no more. She's up the duff. About four or five months gone, we reckon, eh, Lee? Weird, 'cause she never had a boyfriend when she worked 'ere. Do you reckon she's a slag, Dad?'

The colour immediately drained from Michael's face. 'How would I know? Listen, I need to ring your nan. She's still refusing to come to Little Vinny's wedding,' he said, jumping out of his chair. 'I won't be a tick.'

'But what about the fish and chips?' Daniel taunted, as his father bolted out the lounge.

Michael Butler's breathing felt laboured as the fresh air of the back garden hit him. He'd only ever shagged Katy once without a condom. Surely he couldn't be that unlucky? Or could he? Over his dead body was Katy giving birth to his baby.

Vinny Butler never invited birds back to his flat. Brothels or hotels were his usual choice for a bit of sordid entertainment. However after storming out of the club earlier, thanks to the effect that whore Bella seemed to have on him, he'd forgotten to take a lump of dosh out the safe.

Real men didn't carry credit cards, they walked around with a wad of paper money, and when Nadia had told him her gaff was a no-go, Vinny had suggested they go to his. Jay Boy had now officially moved out, was living with his bird Jilly. And no way could he go back to the club to pick up some wonga as he was totally off his face.

'So, what do you do for a living?' Nadia asked.

Vinny didn't indulge in small talk, especially with strangers. 'I'm a monk,' he replied, ramming his member back inside Nadia's mouth. He was reasonably well endowed, and had learned over the years that a mouthful of cock was the best way to shut a bird up.

Positioning himself so Nadia could not move, Vinny became extremely excited as her face reddened and she began spluttering and choking. This was what he got off on: power.

Katy Spencer was in a terrible state. She'd truly believed Michael had loved her, and still did to some extent. 'Once he knows about the baby, Luce, I know he will tell that Bella to jog on. How can he not when I'm carrying his child?' Katy wept.

Lucy Tompkins was no expert on men, especially men like Michael Butler, but she thought it was about time she was honest with her best friend. 'You have to face the fact that he might have been using you, Katy. I know he probably wasn't, but he did tell you he'd been in love with Bella before she'd gone to Italy.'

Mascara running and resembling a panda, Katy sat bolt upright on her pal's bed. 'Well in that case, let's go to his club and confront him.'

'No, Katy. Let's see if Michael contacts you first. Ring your mum and dad again to see if you've had any phone calls. Michael might not have spoken to Daniel or Lee yet. Play it cool.'

'But what if he doesn't contact me tomorrow?'

Lucy cuddled her friend. 'Then we'll both go to his club together and give him what for.'

Daniel Butler was furious. So much so, he'd already raided the fridge and necked two cans of his father's lager. 'He's a fucking pervert, Lee. Katy ain't that much older than us. I told you Dad fancied her, didn't I?'

'We don't know for definite that it's Dad's baby. Perhaps we should just ask him? Katy never stayed here, did she?'

Daniel looked at his half-brother in despair. He was so clued up for his age, so why wasn't Lee? 'As if Dad would shag her here while we were about! I'm telling you now, we've got a half-brother or -sister on the way. Didn't you clock how guilty he looked earlier? Then he ran out the room. I bet Dad was boning her at the club. Gonna be well funny when Bella finds out, eh?'

Lee was alarmed. 'You're not gonna tell Bella, are you?'

Daniel Butler smirked. 'Yeah, probably. At the wedding.'

Vinny Butler only ever enjoyed shagging birds up the rear. Not only was the hole tighter, it saved him from having to look at their stupid faces.

Feeling himself nearing that crucial moment, Vinny put his hands around Nadia's neck. 'You're a whore, Bella. Deserve all that's coming your way, you do,' he spat, tightening his grasp.

Nadia's arms and legs flapping reminded Vinny of a bird desperately trying to fly with an injured wing, and that only heightened the intensity of his orgasm.

'Jesus wept! I needed that. You can get dressed now,' Vinny ordered, rolling onto his back.

When Nadia did not reply, Vinny shook her. 'Wake up. Don't mess about.'

Panic setting in when there was still no reply, Vinny rolled Nadia onto her front. She felt like a dead weight, looked lifeless. He manically pumped at her chest. 'Wake up, girl. Don't do this to me. Fucking open your eyes, will ya?'

CHAPTER ELEVEN

Sweating profusely as he managed to rip out another of Nadia's teeth, Vinny handed the pliers to Carl. 'Your turn to play dentist. I need a glass of water.'

Vinny still felt a bit high, but had sobered up now. He couldn't believe what he'd done, but he'd told Jay Boy and Carl it was a sex game that had gone wrong, and thankfully both seemed to believe him. No way could he have told them the truth: that Nadia was choking and flapping around while he throttled her to death. He honestly hadn't meant to kill her though. Imagining she was Bella was where it had all gone wrong.

Jay Boy had been ordered to go out and steal a motor. Not a flash car, van, or old banger because they were always liable to get a tug off the Old Bill in the middle of the night. A sensible motor. The plan then was to shove Nadia in the boot, drive her miles away and burn her and the car to cinders. Hopefully, with her gnashers removed, the Old Bill wouldn't have a clue who she was. She'd be nothing more than a pile of ashes.

'I've sorted the motor. It's perfect. A Ford Cortina, and I managed to nick a mini-cab aerial an' all, so I've shoved that on the back. Plates have already been changed. We set to go?' Jay Boy asked.

'Not yet. Still trying to get her teeth out.'

Jay Boy sighed. He loved working for Vinny, but seriously didn't need all this other shit that went with his job at the club. He had Jilly and her kid to consider now. 'Well we'd better get a move on. Fuck burning her when it's light.'

The Enemy had become impatient. He'd stalked Vivian a few times now, and whenever he'd been about to strike, something had occurred to stop him from doing so. It was as though God was warning him it wasn't meant to be.

He'd also followed Vinny and Michael on a couple of occasions. They usually had their henchmen with them and the Enemy wasn't stupid. No way did he want to go back inside, which was why he'd now turned his attention to Brenda.

It was common knowledge that Queenie wasn't as close to Brenda as her sons, but she was still her only daughter. He'd also heard through the grapevine that Little Vinny was getting married this weekend, so to spoil the wedding would be an added bonus.

After a bloody long wait, the Enemy finally saw Brenda and her drunken friend stagger from the Eastbrook pub. He crossed the road and glanced around. The pub was situated near traffic lights and he needed to wait for a lull in the passing cars.

After tottering unsteadily along Rainham Road South for a few minutes, the women decided to get some chips. The Enemy was dressed like a nerd again, and pulled the hood of his duffel coat over his head. He'd done his homework. The nearest cab firm was a five-minute walk away, but unfortunately it was within spitting distance of Dagenham Police Station. Would the drunken mingers head there or would they walk home? The Enemy had learned Brenda lived in Oldmead House, which would be a bit of a schlep given the state she was in.

He watched and waited while the girls sat on the pavement, mauling their food like animals. Realizing there were no people or cars in sight, the Enemy put his hand inside his satchel. It was now or never, he thought, as he ran towards Brenda.

Ginger Sharon glanced up as he approached. 'Buy your own fucking grub,' she slurred.

The Enemy didn't reply. He aimed straight for Brenda's stomach, plunging the knife in three times.

When the ginger bird dropped her chips and started to scream manically, the Enemy turned on his heel and ran as fast as he could down Oxlow Lane.

'Bobby Jackson's son. Don't tell the police – tell my brothers,' Brenda gurgled. They were the last words she ever spoke.

Having had no time to prepare for the disposal of this particular body, Vinny Butler ordered Carl to drive the Cortina to Purfleet. He knew the area reasonably well as that was where he'd killed Ahmed and Burak.

Vinny hadn't fancied sitting in the stolen car with his latest victim in the boot, so had chosen to accompany Jay Boy. His pal was driving and Carl was following them.

'Do you wanna talk about what happened?' Jay Boy asked Vinny.

'No point, is there? She's dead. As I told you earlier, it was a sex game that went wrong,' Vinny lied, flicking another of Nadia's teeth out the window as they cruised along the A13. It had been Jay Boy who'd dislodged the last of them. Bastards to get out, they'd been, especially the molars.

'You should try and find yourself a decent bird, Vin. I've never been happier since I settled down with my Jilly. Playing the field ain't all it's cracked up to be at times.'

'Tell me about it. Just drive and don't lecture me, Jay. I'm so not in the mood. My love life has had disaster stamped all over it, ever since I found out what me cock was for. I think we turn off soon. Slow down a bit.'

'I know exactly where to turn off. It's not yet, Vin.'

Eight minutes later, Carl Tanner pulled up behind Jay Boy's motor. He'd felt no nerves driving about with a dead body in the boot. His previous career as a con man had taught him how to control any form of anxiety.

The area Vinny had chosen was that desolate you could've heard a pin drop. 'I think we should burn her separately. I need to make sure she's totally unrecognizable. We can set fire to the motor afterwards,' Vinny said.

Jay Boy was worried. 'Vin, it's nearly four, and it'll be getting light soon. Let's just burn her in the boot and get the fuck out of here. We've got to go home in my motor – which happens to be registered in my bloody name.'

'Want me to do the honours?' Carl offered, waving a petrol container in the air.

Ignoring Jay Boy's advice, Vinny opened the boot and dragged the girl out. She was wrapped in a sheet. He urged Carl to help him pull her along the lane a bit, and with no remorse whatsoever, callously poured the petrol over her, then struck a match.

Jay Boy gagged as the smell of burning flesh hit his nostrils. He was no wimp, but setting fire to random women was something he would never be able to get his head around. The poor bird had only gone out for a drink earlier, must have a family who would be devastated to never see her again. As much as he respected Vinny, now he was planning to marry Jilly and start a family himself, at times such as this Jay Boy did wonder if he should quit his job, while he was still able to.

Vivian Harris had always been a light sleeper, and since her fall-out with Queenie, woke up sporadically throughout the night.

Hearing a car engine, Vivian glanced at her radio/alarm clock, then got out of bed. 'Oh no,' she gasped, as she spotted two coppers get out of a marked car outside Queenie's.

Queenie's heart beat wildly when she opened the front door. Surely Vinny hadn't been arrested? Or worse still, was dead? 'Whatever's the matter?' she asked.

'May we come inside please, Queenie?' DC Marriot asked. He knew the woman well, had often spoken to her around the shops and market.

'It's all right, Queen. I'm here,' Vivian assured, leading her sister into the front room and urging her to sit down. She could tell by the look on the Old Bill's faces that it was extremely bad news. They didn't knock you up in the middle of the night for anything less.

Queenie felt as though she was in a trance as she stared at Marriot.

'I'm afraid we have some bad news for you, Queenie.'

'Not my Vinny or Michael? Please tell me it ain't my boys,' Queenie gabbled.

'There was an incident in Dagenham earlier. A woman received a fatal stab wound and we strongly believe that woman was your daughter, Brenda. Obviously, we will need somebody to formally identify the body,' Marriot's colleague explained.

'Brenda! Stabbed! But she's still alive, right?' Queenie exclaimed.

Their terrible row forgotten, Vivian held her sister in her arms. 'No, Queen. Fatal means fatal. I'm so sorry, my darling. Poor Brenda.'

Slumped in the armchair, Queenie shook her head in disbelief. 'My baby girl. I did love her, ya know. In 'ere I always loved her,' she wept, patting the left-hand side of her ribs.

'What happened? Was Bren at home?' Vivian asked. She couldn't believe their family had been cursed with yet another death. It was surreal.

'Brenda's friend was with her when the incident happened. They'd been drinking in the Eastbrook pub. That is all the information we have at present, but I can assure you the police will do everything in their power to catch the person responsible.'

'Bren's boyfriend beat her up recently. Dave Green his name is. It's got to be him who stabbed her,' Vivian told Marriot.

'Some officers from Dagenham are with Mr Green now. He was in the Cross Keys pub when the incident occurred, and is helping the police with their enquiries,' Marriot's colleague replied.

The last time Queenie had laid eyes on her daughter was when she was lying in a hospital bed. As memories of her final conversation with Brenda came flooding back, Queenie sobbed uncontrollably. 'I told Bren I wished I'd never given birth to her. Told her she was dead in my eyes, and now she is. What a terrible wicked mother I am.'

When Marriot and his colleague glanced awkwardly at one another, Vivian shouted, 'Make yourselves useful, will ya? Pour my sister a brandy, it's in that cabinet. Can't you see she's in shock?'

Jay Boy and Carl were absolutely knackered. After setting fire to the girl and the car, Vinny had insisted they accompany him back to the flat so they could scrub it from top to bottom and wipe away any trace of her. They'd also dumped his mattress and bedding for him. That too had gone up in a puff of smoke.

'I'll get Edna to come in later today and give this one last going over. And I'll need you to pick me up a new mattress, lads. Thanks for your help. There'll be an extra five grand in both your wage packets this week. Remember, nobody must get wind of this, Michael included. It's to be kept between the three of us.'

Jay Boy slouched on the sofa. 'Are you sure nobody clocked you in the pub with the bird, Vin? You absolutely positive she was alone there?'

'She told me she'd never been in that boozer before. Said she'd been out with a mate, they'd rowed, and she'd stumbled in there. We were both pissed, and I swear I only spoke to her for a minute before she suggested going somewhere quieter. I reckon she'd actually had a row with a bloke rather than a mate, 'cause she made it perfectly clear she wanted a good fucking. She said she was starving, hadn't eaten all day, so I told her to go and get something to eat, then meet me where I'd parked my car in half an hour. Which reminds me. Shit! We need to scrub the fucking car an' all. Her fingerprints must be all over it. In fact, I think you should burn that as well. I'll report it as stolen.'

'Jesus, Vin. Let's just wipe it clean, eh? If by any chance the bizzies pay you a visit, don't you think they'll be even more suspicious to see you have a new mattress and your car has been stolen and found burned out? I know you've arranged an alibi for the three of us, but we'll all be in shit-street if you keep setting fire to stuff. Me and Carl will clean the motor for you. Then let's all get some kip.'

'I read an article in the paper recently. It said in years

to come, people will be getting nicked for crimes committed now thanks to advances in DNA technology,' Vinny warned.

'Vin, I can barely keep my eyes open. It's been a helluva long night. Why don't me and Jay give the car a clean, then we can all think a bit straighter once we've slept. Are you sure the Kelly brothers are good for our alibi?' Carl asked.

'Of course. If tugged, I'd better admit I had a beer in that boozer, in case anybody saw me. Then yous two picked me up from the flat in Jay's motor and we drove over to Kent for a card game with the Kellys. That will account for Jay's car being spotted along the A13 – not that it would have been.'

When Vinny's landline rang again, he pulled the plug out the wall. His mother had been constantly phoning while they were trying to clean the flat up, and Vinny guessed it was because she hadn't been able to get hold of him for the past twenty-four hours and was worried. No way was he in the mood to talk to her now, or anybody else for that matter.

'I'll take your car, Vin, and drop it back this afternoon,' Jay Boy said.

Vinny was that tired, he felt stoned. He put his weary head in his hands. 'I can't believe my son is getting married on Saturday, and I've had to deal with all this shit.'

Carl and Jay Boy glanced at one another, both thinking the same. If this ever came to light, they'd be going down as well. For a murder they did not commit.

Michael Butler was having the twenty-four hours from hell. Katy had been far too besotted with him to have been seeing other blokes on the side, so if she was in the family way, it was most likely his. He'd been reaching for the phone to make the dreaded call to her when his mother had rung to inform him his sister had been stabbed to death. Michael couldn't believe it. He might not have been close to Brenda in recent years, but he had when they were kids. She was the nearest to him in age, and he couldn't believe their paths would never cross again. Growing up, Bren had been a vibrant, pretty girl and tears stung Michael's eyes as he remembered the times he'd met her from school. Full of attitude she'd been, a true Butler. Should he and Vinny have done more to help her sort her life out in latter years? Well, that thought would haunt him for ever now. They had tried to help her a few times, but Bren was headstrong, just like they were. Perhaps they should have been more forceful? Made her go into rehab, God rest her soul. She was their only sister, after all.

Nobody had been able to get hold of Vinny, so it was Michael who had the difficult task of accompanying his mother and aunt to identify Brenda's body. The only good thing to come out of all this was that his aunt and mother seemed to have forgotten the stupid argument over his father.

Michael spoke to the police officer alone, then walked over to his mother. 'I think you should let me identify the body, Mum. You'll have plenty of time to say a proper goodbye to Bren once the police have wrapped up their enquiries.'

'No!' A tearful Queenie clenched her sister's hand and shook her head vehemently. 'I gave birth to that girl and I need to see her for myself. You stay here, Viv's coming in with me.'

The police officer led Queenie and Vivian into a room. The whole place smelt awful, an unrecognizable stench that was obviously associated with death. When the man lifted back the shroud to reveal the face, Queenie put her hand over her mouth. There wasn't a mark on Brenda.

She looked asleep rather than dead. 'I'm so sorry, Bren. I did love you. Please forgive me for what I said. I didn't mean it. Of course I wish you'd been born,' Queenie said.

'She looks at peace now, Queen,' Vivian pointed out.

Tears rolling down her cheeks, Queenie nodded. 'Yes. She does, bless her. Maybe being in heaven will do her a favour? I doubt she'll be able to buy booze up there. She'll be able to redeem herself and start afresh.'

'I'm sure she will. Plus she'll have your Roy, my Lenny, Adam and Molly keeping an eye on her. And our lovely mum. What's gonna happen to Tara and Tommy though? Poor little ha'p'orths must be traumatized. We should go and pick 'em up, Queen, take 'em back to yours.'

'They can't live with me. I've got enough on me plate with Ava,' Queenie said bluntly.

'We can't leave 'em with that tosser Dave. They're not even his. And he's an alkie,' Vivian argued.

'Best somebody tracks down Dean Smart then. He's their bloody father,' Queenie hissed.

The copper and mortuary staff exchanged glances. They'd heard some strange conversations in their time, eavesdropping on family members as they identified loved ones, but never one quite as odd as this.

Vinny Butler was disorientated as he sat bolt upright. Had he heard a hammering on his front door or dreamt it?

'Vinny, it's Michael. I know you're in there 'cause I rung Jay Boy. Open the fucking door.'

Relief flooding through his veins it wasn't the Old Bill, Vinny stumbled out of bed. Surely Michael hadn't found out about the bird? 'What's up?' he asked, feeling edgy.

'What's up! What's fucking up! Why ain't you been answering your phone? Mum and me have been trying to get hold of you since the early hours of this morning.'

'Sorry. I had a card game that went on most the night and I've got the hangover from hell. What's the matter? Has something happened?'

Annoyed with himself for not doing more for Brenda, and furious with Vinny for being on the missing list, Michael decided to break the news brutally. 'Er, you could say that. Our sister got stabbed to death last night. I've already taken Mum to identify Bren's body.'

Vinny slumped into the armchair with his head in his hands. 'What exactly happened? That cunt Dave, it's got to be.'

'Is that all you've got to say? Our little sister's dead, Vin. We should've done more for her. It's our fault. She was one of our own.'

'No, it isn't our fault. Well, not mine anyway,' Vinny replied, his face devoid of any emotion. 'While you were focusing solely on your own fucking problems, including that unreliable bit of fluff you're so obsessed with, I was actually trying to help our sister. Found her a nice flat and a decent clinic to get her off the booze, but Bren being Bren, she threw it all back in my face. She was beyond help, unfortunately.'

'You're one callous bastard, Vin. You don't even seem upset.'

'I'm not callous, bruv. I'm real. You feel guilty, that's why you're doing your martyr speech. Whereas I have sod-all to feel guilty about. I'll kill that fucking Dave when I get me hands on him this time, make no mistake about that though. Where did it happen? D'ya know?'

'Nothing to do with Dave, so the Old Bill reckon. They've already let him go. He was in the Cross Keys when Bren got stabbed. She was with a pal and on her way home from the Eastbrook boozer. I don't think the filth have much to go on, to be honest.'

118

'Got to be something to do with Dave. We'll pay him a little visit tomorrow. How's Mum taking it?'

'A bit tearful, but not too bad. She's made up with Auntie Viv, thank Christ. I dropped 'em home on the way here. You need to get your arse round there and take care of things. I can't get out of working tonight 'cause it's gonna be rammed and I'm short-staffed thanks to a flu bug.'

'You should shut the club as a mark of respect, bruv. I'm sure Mum will be upset if you don't,' Vinny warned.

'And are you shutting your club for the foreseeable, Vin?'

'Nah. But I won't be working. Jay Boy and Carl will run it in my absence. Anyway, my club's in Holborn, so it's different. The locals are bound to hear through the grapevine that Bren's been murdered, and it stinks of disrespect, you opening up in Whitechapel.'

'Says who? I've already told Mum the score. I've got some well-known DJ booked, and if I shut the poxy club, it'll cause mayhem with the amount of tickets that've been bought. Mum was OK about it. Had it been any other night, of course I would've closed the gaff.'

Vinny Butler tutted. 'Bang out of order, that is, bruv. Our sister ain't even cold yet.'

Katy Spencer tried on yet another dress, before finally making her mind up. 'I think I'm going to wear the pink one I tried on first, Luce. It shows my bump more, and I still felt sexy in it.'

'Good choice. But more importantly, what you going to say to Michael? Will you mention you know he's seeing Bella?'

'Yes. Then I will tell him I'm carrying his baby and watch him squirm. He's bound to finish with Bella, Luce, so we can finally be a proper family. I've decided to forgive him for lying to me. He was only worried about the age gap, and he truly loves me, I know he does.'

Lucy Tompkins nodded and smiled in a sympathetic manner. Katy was either truly naïve, or obsessed enough to get what she actually wanted. It was one of the two.

Vinny Butler's brain was working overtime. He was so annoyed with his own stupidity. It was too late for regrets though. What was done was done.

'The car's spotless. Up to you, but I don't think you should burn it, Vin,' Jay Boy advised, handing his boss the keys.

'I won't. My head's clearer now. Don't bother getting me a new mattress either. I'm gonna use the one in your old room, that way we only have to get rid of the second bed base,' Vinny ordered.

'We still sticking with the same alibi?'

'Yeah. But if the Old Bill come knocking, I've decided to admit I met the bird, 'cause they wouldn't be knocking if some nosy bastard hadn't spotted me with her. I very much doubt anybody recognized me in that boozer though. It was full of the leftie brigade. I reckon there must have been some tree-hugging rally on in London somewhere. Those unwashed jobless mugs ain't gonna know who I am, are they?'

'If the bizzies do tug you, will you admit you brought her back to your flat?' Jay Boy asked.

'Dunno. But as long as you say you picked me up from here around twelve, all will be cool. The Kellys have two other geezers to back the alibi if need be, and one's a bent cop on their payroll. I'd better get off now, take care of my mum. She's bound to be upset over Bren. It never rains in my world, it always fucking pours.'

'I'm sorry about your sister, mate. Couldn't believe it

when Michael told me. I know exactly how you feel. I felt like my heart had been ripped out when my bro died. Dunno how I'd have coped if it wasn't for you,' Jay Boy admitted. He and Vinny had been sharing a cell in Pentonville when his brother had been stabbed to death back in Liverpool.

'It hardly feels the same, Jay. Your brother was a dude. Whereas my sister was a drunken loser and total embarrassment. It actually ain't a bad thing Bren's departed this world with a bit of folklore behind her. Better than making a cunt of herself and my family for many more years to come, until her liver finally decided it'd had enough of her. But whoever killed her, I will turn them into fucking mincemeat, and that's a promise.'

Queenie Butler was knocking back the sherry. Obviously, she was extremely upset that her only daughter had been murdered, but it wasn't quite the devastation she'd felt when other close family members had been taken from her. She felt more numb than anything.

'I can't believe we weren't talking, Queen, and it's taken something as tragic as this to bang our heads together. I missed you so much. Let's make a pact that if we ever have a fall-out in the future we sort it out immediately. Can you imagine if one of us had croaked it while not talking to the other?' Vivian said. She'd been on the sherry too and was feeling maudlin. Any death in the family always brought her Lenny's back to her.

'I missed you too, but I was so bleedin' angry at the time. You should've just told me you went for a drink with Albie. I'd much rather it'd come from you than our interfering bastard neighbours.'

'I know and I'm sorry. But it didn't seem important at the time. Wait until I see that Nosy fucking Hilda next. I'll give her holding hands, the trouble-making, lying old cow. In fact, I want us to confront her together.'

'We will,' said Queenie, pouring herself another sherry. 'I keep seeing my Bren's face when she was young and pretty. I'd sort of prepared myself that one day there'd be that knock on the door telling me she was gone. I thought it would be the booze that killed her though, not a knife. I wonder how Tara and Tommy are doing? I found it odd they didn't want to come back here. I feel awful, what I said about 'em earlier. I would look after them if push came to shove, you know. They haven't got anybody else, have they?' She looked to her sister, suddenly tearful again as she recalled how Michael had driven her and Viv to Oldmead House where Brenda had lived. Dave had been there with Tara and Tommy, and the kids were insistent they wanted to stay with him and his daughter rather than accompany her back to Whitechapel.

'Tara and Tommy's lives and friends are in Dagenham, Queen. And apart from them being upset when they turned up on your doorstep that time when Bren and Dave had the fight, they genuinely seem fond of him. Especially today. He was cuddling 'em like they were his own.'

'All false. Probably him that arranged Brenda's death,' Queenie spat.

'You can't come in, girls. I'm sorry, but it's ticket only tonight,' Michael's doorman told Katy and Lucy.

'But you must recognize me? I'm Michael's ex-employee. I used to look after Daniel and Lee and cook and clean for him,' Katy reminded the large man with the squashed nose.

Gerry sighed. 'Yes, I do recognize you, but I'm under strict orders from Michael not to allow anybody in without a ticket. The place is already heaving.'

'But my friend needs to see Michael. It's urgent,' Lucy piped up.

Donny, who usually worked the door with Gerry, was off with the flu, and his stand-in Black Troy laughed. 'Lots of ladies urgently want to see Michael, but that man is taken. So off you trot. Yous two are far too young for the boss anyway,' he chuckled.

Lucy clocked the shell-shocked tearful look on her pal's face and bravely poked Black Troy in the chest. 'Too young for your wonderful boss, are we? Well, look at my friend's stomach. Turn sideways, Katy, go on. See that bump? My mate is carrying Michael's baby, so I guess you can let her in after all. As for me, I plan to be godmother, so I guess I won't need a ticket either.'

Gerry suddenly felt anxious. 'Shut the fuck up, Troy, I'll deal with this. Ladies, wait here a tick. I'll go and find Michael.'

Vinny Butler was holding his beloved mother in his protective arms. Vivian had sodded off back to her own gaff as soon as he'd arrived, then minutes later the Old Bill had turned up. They seemed to have no leads in the hunt for Brenda's murderer, and according to them her pissed-up mate had been about as much use as a chocolate teapot. She hadn't even been able to give them a decent description of the killer.

'I'm telling you now, Mum, no way was that a random attack. If it was some nutter, he would've stabbed Bren's mate an' all. The Old Bill are hopeless. I've got more chance of finding out who killed Bren than them. It's either someone Bren's upset, or it's a direct attack on this family. I'll shoot down to Dagenham with Michael tomorrow. We'll do a bit of investigating ourselves, starting with Dave. He could've easily organized it, him. But he was petrified when

I threatened him after he hit her, so part of me thinks it ain't him. But who knows? Perhaps the shitbag had Bren insured, decided it was worth his while to take the risk.'

'Does Little Vinny know yet?'

'Yeah. He offered to postpone the wedding, but I told him not to be so stupid. It's cost Sammi-Lou's dad an arm and leg. He might be an arrogant prick, Gary Allen, but hats off to him for pushing the boat out.'

'Answer the door for me, Vin. I'm really not in the mood to see anyone other than family, boy.'

Vinny opened the front door and stared at the ugly ginger bird. She was obviously pissed. Her eyes looked glazed and he could smell the fumes. 'Who the fuck are you?' he snarled.

Still in shock, the girl burst into tears. 'I've got a message from Brenda for ya,' she slurred.

Vinny pulled the door to as he didn't want to upset his mother. 'What are you, a fucking psychic?'

'No. I'm Ginger Sharon. Bren knew who killed her, Vinny. Before she died, she told me to tell ya.'

Michael Butler was horrified as Lucy marched into his office with Katy, pointing at Katy's stomach and shouting abuse at him.

'You want me to hang around, boss?' Gerry asked awkwardly.

'No. You go back to the door.' Michael turned to Lucy. 'Do you mind if I speak to Katy alone, please?'

'Yes, I do mind. You've messed Katy about and lied to her, so I want to hear what you've got to say for yourself,' Lucy replied bravely. She wasn't usually a big drinker, but had been so nervous about accompanying Katy to the club, she'd drunk a whole bottle of Asti Spumante to herself.

'Lucy, I'll be fine. Please wait outside while I talk to Michael. I'll call you if I need you, I promise.'

When Lucy slammed the door, Michael got straight to the point. 'So is it true? Are you pregnant?'

Katy stood sideways and pushed her bump out as far as she could.

'And how can it be mine? Whenever we had sex, I used a condom.'

'Not always. Twice we did it without a condom,' Katy reminded the man she loved, her bottom lip trembling. She'd been hoping he'd be pleased to see her, but Michael was looking at her so coldly.

'Once, not twice,' Michael spat. 'Was you sleeping with anyone else around that time?'

'How could you even ask me that? I'm not a slag! Is that what you think of me? I loved you and I thought you loved me. And it was twice we did it without a condom,' Katy retorted, tears of anger beginning to fall.

'I'm sorry. I didn't mean it like that. I don't want another child, Katy, so you're gonna have to get rid of it, darling. I'll book somewhere private, come with you. It's for the best, trust me.'

'No way am I having an abortion. I hear you're back with Bella. Is she the reason you ended our relationship and sacked me?'

Michael punched his desk in frustration. If being brutal was the only way to make the stupid tart get rid of this unwanted baby, then so be it. 'We were never in a fucking relationship; it was just sex, end of. I love Bella, not you. I was gutted when she sodded off back to Italy, and you were – well, available. You made it perfectly clear what you wanted, turning up at the club with hardly any clothes on, like some fuckin' stalker. Me being a man, I gave you what you were begging for. It meant nothing to me. You mean nothing to me, and neither will that brat in your stomach. So let's do the sensible thing and get rid of it, shall we?'

As the harsh reality of Michael's words hit home, Katy stood open-mouthed. Furious with herself and him, she picked up Michael's mobile phone and aimed it at his head. She then ran from the office, sobbing.

'Bren did love you, Queenie, deep down. And she was so proud of her brothers in her own way. She felt left out at times though, I know she did. A bit unloved, like she wasn't an important part of the family. I'm gonna miss her so much, bless her. She was my bezzie.'

Aware that tears were streaming down his mother's cheeks, Vinny gently grabbed hold of Ginger Sharon's elbow. 'You get off now, girl. Cheers for coming round – and keep what you've told us to yourself. There's a cab firm round the corner. Take that and get yourself home safely,' Vinny urged, giving the lush a score. She was getting on his nerves now, big time.

'You will get revenge for Bren, won't you? When will the funeral be? I'm gonna be lost without her, Vin.'

'And won't we all be. My mum'll let you know the funeral arrangements. She's got your number now. You take care, love,' Vinny said, virtually bundling Sharon out the front door.

Queenie shook her head dismally. 'Jake Jackson. I remember him when he was knee-high. What did Bren ever do to upset him, eh?'

Vinny said nothing. He knew Brenda's murder was payback for his own actions. True enemies always came from past sins. He'd disposed of Jake's grandfather Kenny many years ago. It wasn't common knowledge – very few of the murders he'd committed were. About the only exception was the killing of Jake's father, Bobby. Believing him to have been responsible for Molly's death, Vinny had slung him through a bookie's window and beat him senseless in front of witnesses. Bobby had died due to his injuries, landing Vinny with a lengthy prison sentence.

'Made me feel bad, what Sharon said. We always tried to help Bren, didn't we?'

Vinny kissed his mother on the forehead. 'Don't take to heart what Sharon said, that was just the drink talking. Bren was far too wrapped up in herself to be discussing us.'

Queenie stroked her eldest's face. 'Be careful, won't ya? I don't want you going away again.'

Vinny stood up. 'I'm gonna ring Geary, find out where the shitbag lives. Don't worry. I'll make sure our Brenda's memory is honoured, Mum. In true Butler style.'

Daniel Butler nudged his brother to wake him up. 'Dad came home about an hour ago and someone else has turned up now. Let's creep downstairs and see if it's Katy.'

Careful not to tread on the creaky floorboard, Lee followed his brother. There were muffled voices coming from the front room and the door was shut.

'It's Vinny,' Daniel whispered, putting his ear to the door.

Daniel's eyes widened as he learned Jake Jackson had killed Brenda. He remembered Jake getting put away for stabbing some random people in a carvery and hadn't realized he was now free.

'Where does he live?' Lee heard his father ask.

It was clear from the rest of the conversation that his dad and Vinny planned to kill Jake, which alarmed Daniel. Gesturing to his brother to follow him back up the stairs, Daniel wrote Jake's address down.

'Why you doing that?' Lee asked.

'Because we're gonna pay Jake a visit. No way can we chance Dad getting nicked, Lee. If he goes to prison, we'll get put into care. No one else is gonna want us living with them, are they? Nan ain't got no time for us and Granddad can barely take care of himself. As for Vinny, he don't even live with his own daughter.'

'What we gonna do then? Warn Jake?'

Daniel raised his eyes in exasperation. 'Course we ain't gonna warn him. We're gonna set fire to his flat with him inside.'

'How d'ya know he even lives in a flat?'

''Cause I heard Vinny say it's a tower block. If we pour loads of petrol through Jake's letterbox then set fire to some newspaper, he won't be able to escape, will he? Not unless he throws himself out the window. And if he does that, he'll be dead anyway.'

CHAPTER TWELVE

Vinny Butler checked over the van, then handed Mick the Greek the dosh. 'Keep it garaged, and I'll bell you when I'm ready to collect.'

'No worries, Vin. And good luck tomorrow. Hope it all goes smoothly.'

'Cheers, pal.'

Vinny switched on the ignition and cranked up the volume of his Roxy Music cassette. He'd spoken to Michael again this morning and the two of them had decided to do away with Jake alone. No matter what Brenda might have turned into, she was still their bloody sister and young Jake Jackson had taken a huge liberty. The little shit was certainly no older than eighteen.

His sister might not have wanted his help while alive, but Vinny was determined to do her proud in death. Firstly though, he had a wedding to attend. His son's.

Lee Butler nervously chewed at his fingernails as his brother explained the plan in more detail. He had serious reservations over the whole thing, but had always gone along with whatever Daniel had wanted to do in the past. 'But say the whole block of flats burn down and we kill innocent people an' all?' Lee warned.

'Tower blocks ain't made of wood, you numpty. What we'll do is after school one day, we'll take a trip to Dagenham and check the flats out. Then we need an alibi before we strike.'

'Who's gonna give us an alibi then?'

'I dunno. I haven't thought that far ahead yet, but we'll get one. Trust me with this, Lee, will ya? I know what I'm doing, and we won't get caught.'

Lee forced a smile. His brother was a born leader and usually right. 'OK. I trust you.'

Little Vinny hadn't wanted a stag do. He rarely touched alcohol since Oliver had been born and would've been quite happy to spend the night before his wedding at home alone, chilling and watching TV. His father, however, had other ideas and they'd compromised on going out for a meal.

'Hello, boy. How you feeling? Excited? Nervous? Or like a condemned man being led to the gallows?' Albie joked. His eyes were still red from crying over Brenda's murder – he couldn't believe his daughter was dead. But he was determined to be jovial for his grandson's sake.

Little Vinny grinned and hung his suit on the door frame. 'I'm not nervous at all. I can't wait to put that ring on Sammi's finger. Here it is. Put it away safely and for Christ's sake don't have too much to drink and lose it, Granddad.'

Unlike most lads his age, Little Vinny had no close friends. The only good mate he'd ever had was Ben Bloggs, and seeing as he was six feet under, Little Vinny could hardly dig him up and ask him to be best man. After discussing the matter with Sammi-Lou, both had agreed that Albie was the perfect choice. Little Vinny felt he owed his grandfather big time. Nobody else had wanted him living with them when his dad got banged up, and if it wasn't for his granddad moving to Barking to take care of him, Little Vinny would've been left in limbo.

Albie poured himself a brandy. His nerves were shattered over this best man lark. His grandson had only asked him a fortnight ago, and he hadn't told his father. None of the family knew yet, bar Michael, whom Albie had told to keep his trap shut. Queenie was going to have a fit when she found out, and even though Albie was honoured to be asked, he wished he hadn't been. Truth was, he couldn't wait for the bloody day to be over. And to add insult to injury, he had to wear an awful cream suit that made him look like an old pervert.

'Don't worry, Granddad. Everything's gonna be fine,' Little Vinny said in a reassuring tone. 'I'll tell Dad over the meal tonight. Once I've explained my reasons, I promise you he'll understand.'

Remembering how Vinny had once kicked seven bells out of him for having an affair with Judy Preston, Albie flinched. He'd suffered two broken legs, numerous broken ribs and been laid up in hospital for weeks after that attack. His eldest son might be a lot of things, but understanding was not one of them.

Feeling as guilty as hell, Michael rang Bella. He hadn't spoken to her since he'd informed her of Brenda's death. 'You all right, babe? Sorry I haven't been in touch since yesterday morning, but as you can imagine I've had a lot on my plate.'

Sowing the seed for her no show at tomorrow's wedding, Bella put on her best not-feeling-well voice. 'I understand. Any news? Have the police got any leads yet?'

'Nope. I rung them again earlier and they have nothing

new to tell us. What's up with you? You got a cold?' Michael asked. He would never tell her about Jake. That was men's business.

'No. I wish I did have. A cold would be far more pleasant than the bug I've got. I was on and off the toilet all night, Michael. And today, I've been sick three times. I've sent Antonio round to my friends'. They are picking him up from school and he'll stay with them tonight. I don't want him to catch this.'

'Poor you. Do you want me to pop round later this afternoon and bring you some medicine and stuff? A bottle or two of Lucozade might perk you up.'

'No, but thanks anyway. I'm going to take myself off to bed. Hopefully, it's only a twenty-four-hour bug and I'll feel fine by the morning. I'm so looking forward to the wedding and spending the day with your family,' Bella lied.

For the first time ever, Michael was actually relieved Bella didn't want to see him. He'd taken his pal Kev's advice, contacted Katy, and she'd agreed to meet him to talk things through. He was picking her up from the top of her road at four. 'I'll let you get some kip then, sweetheart. I've got that pre-wedding meal tonight. Dreading it, I am. Vinny's bound to go ballistic when he finds out Little Vinny's asked our father to be best man. I love my brother dearly, but he can be a proper psycho at times.'

Bella squirmed. 'Michael, I have to dash. I think I'm going to be sick again.'

Over in Whitechapel, Queenie and Vivian were discussing the police's latest visit regarding Brenda when the doorbell rang.

Queenie peeped through the curtain, but couldn't see anybody because they were obviously standing on her actual doorstep. 'Answer that, Viv. Whoever it is, tell 'em to sod off. I'm really not in the mood for nose-ointments.'

'I want to answer the door,' Ava insisted, lip pouting.

'No. Get Fred off Auntie Viv's leg and let her answer it,' Queenie ordered sharply. Ava had driven her mad these past couple of days, behaving like a proper spoilt brat.

'Horrid little ratpig needs its nuts chopped off,' Vivian moaned, as she stomped into the hallway. 'And what do yous two meddling pair of trouble-making old trouts want?' she yelled, seconds later.

Guessing immediately who the unwanted visitors were, Queenie leapt out the armchair. Nosy Hilda was holding a card, Mouthy Maureen a bunch of flowers. 'You've got some fucking nerve, knocking 'ere after the trouble you caused. Get off my doorstep. Go on, scarper,' Queenie shouted.

Petrified, both Hilda and Maureen did a backwards walk away from the house. 'We heard about Brenda. We're truly sorry for your loss. I'll leave the card here,' Nosy Hilda gabbled, placing it on the bush.

'And the flowers are to say sorry that we got things so very wrong. We never meant to cause trouble between yous two, nor Albie. We're your neighbours and we think the world of you,' Mouthy Maureen apologized, the sob in her voice genuine. She might not like Queenie and Viv much, but nobody wanted to fall foul of the Butlers. Only a person with a death wish would contemplate upsetting Vinny's beloved mother or aunt.

Absolutely livid, both Queenie and Viv flew out the house. Queenie ripped the card into shreds. 'I don't want or need your sympathy. And if you ever darken my doorstep again, you'll know all a-bleedin' 'bout it.'

Picking up the flowers, Vivian smashed them against Hilda and Maureen's heads as she chased them across the road. 'I'll give you holding hands with Albie, you pair of lying old whores.'

Hearing the commotion, Notright Norman – who lived with his equally notright mother in the house between Queenie and Viv's – opened his front door. 'Howdy, ladies. Just checking everything is OK?' he chirped, tilting his cowboy hat with one hand, and placing his other on the plastic gun in his holster.

Fred was a friendly dog as a rule, but had a huge dislike for Norman and as Ava opened the front door, the small mutt with a big personality darted towards his enemy, baring his teeth and yapping until Norman scarpered indoors.

Ushering a giggling Ava, the dog and Vivian indoors, Queenie saw the funny side. 'The look on Hilda and Maureen's faces as you clumped 'em with those flowers. It truly was a picture,' she roared.

Vivian held her crotch as she literally cried with laughter. 'And Norman's face. There he was, all big and bold, stood there like John bastard Wayne, and that scrote of a ratpig had him running for his life! He even dropped his plastic gun as he bolted back indoors.'

Not really understanding the conversation, Ava jumped up and down, joining in with the laughter. 'I am glad you and Nanny are friends again, Auntie Viv.'

Still laughing like hyenas, Queenie and Viv hugged one another. 'And so are we,' the sisters said in unison.

Michael Butler felt physically sick as he saw Katy walking towards him. He was dreading the conversation he was about to have with her. So much so, he would rather be chopping up or burning bodies with Vinny. And that was another huge dislike of his.

As she approached his BMW wearing a tight-fitting peach

Lycra dress, Michael stared at her stomach. He could barely see a bump, so perhaps she was lying? Or she'd purposely got up the duff by somebody else after he'd dumped her to try and pretend the child was his to snare him? He only hoped Kev's joke would turn out to be true and, if Katy was up the spout, the baby would pop out black. That'd certainly be the answer to all his prayers.

Having been absolutely appalled and so very disappointed at the way Michael had spoken to her last night, Katy had thought long and hard about his reaction since. She'd cried herself to sleep, but had woken this morning with a fresh determined strength. She was no fool. Back in school she'd had all the lads eating out the palm of her hand, and every lad she'd ever dated since she'd ended up dumping them. Perhaps it was because Michael was an older, incredibly handsome gangster that had kept her from seeing things so clearly. But she had seen the light now, and was not about to let Michael walk all over her.

'Hi, Katy. I wanna apologize for last night. It was such a bloody shock, and what with my sister being murdered, I just couldn't think straight. I'd had a fair bit to drink an' all, but I should never have spoken to you the way I did,' Michael grovelled, as the dumb tart he wished he'd never laid eyes on parked her arse on his passenger seat.

Looking directly at Michael's handsome face, Katy wanted to hug him, tell him she loved him and was so sorry about his sister, but she did nothing of the sort. His words had hit her like a sledgehammer and she had to act tough and grown-up. Like Bella, who he was obviously so in fucking love with. 'Can you please drive somewhere, Michael? I don't want any of my neighbours to see me in your car in case it gets back to my parents. Oh, and in case you're wondering, our baby is due early November. I'm four and a half months pregnant.'

Feeling like he'd suddenly contracted Parkinson's disease, Michael put his trembling hands on the steering wheel, and somehow managed to steer the vehicle.

Aware that his son wanted a chilled evening before his wedding, Vinny Butler had organized the meal at Nick's Restaurant in Stratford, a venue that he partly owned. He'd invited male family members, apart from his tosspot of a father. Plus Eddie Mitchell and Jay Boy. Carl, Pete and Paul were running the club in his absence.

'You're early. I said seven, not five,' Vinny complained as Jay Boy let himself in his flat with the spare key.

'I need to talk to you. Not here. Let's go for a quick walk.'

'But I was about to get ready.'

'Do that afterwards,' Jay Boy urged, gesticulating for Vinny to follow him.

Guessing by the look on his pal's face that the news concerned Nadia, Vinny followed his pal outside, then along the street.

'The body's been found. Gnasher heard it on the news earlier,' Jay Boy explained.

'Gnasher! You ain't fucking told him what happened, have ya?' Vinny asked, alarmed. It'd been Gnasher he'd paid to get rid of Joanna. The tosser had been happy enough to kill Vinny's ex-wife, but when he found out that her boyfriend's young son was in the back of the motor when he rammed it into the ditch, Gnasher had been none too impressed. The kid had survived, and Vinny had paid Gnasher more dosh to keep him sweet, but he'd never had any dealings with him since and had no desire to.

'Course I never told Gnasher! I met him for a bit of scran earlier and he just mentioned hearing on the radio that the burnt remains of a body and motor had been found in Purfleet. He reckoned it was probably a bird he knew who'd been reported missing. She was one of the regulars at Elliots, and her boyfriend was a drug dealer who used to clump her – one time he got stuck into her in the club and Gnasher had to drag the geezer outside and give him a proper hiding. He said the minute he heard she'd gone missing, he thought the boyfriend must've done her in.'

'So he didn't mention no names?'

'No. And it would've looked well dodgy had I asked. I assume he was talking about Nadia though, unless another bird has been reported missing. Did Nadia say where she lived?'

'I was out of my nut, Jay Boy. And no, far as I remember we skipped the formalities in favour of fucking, so I can't tell you where she lived.'

'Well, if it is her, Gnasher said she had two young kids.'

Vinny shrugged. 'Oh well, shit happens.'

Michael Butler was astounded by the change in Katy. He'd driven her out to a quiet boozer in a country lane in Essex and she was currently sipping lemonade in the beer garden, with a steely look in her eyes. Gone was the stupid love-sick young tart he'd made the mistake of shoving his penis up. And in its place was a very determined young lady.

'Of course I know you're not a slag. I've already said sorry, yesterday was a bloody difficult day for me. My nut was in overdrive. A man can only deal with so many shocks at once.'

Michael had never taken her anywhere before, apart from to bed, and Katy was chuffed she finally had his undivided attention. She was also pleased that the man she was and probably would always be in love with, was treating her respectfully. 'I'm so sorry about your sister,

Michael. I'm all over the place too. I only realized I was pregnant recently,' Katy fibbed.

'Don't give me that old flannel. You must have had an inkling beforehand. I've been a father in the past remember, Katy? It ain't rocket science when a woman's periods stop there's a chance she's up the fucking duff.'

'For your information, my periods have always been irregular,' Katy lied again. She'd lain in bed last night wondering how Bella must look and act. Katy was very aware of her own beauty, and wondered if she resembled Bella. She knew Michael's ex was much older than her, hence Katy's plan to act much more mature herself. 'And swearing at me isn't going to get us anywhere, Michael. Whether you like it or not, we have a baby on the way that I've yet to even tell my parents about. What am I meant to say to them? They are very religious, and will be horrified. So will my brothers. My eldest brother's a solicitor.'

'Solicitor! For fuck's sake, you kept that one quiet, didn't you? I didn't even know you had any brothers. You winding me up?'

'No. I'm not close to my brothers. They're much older than me and left home years ago,' Katy replied truthfully.

If Michael thought his day could not get any worse, it just had. 'Katy, you can't tell your parents or brothers that baby is mine. In fact, you can't tell any bastard. Who else have you told, other than your mate you brought to the club?'

'A few of my other close friends.'

'Well, this is what you have to do. I want you to convince your mates that baby ain't mine. Say you lied, that you slept with somebody else – make out it was some random geezer. If you do that, I promise to look after you and the kid. I'll even rent or buy you a gaff to live in. But only if you keep my name out of it. You know the world I'm part of, Katy, and if it gets out that I've knocked up somebody as young as you, everybody will look at me as some fucking pervert. My mother and kids will probably disown me,' Michael pleaded. He didn't mention his biggest worry: what would happen if Bella found out.

'But I want our child to have a dad that's part of his or her life. I'll agree to what you've asked, but only if you agree to play Daddy and visit regularly.'

Michael's brain felt as if it was about to explode. Katy had always come across as pleasant, but very naïve. Was she actually a clever calculating bitch who'd had a plan to trap him all along? Well, whatever she was, he had no option but to try to keep her silent and sweet. 'Of course I'll visit you and our child, but the gaff I get you can't be local. I'll find you somewhere nice, in the sticks.'

Katy smiled. She still had high hopes that once Michael laid eyes on their baby, he would finish with Bella and they could finally be a real family. So what if she was a lot younger than him? She was hardly a bloody child. 'OK. I'll tell my parents I had a fling, and my friends the same. I won't let on the baby is yours.' She took another sip of her lemonade and smiled. 'I hate living where I do anyway. It's a dump.'

Vinny Butler was aware of all eyes in the restaurant on himself and Eddie Mitchell as they greeted one another warmly. Both were equally well known in this neck of the woods, and Vinny had no doubt that the star-gazing gawpers would be full of this story for years to come. The night they dined out with him and Eddie – the mugs.

'You nervous, lad? I remember being shit-scared in the days leading up to marrying my Jessica. She was lucky I even turned up,' Eddie Mitchell joked, shaking hands with Little Vinny.

'Nope. Not nervous at all, me. In fact, I can't wait. We plan to try for another baby as soon as the big day is over, so the honeymoon should be fun. We don't know where we're off to yet though. Sammi-Lou's dad wants to surprise us.'

'Is this it? Only the three of us? You not invited any of your pals, Vin? And where's Michael?' Eddie Mitchell asked.

Handing Eddie a glass of champagne, Vinny answered for his son. 'Michael's running late, but he'll definitely be here with his boys. Jay Boy's on the way too. We like to keep things close to home, so Little Vinny didn't invite any pals. It's not a proper stag night. And after what happened to Brenda, we thought a quiet celebration was far more appropriate.'

'So sorry about your sister, mate. Proper tragic,' Eddie sympathized. He and Vinny had already discussed Brenda's death on the phone.

'Carl, Pete and Paul would've come, but the club's busy on a Friday and I needed 'em there. Where're your boys? I thought they were coming with you, Ed?'

'Gary and Ricky are out clubbing. Got a different bird on the firm every week, those pair. And I didn't bring Joey, 'cos Frankie would've gone right into one that she weren't invited. Twins are a pain in the arse, trust me,' Eddie chuckled.

'Kids are a pain in the arse, full stop. Caused me nothing but grief when he was younger, my boy. But look at him now. All grown up and about to get hitched. Ava's a proper little madam an' all. Gonna be a handful, she is. The only one that never caused me any problems was my Molly, God rest her soul.'

As an image of his sister flashed into his mind, Little Vinny, who'd only ordered an orange juice, suddenly felt the urge for a glass of champagne after all.

*

Michael Butler rarely used cabs. But after the traumatic day he'd had, he needed a bloody good drink, so he'd left his motor at home. It was bound to all kick off when Vinny found out who the best man was, and Michael hoped by that time he'd be as drunk as a skunk.

Lee and Daniel were in the back of the cab, so Michael turned his head. 'When we get there, yous two go straight inside. I've got to make an important phone call.'

'Who you got to ring then, Dad?' Daniel asked, nudging his brother.

'Bella. She's not well.'

The cabbie had the radio on, so Daniel leaned across to Lee and whispered in his ear. 'I bet he's ringing Katy to talk about the baby. Bella ill, my arse.'

Having scoffed a big plate of mussels and garlic bread for starters, Little Vinny was full up halfway through the main course.

'What's up? Surely you're not going to leave that steak? Mine was gorgeous, melts in your mouth,' Jay Boy said.

Plonking the rest of his steak on Jay Boy's plate, Little Vinny decided to have another glass of champagne. He studied his family while sipping it. Michael was knocking the booze back like there was no tomorrow, and had left his main course also. Daniel was sulking big time after being given a quarter of a flute of bubbly, then being refused any more. And his father seemed obsessed with Eddie Mitchell and had barely spoken to anybody else.

'Why isn't Granddad here, Vin?'

Little Vinny ruffled Lee's hair. He seemed to be the only family member other than himself acting normally this evening. 'Your granddad's saving himself for tomorrow. He wanted an early night.'

'D'ya know how Dave Fraser's doing, Ed? I heard the bastards shipped him out to Franklyn,' Vinny asked.

'Dave's doing OK. My dad bumped into his wife and daughter, Rachel. They were on their way to visit him. Talk about taking a condemned man away from his family, eh?'

'They're arseholes, mate. I've got a lot of time for Dave – top geezer,' Vinny replied, before shoving the last of his T-bone in his mouth.

Having waited for his father to finish his dinner, Little Vinny now decided to speak up. 'I've got an announcement to make.'

Vinny Butler grinned. 'Spit it out, then,' he urged. He was hoping his son had decided not to make him or Michael wear those ridiculous suits after all.

'Please don't be upset with me, Dad, because I know you don't see eye to eye with him. But me granddad's gonna be my best man. If it—'

Vinny stopped his son mid-sentence. 'You having a fucking laugh with me, or what?' he bellowed.

'Tone it down, Vin. The whole restaurant's looking at us,' Michael ordered. 'Let the boy finish what he's got to say, for Christ's sake. It's his wedding.'

Vinny Butler took deep breaths as his son explained his decision and reasons. If it wasn't for Eddie Mitchell's presence, Vinny would've picked up his empty dinner plate and smashed it over his son's dumb fucking head. Instead he mumbled the words, 'Your wedding. Your choice,' while seething.

CHAPTER THIRTEEN

'Noooo! Don't like it. Hate it! Not wearing it,' Ava screamed, as Queenie encouraged her granddaughter to put the bridesmaid dress on.

'You've got to wear it. I swear to you, Ava, if you don't do as I say, Fred won't be coming to the wedding. I shall leave him here all day with no food and bastard water,' Queenie yelled. She didn't often blow her top with her grand-daughter, but by Christ the kid had been testing her patience to the limit lately.

Ava burst into tears and threw her arms around her beloved dog's neck. 'I hate you and so does Fred,' she sobbed.

Vivian dragged her sister out of the bedroom. 'Let her calm down and I'll talk to her in a bit. The worst-case scenario is we let her wear what she wants, then Vinny can make her put the sodding dress on when we get there.'

'I wish we'd stayed in that posh manor house after all now. Would've saved all this stress. Getting far too big for her boots, that child is. Molly was so different, would never've behaved like her. Been thinking about Molly all morning, I have. She'd have made such a beautiful bridesmaid. Miss that little angel so much. Life is so fucking unfair at times.'

Aware that her sister was near to tears, Vivian hugged her. 'I know how you feel. I laid awake last night imagining my Lenny in his wedding suit. I bet he'd have been the DJ there an' all. Let's not be sad today of all days though, Queen. A wedding is meant to be a happy occasion and we'll spoil it for everyone if we turn up with faces like smacked arses. As for staying in that posh manor house, we'd have hated it. You know how private we are. Sod having a dump, then Sammi-Lou or her mother are stood outside the khazi waiting to do a wee. My shit might smell of roses, but yours ain't too clever at times,' Vivian joked.

Queenie managed a smile. Gary Allen had rented out some plush manor house in Essex and invited herself, Viv and Ava to stay there the night before the wedding along with Sammi-Lou, female members of his own family, Sammi-Lou's other bridesmaids and friends. 'That menu we saw was enough to put me off. I mean, who wants smoked salmon for breakfast? I've never heard anything like it. And what's "Eggs Benedict" when it's at home?'

Vivian chuckled. 'Don't be asking me. We'd have been like fishes out of water there, that's for sure.'

'Who the bleedin' hell's that ringing my bell? Tell 'em to do one, Viv,' Queenie ordered.

Vivian ran down the stairs, then shouted out, 'Queen, it's the police!'

Vinny Butler stared in the mirror with a twisted expression on his face. He had never felt or looked such a twat in his life as he did in this suit. 'Look at us, Michael. What are the Mitchells gonna think? We look as bent as nine-bob notes.'

'Shut up about the poxy suits, will ya? My head's banging,

144

and I've just rung Bella and she's too ill to make today. Mum's gonna be proper gutted. She was looking forward to spending the day with her and Antonio.'

'Fuck Bella,' Vinny spat, remembering the time that he had. 'Mum's gonna be far more pissed off about our alcoholic of a father being best man than your unreliable bird and her son not turning up.' Vinny knew if he'd phoned his mother and told her the news, she would probably refuse to attend the wedding, which was why he planned to tell her on arrival.

'Don't start on Dad today, and I mean that. Little Vinny explained his reasons. Let's leave it at that, eh?' Michael urged.

'And what you gonna do about it if I do start?'

'Oh, do what you fucking like, Vin. If you wanna ruin your own son's wedding, then that's up to you. It certainly won't be the first time you've made a complete cunt of yourself, and I doubt it'll be the last.'

When Michael slammed the bedroom door and stomped down the stairs, Vinny allowed himself a smirk. Little did his mouth-almighty brother know the real reason why Bella wasn't coming to the wedding. The smirk turned into a grin as he recalled the night she'd come with him. Three times, if he remembered correctly.

Sammi-Lou Allen giggled excitedly as she was shown her hair and make-up in the mirror. 'Oh my God! Thank you so much for making me look so beautiful,' she squealed with delight. It had been her mum's idea to hire a professional hairdresser and make-up artist; she'd never felt so spoilt.

'You are beautiful, darling. But today you look like the princess of all princesses. Your dad's bound to cry when he sees you, and Little Vinny will be blown away,' Meg Allen gushed.

'I can't wait to see Oliver's reaction as well. I hope he's OK with Dad.'

'Of course he's OK. I spoke to your father earlier, and he was about to give Oliver his bath,' Meg reassured her daughter.

'Who wants another glass of champagne?' Kym asked.

Meg glared at her dysfunctional sister. Instead of finding herself a decent husband like Gary, Kym had wed a complete lowlife who'd run off with a neighbour's eighteen-year-old daughter. Gary had seen to it that the hubby got a bloody good hiding, but it had left Kym with issues. She swallowed Valium like Smarties and alcohol like water. 'You don't want any more, that's for sure,' Meg hissed.

'Don't be so boring. It's my niece's wedding day and I want to celebrate her finding the man of her dreams. I never bloody did.'

Sammi-Lou chuckled. Her aunt always got drunk, but she didn't mind. Neither did her friends. They found her aunt hysterical, especially when she danced. 'It's my big day, so I get to make the decisions. Of course you can have another drink, Auntie Kym.'

Meg Allen was not impressed, and neither would her daughter be if she'd witnessed what'd happened in the past. Little Vinny had brought his father's friend Ahmed to her fortieth, and Kym had been all over the Turk like a rash. Meg had then spotted them having sex in the grounds of her beautiful property. She'd never told Gary. He would've disowned her sister. And as far as Meg was aware, neither Little Vinny nor Sammi-Lou knew. Talk about bring shame on the family.

'You look proper dapper, Granddad. I hope I'm as handsome as you when I'm an old man,' Little Vinny said sincerely.

'Cheers, lad. Make me feel ancient, why dontcha,' Albie chuckled. He poured himself another brandy. To say his nerves were jangled was putting it mildly. 'You sure your dad was OK about it, boy? I bet your nan bleedin' well ain't.'

'Stop worrying, will ya? I've told you three times already that Dad was cool. "Your wedding, your choice" were his exact words. Nan'll be OK too. Dad's bound to have told her and she would've been on the phone this morning ranting and raving if she were that bothered. I doubt she's jumping for joy at the news, but you know what Nan's like. She won't wanna show herself up in front of Sammi's parents. When her and Viv met them last time, they were full of airs and graces. Acted all posh,' Little Vinny laughed.

Albie sighed. His grandson obviously didn't know his nan as well as he thought he did. Queenie could show herself up alone in a dark fucking room.

'Smile, look happy,' Queenie ordered Vivian, as they stepped out of the front door. The white limousine that was to carry them to the venue was stunning, tinted windows and gleaming paintwork, and Queenie knew the neighbours would be out in full force. No way did she want them nosy bleeders knowing she'd had the morning from hell.

Queenie was dressed in a peach suit, Vivian's was jade green. Both wore hats and sunglasses so ridiculously over-sized you could barely see their faces.

'You look stunning, ladies, may I say. I hope the wedding goes well, and do give my regards to Little Vinny,' Big Stan grinned. A crowd of about thirty had gathered, including half a dozen scrawny-looking kids staring incredulously at the motor.

'I heard about your Bren. Is that why the police came

round earlier? Such a shame, my heart goes out to you. Have they caught the killer yet?' Fat Beryl asked.

Annoyed that Fat Beryl had the nerve to show her face, let alone mention Brenda's death today of all days, Queenie immediately forgot her happy act. 'Nope! And that silly pisshead old priest you swore by didn't bring me much luck, reciting bollocks and spraying his holy water round my home, did he now?'

'I'm sorry, Queen. My friends all swear by Father Patrick. I was only trying to help. Anyway, I hope today goes well. Give my love to all the family,' Fat Beryl replied, awkwardly. She'd known Queenie since they were knee-high. They'd gone to the same school.

Too afraid to leave the house in case Queenie and Vivian tried to attack them again, Mouthy Maureen and Nosy Hilda were peering through Hilda's net curtain. 'Pair of old witches,' Maureen mumbled.

'Look at that car though, Maur. I'd give my right arm to have a ride in that. And they've got a proper chauffeur. He's even got a peak cap on. Apparently, he's loaded, that Sammi-Lou's dad. Money always goes to money, eh?'

'Don't bring the Butlers no luck though, Hild. Dirty money, that's why,' Maureen snapped.

'Why isn't Ava wearing her bridesmaid dress? Destiny said she was a bridesmaid,' Stinky Susan asked Queenie.

'She is, but we would hate Ava to get the dress creased or dirty. She'll be putting it on at the venue,' Queenie replied haughtily. Anything was better than admitting she had no control over her wayward granddaughter.

'Come on, Ava. Get Fred in the limo, darling. Our chauffeur is waiting,' Viv shouted out.

'Fred wants a poo-poo. He's been scared since Nanny was wicked to him,' Ava shouted back, lip pouting and still sitting on the doorstep.

'I'll deal with her. Get in the motor, Viv,' Queenie hissed. 'Come on, sweetheart,' she coaxed, grabbing the dog's lead with one hand and her granddaughter's arm with the other.

At that precise moment, the notrights next door appeared. 'That's a nice car, Queenie. What make is it?' Doll asked.

'It's a Ford Cortina,' Queenie replied sarcastically, before literally dragging Ava and Fred down the path.

Once the mutt and her horrid granddaughter were seated, Queenie allowed the chauffeur to help her inside. Then, as the vehicle slowly pulled away from the kerb, she waved and smiled at the well-wishers in true Her Majesty style.

A magazine article about a famous American celebrity's wedding had given Sammi-Lou the idea for hers. She'd shown it to Little Vinny and he'd loved the idea also.

The Allens were Catholic, but not overly religious, so when Sammi had suggested her dad cancel the church and let the service take place in the huge grounds of her parents' home, both Gary and Meg were in agreement. Gary knew a man who could grant them a licence. Whatever made their daughter happy made them happy too.

'Do you think one day I will get married and look beautiful like you, Sammi?' asked nine-year-old Millie.

Sammi-Lou hugged her sister. 'Of course you will. You look amazing today in your dress. You will definitely be my prettiest bridesmaid, unlike Tonya.'

'Now, now. Be nice,' Meg Allen chuckled. Sammi-Lou had chosen five bridesmaids. Her sister, her best friend Charlene, Ava and two of her oldest school mates. The only disagreement Meg'd had with her daughter over the entire wedding plans was that she must ask Tonya to be a bridesmaid also. Tonya was Kym's fourteen-year-old daughter and Meg had to admit she wasn't the most pleasant or prettiest of girls.

'I swear, Mum, I'm pushing her towards the back when the photographer arrives. No way is she spoiling my photos.'

'Don't be nasty, love, it's not in your nature. We all know Tonya is a horror, but she's your cousin, and your Auntie Kym would've been dreadfully upset if you hadn't asked her to be a bridesmaid.'

Millie giggled. 'She's also fat, like an elephant.'

'Right, enough of this horrid talk. Let's go downstairs and join everybody else. And if yous two are horrible to Tonya, you'll have me to deal with. Understand?'

Sammi-Lou and Millie both laughed. 'Yes, Mum,' they said in unison.

Vinny Butler raided his brother's drink's cabinet and poured himself a large Scotch. Everybody else was over the road in his father's house, but Vinny couldn't face being in close proximity to that old tosser for any longer than necessary.

Vinny stared out of the window. The limo had been due to pick his mother up at half ten, so should be here soon.

The minute it came into view, Vinny ran outside and opened the passenger door, urging his mum to follow him. 'Everyone else is in me dad's gaff, Auntie Viv. Take Ava and the dog over there and we'll be over in a bit. I just need to have a quick word with Mum about something.'

As soon as Vinny shut the front door, Queenie asked, 'Have the police been in touch with you an' all? Turned up at mine earlier and they have sod-all to go on, bar one sighting of a lad running away. Good news, eh?'

'That is good news. Now drink that,' Vinny ordered, shoving a brandy in his beloved mother's hands. She was going to go apeshit, no doubt about it.

'So, did the police visit you an' all?' Queenie asked again.

'No. It's the wedding I needed to speak to you about.'

'Oh, Jesus! Please don't tell me Little Vinny's got cold

feet. The neighbours were out in their droves as we left. That's all I need, having to explain the wedding never took bastard place.'

'Little Vinny's fine, Mum, but his choice of best man isn't.'

'Why?'

'He's asked me father to do the honours.'

Queenie was that shell-shocked, the glass slipped out of her hand, and the contents splashed all over her lovely, expensive peach suit.

Gary Allen's breath was literally taken away as his stunning daughter walked towards the carriage that awaited her. He could remember the day she was born as though it were yesterday, and here she was at nineteen, all grown up and ready to become a wife herself.

'Mummy,' Oliver squealed, trying desperately to wriggle out of his grandfather's arms.

'No, Ollie. Wait for Mummy, else you'll have grass stains all over that suit and she won't be happy,' Gary said.

Sammi-Lou put her hand over her mouth as she approached the two striking white horses and stunning glass carriage.

'Well? What do you think?' Meg Allen asked, linking arms with both her daughters.

'Can I go with Sammi and the horses?' Millie asked.

'No, darling. Only Daddy and Ollie are going with your sister because they have to walk down the aisle with her. You're coming in the limousine with me,' Meg explained.

'But I have to follow Sammi down the aisle too. Please, Mummy,' Millie begged.

'Millie can come with us, Mum. She can look after Ollie.'

Gary Allen handed his grandson to Meg and held his daughter in his arms. He couldn't stop the tears from falling. 'You look amazing, and I am so very proud of you.'

'Don't cry, Dad, else you will start me off and my mascara will run. Thanks so much for everything. I really do love you, y'know.'

Pulling himself together, Gary smiled. 'And I love you, more than you'll ever know.'

The atmosphere in the other limo, currently pulling out of Barking, was none too cheerful. Queenie was furious, but both she and Vinny had made a pact not to make a scene today, as neither wanted to make a fool of themselves in front of the Allens.

The chauffeur had been in his job a long while, but never had he come across a family quite as strange and scary as this one. The nan and aunt certainly hadn't been to finishing school, and the men had villain stamped all over them. Even the children seemed unhappy, especially the grand-daughter. She hadn't stopped whinging since they'd left Whitechapel, and her dog had pissed up the seat of his beloved vehicle.

'Look at the state of me suit. You can still see the stain. All your fault,' Queenie growled at Albie.

Instead of arguing, Albie looked out the window. Queenie had actually taken the news of him being best man better than he'd expected, but he'd still be glad when the whole bloody day was over.

'I think Dad looks like a paedophile in his suit, don't you, Mum?' Vinny mocked, trying to brighten her mood.

'He is one. How old exactly was Judy Preston when he knocked her up?' Queenie snarled.

Vivian glanced sympathetically at Albie, but kept her mouth firmly shut. After being accused of having a bloody affair with the man, no way was she going to pipe up in his defence.

'Shame Bella isn't well, Michael. I was looking forward to

spending the day with her and Antonio. Such a classy woman. You did well for yourself there, son,' Queenie commented.

'She's probably pissed off back to Italy and left him in the lurch like she did last time,' Vinny sniped.

'Stop the car, mate,' Little Vinny bellowed, slamming his fist against the leather seat. 'Right, enough is e-fucking-nuff. This is meant to be the happiest day of my life, and all yous lot have done so far is moan and bicker. Granddad being my best man was my choice. He took me in when Dad got banged up and, let's be honest, nobody else wanted me at the time, did they? Now you lot can either put a smile on your miserable faces before we reach the venue, or fuck off home. I'm sick of it. Sammi-Lou's dad has spent a fortune on this wedding, and I will not be made to look like a prick.'

Looking in his interior mirror, the driver nigh on jumped out of his skin as the dog began to bark like a maniac. Even that wasn't normal. If this was the way this mob behaved when sober, no way was he taking them home later when they were all inebriated. He would call his boss this afternoon and tell him he was sick. Let another driver have the pleasure.

The journey in the glass carriage was one of the most amazing experiences of Sammi-Lou's life. Apart from meeting Little Vinny and having Oliver, she could think of no better.

Lots of van drivers, cabbies, and plain old motorists were waving and shouting out good wishes, and Sammi-Lou truly felt like a princess.

As the horses were brought to a halt at the traffic lights, a Mercedes pulled up next to it. The driver opened his passenger window, leaned across the seat and yelled. 'Good luck, Gal. And you, Sammi. See you at the reception later.'

'Who's that, Dad?' Sammi-Lou asked, as the horses began to trot once more.

'Tony Garnet. I do a bit of business with him, and his daughter goes to Millie's school.'

'I don't like Leisha Garnet, Daddy. Will she be coming to the reception too?' Millie asked.

'I should imagine so. Yous two fallen out? I thought you were pals,' Gary replied.

'We was. But then she said some nasty things to me.'

'Dad, take Ollie. He keeps leaning against my dress. We shouldn't have put that bloody Brylcreem on his hair until we got there,' Sammi-Lou said.

Gary Allen lifted his grandson up, then asked Millie, 'What nasty things did Leisha say to you, love?'

'I don't want to say,' Millie muttered.

'Millie, there are no secrets in our family. Tell Dad what Leisha said, otherwise I won't allow you to be my bridesmaid,' Sammi-Lou threatened. If her little sister was being bullied, Sammi wanted to know about it. She was once bullied at school by a friend she'd fallen out with and it was the worst feeling in the world.

Eyes brimming with tears at the thought of not being allowed to wear her beautiful dress, Millie replied: 'Leisha said you were making a mistake marrying Little Vinny. She said her dad told her the Butlers were terrible people and you would probably end up dead.'

Handing Oliver back to Sammi-Lou, a furious Gary Allen moved seats and hugged his youngest daughter. 'Dry those eyes, sweetheart. You don't have to worry. Leisha and her family won't be coming to the reception after all. Neither will Leisha be horrible to you at school any more. Daddy will make sure of that, trust me.'

After all the drama leading up to his big day, Little Vinny was pleased that his abrupt speech in the limo seemed to have worked, and now they had arrived at the venue, all his family were not only acting normal, but even had smiles on their faces.

Gary Allen had done himself and Sammi-Lou very proud indeed, and as Little Vinny stared in awe at the wedding venue the Allens had created in the beautiful grounds of their property, he couldn't help wondering why his father and Uncle Michael had never branched out. Neither of their properties were anything special and since Little Vinny had seen how the other half lived, he found that rather embarrassing. The East End and surrounding areas were shitholes now, so why were his supposedly wealthy family still living there?

'Looks the bee's knees, eh, boy?' Albie said, putting a protective arm around his grandson's shoulders. There were two gigantic marquees, and everything including the aisle was pure white, apart from the flowers. There were waiters handing out the finest champagne to the numerous guests who suddenly seemed to be arriving all at once. Truth be known, Albie would've felt far more at ease in an East End working man's club had his grandson chosen to hold his big day there. Posh just wasn't his bag.

The Allens had left no stone unturned in preparation for their daughter's big day and it was left to the Master of Ceremonies to announce, 'Can we all be seated now, please. Apart from the groom, of course. Providing he hasn't drunk too much champagne, he needs to remain standing. The bride will be with us shortly. It seems she hasn't done a runner after all.'

When the guests laughed, Little Vinny glared at the silly perverted-looking old bastard in the red felt jacket. He'd never been a fan of comedians, even at his dad's old club, and this geezer was far less funny than those.

*

155

Kimberley Chambers

Sammi-Lou's dress was big, bold and had cost her father a hell of a lot of money. It had been hand-made by a West End designer, and as Gary linked arms with his daughter, he couldn't help but think it was worth every penny, plus more. 'You ready, sweetheart?'

Sammi-Lou grinned, nodded, then held her son's hand. She'd insisted that Oliver must walk down the aisle the other side of her. It seemed only right. Oliver had completed her perfect family for now, and hopefully more children in the future would make Sammi-Lou the happiest woman alive. She and Little Vinny were such great parents; they'd both decided the more kids they had, the merrier.

As the organist's fingers sprung into action playing 'Here Comes the Bride', Little Vinny turned around and gasped in awe. Sammi-Lou looked incredible, and his beloved son so dapper. The past was the past and there was sod-all he could do about that now. Walking towards him was his future, and he was determined to enjoy every single second of it.

156

CHAPTER FOURTEEN

The ceremony was short, sweet, yet perfect. And as Little Vinny and Sammi-Lou exchanged vows, there was laughter and tears all round when young Oliver interrupted by shouting out, 'Love you, Mummy. Love you, Daddy.'

The seating arrangement at the top table wasn't the norm. No way was Vinny sitting anywhere near his father, neither was he wearing that awful suit for a moment longer than need be, so he'd opted to sit with his mother on the table facing instead. When explaining the last-minute change of plan to the Allens, Vinny had blamed Ava. 'She's besotted with that mutt I bought her. Won't go anywhere without it and we can't have Fred on the top table,' he'd joked to Gary and Meg during the hundreds of photos that were taken of him looking like a complete and utter prick.

Queenie put her knife and fork down with a look of distaste on her face. 'Looks a bit pink to me, that chicken. Don't eat it in case you get salmonella. Little Vinny told me the Allens had hired the best catering firm in Essex. Wouldn't want to meet the worst, would you? Even my prawn cocktail weren't all that. Too rich, that bloody sauce.'

'My chicken looks all right,' Vivian replied, prodding it with her fork.

'Watch this,' Queenie cackled.

Albie was scared as he glanced up and saw Queenie marching towards him, plate in hand. Surely she wasn't going to smash it over his head? 'Whatsa matter?' he mumbled.

Shoving the chicken quarter on Albie's plate, Queenie replied, 'Nothing. I'm full up, and I know how you like your chicken. Hate seeing things go to waste, so make sure you eat it all up.'

Feeling much more comfortable now he was dressed in his dark grey Armani, Vinny nudged Michael. 'What's up with you? You look as miserable as sin. Told you to bring a whistle to change into, didn't I?' he chuckled.

'I'm OK. I just wish Bella was 'ere, that's all,' Michael replied. The truth was, he was thinking about Katy. The thought of her giving birth to his child made him feel ill. Had it been Vinny in this situation, Michael had no doubt that Katy would be involved in some fatal accident before the baby arrived. But even though that thought had crossed Michael's mind, he knew he could never live with himself. Vinny had no scruples whatsoever when it came to women, but Michael could never go through with something so awful, even if the alternative was losing Bella.

'She looked over at me again,' Daniel whispered in his brother's ear.

Lee looked over to the table where the Mitchells were seated. Frankie was pretty, but unlike Daniel, who obviously fancied her, Lee found her a bit scary. She looked as if she could hold her own in a fight with a girl or boy. 'She ain't looking now. But if you like her, you should ask her out on a date,' Lee whispered back.

'Say she says no? And where am I meant to take her?'

Lee shrugged. 'The pictures. Or what about McDonald's?'

'I dunno. Let's get our hands on some booze later and get drunk. Then I might ask her.'

'What yous two whispering about?' Queenie asked.

'Nothing,' Daniel replied.

'Nan, I do like my dress now. But that fat girl doesn't look nice in hers,' Ava said loudly, pointing towards the table opposite.

'Right, let's take Fred outside for a wee-wee,' Queenie said, grabbing the dog's lead and her granddaughter's arm.

Aware that Sammi-Lou had most certainly heard Ava's comment, Viv mumbled, 'I'll come with you.'

'Talk about show us up, Viv. I'm sure Meg's sister clocked what Ava said and the fat bridesmaid is her daughter,' Queenie said, once outside.

Vivian chuckled. 'So did Sammi. But I'm sure I saw her smirk.'

'It's not bastard-well funny. Look how the little mare behaved earlier when I tried to put the bridesmaid dress on her. Vinny asks her to wear it and, like a little angel, she does exactly what he bloody tells her. Now she has the cheek to say she likes the poxy dress.'

Lighting up a cigarette, Vivian handed one to Queenie. Ava was now running around, being chased by that devil dog of hers. 'She did have a point though. What a moose that other child is. Not seen it smile all day. No hope for that when it's older. She'll never find a husband.'

'And what about its mother? Looks like a bundle of shit tied up ugly in that outfit. The skirt's up its arse and the lils are on show. Been knocking back the booze like it's going out of fashion an' all. A definite old slapper, she is.'

'Anyone ever tell you you have a way with words, Queen? No wonder Ava comes out with the stuff she does. Spends too much time with me and you,' Vivian laughed.

*

159

When Gary Allen stood up and delivered a wonderful, heartfelt speech, Albie's nerves started to kick in. He was confident when belting out a song, but had always hated giving speeches.

Gary Allen told them all how proud he was of his daughter and what fantastic parents her and Little Vinny were. 'I'm not going to lie, when Sammi-Lou first introduced us to her choice of man, I did have my doubts. But what father wouldn't? We only want the best for our children and I now know that's what Sammi has got. Welcome to the family, son,' Gary Allen proclaimed, shaking Little Vinny's hand.

Gary then waved an envelope in the air, before handing it to his daughter. 'Your mum and I searched high and low before booking this. We know you wanted to take Oliver on honeymoon with you, and not only is this gaff truly five-star, it has so much going on for the little 'un. Enjoy.'

When Sammi-Lou squealed, 'We're going to Spain on Monday,' at his son, Vinny Butler smirked. He didn't hate the Allens, but they weren't exactly his cup of tea. A bit too flash for his liking, hence the fuck-off extravagant wedding. Well, he'd top that Spanish honeymoon in his speech, that was for sure.

Outside the marquee, Daniel urged his brother to take another gulp of the revolting-tasting wine he'd swiped off a table.

Lee did as he was told, then turned his nose up as he handed the glass back. 'You drink the rest. It's 'orrible.'

'I saw yous two sneak out here. Aren't speeches boring? Give us that. I'll drink it.'

When Frankie Mitchell snatched the glass out of his hand and sank the contents in one, Daniel Butler grinned at her

in awe. Sod Katy Spencer, this was the girl he was in love
with now.

After telling a few crap jokes that everybody bar the groom
seemed to find funny, the Master of Ceremonies finally
handed the microphone to Little Vinny.

Clearing his throat, he turned towards his in-laws. 'Firstly,
I would like to thank Meg and Gary for not only welcoming
me into their family, but also giving Sammi-Lou and I the
best wedding ever. We truly appreciate it, and can't thank
you enough for all the effort you've gone to in order to
make our big day so special. Cheers, guys,' Little Vinny
said, raising a glass.

Queenie mumbled the words 'To Meg and Gary' before
turning to her sister and hissing, 'I swear if he mentions
that old goat and not me, I'll be giving a bleedin' speech
meself.'

'I'm not much of a public speaker, so rather than bore
everybody I will keep the rest of this short and sweet. I
want to thank my own family for all they have done for
me over the years. But most of all I want to thank
Sammi-Lou and Oliver for making my life complete. I'd
never truly been in love in the past, and the moment I
laid eyes on Sammi, I knew she was the girl I one day
wanted to walk down the aisle towards me. I love you
Sammi-Lou and our wonderful son, more than words
can say.'

'Let's all raise our glasses to Sammi-Lou and Oliver,
please,' the Master of Ceremonies announced when the
emotional bridegroom handed back the mike.

To say Vinny Butler was livid was the understatement
of the century. Not only had his son barely given his own
family a mention, his failure to remember those who were
unfortunately no longer alive was a true insult in Vinny's

161

eyes. His son had not done him proud with that speech at all, and when he stood up to give his, Vinny would most certainly fucking correct that. How dare he not even mention Ava? Or worse still, Molly.

'So what school do yous two go to?' Joey Mitchell asked Daniel and Lee Butler. He'd seen his twin sister sneak out, and bored shitless by the speeches, he'd quickly followed suit.

A grinning Daniel handed Joey the whole bottle of wine he'd just stolen. 'A crap school in Barking. Now neck some of that,' he ordered, showing off in front of Frankie. She looked nothing like Katy Spencer. Frankie had long dark hair, and massive eyes that made his stomach flutter every time she looked at him.

Lee was slightly concerned. He could tell Daniel was only knocking back the booze to give it the large in front of Frankie Mitchell, but his eyes already looked glazed. 'Let's go inside and listen to the rest of the speeches, eh, bruv? We can all get drunk together later, on lager, or cider. Dad'll go mental if we don't show our faces again soon.'

'Dad'll be too busy worrying about our so-called babysitter he's knocked up to be concerned about us,' Daniel replied, grinning stupidly at Frankie.

Joey Mitchell put his hand over his mouth. 'No way! Your dad has got your babysitter pregnant? And why have you got one of those at your age?'

About to explain the situation, Daniel was stopped from doing so by a none-too-happy-looking Eddie Mitchell poking his head around the side of the marquee. 'Joey, Frankie, get your arses back inside now,' he bellowed.

When Joey and Frankie immediately did as they were told, Lee shook his head dismally. 'You should never have said that about Dad, Dan. And as for calling Katy our babysitter, you made us sound like right divs.'

Even though he'd drunk enough Dutch courage to grow a pair of clogs, Albie's hand still shook as he took hold of the microphone.

Apart from slinging a quarter of a chicken on his plate, which Albie wouldn't put it past Queenie to have added arsenic to, she'd glared at him all day. As for Vivian, that poor woman was too scared to look his way, but he could fully understand why.

Realizing Albie was struggling, Little Vinny grabbed hold of the microphone. 'Let me properly introduce my best man to you. An unusual choice for most lads, I know, but he's my granddad and I owe him big time. He helped me become the man I am today,' he announced, unaware of the glares being levelled at him by his father and grandmother.

Queenie leapt out of her seat. 'What about me? Have you forgotten you also lived with me all those years?'

'Oh, and can you raise your glasses to my lovely nan, Queenie. When my mum died I went to live with my nan,' said a red-faced Little Vinny.

'I should bleedin' well think so too,' Queenie hissed, as Vinny grabbed her arm so she'd sit back down. 'Cheeky little bastard,' she added.

'I'll sort it in my speech. Be quiet now,' Vinny whispered in his mother's ear.

Wishing the ground would open up and swallow him, Albie was handed the microphone again. 'Erm, I'm not much of a public speaker and nobody wants to listen to an old fogey like me for long, so I won't bore you all. I'll get straight to the point.'

'Truest thing he's said in years,' Queenie hissed.

Avoiding eye contact with the table where Queenie was sitting, Albie spoke from the heart. 'Not only am I honoured to be my grandson's best man today, I am also so very proud of the way he's turned out. He wasn't always perfect, but then again, how many of us here today can proclaim that we were?'

'You can say that again,' Queenie muttered.

'Shush, Mum,' Michael ordered.

'Meeting Sammi-Lou has been the making of my grandson. Sammi's a wonderful girl and Oliver is extremely lucky to have two such loving parents. I wish my grandson and his wife all the luck and happiness in the world for their future together – not that they'll need it. They truly are soul-mates.'

'That was a lovely speech and if you think you're an old fogey, then what does that make me?' the Master of Ceremonies joked, before urging everybody to join him in a toast to Albie.

Vinny Butler winked at his mother. 'Chin up, sweetheart. My speech is next.'

'There you are! Whatcha been doing out 'ere?' Michael Butler bellowed.

'Talking to Frankie and Joey Mitchell.'

'Where are they then? I can't bloody see 'em. Invisible are they?' Michael grilled his sons.

'Their dad came out and got 'em,' Lee explained.

Michael turned to Daniel. 'What's up with you? Cat got your tongue?'

'No. It's the speeches. They're boring, so we came out here,' Daniel mumbled.

'You can get your arses back inside now. And if I find out you've been drinking alcohol, I'll sell your pool table and the gaming machines. Comprende?'

'Fucking wanker,' Daniel hissed in his brother's ear.

'Shush. He'll hear you.'

'Can I have your attention, please? Our page boy has decided he's not shy after all, and now wants to say a few words,' the Master of Ceremonies announced, crouching to hold the mike towards Oliver.

Little Vinny lifted his son off the seat. 'Talk,' he whispered.

Aware that all eyes were on him, Oliver put his finger in his mouth and glanced at the floor. 'My name is Oliver and I'm a page boy.'

As laughter and murmurs of 'Awww' and 'Bless him' filled the marquee, Oliver suddenly felt brave and grinned. 'I love my mummy, daddy, nanny, granddad, Millie and Pebbles the cat,' he shouted at the top of his voice.

Once again, Queenie was livid. 'Fucking cheek. Like father, like son. Even he never mentioned us,' she said, knocking back her drink.

'He's only a kid, Queen. And he did say "granddad",' Vivian added.

'Exactly! Granddad! Not granddads! Has he only got one then? And what about us? Don't he love us as well? Last time I buy him any toys,' Queenie retorted.

'And last but certainly not least, the groom's father wants to say a few words. I wondered why our groom was referred to as Little Vinny when he towers over me, but now I've met his dad I understand. Up you come Big Vinny. Wouldn't fancy my chances in a scuffle with you,' the Master of Ceremonies joked, making boxing punches with his hands while laughing at his own wit.

Vinny Butler sauntered towards the top table as though he owned the gaff, stood next to his son and snatched the mike. He also found the Master of Ceremonies an irritating old bastard. His jokes were on par humour-wise with finding out you'd caught a dose of the clap.

'Afternoon, everybody. Been a lovely day so far, hasn't it? Perfect weather an' all.'

As most of the guests began nodding and murmuring words such as 'Beautiful', 'Lovely day' and 'Brilliant', Vinny Butler smirked. Apart from Jay Boy, Pete, Paul, Carl and their nearest and dearest who were seated right at the back. Plus the Mitchells, who were also seated near the rear, Vinny didn't know a soul bar his own family at this poxy jumped-up wedding.

Aware that he now had everybody's full attention, Vinny continued, 'Right, let's get this done and dusted so we can all go and party the night away in marquee number two. Meg and Gary,' Vinny said turning towards the couple. 'What a wedding! Totally unforgettable. I've never seen one like it in the past, and I'm sure many of yous lovely people will agree?' Vinny added, turning back to the guests who were now eating out of the palm of his hand.

'What you laughing at?' Jessica Mitchell asked her husband, as they toasted Meg and Gary.

Eddie Mitchell knew Vinny was being sarcastic. They'd had a chat before the ceremony and both agreed how over the top and showy it all was. 'I'm not laughing, I'm smiling. It's a wedding, people are meant to be happy,' Eddie informed Jessica.

Vinny turned to his daughter-in-law. 'Firstly, I must say how incredibly stunning you look today, darling. A truly beautiful bride, with a soul to match. I can't thank you enough for putting up with my son and taking him off my hands. I never thought anybody else bar his own family would ever suffer him.'

When everybody laughed, Little Vinny included, Vinny added, 'I'm only messing, well sort of. Nah seriously,

Sammi-Lou has been the making of my boy, and I can't thank you enough for that, sweetheart. I also can't thank the pair of you enough for making me a granddad at such a young age. Ollie is a blinding kid, and I'm sure you'll go on to have many more. Such brilliant parents. I wish you every happiness for your future together, which is why I want to give you this.' Vinny took an envelope out of the inside of his jacket and handed it to his daughter-in-law.

Sammi-Lou stared at the cheque, then put her hand over her mouth. 'Oh my God! Twenty thousand pounds! We can't accept that, Vinny. You've already bought us a lovely present.'

'Of course you can accept it. It's a gift, for you to put a deposit on a gaff of your own. My son has got to man up now you're married, Sammi. You can't be living in one of your dad's properties for ever. Be an investment for Oliver and any future kids you might have.'

'And what exactly the fuck is wrong with 'em living in one of my properties?' a furious Gary Allen whispered to his wife. He charged them no rent, wanted them to enjoy their lives while young, and spoil his grandson rotten.

Meg glared at her husband. 'Smile and shut up. We'll talk later,' she hissed through gritted teeth.

Little Vinny stood up and shook his father's hand. 'Thanks, Dad.'

Sammi-Lou hugged Vinny. 'Thanks ever so much. That's so kind of you.'

Vinny held the mike close to his mouth. 'The pleasure is all mine. Welcome to the family. You're a Butler now.'

'Only by fucking name,' Gary mumbled. Meg kicking him under the table stopped him from saying any more.

The Master of Ceremonies held up a glass. 'May we all have one last toast to Big Vinny, Little Vinny and Sammi-Lou,' he bellowed.

'Hold your horses. I haven't finished yet,' Vinny told the

prick. He turned to his son. 'Very proud of the way you've turned out, boy, but I wasn't very impressed with that speech you gave earlier. I think you should give another and this time give each of your family a proper mention.'

Little Vinny looked at the confusion on the guests' faces, then in horror as his father said, 'And don't forget to mention family that are no longer with us. Your cousin Adam, Uncle Roy, Champ, and your amazing little sister Molly. She would've been a bridesmaid today, God rest her soul, and deserves to be properly remembered,' Vinny glared.

'Fucking cheek, mentioning my Lenny. It was him that killed him,' Vivian spat.

When his father tried to hand him the mike, Little Vinny leapt out of his seat. 'I can't do it. I'm sorry, OK?' he screamed, before running past the open-mouthed guests and out of the marquee.

The entertainment consisted of a band and a DJ who would take it in turns to entertain the guests. Another two hundred plus guests had been invited to the evening reception, which was why the Allens had hired a security firm to keep a close eye on proceedings.

When the band kicked off their set with The Drifters' 'There Goes My First Love', Gary Allen mumbled, 'And there goes our perfect-fucking-day.' He was still fuming. Not only had Vinny deliberately tried to upstage him by handing his daughter a twenty-grand cheque, he'd also ruined the whole bash by picking on his own son and upsetting him with his speech.

Meg was doing her best to appease her husband. 'The day hasn't been ruined at all, Gary, and we still have a large chunk of it to get through. Little Vinny seems fine now. He's outside chatting to Sammi and playing with Oliver.'

'No wonder he barely gave his own mob a mention.

Neither would I if they were my family. That nan and aunt are a pair of old witches. All they did was spout their mouths off during the speeches. I dread to think what all our friends must think.'

'Old school East Enders like Queenie and Viv don't think before they speak, Gary. My Auntie Lil was the same, wasn't she?'

'She weren't as bad as those two old trouts. I still can't believe Vinny tried to mug me off by giving out the cheque during his speech. Why didn't he just hand it to 'em on the quiet?'

'You've got to look at the bigger picture. Sammi-Lou and Little Vinny will now have twenty grand in their bank account. Even if they did look for their own place, they wouldn't need nowhere near that amount for a deposit, so there will be lots left over for them to enjoy themselves with and spend on Oliver. I know you're a proud man, Gary, but you've not been overshadowed. This is the wedding of all weddings, and our friends know you paid for the bloody lot. You should feel grateful that Sammi-Lou now has two wealthy families behind her. I am.'

About to reply, Gary was tapped on the shoulder by one of the security men. 'That bloke you told us not to let in is here with his family. I told him to wait at the gate.'

'What bloke?' Meg asked.

Gary kissed his wife on the forehead. 'It's something and nothing, dear. You mingle with our guests and I'll be back before you know it. And I promise I won't kick off later, OK? You're right. Our Sammi is twenty K better off, so let's celebrate.'

Meg smiled and hugged the love of her life.

'Even if it is dirty money,' Gary muttered as he walked away.

The Garnets were waiting none too patiently at the gate.

169

'I don't get what the problem is. As you can clearly see, we have our invitation,' Michelle Garnet said loudly, thrusting the invite towards the huge black security guy for the third time.

'I don't wanna see the invite. Your name is down as ain't coming in. Let the main man himself sort it. Big Al's gone to get him.'

'Why aren't we allowed in, Dad?' Leisha Garnet asked, tears in her eyes. She was an only child and spoiled rotten.

'There isn't a problem, Mich. Must be a mistake. I saw Gal today on his way to the wedding on that horse-and-trap creation. I even spoke to him. Look, 'ere he is now.'

After the day he'd had, Gary Allen had fire in his eyes as he marched towards Tony Garnet. 'Let's speak in private. Follow me,' he ordered.

'What's up, mate?' Tony asked, as they walked round the side of the massive property.

Once the wife and child were out of view, Gary punched Tony hard in the stomach. Tony was sturdy, but lacked in height and Gary had often joked in the past to Meg that he had 'short man syndrome'.

'Jesus, Gal. What was that for?' Tony asked.

Grabbing the man by the thick of his neck, Gary hissed, 'You ever mouth off about my family again, I will make sure no bastard ever does business with you in the whole of Essex.'

Tony was mortified. 'But what am I meant to have said?'

'Ask your daughter. She's the one been trapping off to my Millie and upsetting her at school. And that's another thing, you tell Leisha to steer well clear of my baby in future. I swear, if you don't, not only will you not have a business left; I will repeat everything I hear to Big Vinny. Me and the Butlers are family now, aren't we?'

The expression of Tony Garnet's petrified face was priceless, and as Gary walked away, he couldn't help but chuckle. Perhaps Sammi-Lou marrying a Butler wasn't such a bad thing after all.

Outside the marquee, Vinny Butler and his son were having a heart to heart.

'Perhaps I was a bit tough on you, boy, but you know family means the world to me, and I was upset you only bigged up the Allens. How do you think your nan felt when you gave your granddad a glowing accolade, but not her, eh? That's why she stood up. I know you ain't great with speeches, so if you ever have to do any more, make notes first so you don't leave anybody out. You didn't even give Ava a proper mention, let alone poor Molly. You can't forget your sisters, dead or alive, especially on occasions such as this.'

When he'd run from the marquee earlier, Little Vinny had barely been able to breathe. He'd locked himself in the toilet and drunk a bottle of champagne just to calm his nerves.

Since becoming a father himself, Little Vinny truly regretted his past, which was why he never allowed himself to think about it. He still had the odd nightmare when he'd wake up in a sweat having seen Molly's terrified eyes bulging as he strangled her, but other than that, he had banished the event from his mind. He'd had to for the sake of his sanity, Sammi-Lou and his son. No way could he have given a speech today mentioning her. It beggared belief now how he'd stood up at Molly's funeral and read out a poem he'd written about her. He must have been a callous bastard back then, but in his eyes, he wasn't now. He was a caring, loving husband and father.

Having prepared an excuse carefully whilst sitting in the toilet, Little Vinny turned to his father with genuine tears of remorse in his eyes. 'I was gonna mention every-body, even Brenda, but I didn't want to cause trouble or upset Auntie Viv. She still blames you for killing Champ and I couldn't leave him out. That's why I chose to mention nobody. I also wanted my wedding to be a happy occasion. I still blame myself for Molly's death and always will. If I hadn't have fallen asleep that day, Jamie Preston would never have abducted Molly and she would still be alive. That's why I try not to think or talk about my sister any more. I find it too upsetting and it makes me hate myself.'

Tears in his own eyes, Vinny embraced his son. 'Never blame yourself, boy. You didn't put your hands around Molly's throat and throttle her. Jamie Preston did, and one day that piece of scum will pay for his wrongdoings. Karma has a funny way of rearing its ugly head.'

'Vin, you got a minute?' Jay Boy interrupted.

'Yeah, one tick,' Vinny replied. He turned to his son again. 'Get your arse back inside that marquee and enjoy your wedding night, boy. I'll be in there partying with you in a bit.'

Relieved that he wouldn't have to speak about Molly any more, Little Vinny grinned. 'Thanks, Dad. For every-thing. I know I don't say it much, but I do love you.'

'And I love you too.'

When Little Vinny wandered off, Jay Boy sat down. 'I wanted to catch you while you were alone. Gnasher reckons Nadia's boyfriend has been arrested.'

'You didn't mention her fucking name, did ya?'

'Of course not. What do you take me for? Gnasher rung and while we were chatting said "They've nicked that geezer." Apparently a few witnesses had come forward to say they'd seen him and her having a barney in a boozer up town on the day she went missing. I joked he was proper on the ball and would've made a good bizzie. Then I asked what the bird's name was so I could look out for the case in the papers. He said it was "Nadia Konchesky", and that was it – I changed the subject after that. I think we should tell Carl though. He's bound to see it on the news or somewhere and I'm sure he'll be relieved, seeing as we were all involved.'

'They can't've identified her body. It was virtually a pile of fucking ashes by the time we drove off. Yeah, we'll tell Carl, but not here. Let's tell him tomorrow. Right now I think we should celebrate. Looks like we've got away with murder,' Vinny grinned, slapping his pal on the back.

About to remind Vinny that it wasn't he or Carl who had actually murdered Nadia, Jay Boy instead bit his tongue.

'Oh my gawd! Look at the trollop now. She's gone for a burton. Look! Flat on her face showing her crotch,' Queenie shrieked, nudging Viv.

Watching Meg Allen trying to lift her horrendous sister up was like something out of a *Carry On* film. Vivian couldn't stop laughing. She had been furious earlier when Vinny'd had the cheek to mention her Lenny in his speech, but as Albie had once said, 'Bitterness will get you nowhere.' So Viv was now knocking back the sherry and making the most of a rare night out.

'Oh, how funny. The DJ's put on that silly rowing song 'cause they can't move her. She's comatose. They're holding her up like a fucking rag doll,' Queenie roared.

Vivian stared in disbelief at all the silly guests swaying from side to side while chanting 'Oops Upside Your Head'. 'What a sight! And we thought our family was abnormal.'

*

Outside the marquee, Daniel Butler was trying his hardest to impress Frankie Mitchell. It was difficult to chat her up though, as her twin brother seemed to be glued to her side. Daniel wasn't too keen on Joey. He seemed a bit gay.

Taking another gulp of the champagne Frankie had swiped, Daniel suddenly felt brave. 'Follow me. I wanna ask you something, but not in front of Lee and your brother,' he whispered.

When Daniel wandered off, Frankie waited a couple of minutes before announcing, 'I'm going to the toilet.'

Joey, who was chatting to Lee, stood up. 'I'll come with you if you want.'

Frankie laughed. She loved her twin dearly, but sometimes he was a bit too clingy. 'I'm quite capable of going for a wee on my own, Joey. You keep Lee company.'

Daniel felt nervous as he saw Frankie walk around the back of the marquee. Apart from trying to chat her up, then masturbating while thinking of Katy Spencer, he'd had little experience with girls.

'What do you want to ask me then?' Frankie asked boldly.

'Have you got a boyfriend?' Daniel blurted out.

'No. Tell me what happened with your dad and the babysitter?' Frankie urged.

'I was joking when I said Katy was our babysitter. My dad employed her as a housekeeper after my mum committed suicide.'

Frankie held Daniel's hand. 'That's sad about your mum. Mine drives me mad, but I'd miss her so much if she died. So did your dad really get her pregnant?'

Thrilled that Frankie was holding his hand, Daniel decided to open up, even though Lee had forbidden him to. 'Yeah. Dad says it ain't his baby, but me and Lee know it is. I hate my dad at the moment. Now that he's back with Bella, his ex, he never spends any time with me and

Lee. I might leap on the stage later, grab the mike off the DJ and give a speech myself. Apart from me and Lee, I don't think the rest of my family know he's got Katy up the duff.'

'That would be so funny. I'd love to see the look on everybody's faces. You must do it.'

Feeling brave again, Daniel said, 'I will if you agree to go out with me.'

When Frankie Mitchell suddenly lunged towards him and gave him his first ever proper French kiss, Daniel Butler thought all his Christmases had come at once. The feel of her tongue in his mouth was immense, and he immediately felt an erection.

'Does this mean we're boyfriend and girlfriend now?' Daniel asked, swiftly pulling away. He would hate Frankie to know he had a hard-on. That would be so embarrassing.

Frankie Mitchell laughed. 'It all depends if you give that speech. I'll definitely be your girlfriend if you liven up this wedding. I'd best get back to Joey now. He'll be wondering where I am, and so will my dad.'

When the stunning Frankie Mitchell skipped away in her pretty red frock, Daniel Butler punched the air with delight. Not only were they roughly the same age, with their fathers both being notorious, they had lots in common. And if embarrassing his father would help him get his girl, Daniel was prepared to risk that. It would serve his dad right for knocking Katy up in the first place.

Because of the earlier drama, it was nine p.m. when Little Vinny finally gave the DJ the nod to play his and Sammi-Lou's special song. Wham's 'Careless Whisper' had been in the charts around the time they'd first got together and even though Little Vinny was no Wham! fan, he did like that song because it reminded him of Sammi.

As the young couple gazed lovingly into one another's eyes, Queenie said, 'I'd better go and check on Ava.' Her granddaughter was outside with Fred, playing with some other young children.

Knowing Albie was also outside, Vivian said, 'I'll go. You watch the rest of their dance.'

Spotting Ava playing happily, Vivian had a look around for Albie. She'd not even spoken to the poor sod all day, had been too bloody scared to.

Albie was sitting alone at a table. He smiled as Vivian walked towards him. 'Hello, love. You OK?'

'Fine, thanks. I wanted to apologize because I haven't had a chance to speak to you properly. You know how it is. But I wanted to say I'll never forget your kindness when me and Queen weren't talking. Our laughs on the phone really did keep my spirits up.'

'You're very welcome. Whenever I'm low I always think of that story you told me about your name being spelt wrong on your birth certificate. That's a classic, always makes me smile,' Albie chuckled.

'I miss our chats. If you're ever indoors bored of an evening, you can always ring me. Queenie's never in mine, I'm always in hers, so she'll never know.'

'I might just do that,' Albie winked.

'The band announced earlier if anybody wants to get up and sing later, put in a request. I've got one. I want you to sing "Spanish Eyes". Love the way you sing that, Albie. You sound exactly like Al Martino.'

'OK. You'd better get back inside now. The last thing I need is Her Majesty catching us chatting after she's been on the sherry all day.'

Vivian laughed. 'You take care, and we'll catch up properly on the rag and bone.'

*

'Sorry I'm late, Vinny, and couldn't accept your invitation for the actual wedding. Sod's law, eh? You don't get a wedding invitation for Christ knows how long, then you get two for the same day. My lady friend's niece got married so I couldn't get out of it,' Harry Mitchell explained.

Vinny shook hands with the head of the Mitchell family. 'No problem, Harry. It's nice to see you again. Eddie and Jess are over in that corner. Ed gave me the nod over Ronny. Cheers for that.'

'Oh, he's a fucking nuisance at weddings, him. Caused punch-ups at the last three we've been to. I love him, but not in bloody drink. Eddie's your mate, and Ronny and Paulie knew I was going to the other wedding. There was no need to invite either.'

'Cushty. There's some lovely grub over there, Harry. I know you like a bit of seafood and there's plenty of that. The catering's been top drawer today, I have to say. Now, before I take you over to Eddie, let me introduce you to Gary and Meg, my new family.'

Harry Mitchell chuckled. 'Ed said you aren't overly struck.'

'They're too Essexy for my liking. Done Gary up like a kipper in my speech earlier. I'm very fond of Sammi-Lou though, so that's the main thing.'

'What's up with the ratpig?' Vivian asked, as Queenie carried Fred in her arms and placed him on the seat next to them.

'He's pissed, that's what. Went outside to check on Ava, and caught her giving him wine. Christ knows how much he's had, the poor little mite. I dunno whether to rush him off to a vet. His legs were all wobbly.'

'Is Fred going to be OK, Nanny?' Ava sobbed, stroking her beloved pet.

'You need to be truthful with Nanny and tell me how many glasses of wine you've actually given him, Ava, before I can answer that question. Was it one? Two?'

'He was thirsty and he liked it,' Ava wept.

'Yes, but how many glasses did you pour in that bowl?'

'Three.'

'He'll be fine, apart from a doggy hangover in the morning. No need to take him to a vet,' Vivian said, staring at the horrid little creature. This was the first time she'd ever seen the bastard thing so quiet, and if it croaked it with alcohol poisoning, she wouldn't be grieving, that's for sure.

When Albie got up on stage to croon 'Spanish Eyes', Meg's drunken sister couldn't take her eyes off the man.

'How would you like him as your new daddy, eh?' Kym asked, nudging her miserable daughter.

'Yuck. He's well old.'

'Very handsome though,' Kym slurred, before making her way to the front of the makeshift dance floor to sway and sing in front of Albie.

Opening Fred's eyelids to make sure he was still alive, Queenie turned to Viv. 'I thought it wouldn't be long before that old toad made himself busy. He's pulled the lush now, look!'

Vivian made eye contact with Albie and couldn't help but smile. Queenie would have an absolute fit if she realized he was singing that song just for her.

'What you gonna say, Dan? I really don't think you should give a speech. Dad will kill us if he finds out we've been drinking,' Lee advised.

Frankie Mitchell squeezed Daniel's hand under the table. She and Joey had found an empty table over the other side of the marquee away from the prying eyes of their parents

178

and grandfather. 'I think Dan will do a good speech,' Frankie piped up.

Looking into Frankie's mischievous eyes, Daniel grinned, then marched up towards the stage. He felt like a king on a mission to win his queen.

Michael Butler had just sat down next to his brother on the Mitchells' table, when the band finished their version of The Beatles 'She Loves You' and announced Daniel was going to make a speech.

Daniel grabbed the microphone and stared at Frankie. 'I would like to wish my cousin Little Vinny and Sammi-Lou all the best for the future. And I also want to let everybody here know that my wonderful father got mine and Lee's housekeeper up the duff. That's why she don't work for him no more.'

'Gordon Bennett!' Queenie shrieked, when Michael ran towards the stage and dragged Daniel off by the neck.

'What must the Allens think? D'ya reckon it's true?' Vivian gasped.

Frankie Mitchell nudged her brother. 'How funny is this?'

Lee Butler was mortified. So were Little Vinny and Albie.

Vinny Butler couldn't stop laughing. 'Well, that's a turn-up for the books, eh? Never a dull moment with my mob,' he said to Eddie and Harry Mitchell. 'And you thought your Ronny would spoil the occasion,' he added.

'You get outside an' all. Now!' Michael shouted at Lee, as he bundled Daniel in an armlock past the stunned guests, plus Meg and Gary, who both had faces like thunder.

Jessica Mitchell stormed towards her daughter. She could see her laughing like a hyena and Jess knew her only too well. Joey was a good lad, a true mummy's boy. But Frankie took after her dad, and had unfortunately inherited his sometimes warped sense of humour. 'If I find out you had anything to do with that, there'll be trouble, young lady.'

Frankie held her hands outwards to proclaim her innocence. 'How was that anything to do with me? I didn't know Michael Butler had been shagging the housekeeper, did I?'

'Get over there now! You sit with me and your father for the rest of the night, and you don't move. Same goes for you, Joey.'

'Cheers, sis,' Joey mumbled.

Queenie Butler was in a state of shock. She knew Michael had probably had more birds than she'd had hot dinners back in the day, but he truly loved Bella, and Queenie could not believe he had cheated on her with some silly wet-behind-the-ears young girl.

Shame-faced, Queenie marched outside the marquee. What a show-up this was for the family. 'Where's Michael?' she asked Little Vinny.

'I don't know, but Granddad just walked towards the other marquee, so maybe he's over there. This is a disaster, Nan. Sammi-Lou's mum and dad aren't impressed, ya know.'

'Bollocks to them. All I'm bothered about is Michael.'

There was a massive queue for the portable toilets, so Albie Butler had decided to clear his head by walking over to the ones outside the marquee where the earlier reception had been held. He felt so sorry for Michael. It was all such a shambles.

'You do have a nice voice. You married?' Kym asked Albie.

Wishing the awful woman would stop following him, Albie replied, 'No. I'm happily divorced, and that's the way I shall stay.'

'Shame. I think you're very handsome. I'm sick of blokes my age. I've been looking for an older one to take care of me and you fit the bill nicely,' Kym slurred, before stacking it as her heel got stuck in the grass.

Always the gentleman, Albie bent down to help Kym on her feet. 'Stop it. No,' he urged, as she threw her arms around his neck with such force, he toppled straight on top of her.

Unfortunately for Albie, Queenie appeared at that very second. 'You dirty, disgusting old bastard! You never fail to disappoint me, you filthy old ratbag,' she screamed, kicking him with her pointed shoes.

Albie leapt up. 'I haven't done anything. I swear! I only wanted a piddle, and she followed me.'

'Get back on top of me, Albie,' Kym slurred.

Treating Albie to the hardest slap around the face she'd ever given him, Queenie hissed, 'I despise you with a passion and hope you die very soon. If Michael has ballsed up his life by not being able to keep his dingle-dangle in his pants, it really is no wonder. What chance did any of our children stand with you being their cunting father?'

Half an hour after his little outburst, Daniel Butler was back on the stage with the microphone in hand. 'I'm very sorry for what I said earlier. It wasn't true, but I was angry with my dad over something else. I truly do apologize if I have ruined anybody's evening.'

Frankie Mitchell stared at the grovelling Daniel Butler in total disappointment. No way was he ever going to be her boyfriend now.

By the time the fabulous firework display was let off at midnight, most of the Butlers had left the bash.

Vivian was both amazed and distraught by Albie's

behaviour. She hadn't quite believed it at first, until she'd seen the grass stains all over his light suit. She'd thought he was a changed man, but more fool her. Leopards never changed their spots, and now she wanted no more to do with him either.

Viv and Queenie had left the reception with Ava and Fred. Unfortunately for Viv, the ratpig seemed to have recovered from his drinking session and trotted towards the limo in a straighter line than she and Queenie could manage.

Michael chose to share a cab home with his dad and sons. No way could either he or his father face sharing the limo with his mother. It had already been a disastrous day for both of them, to say the very least.

Vinny Senior was the only Butler family member left when his son and Sammi-Lou were waved off to begin their married life together. Vinny had had a blinding day. Not only had he mugged Gary Allen off, he'd also found the incident with his father and the lush highly amusing. The drama of Michael's love life had probably topped the lot though. His brother had insisted that Daniel was pissed and lying, but Vinny knew him well enough to guess something was wrong. Now it all made sense. Hopefully, Bella and Michael wouldn't be living in complete bliss after all. That would be a right fucking result.

Little Vinny put an arm around his wife. Oliver was fast asleep on their laps. 'I'm so sorry about my family, babe. I will phone your parents and apologize first thing tomorrow. No wonder I'm a notright at times, eh?'

Suddenly seeing the funny side, Sammi-Lou chuckled. 'My family are hardly normal either. My aunt got caught snogging your granddad, and she fell over at least five times throughout the day.'

'Your aunt weren't half as bad as my mob. I'll make it up to your mum and dad, I promise.'

'You're perfect and that's all that matters. I love you.'

'And I love you too.'

When Sammi-Lou blissfully snogged her child killer of a perfect husband, she could never have predicted the misery that their future held. Nobody could.

PART TWO

'Tis better to have loved and lost
Than never to have loved at all.

Alfred, Lord Tennyson

CHAPTER FIFTEEN

Autumn 1991

Vinny Butler glanced at his watch while cursing. As per usual, there was no bastard even working on the so-called roadworks.

Hearing a thumping noise next to him, Vinny glared at the five grinning buffoons in the Ford Capri. Every one of them looked out of their nuts, and their music was that loud the car was vibrating. 'Turn that crap down,' Vinny ordered.

'Whaddya say, mate?' one of the blokes yelled.

Traffic at a standstill, Vinny stepped out of his motor and poked his head through the Capri's passenger window. 'I said turn that fucking crap down.'

Ecstasy was the drug of love, not hate, so the driver happily complied with Vinny's orders. 'Really sorry, mate.'

Having not had much sleep, Vinny wasn't in the greatest of moods. Neither did he understand or like the stupid rave scene that seemed to have taken over the nation. Grown men dressed in bright colours chucking themselves around a dance floor or field needed putting to sleep with an injection in Vinny's eyes. 'I ain't your fucking mate, OK?'

'Yeah, OK. Sorry,' the driver said, nudging his pal in the hope he would close the window.

By the time Vinny arrived at his mother's house, he was half an hour late. He had no idea why she'd insisted on him turning up so early and his heart lurched when he spotted Michael's car. Surely she hadn't found out about him and Bella?

Convincing himself that she'd sounded far too calm on the phone for this to be anything too serious, Vinny let himself in with his own key. 'Sorry I'm late. I'm sure some prick with no life must get great satisfaction at partially shutting off roads for no viable reason. Not a workman in bastard sight.'

'Mum's popped round the shop. What's this all about? D'ya know?' Michael asked.

Vinny shrugged. 'Search me. How's Mum seem?'

'Jovial enough. Perhaps she wants someone dealt with?'

Queenie's arrival spelled an end to the speculation. 'This is more like it. Both my boys in my house, at the same time. Rarity these days that, isn't it?'

'We've both got clubs to run, Mum. Lead busy lives, don't we?' Vinny reminded her.

'I don't care how busy your lives are. Family comes first. And when do we ever do anything as a family any more? If Michael and Bella visit, you're always busy, Vinny. And vice versa when Vinny visits with you, Michael. So what's the problem? Is it Bella? Only as far as I'm aware, yous two haven't fallen out.'

'Bella's fine, Mum. She loves spending time with you and Auntie Viv, you know that,' Michael insisted.

Looking at her eldest son, Queenie probed some more. 'I don't think I've ever been in the same room as you and Bella, boy, apart from at your fortieth. Oh, and once when you popped in and she was 'ere. She's your brother's other half. Don't you like her or something?'

Wanting the floor to swallow him up, Vinny managed to keep his cool. 'I don't really know Bella, do I? And I don't wanna be listening to a houseful of women rambling on. You know what I'm like, Mum. A man's man.'

'But you used to mix with Nancy,' Queenie snapped.

'I was with Jo back then and they were pals, so the four of us could do stuff together. It's different when you're single, ain't it?'

'I get where Vin's coming from, Mum. I'd feel the same if I were single,' Michael piped up. He knew full well that Vinny was jealous of what he had with Bella, and would probably do his best to throw a spanner in the works given the opportunity.

'Oh, well. At least I've got yous two all to meself for once. Now who fancies one of my legendary fry-ups?'

'Lovely jubbly,' Vinny grinned.

'Not arf,' Michael added.

Deep in thought, Queenie put the sausages in the pan. Something didn't quite add up, but it was good to hear her boys laughing in the lounge.

Little did Queenie know at that point, she'd never hear them laugh in quite the same way ever again.

Sherry McIntyre glanced around furtively as she walked in the direction of the postbox. She knew she was doing the right thing, but it still made her feel like a criminal. Her husband would be furious if he found out she'd posted it. Gavin had insisted she destroy the bloody thing, but how could she? She was a mother to a little girl herself.

Finding a hidden safe in a house you'd owned for years certainly wasn't all it was cracked up to be. The huge amount of money was a worry, especially as her husband planned to spend it. The property had previously belonged

189

to Anna and Ahmed Zane, and rumour had it the husband had been a Turkish gangster who'd disappeared.

It was the taped confession that had caused Sherry continuous sleepless nights though. She'd listened to it numerous times, had even gone to the library and searched through the archives. The case had been headline news at the time, and Sherry had wept as she'd stared at the photos of that innocent child. Molly Butler had been so beautiful, and Sherry knew she could not live with herself unless she tried to get justice for her.

Hands shaking, Sherry popped the envelope inside the postbox. The police needed to know the truth. They'd locked up the wrong boy and Molly's evil brother had literally gotten away with murder.

Over the years, Queenie Butler had made her dining area a shrine to her beloved. Dead or alive, there were pictures of all her family, apart from Albie, obviously. But today, Queenie was in an unforgiving and strange mood. Even after their hearty breakfast, Vinny and Michael would not be pinned down to visit her together for a Sunday roast any time soon, which had given her the hump. So she'd now decided to replace the photograph of Daniel, Lee and Adam, with one of Adam, alone.

'Stupid little bastards,' Queenie muttered, swapping the snaps in the frame. Not only had Daniel and Lee been responsible for Adam's death, they'd also stopped the family from getting retribution for Brenda's.

It had been shortly after Little Vinny's wedding when Vinny had informed her that he and Michael were waiting outside the tower block Jake Jackson lived in when they'd heard a commotion and seen Daniel and Lee being chased by a gang of burly-looking blokes. The silly little sods had taken it upon themselves to set fire to Jake's flat with him inside and been caught red-handed. Their intention had been to kill Jake, but the only life they'd managed to snuff out was some poor unsuspecting kittens. Jake, obviously realizing the Butlers were on to him, had never been seen since.

The police still didn't have a clue who was responsible for Brenda's murder, and at one point Queenie had been insistent on telling them. Vinny had urged her not to though. He reckoned Jake would get away with what he'd done if the Old Bill had no evidence and assured her that one day he would find out where the scumbag was and deal with him, properly.

'Cooey, Queen. What you up to?' Vivian asked.

'Took Daniel and Lee off the wall. They're grating on me.'

'Why? What they done now?'

'Nothing. Been thinking about Bren, that's all. If they hadn't stuck their trunks in she'd be resting in peace.'

'But they were only kids back then. Thought they was doing the right thing at the time, didn't they?'

Conveniently forgetting about all the lives Vinny had snuffed out, Queenie hissed, 'Those poor kittens were burnt alive.'

About to remind her sister she didn't even bloody like cats, Vivian decided to keep her trap shut. Queenie's odd morose moods never tended to last very long and it was best to let her snap out of it without fuelling the fire.

Shirley Preston shuffled inside the prison and took her place in the queue. Chelmsford was an awkward journey from Poplar, especially when her arthritis was giving her gyp. But wind, rain, hail or shine, Shirley made the trip to see her grandson. He was all she had.

She had never believed for one minute that her grandson was guilty of Molly Butler's murder. The so-called evidence against him was all circumstantial, but the Old Bill needed a scapegoat and once they found Jamie they looked no further.

Because of the nature of the crime, Jamie had suffered terrifying attacks when he'd first been sent to Feltham, then Wandsworth. That had all changed though when Glen Harper had taken her grandson under his wing in Chelmsford. Glen was a lot older than Jamie, highly respected, and it was such a weight off Shirley's mind to know her grandson was safe.

Jamie Preston stood up and greeted his nan with a big hug. She was the only family member who had stood by him, and he was ever so grateful.

'Your hair looks nice.'

'Thanks, love. I tried a new hairdresser down the Roman that Madge goes to.'

'I don't like you going over that way. It's too near Butler territory and everyone round that area sees me as guilty.'

'But you're not. Don't you be worrying about me. Walk along with me head held high all day long, I do. Bollocks to the disbelievers and haters.'

Jamie smiled. 'So what did Johnny Junior have to say?'

Johnny Junior was Jamie's cousin. His dad, Shirley's son, had put a gun to his head and blasted his brains out after his daughter's car was rammed off the road by a truck, killing her and her fiancé. The driver responsible had never been caught, but everyone knew Vinny Butler had wanted Joanna out of the way so that Ava would be his.

'Didn't have much to say for himself, to be honest. Asked how I was and if I'd heard anything about Ava.'

'Did he mention Deborah?' Jamie asked. Johnny's mother had been sectioned not long after the deaths of her husband and daughter.

'Yes. She's still in the funny farm. Johnny reckons that electric shock treatment did permanent damage to her. She rocks in a chair by all accounts, mumbling crap that doesn't make sense. Johnny said last time he visited her, she didn't even know who he was.'

'Poor cow. I know yous two never saw eye to eye, but it sounds like she'll spend the rest of her life in that joint.'

'Couldn't give a shit – and don't you be feeling sorry for her. It was that fat cow who put the kibosh on your Uncle Johnny going to the police. He believed you were innocent, I know he did.'

When Jamie squeezed her hand, Shirley asked what he'd done to himself. On both fists, his knuckles were scratched and swollen.

'I had to give a geezer a dig yesterday, but don't worry, it's all sorted now.'

'What did the man do to upset you?'

'Yelled out in front of everyone that I wasn't a Preston, I was a Butler. I know it's common knowledge since the court case that Albie's my dad, but I don't wanna be reminded of it, thanks. The geezer was on a wind-up, so I had to give him a clump. You can't let men take liberties in 'ere, Nan.'

Shirley sighed. What a tangled web her family was. Her daughter Judy, who neither herself nor Jamie had anything to do with any more, had once had an affair with Albie Butler. Jamie was the outcome of that liaison, which meant he was Vinny and Michael's half-brother. That's why the press had gone to town with the case. In their eyes, Jamie had throttled his own little niece to death.

'Nan, chill out. I'm twenty-five years old, not ten. Anyway, I have some good news for ya. The parole officer came to see me. Reckons even with my bit of bad behaviour I've got a good chance of getting out of this dump soon. Glen was released last week, so he's gonna sort us out somewhere to live. I might have to stay in a probation hostel first though.'

Shirley Preston's eyes welled up. She was thrilled for her grandson, but extremely worried that the moment Jamie stepped through those prison gates, the Butlers would kill him. If that were to happen, Shirley knew it would be the end of her. Her heart would be broken beyond repair.

Queenie and Vivian were sitting in Queenie's back garden catching some autumn sun whilst sorting through a huge collection of old photographs.

'Awww, look at Mum in that one. Weren't she beautiful before that bastard started beating the living daylights out of her?' Vivian remarked.

'Stunning, bless her. And I do hope that old shitcunt is rotting in hell,' Queenie spat, referring to their father.

'Look at my Lenny in this one, Queen. Size of his chubby legs in those shorts.'

Her earlier foul mood now fading, Queenie joked: 'I remember those shorts well. He had them on the first time he flopped his dingle-dangle out to Old Mother Taylor over the cemetery.'

Vivian chuckled, and sifted through more photos. She still thought about her Lenny every single day, but rarely cried any more. Time was a great healer, and Vivian now preferred to remember the good old days with a smile on her face. Time would never heal the fact that Vinny had killed her beloved son though. Viv could never forgive him, although she did try to keep the peace for the sake of her sister.

'That's a lovely photo of us at Vinny's fortieth. We should get it blown up,' Queenie suggested.

'Stunning! We look so glamorous,' Vivian crowed. Neither

she or Queenie had ever lacked self-confidence. Viv was sixty-one now and Queenie would be sixty-five soon, and neither of them were ready to become part of the blue rinse brigade just yet. Both still had their straight, shoulder-length hair dyed blonde, and wouldn't dream of walking out their front doors without their bright-red lipstick, foundation, eyeliner and mascara. In their eyes, they truly were the bee's knees.

'Look, Queen. Poor old Harry Mitchell. Such a nice man an' all. I must've been trying to get some sneaky photos of our handsome Eddie when I took these at Little Vinny's wedding. I wonder how he's doing?' Vivian said, handing her sister the photos.

Queenie had a lump in her throat as she stared at the photos. There had been some awful things happen in the country since Little Vinny's wedding. The fire at King's Cross Station, the Hillsborough disaster at the FA Cup Semi-Final, the *Marchioness* sinking on the Thames. So many people had died in those terrible tragedies and both herself and Vivian had shed many tears whilst watching the dramas unfold on TV.

Lots had happened to affect Queenie and Viv's lives on a personal level also. Dirty Den had left *EastEnders*, which had made the soap as dull as dishwater ever since. John Major had taken over as leader of the Tory party when Maggie had resigned, which had angered Queenie and Viv as they both loathed the man. The absolute tossers who were in charge at Tower Hamlets council had dragged the carpet from under the renowned Roman Road market when they'd stopped free parking in surrounding areas, and brought in a horde of traffic wardens to fine every poor bastard who worked or shopped there. There were no proper parking facilities in the bloody area, therefore Queenie and Vivian's beloved market had all but died on its feet overnight, which had upset the sisters greatly.

No event had shocked or saddened Queenie and Vivian as much as the demise of the Mitchell family though. Christmas 1987 it was, when Eddie had rung Vinny to tell him the awful news that his father had been beaten to death by an unknown intruder. Poor old Harry had been asleep in bed when he'd been so viciously attacked and his killer or killers had never been caught.

Harry's death had sent shockwaves through the underworld and East End, but nothing could be more astounding than what happened the following year. In the spring of 1988 Eddie Mitchell had blasted his beautiful wife Jessica to smithereens, killing her and their unborn baby instantly. It had been a case of mistaken identity. Eddie had fired away like a maniac thinking he was aiming at his daughter's gypsy boyfriend, Jed O'Hara. By all accounts, poor Jessica had only gone to Tilbury to try and smooth things over for the sake of their troublesome daughter. But she'd done so without Eddie's knowledge and when her husband had unexpectedly turned up, Jessica had panicked and hid under the bed.

'Shall we take a break from the photos? How about I pour us a nice gin and tonic and stick on some Chas and Dave?' Vivian suggested.

Queenie smiled. 'Yeah. That'll cheer us up.'

'Calum, Regan, no! You've got chocolate all over your hands and you'll get Daddy's suit dirty. Sammi, where are you? Sort these boys out for Christ's sake,' Little Vinny yelled.

Sammi-Lou appeared a minute later with Oliver in tow. 'Sorry. I was just getting changed and thought you were looking after the two little monkeys. What time's your meeting?'

'Two. I'm meeting Finn at one. We'll probably go for a bite to eat and a few drinks afterwards, so that'll give you and Charlene some quality time together.'

Sammi-Lou wiped her sons' hands before hugging her amazing husband. 'I can't wait to show off our beautiful new home to Charlene. I still can't believe it's ours.'

Little Vinny grinned. He too was extremely proud of their new gaff in Emerson Park, and he'd bought it without having to ask his father or Gary Allen for help. Meeting Finn and getting into the rave scene had earned Little Vinny a hell of a lot of money. He and his new best pal were wizards at organizing such events. 'I'll stop at the chinky on the way home, save you cooking, babe.'

'Can I come with you, Daddy?' Calum begged.

Regan pushed his brother out the way. 'No. Me.'

Little Vinny crouched down. Unlike Oliver, his youngest two were a bloody handful. Sammi-Lou often joked it was because they looked like him rather than her. 'I've got to go out on business. You behave for your mum, OK? Else you won't get a present later.'

'What about me, Dad?' Oliver piped up.

Vinny Butler picked up his eldest son. If it was wrong to have a favourite as a parent, then he was guilty of that. His blond-haired, brown-eyed, first-born would always have that special place in his heart. The other two, as much as he loved them, reminded him too much of himself.

Queenie and Viv were munching on cheese, crackers and pickled onions while discussing how useless the police were.

'Funny how they seem to solve your average Joe Bloggs's murders, but not Bren's or Harry's. Don't want the likes of us on the streets that's why,' Queenie said bitterly.

'They solved Molly's,' Vivian reminded her sister.

'That's because she was a child and the press were all

over it like a rash. Had no choice but to pull their fingers out then. My Bren never even got a mention in the nationals.'

'Harry's did. It was front page of the *Sun*.'

'The Old Bill was never going to fall over backwards to catch Jake. They hate my boys, that's why,' Queenie snapped.

Vivian had always found the police quite polite and helpful, but said nothing. When Queenie was in one of her 'it's the world against my boys' moods, it wasn't worth arguing with her.

'Nan, can I have some money? Me and Destiny wanna go shopping down the market.'

Queenie glared at the ten-year-old bane of her life. 'I think you forgot to say the P word.'

'Piss,' Ava mumbled under her breath.

Destiny giggled.

'What did you say?' Queenie bellowed.

'Please. I'll say it again, shall I? Please can I have some money, Nan?'

'Take Fred over to Mrs Agg's first then, so he can play with Mabel. I'm not having him trampling over all these photos,' Queenie insisted. She currently had the right hump with Fred. Whenever Vinny and Ava took him over the park, he came trotting back to them like a little angel. But whenever she let him off his lead, he refused to go back on the bastard thing. Over two hours it had taken her to catch the little sod recently, and she'd vowed never to take him out again.

Mrs Agg lived next door to Nosy Hilda with Mabel, her Jack Russell, and as Ava skipped away happily, Queenie mumbled, 'She'll be the death of me, that child.'

Vivian chuckled. 'She's no worse than Little Vinny was at that age.'

Queenie sighed. Girls were so much more of a worry than boys, especially in this day and age. And Whitechapel certainly wasn't safe any more. Gangs hung around the High Road of an evening, and crime was rife. In the good old days you never heard of anybody getting burgled or mugged, but that's all you heard now. Vinny had begged time and time again for her to let him buy her and Viv a nice gaff out in Essex, but Queenie wouldn't budge. She was an East Ender through and through, and couldn't bear the thought of living anywhere else.

When Ava had reached primary school age, Vinny had sent her off to a posh private school. The little cow had hated it and hadn't lasted a week there. On her final day, she'd climbed over the gates and made her own way home. She now went to the local primary.

'You all right?' Vivian asked.

'Yeah. I worry about the future, that's all. Ava'll be getting to that age soon where she wants to stay out a bit later, and over my dead body is she ever roaming the streets round 'ere.'

'Too bleedin' right. I haven't been out after dark since Fat Beryl got her purse snatched.'

'Me neither. Wish we could go back to the good old days. Things ain't what they used to be and that's a fact.'

Finn O'Marney was a smooth-talking, extremely savvy, handsome young entrepreneur. Born in Limerick, Finn's parents moved to London when he was a small child, and after starting out his working life in the city, he branched out on his own before joining forces with Little Vinny.

'No. I can't go to four thousand. Three and a half is our limit. The clean-up costs a fortune, and we're paying for that also, remember?'

'Three eight,' the landowner bartered.

199

Finn spat on his right hand before holding it out. 'Three seven and you've got yourself a deal.'

When the geezer accepted the handshake, Little Vinny smirked. Even with the cost of the land, clean-up, security and DJs, he and Finn would be quids in. Three thousand ravers at a tenner per head was a very tidy profit indeed. And on top of that was their cut from the pills. No way did Finn or Little Vinny want punters dropping down dead at their raves, hence them employing their own dealers. Decent ecstasy tablets, rather than the ones cut with strychnine, made their job a whole lot easier.

Walking away from the landowner, Finn asked, 'You happy?'

Rubbing his hands together, Little Vinny grinned broadly.

'Right, let's go celebrate. I know a nice little restaurant not far from here. It's the other side of Braintree.'

'Stick the roof down, eh?' Little Vinny suggested.

'Yes, boss,' Finn chuckled. He'd first met Little Vinny a couple of years ago when he'd paid a random visit to his father's club with some clients. They'd hit it off immediately and six months later had become business partners. At twenty-eight, Finn was three years older than his pal, but Little Vinny reminded him of himself in so many ways. Both liked to work out, and look after themselves and their image. It was all about creating a name and persona in their world. Designer clothes and watches, fast expensive cars and being seen at the trendiest restaurants and clubs was all part of the job. To be a somebody, you had to look a somebody, and Little Vinny being a Butler was an extra-big fucking bonus. Nobody wanted to mess with them.

For the time of year, the weather was very warm, and as the wind swept through his hair, Little Vinny shut his eyes and smiled. He still worked part-time at his dad's club, even though he didn't need to any more. Life had changed so much for the better since he'd met Finn. It was great to have a best mate again and be a success in his own right. His dad was really proud of him, and so was Sammi-Lou.

'What you thinking about?' Finn asked.

'Life. I've got a beautiful wife, three wonderful sons. You as my business partner, and we're fucking cake-o. Ain't life grand?'

With Ava bathed and tucked up in bed with Fred, Queenie and Viv were sorting through the rest of the photos.

'I've got some good ones 'ere. Look,' Queenie said.

Vivian peered over her sister's shoulder. 'Christ, don't Little Vinny look cute there. I don't ever remember him wearing suits at that age though.'

'How many gins you had? I think you need a trip to the opticians, you daft old bat. That's Antonio, Bella's son. Look, that's Ava in the background. These were taken at Vinny's fortieth.'

'Gawd, stone the crows!' Vivian exclaimed, flicking back through her own pile of photos. She put the one of Little Vinny smiling as a young boy next to the one of Antonio. 'Now tell me I'm a daft old bat. They could be twins.'

Queenie studied the photos carefully, then laughed. 'OK, I'll take the daft old bat bit back. Jesus! They do look alike, don't they? I never noticed that before. Antonio's even got the infamous Butler eye colour.'

'Don't reckon he's Michael's kid, do you?'

'Nah. Why would Michael and Bella keep that secret? I must show Vinny though. Uncanny, ain't it?'

'Freaky.'

When Queenie put the two photos in an envelope and stuck them in the drawer, she had no idea of the can of worms she was about to open. If she had, she'd have burnt the fucking photos there and then.

CHAPTER SIXTEEN

Daniel Butler put the flowers on his brother's grave and stared at the headstone in silence. Today was Daniel's nineteenth birthday and it would have been Adam's seventeenth, had his brother lived that long.

Michael Butler glanced at his watch. He'd promised to be in Tunbridge Wells by noon, and Katy was bound to have one of her infamous tantrums if he was late. What a bitch she'd turned out to be. A nasty, blackmailing, money-grabbing cow. Michael had no choice other than to keep her sweet though. It was the only way to keep his dirty little secret safe.

'I'm starvin'. Fancy a fry-up, Dan?'

'Yeah. I'm still lagging after last night. Need something to soak the booze up.'

'I'll have to drop you at a café near home, lads. I'm meeting a pal this afternoon in Kent.'

'Who? And why you gotta meet him? Every year you disappear all day on my poxy birthday,' Daniel complained.

'I'm sorry, son. Important business,' Michael replied guiltily. Only he could produce three sons that were all born on the same fucking day. What were the odds on that? And Katy had him by the short and curlies. Insisted if he could not make a fuss of their son on his birthday, then she might as well send a letter to Bella explaining everything.

Michael drove towards home deep in thought. He'd moved out to Warley, a suburb of Brentwood, when Bella had fallen pregnant with Camila. He'd bought a bit of land and had their dream home built from scratch. He'd also had a separate bungalow built there for Daniel and Lee. He knew Bella didn't particularly want his sons living with them. She felt they were a bad influence on Antonio. The set-up had worked out reasonably well, apart from the occasions when his sons rolled home pissed and woke every bastard up. Michael had forbidden Daniel and Lee to bring any birds or pals back in future, told them it wasn't fair on Camila.

Listening to his sons bantering about the two sisters they'd pulled the previous evening, Michael smiled. Daniel and Lee both worked for him at the club now. Music had changed beyond recognition and it had been his sons' idea to move with the times. Soul, disco and pop were seen now as old hat. House, garage and trance had taken their place, so Michael's club was now full of ravers, pilled up to the eyeballs on Friday and Saturday nights. All his new punters seemed to drink was bottles of water, so Michael charged a quid for those and twelve quid entrance fee to make up for the profit he lost on booze. Thursday was an old school disco night. Sunday lunchtimes the strippers still went down a treat, and the grab a granny night on a Monday had always been busy.

'You gonna see these birds again?' Michael asked.

Daniel burst out laughing. 'Lee is. He likes a pig.'

Lee playfully punched his brother's arm. 'You can talk. What about that Tessa bird you shagged? She was well fat and ugly. Ten-Ton Tessa.'

When Daniel got Lee in a headlock, Michael chuckled.

His sons were no longer the lairy teenagers who'd he'd given a good hiding to for being thick enough to set Jake Jackson's flat alight. They were now bright, six feet tall, handsome, strapping lads. Remembering his own plight, Michael decided to dish out some fatherly advice. 'Enjoy yourselves by all means, lads, but always use protection. Birds'll be queuing up to trap yous two. You're Butlers, the perfect catch.'

Vinny Butler grinned as his daughter came out of the shop changing room in Romford.

'I didn't like two of the dresses, Dad. But I like all of these,' Ava said, clutching an armful of clothes. 'And Destiny likes that white dress, so will you buy it for her?'

'No, Ava. My mum gave me some money,' Destiny said, embarrassed. Ava's dad was extremely generous to her as it was, and she hated taking liberties.

'Put your money away, girl. I insist,' Vinny said, as poor Destiny began pulling out fifty-pence coins from her purse. When his daughter had first started knocking about with Stinky Susan's child, Vinny had been anything but impressed. Over the years though he'd grown fond of the kid. Unlike her mother, who was greasy-haired, soapy-looking and obese, Destiny was a pretty little slim girl with a lovely disposition.

When Ava snatched the two fifty-pound notes out of his hand and marched up to the till, Vinny winked at the two women who were gawping at him. He'd recently turned forty-six, still looked as suave as ever, but really couldn't be arsed with birds any more, not even prostitutes. All they'd ever done was cause him grief.

Bella giving birth to Camila had sent Vinny on the bender of all benders, and he'd very nearly throttled another brass. He'd been out of his head on Scotch and cocaine, and the following day had decided enough was enough. He'd had more lives than a cat when it came to getting away with murder, and he knew if he didn't clean up his lifestyle his luck would run out sooner rather than later.

These days Vinny was a saint in comparison. He never touched the gear, rarely got steaming drunk, and his sex life was that of a monk's. The only vice he did have was the porn and snuff films. A punter at his club sold the real hardcore stuff, and Vinny would satisfy his own sadistic urges while watching birds getting murdered, raped, strangled or tortured. He often imagined the women were Bella, especially when they were dark-haired and attacked from behind. Vinny never saw himself as a saddo or a wanker. Unlike other perverts who watched such films, he was only doing so for a legitimate reason. It beat doing another long stretch, and his daughter and mother needed looking after in life.

'Happy birthday, Daniel,' Camila said, holding out the card her brother Antonio had helped her make.

Daniel crouched down and ripped open the envelope. 'Wow! Did you write all this yourself?'

'Yes,' Camila grinned. She loved all of her brothers, but Daniel was her favourite.

'Happy birthday,' ten-year-old Antonio said, handing Daniel the wrapped-up bottle of aftershave his mother had bought from Harrods.

Daniel ruffled Antonio's hair. 'Cheers, pal,' he replied, before lifting Camila in the air and giving her lots of kisses.

Bella put her arm around Antonio's shoulders. Daniel and Lee doted on their little sister and even though they were always kind and polite to Antonio, she feared he felt left out at times. When her son was a toddler, he'd been so happy and vibrant. Then she and Michael had decided to move in together. They'd rented a place first, and that had been a nightmare. Daniel and Lee were fifteen at the time, and very boisterous. Antonio had become withdrawn and even though he was very bright and doing extremely well at the private school he now attended, he'd never got his old bubbly personality back.

'Is it OK if I go to my room, Mummy? I have lots of homework to do,' Antonio asked.

'Of course you can, sweetheart.'

Michael Butler glanced at his watch anxiously. When Daniel had suddenly felt sick and decided he needed to stop at the nearest café, Michael had agreed. He'd rung Katy from outside, explaining he was going to be late, but as usual, she wasn't happy.

'You OK, Michael?' Bella asked.

'Fine, but I'm running late for that business meeting I told you about. Make a fuss of the kids, eh? I won't be home too late.'

When Bella kissed Michael goodbye, she had no idea he was off to visit the illegitimate son that had been conceived while she'd been in Italy. Bella had inherited her father's temper, and had she known, she'd probably stab Michael, chop his dick off, or both.

Vinny Butler had just ordered food in the Pizza Hut when he spotted Joey Mitchell having lunch with another lad. He craned his neck wondering if the other geezer was a pal or lover.

Eddie Mitchell's twins had turned out a proper disappointment. It was now common knowledge among villains that Joey was as bent as a nine-bob note, and as for his sister, she'd turned out to be the wrong 'un of all wrong 'uns. It was Frankie's fault that Jessica was dead. The silly little cow had gone and got herself knocked up by the son of Jimmy O'Hara. Not only were the O'Haras a villainous gypsy clan, Eddie despised them with a passion because of a feud that dated back as early as 1971.

'Who you looking at, Daddy?' Ava asked.

'Joey Mitchell, and I think he's spotted me. Stay 'ere with Destiny, babe, while I go and say hello.'

'Is that the son of the man who shot his wife?' Ava asked loudly.

'Shush,' Vinny ordered, when the people on the next table all looked around.

Joey looked sheepish when Vinny strutted over to him. He stood up and held out his right hand. 'Hi. How are you? This is Dom, my erm, friend.'

'I'm all good, cheers. How's your dad?' Vinny enquired. Eddie had written to him a few times, but had never sent a VO. Since being sentenced, Ed would only be allowed limited visits, so Vinny guessed he used such for family.

'Dad's doing OK,' Joey replied, glancing at Dominic. His father had actually disowned him since finding out he was gay, but no way was Joey giving away such information in the middle of the Pizza Hut.

'When you speak to the old man next, tell him I'm due another letter. How you and your sister doing?'

'Not bad. Obviously life has never been the same since Mum died, but you have to carry on, don't you? Frankie's got two kids now, Georgie and Harry.'

'Nice,' Vinny replied sarcastically. Eddie might not have had a lot of luck with his twins, but he'd had a proper touch when his case went to court. His brief and QC had played a blinder, and by all accounts nobody could believe it when he'd got a 'Not guilty' for murder and manslaughter. The only charge his pal had been found guilty of was possession of a firearm. Good behaviour permitting, Eddie should be out in the next few years and Vinny couldn't wait. He'd missed his mate big time. 'Oh well, best I get back to my Ava and her mate now. You take care, lads.'

When Dominic stood up and shook his hand, Vinny smiled politely, before sauntering back to his own table. His heart went out to Eddie Mitchell, it really did. He could understand why his pal didn't want many visitors. Vinny knew how tough it was to suffer a bereavement of a loved one, then be confined to a cell. How he'd got through his stretch after Molly had died, he would never know. He also knew how other inmates would try to wind you up, and Ed had more to feel humiliated about than most. Not only had he accidentally killed his own wife and unborn child, it would be common knowledge in a prison that his son was gay and his daughter was shacked up with a gypsy. Poor fucking Eddie.

Another Butler dining out was Michael. The opening of the M25 had been a godsend for his secret life, especially on a day like today when there'd been no accidents or roadworks, and he'd been able to keep his foot full on the throttle.

Katy Spencer flicked back her expensive blonde curls. Now Nathan was at school she could spend lots of time in the West End, shopping and pampering herself, so that's what she did. She still loved Michael with a passion, but he'd made it perfectly clear that he was in love with Bella, and the only thing between them was their child. That's why Katy had decided to rinse him financially. If she couldn't have the man she idolized, his money was the next best thing.

Michael ruffled Nathan's hair. The lad thankfully had his looks and nature. 'What do you fancy to eat, son? Shall Daddy help you choose?'

Nathan grinned. 'Burger and chips.'

Waving her hand frantically, Katy finally caught the attention of a waitress. 'We'd like to order our food now. And could you also bring over a bottle of finest champagne? It's our son's fifth birthday today,' Katy proudly announced, in that extra-loud tone Michael despised.

Nathan not only looked like Adam had at a similar age, his sweet nature was the same. Michael truly felt guilty every day of every week for not allowing Nathan to be part of his family's lives, but what could he do? It was an impossible situation he'd found himself in, and he couldn't lose Bella and Camila. There was also Bella's father to contend with, but that was another story. As for his own mother, Michael knew she'd never speak to him again if she found out he'd been keeping such a beautiful grandson from her for all these years.

'Lucy Kendall is over there. Her son William is in Nathan's class, but he isn't with her. William's with his dad this weekend. If she comes over here, you know what to say,' Katy warned.

Michael stared at Katy as she marched off. There was no denying she was a pretty girl, with a figure worthy of a Page Three bird, but he felt no desire whatsoever when he looked at her. The only good thing ever to have come out of Katy's mouth or body was Nathan.

'Daddy, why does Mummy always say "You know what to say" to you?'

Michael chose his words carefully. His name was not on Nathan's birth certificate as he'd put his foot down on that one, and as far as his son, Katy's family and every other nosy bastard in Tunbridge Wells was concerned, he was a rich banker from London who was still in a relationship with Katy, and went by the name of Michael Jones. 'It's because Daddy has a secret job at the bank, boy. I have to travel around the world a lot, that's why your mum says such stuff. That's also why I don't get to see you half as much as I'd like to.'

Nathan put his arm around the waist of the man he adored. 'I love you, Daddy.'

'State of her, look! All fur coat and no knickers,' Queenie said, nudging her sister.

'Who? Where?'

'Outside that shop with the blue sign. Got a my-shit-don't-stink look on its boat race an' all.'

Spotting the miserable-looking trout in question, Vivian chuckled. 'That's one of them posh coffee shops, I think. Looks like they sell fancy cakes an' all. Shall we try it out?'

Lakeside Shopping Centre was the sisters' new haunt since the Roman had gone down the pan. It was a cow-son to get to by public transport though, so Queenie and Viv only shopped there if one of the boys was free to take them and pick them up. It was ever so glam though, and they never got wet like they had down the Roman many a time.

'I don't like bleedin' coffee. Christ! Don't that bloke in a tan leather jacket look like a young Albie in the face? I bet he ain't a pervert though,' Queenie said bitterly. She'd never allowed Albie into her home since he'd embarrassed himself at Little Vinny's wedding. The only time she ever had to face him these days was at the odd family event, thankfully.

'I saw Albie this morning as I went to get the papers. Looked like he was heading towards Michael's club. He didn't see me, I crossed over the road,' Vivian informed her sister.

After the fiasco at Little Vinny's wedding, Albie had rung Viv to proclaim his innocence. He'd sworn on Michael's life that he wasn't fornicating with Meg's lush of a sister, but Vivian hadn't believed him and had told him where to go. She'd been bitterly disappointed with his behaviour. No way would Queenie lie about what she'd seen. Albie Butler couldn't keep his dingle-dangle in his trousers, not even on a day when he'd sung 'Spanish Eyes' just for her.

'You OK, babe? Sorry I've been ages,' Michael apologized, kissing Bella. Apart from spending time with Nathan, Michael had had a crap day. He hated it when Katy invited friends of hers to sit in restaurants with him and he had to play the happy couple charade. Katy seemed to get a kick out of such situations, and it made Michael squirm when she'd hold his hand and try to kiss him in front of people.

'You've just missed Dan and Lee. I heard them go out in a cab about ten minutes ago. They've been well fed and I saved you some lasagne. Do you want me to heat it up now?'

'I'll have it in a bit. So what you been up to all day?' Michael asked, squeezing Bella's buttocks with his hands while rubbing himself against her.

'Stop it! Antonio's upstairs with a friend. I've had a very productive day actually. The Gilbeys picked Camila up to take her out with Chelsey, so I was able to get plenty of work done. I also had a lovely catch-up with my parents, and I have some very exciting news.'

'What?' Michael asked, a feeling of dread in the pit of his stomach. Four times Michael had met Bella's parents, and each time her father had scared the shit out of him. His worst fears were confirmed on his first trip to Italy last year. The old man was definitely Mafia. And Michael had since convinced himself he was at the top of the fucking Mafia tree.

'Mamma and Papa are spending Christmas and New Year with us, Michael. I'm so excited! Two whole weeks they're staying for,' Bella beamed.

'What here? Or in a hotel?'

'Here, of course. Why would they need to go to a hotel when we have plenty of room?'

Michael faked a big grin. 'That's what I meant, they should stay 'ere.'

Eyes sparkling with happiness, Bella said, 'I haven't told Antonio or Camila yet. I thought we'd tell them tomorrow, together. This is going to be the best Christmas ever, Michael.'

Michael nodded in agreement, then poured himself a large Scotch. He hadn't thought his day could get any worse, but it just bastard-well had. Katy would insist he visited Nathan lots over the festive season, and how the hell was he meant to do that with Mr Mafia's eagle-eyes watching his every fucking move?

When Queenie's eldest son decided not to rush off, Vivian left them to it, insisting she was tired. Queenie didn't mind. Viv had abruptly thanked Vinny for the lift and fish and chips earlier, so relations were improving between the two, if only slightly.

'What's that little bastard barking at? Probably heard a fox or cat. I bet Ava's awake now. Pain in the arse, he is.'

Vinny chuckled. Fred had his mother right in the palm of his clever little paws, and all the family knew it. 'You love him really.'

'No, I don't! I only keep him for Ava's sake. Oooh, that reminds me: me and Viv were sorting through some photos the other day and we couldn't believe the res—'

The sound of the doorbell ringing stopped Queenie from finishing her sentence, and she was horrified when Vinny answered the door, then returned with two Old Bill in tow.

'It's OK, Mum. Don't panic. The police have some news about Brenda's case.'

Relief flooding through her veins, Queenie asked, 'Well?' Her daughter had finally been buried five weeks after her death. Not wanting a big fuss, Queenie had agreed to the funeral leaving Brenda's home in Dagenham, rather than hers. Her daughter was then laid to rest in Plaistow Cemetery, near all her relations.

The taller of the coppers explained the situation. 'A few days ago, we arrested a young man on a separate charge to that of your daughter's murder. This young man has since provided us with important information that we believe to be true. Does the name Jake Jackson mean anything to you?'

'Bobby Jackson's son, Jake?' Vinny asked, faking a look of surprise.

The copper nodded.

'But I thought he was locked up?' Queenie questioned. She had to act dumb.

'Jake was released in 1986, and was living approximately a mile away from the incident with Brenda at the time of her death. From the information that's recently come to light, we strongly believe he can help us with our enquiries to finally solve your daughter's murder.'

'So have you caught him?' Queenie asked.

Suddenly finding his voice, the shorter of the policemen replied, 'No. We're not actually sure of Jake's whereabouts at present. The information we have suggests he moved to Greece in 1988 to work as a DJ. I can assure you we're doing everything in our power to track him down. We've already contacted Interpol.'

Queenie leapt out of the armchair, frantically waving a finger. 'Absolutely useless, yous lot are. You couldn't catch the little bastard when he lived a spit's throw from the murder scene, so what chance you got of finding him in Greece? He could be anywhere in the world right now and he's bound to have changed his name and be using some kind of false documentation. Wouldn't you be, if you'd murdered some poor bastard's daughter?'

Shocked at the hatred on the woman's face, the shorter officer took a step backwards. Everybody knew of the Butlers, but he hadn't been in the force that long, and this was the first time he'd had any dealings with them. Vinny was a scary-looking man. Sinister, with evil green eyes. As for the old trout, even he wouldn't fancy his chances in a fight with her.

'We'll be going now, Mrs Butler. But we'll keep you informed of any developments,' the taller plod said.

'Off you go then. As for any developments, I won't hold my bastard breath. I've got more chance of finding a cure for cancer than you mob have of tracking down Jake Jackson. Close the door behind you.'

As the Old Bill scuttled off with their tails between their legs, Vinny Butler couldn't help but smile. His mother was a legend, she truly was.

CHAPTER SEVENTEEN

Michael Butler glared at the back of his mother and aunt's heads. 'Never again,' he vowed out loud.

Huffing and puffing, Queenie and Vivian sat in the back of the Jaguar, leaving Michael to load all their shopping in his boot.

'Never seen so many loonies in all my life, and how I stopped meself clumping that fat monster with the moustache I'll never know. She rammed her bastard trolley straight into me,' Queenie complained. Both she and Vivian hated supermarkets. They were old school and preferred to buy fresh produce daily. Back in the day, people didn't have the luxury of fridges. You kept your grub in the larder, ate it before it went off, and if you were lucky to have any pennies or shillings left in your purse, replaced it soon after.

'Reminded me of the days when food was rationed, and even then people didn't push and shove like those load of plonkers. Never seen anything like it, and I will never visit one of those poxy places again,' Vivian insisted.

'Butler by name and nature, me,' Michael moaned, as he fired up the engine. Sick of Bella banging on about her parents' imminent visit, it had been his suggestion to take his mother and aunt to a big supermarket so they could do a pre-Christmas shop. He seriously wished he hadn't bothered now. The pair had moaned even more than Katy had on the phone earlier. That bitch was well pissed off when she heard Bella's parents were visiting for Christmas, and had threatened if he didn't see enough of Nathan she would turn up at his house with their son in tow. She knew where he lived as well, had snooped through his pockets one day and found his address on a letter.

'You're a right miserable bastard today, you are. Whatsa matter? Had a row with Bella?' Queenie asked.

'Pot calling kettle,' Michael mumbled.

Queenie softened. 'I gave birth to you, Michael Butler. Tell me what's wrong.'

Michael sighed. 'Bella's invited her parents to stay with us over Christmas and New Year. Dreading it, to be honest. They're nice people, but not my cup of tea.'

'Oooh, I'd love to meet Bella's parents, wouldn't you, Viv? You must bring them to my house. I'll lay on a big spread.'

'They don't speak very good English, Mum,' Michael lied.

'Don't matter. Me and Viv'll teach 'em some new English words. Bring 'em round – I insist. Or, if you'd prefer, me and Viv will come to yours?'

Wishing he'd never mentioned Bella's parents, Michael muttered, 'We'll see.'

Jamie Preston sat down opposite his nan. He hated worrying her, would've cancelled her visit if he could.

'Oh my God, Jamie! What happened? Who did that to your face? Are you hurt anywhere else?' Shirley asked, tears in her eyes. Since Glen Harper had been released, Shirley had known by her grandson's tone on the phone that he'd been having a tough time of it.

'I'm OK, Nan. Looks worse than it is,' Jamie lied, as another sharp pain shot through his ribs.

Shirley leaned forward. 'What's going on?' Jamie's handsome face was smothered with fresh-looking cuts and bruises, and one of his eyes was that swollen it had virtually closed up.

'That geezer who I clumped for taunting me about Albie has been giving me grief. He and his pals did this in the shower this morning. I told the screws I slipped. He's gonna get it soon, I'm telling ya. Nobody messes with me.'

'Please don't do anything silly, nothing that'll jeopardize you getting out of 'ere. Break my heart, that would.'

'What am I meant to do, Nan? Keep letting the arseholes beat me to a pulp? I'm no man's fool, trust me. I'll have that bastard when nobody's looking. I have to stick up for myself, otherwise the only way I'll be leaving 'ere is in a bloody coffin.'

When Shirley Preston continued to plead with her grandson not to lose his rag, neither she nor Jamie had a clue that the attacks on him had been carried out on the orders of Vinny Butler.

Michael Butler clapped his hands when Nathan finally got the hang of driving his new motorized car. 'That's it, son, now turn it around and drive slowly towards me.'

Watching from the window, Katy Spencer smiled. She loved watching her boys play together. Nathan was a ringer for his father, so much so, the likeness made her heart melt.

Studying Michael's handsome features, Katy sighed. She'd dearly like another child. It had even crossed her mind to blackmail Michael into impregnating her again. Katy had recently read up on artificial insemination, so knew it was possible to achieve without Michael having to betray Queen fucking Bella.

Katy walked into the garden and stood next to the love of her life. She'd never slept with another man since Michael, had no desire to. Instead, she would satisfy herself regularly with a vibrator, while remembering Michael's touch and their love-making. 'Shall we take Nathan for a pizza soon? He said earlier that's what he wanted for dinner.'

'I've got to shoot, Katy, but I'll leave you some money to take Nathan out.'

Crestfallen, Katy whined, 'But you've only been here an hour!'

'Please don't start, Katy. Nath said it's half-day at school on Friday, so I'll pop back then and we'll take him out somewhere.'

'I've already made arrangements for Friday. I'm going out with the school mums.'

'Well, I'll pop over Saturday daytime then, bring the rest of his presents.'

'No, you will not!' Katy snarled. 'You'll visit your son on Christmas Day; otherwise I will come to your house and tell Bella everything in front of her parents. And I don't mean just a flying visit either, Michael.'

Not wanting to raise his voice in front of his son, Michael grabbed Katy by the wrist and edged her towards the kitchen. 'You gotta stop blackmailing me like this. If I could get here on Christmas Day, I would. Bella went ballistic when I disappeared for hours last year. No way can I fuck off out when her parents are there. I do a lot for you and Nathan. Neither of you want for anything. You need to give me a break, 'cause I can't live like this any more. I'm seriously debating whether to tell Bella the truth, and if I do that, believe me: you won't be living in this lovely gaff, or get half as much dosh as you do every week. Bella's bound to kick me out, therefore I'll need to keep her in the life she's accustomed to, and support my bastard self.'

Positive Michael was bullshitting her, Katy smirked and in a silly, high-pitched voice, recited his address. 'I'll give you until six p.m. on Christmas Day. If you haven't arrived by then, I'm driving to Warley with Nathan. Don't forget to save us some turkey.'

Nigh on foaming at the mouth, Michael grabbed Katy by the neck, before quickly releasing his grip. He couldn't afford to lose his temper. This truly was destined to be the Christmas from hell.

Vinny Butler was in the office of his club when what his staff referred to as his 'dodgy mobile' rang. The handset wasn't registered in his name.

'Good hiding in the shower this morning. Not a pretty sight,' Richie Woods mumbled.

'How'd he take it?'

'Like a man, but we deffo broke some ribs and his face is a proper mess. Can you drop some more cash off to Kaz before Christmas? She's boracic, you know how it is. Five kids to buy presents and grub for.'

'Of course. I'll get one of the lads to drop a grand round to Kaz later today. Keep doing what you're doing, and there's plenty more dosh where that came from. I want ya to make that cunt's life as miserable as humanly possible, OK?'

'Will do.'

When the pips went, Vinny poured himself a small celebratory Scotch, and slouched back in his black leather chair. Richie Woods wasn't a bright spark by any means. He'd got caught robbing a local bookies when he'd dropped his keys as he'd legged it with the dosh. His key ring had contained a photo of his five kids, the muppet. But Richie was no snitch. Vinny had known him for years and knew he didn't have loose lips. With a piss-poor wife and five kids to feed, Richie was Vinny's ideal man on the inside to do his dirty work. Now Glen Harper wasn't around to protect that evil child-killing scumbag, Preston was nothing, a nobody.

Michael Butler put his arms around Bella and squeezed her tight. 'How was your day, babe? Did your meetings go well?'

As much as Bella loved her children, she'd never been a seven-day-a-week stay-at-home mother. Her modelling agency was very important to her, and she liked to spend at least two days a week at her office up town.

'My first meeting went fantastically well, the second not so good. I cannot work with ignorant spoiled little bitches. How was your day? You look tired and stressed.'

'If you went supermarket shopping with my mother and aunt, you'd be tired and stressed too. Love 'em to bits, but they're a nightmare at times. Wanted to fight half the shoppers, then all I got in my earhole all the way home is "It's supermarkets that have caused the rise in cancer because their food isn't as fresh as what it was in the good old days." Perhaps they should've been scientists, eh?'

Bella chuckled. 'You should invite them over to meet my parents. I'm sure my mamma and papa would love Queenie and Viv.'

'Not on your nelly! Where're the kids? And what's that lovely smell? It certainly ain't your cooking.'

'Juanita has taken Antonio and Camila shopping. They wanted to choose their own Christmas presents for the family this year, bless them.' Juanita was Bella and Michael's housekeeper, cook, cleaner and nanny. She truly was a godsend and lived rent-free in the tiny bungalow they'd had built for her at the back of their property.

Michael positioned Bella so she was lying on the sofa,

then clambered on top of her. 'Let's make the most of being alone for once, eh?'

'Not here. Say Dan and Lee come in for their dinner? Or Juanita brings the children back?'

'Dan and Lee are checking out some bars for me. I'm thinking of scrapping the disco of a Thursday and instead having a karaoke night. It's the new big thing. As for Juanita, we'll hear her car pull up,' Michael said, expertly ripping Bella's thong off in one split second.

Bella groaned with ecstasy as Michael's tongue made contact with her clitoris. She'd had a tough day at the office, and this was just the release she needed. 'Stop. I'm nearly there; I want us to come together with you inside me.'

As hard as a bullet, Michael sighed with ecstasy as he penetrated Bella. 'I love you so fucking much, babe,' he whispered.

Bella stroked Michael's handsome face. He was forty-two now, but hadn't altered much over the years. He still reminded her of David Essex back in the day, had the same cheeky twinkle in his eyes and boyish grin. 'I love you too, Michael. More than you'll ever know. You and the children are my world.'

When Michael brought Bella, then himself to an orgasm, he temporarily forgot all his worries, Katy included. If only life could be like this every second of every day.

As usual when Vinny turned up at Queenie's of an evening, Vivian was polite, but then chose to make a quick exit back to her own house. 'I'll leave yous two to catch up. Wanna watch me *Darling Buds of May* video, refresh the old memory before the Christmas special.'

'Night, Viv. See you tomorrow, love,' Queenie said, before hugging her first-born. 'Want a sandwich or something, boy?'

'No thanks, Mum. I've already eaten. Pour us both a drink. We've got a little something to celebrate.'

Queenie excitedly did as she was told. 'Let me guess. You've found out where Jake Jackson is?' she said, handing Vinny his Scotch.

'No. But I have put the feelers out again. I've now offered George Geary twenty grand if he finds Jake.'

'What we celebrating then?'

When Vinny explained all about the torture and torment Jamie Preston was currently enduring, Queenie clapped her hands together with glee. 'Serves him right. What goes around comes around. I hope our Molly is watching him suffer an' all. My little angel, she was.'

Vinny put an arm around his mother's shoulders. 'Mine too, but let's not depress ourselves. All we can do for Molly now is make sure revenge is served up as cold as fucking ice.'

'Yep. You're right, boy. And we're lucky we have Ava to focus on. Destiny's spending Christmas with us now an' all. Stinky Susan's going to her mother's and the little 'un didn't wanna go.'

'She's turned out a good kid, her, and a nice friend for Ava. That's spending time with us, that is. She'll do OK in life now. Destiny's destiny was obviously to be included in our family.'

'Speaking of Ava has reminded me: I never showed you that photo. Proper uncanny me and Viv thought it was.'

'What photo? Not a ghost in the background is there? You know I don't believe in all that old flannel,' Vinny chuckled.

Queenie took the photo out of the drawer and handed it to her son. 'Don't they look like brother and sister? And don't he look like Little Vinny at that age?'

A bit taken aback, Vinny stared at the image. He could

see Fred as a puppy in the background and guessed it must've been taken at his fortieth. 'Blimey! Who is the boy, Mum?'

'It's Antonio. Bella's boy. Don't he look like a Butler? Then again, she's Italian, isn't she? Which would explain his black hair and dark skin. It was the eyes me and Viv couldn't get over. Bella has blue eyes and Antonio's are exactly the same colour as the males in our family. Freaky, eh?'

Unable to take his eyes off the photo, Vinny's heart beat wildly as he managed to mumble, 'How old is Antonio?'

'Ten. Me and Viv went to his birthday party earlier this year. You look a bit pale, boy. You OK?'

Feeling dizzy and slightly sick, Vinny took some deep breaths. 'I'm fine. When was his birthday party?'

'Erm, now let me think. The weather was warm because we sat in Michael's lovely garden. May, it was. Definitely May, because I remember it being near Molly's birthday.'

Vinny couldn't speak. Finding out Ava existed had been a shock, but nothing compared to this. He remembered the dates so well. August 1980 it was when he'd fucked Bella senseless. How could he ever forget? Not only had she been the most memorable sexual encounter of his entire lifetime, Molly had gone missing shortly afterwards.

Queenie put her hand over her mouth. 'Oh dear Lord! Viv said she thought Antonio was Michael's – he is, isn't he?'

Legs trembling, Vinny stood up. 'Nah. Antonio isn't Michael's. I've gotta go, Mum. Just remembered something I've forgotten to do.'

'Vinny! Come back 'ere,' Queenie ordered, when her ashen-faced son bolted from the house with the photo still in his hand.

Ignoring his mother, Vinny jumped in his Merc and drove off like a lunatic. He skidded around the corner, slammed his foot on the brake, then switched on the interior light. Vinny stared at the photo again, and as the bile reached his throat, swallowed it back down. He smashed his fist against the steering wheel. 'You no-good, lying, Italian fucking whore.'

CHAPTER EIGHTEEN

'Viv, you awake?' Queenie asked.

'I wasn't, but I bloody well am now. It's not even six. Whatever's wrong?'

'Something terrible's happened. Can you come in mine? I haven't slept all night.'

Five minutes later, Vivian let herself in her sister's house. 'What's the matter?' Queenie was red-eyed and had clearly been crying.

'It's Antonio.'

'Is he ill? Dead?' Vivian asked, alarmed.

Queenie shook her head. 'I think he's Vinny's son.'

Vivian looked at her sister, wondering if she'd gone mad. 'Of course he ain't Vinny's son. Whatever would make you think that? You haven't banged your head, have ya?'

Explaining Vinny's reaction when he'd seen the photo, Queenie said, 'It all makes sense now. I laid awake thinking about it all night. Vinny's always hated Bella with a passion, will never be in her company, and he has nothing to do with Camila. I think he's only seen that little girl twice, and don't you remember he acted all weird when she was here with Michael that time? Me and you spoke about it. He couldn't get out the house quick enough.'

Vivian sat next to her sister and squeezed her hands. 'I really think you're barking up the wrong tree, Queen. No way would Bella ever have anything to do with your Vinny. She's far too classy, and clearly adores Michael.'

'I know my own son, Viv, and I've never seen him go so pale as he did last night. He looked at that photo and it was like he'd seen a ghost. Then he started questioning me on how old Antonio was and what month was his birthday. That boy is his, I'd put my house on it. As for Bella, how could she do this to my Michael? That boy's heart will be broken in a thousand pieces when he finds out.'

'I still think you're wrong, Queen. There must be some simple explanation, surely? But if what you're saying is true, how could Vinny keep it from Michael an' all?'

'Vinny didn't know the kid was his until last fucking night. That lying whore told everybody Antonio's father was a yank called Clint. She's driven a wedge between my boys for years, her. And now I know cunting-well why.'

'So, what you gonna do? You can't start having a go at the girl without actual proof.'

'Oh, I'll get proof all right. We'll get a cab to Vinny's now, me and you. Even ran off with the photo in his hands, he did. What more proof do I need?'

'And if he admits it?' Vivian asked.

'Then he tells Michael, or I do. I will not have that boy lied to any more. As for that Iti slut, I'll fucking kill her.'

Vinny poured himself another Scotch and stared at the photo again. He hadn't slept yet, had been drinking and thinking all night.

Sighing, Vinny lay back on his pillow, hands behind his head. Michael could never find out Antonio was his, that was for sure. Such knowledge would destroy his brother and their relationship for ever. And if that meant Vinny never getting to know his son, then so be it. He'd never met Antonio anyway, would rather have his brother in his life than a child he did not know.

Bella had already ruined his and Michael's relationship to an extent. For obvious reasons, they could do nothing as a family together. But if Bella was out of the picture, things would be different, like they used to be. For once he had the upper hand over the bitch. She either moved back to Italy with his son, or he would tell Michael everything and demand parental rights.

He was staring at the photo, wondering what Antonio was like, when the buzzer made him jump. Vinny decided to ignore it, but then it was pressed continually, so he leapt out of bed. 'Who is it?'

'Your mother. Let me in now, Vinny!'

Vinny strutted up and down the flat with his unshaven face in his hands. If his mum had guessed the truth, he'd have to bluff his way out of it somehow.

Opening the door, Vinny was horrified to see his aunt as well. Both had faces like thunder. 'What's the matter? Has something bad happened?'

'Viv, go in the kitchen and put the kettle on,' Queenie ordered.

'Spit it out then,' Vinny demanded in a nonchalant tone.

'Look at the state of you. Been drinking all night, have ya?' Queenie remarked, pushing her son towards the sofa. 'I'm not stupid, Vinny. I know.'

Slumping backwards on the sofa, Vinny mumbled, 'Know what?'

'That Antonio is your son.'

'You're having a laugh, ain't ya? I've heard some bollocks in my time, but Jesus wept, that's insanity. How is Antonio mine? I've never even met the kid.'

After a night spent praying that she had been wrong,

one look in her son's eyes told Queenie she wasn't. She'd always known when Vinny was lying, even as a toddler.

If Vinny had been sober, he might've been able to lie himself out of the situation a bit better, but unfortunately for him he wasn't. 'I dunno who Antonio's father is, but when I saw the photo, I thought he must be Michael's, OK? That's why I ran out your house. I wanted to get the truth out of Michael, but I ain't been able to get hold of him yet.'

Insulting her intelligence was Queenie's biggest pet hate, especially by one she'd given birth to. Unable to stop herself, she began slapping her eldest around the head. 'A liar's worse than a thief, I always drummed that into you. Now tell me the bastard truth.'

Like a rabbit caught in the headlights, Vinny punched the wall. 'It was a fling, a one-night stand. And the slut told me her name was Izzy. I hate her, Mum. Fucking hate her.'

Unaware of the drama currently surrounding them, Michael and Bella were having an early-morning grope.

'Stop it! The children will hear us, and say Camila walks in on us again,' Bella giggled, when Michael's middle finger made contact with her vagina.

'Well, they've gotta learn how they were created one day,' Michael joked. Yesterday was the first time he and Bella had made love in a few weeks, and it had reminded Michael of what they'd been missing. What with the kids and work, it was difficult at times. Then there was Katy. Michael had been so stressed over her constant demands, no wonder his libido had suffered.

'If we're to beat the Lakeside traffic, we should be getting showered now,' Bella tormented, stroking Michael's penis.

Michael was about to enter Bella when Camila burst into the room. 'My toy duck is broke,' she cried.

Michael's erection deflated as rapidly as a burst balloon. 'Happy days,' he chuckled.

'I'll leave you to it. Gonna have a wander, find a paper shop,' Vivian said. Vinny had only recently moved to a flash new apartment in Canary Wharf and she had no idea where she was heading. Anything was better than being around that no-good snivelling wreck though. Vivian's heart went out to Michael, it really did. That poor bastard's world was about to be blown apart, thanks to the evil one, just like hers had.

When the door slammed, Queenie slapped her eldest hard around the face. 'Crocodile tears don't wash with me, boy, so man up. I want to know everything, from the very beginning.'

Vinny took a series of deep breaths, before swallowing the rest of the black coffee his mother had forced him to drink. 'I met her in a club up town. I remember exactly when it was, because it was shortly before Molly went missing. She was all over me like a rash, made it very clear what she wanted, so we headed off to some hotel. I hadn't been happy with Jo for ages, so weren't gonna look a gift horse in the mouth. She turned out to be a proper wild one. Wanted me—'

'For goodness' sake, Vinny! Spare me the gory details,' Queenie interrupted. 'When I said I wanted to know everything, I didn't mean filth. When did you see her next?'

'When I woke up in that hotel the following morning she was gone. Hand on heart, I never saw her again until Michael brought her to my fortieth. She bolted as soon as she recognized me. I only knew her as Izzy; turns out her real name is Isabella, which explains the confusion. I collared her outside when Michael went to get the car. Warned her if she ever messed my brother about I'd slice her up. I didn't know what else to do. It was all such a shock, and me and Michael had only recently got back on track. It would've destroyed our relationship for good had I told him. I couldn't do that. I love him way too much.'

'You should've told me. I would've sorted it,' Queenie retorted.

She was so very disappointed with Bella. She'd always liked her, thought she was so beautiful and classy, but deep down she was nothing more than a whore. Having only ever slept with Albie, Queenie hated loose women. It had been harlots like Bella who'd broken up her own marriage. 'No wonder the slapper sodded off to Italy for months straight after your fortieth. Shame she ever came back. What contact have you and her had since? And don't lie to me, Vinny.'

'Very little. When Bella returned from Italy I made her meet me in a boozer. Did my utmost to get her out of Michael's life for good, but she refused to leave him, said she'd rather tell him the truth and take her chances. So we agreed to stay out of one another's way. That's why she was supposedly ill when Little Vinny got married, and our paths never cross at any other family do's. Michael was and still is so in love with her. How could I burst his bubble?'

Queenie pursed her thin lips. 'Well, I can assure you Michael won't be in love with that tart any more, not when he finds out she's had hold of your dingle-dangle an' all.'

Vinny was horrified. 'We can't tell him, Mum. Not ever!'

Michael and Bella were Christmas shopping. They'd driven to Lakeside early and sat in the car park for an hour sipping coffee to be the first in the doors and avoid the crowds.

'Who the bloody hell's that for?' Michael asked, when Bella picked up an Arsenal kit. He wasn't a massive football fan by any means, but he and Vinny always referred to themselves as Spurs supporters. They'd actually had a top day out at Wembley earlier this year, when Vinny had blagged some free tickets for the FA Cup Semi-Final in an executive box. Not only had Spurs stuffed the Arsenal, Gazza's free-kick was the stuff legends were made of.

'It's for Antonio.'

'But he doesn't even like football.'

Bella chuckled. 'He does now. His new friend Edward is an Arsenal fan, so Antonio told me he wants to be one too.'

Michael raised his eyebrows, and not having a clue how very apt his words were, joked, 'That boy's father must've been a proper wrong 'un.'

The journey home was a silent one. Both Queenie and Viv had always hated taxis of any kind. Cabbies were nosy bastards, and if they weren't asking questions, you could guarantee they were earwigging.

'Go in mine and put the kettle on. I'm gonna knock at Stinky Susan's, make sure Ava got off to school OK,' Queenie said, when the cab pulled up outside hers. She'd had to wake Stinky Susan up at dawn this morning. Ava had been fast asleep with Fred snoring beside her, so Queenie had left a note next to her bed saying she'd had to pop out. Ava was very grown up for her age, and quite capable of making her own breakfast. Leaving her sleeping blissfully was far better than letting the child know that something was dreadfully wrong, and Susan had promised to knock at Queenie's to check on her.

Queenie shut the front door. 'Ava was fine. She took Fred over to Mrs Agg's before she went to school.'

'What did Vinny have to say then? How could he keep something like that to himself, Queen? Poor Michael.'

'I know. It's such a bloody mess. Vinny's begged me not to tell Michael, but he has to know, Viv. Gonna break his heart, but it's better than living a lie with that scheming whore,' Queenie said, before repeating Vinny's version of events.

'Are you going to tell Michael? Or is Vinny?'

'I don't know yet. I've told Vinny to get some sleep then pop round later. No point trying to talk to him while he's still half-pissed. I'll cook him a roast or something, help soak up the booze.'

Vivian looked at her sister in astonishment. 'You're cooking him a roast! That's his reward for shoving his todger up his brother's other half, is it? Poor bloody Michael, that's all I can say. Yet again Vinny has ripped this family apart, and yet again you forgive him.'

Unusually for Queenie, she burst into tears. 'Don't you think I've had a bad enough day without you starting on me an' all? Of course Vinny should've said something. He should have told me after his fortieth. But he didn't. He wanted to protect his brother. You can't just blame him, Viv. What about her? She's the one lying in bed with my Michael of a night knowing full well what she's done. It takes two to fucking tango.'

Antonio had his own personal driver who took him to and from his private school, and as soon as her son arrived home, Bella urged him to take off his uniform, freshen up and put something smart on.

'Why, Mum?'

Bella hugged her handsome son. Due to work commitments, it was rare she and Michael spent the whole day and evening together so they'd decided to make the most of it. 'Because you've broken up from school, Michael and I thought we'd take you out to celebrate. I managed to book us a table at your favourite restaurant. Camila's coming too.'

Antonio grinned. 'Can I have lobster?'

'You can have whatever you want.'

'Bell, I'm just gonna pop outside to make a couple of business calls,' Michael shouted out. He could hear Camila crying, so it was the ideal opportunity to excuse himself to ring the bitch.

Katy answered within seconds. 'Remembered me and Nathan exist then, have you? I've been trying to call you all day, but your phone's been switched off. Our son has been ill.'

'I'm sorry. My battery was out of juice. What's wrong? Is Nath OK now?'

'No, he isn't. I had to keep him off school. Been vomiting all day, and he has a high temperature,' Katy lied. Her son was actually asleep on her lap and as fit as a fiddle.

Having had a wonderful twenty-four hours with Bella, all Michael's worries came flooding back. Feeling guilty, he promised to visit Nathan the following day.

Yelling, 'Only if you can be bothered,' Katy smiled and ended the call.

Nathan opened his eyes. 'You OK, Mummy?'

Katy stroked her son's hair. 'Fine, darling. Daddy's coming to visit us tomorrow, and we're going to tell him a little fib. If we pretend you haven't been well, then Daddy will stay with us longer, won't he?'

'You shouldn't have gone to the trouble of cooking for me, Mum. My stomach's in knots and I don't feel a bit hungry,' Vinny said. He was actually quite surprised by his mother's reaction to the latest drama in their lives. He'd always been worried that, if the truth came out, she'd disown him and side with Michael.

'Just eat what you can. Starving yourself ain't gonna solve this particular problem.'

Vinny did as asked, then sat opposite his mother in the armchair. 'I've thought of a plan. I'm going to tell her I know and try and force her to go back to Italy. That way Michael need never know.'

Queenie was horrified. 'You will do no such bloody thing. That bitch has denied me a grandson for years and no way is she taking my granddaughter away from me as well. Sometimes I wonder if there's a brain in that head of yours. How heartbroken would your brother be if she sodded off back to Italy with his only daughter, eh? Use your loaf, for goodness' sake.'

'It's better than Michael knowing the truth, Mum. He'll never forgive me, or her, I'm telling ya. If you wanna split our family in two, then go ahead and tell him.'

'This family is already split in two, don't you see that? That manipulative whore has driven a wedge between you and your brother for years. How often do you socialize with Michael now?'

'I had a drink with him about a month ago. He didn't stay long though.'

'My point exactly. Look, Vin, it's obviously going to be a massive shock to Michael and he's going to hate you at first. But he'll hate her more. I cannot believe she's been lying in Michael's bed all this time after what she's done. A cold, calculating, heartless old tom, that's what she is. And to deny you a son and me a grandchild is truly despicable.'

Vinny put his head in his hands. 'Call me a coward, call me whatever you like, but I can't be the one to tell Michael, Mum. You'll have to do it.'

After her earlier show of weakness, Queenie was back to her usual tough-as-old-boots self. 'Neither of us are gonna tell Michael. Let that slut look him in the eyes and tell him what she's done. Arrange to meet her in a pub or somewhere where nobody knows us. I'm coming with you to confront her.'

'She's bound to deny Antonio's mine.'

'Then we demand proof. A DNA test will shut the slapper up. Whether she likes it or not, Antonio is your son and you're his father. Only got herself to blame. Should've kept her legs shut and her hand on her ha'penny.'

'So, how was your last day at school? Did you do Christmassy things?' Bella asked. She and Michael had gone to watch Antonio in his nativity play a couple of weeks ago. He'd played one of the three kings and they'd both been so proud of him. He'd been very self-assured on stage, a natural.

'We did Christmassy things this afternoon, but this morning Mr Abbot wanted us to make a list of three professions that we would like to do when we're older, then we had to stand up and tell him why.'

Michael ruffled Antonio's hair. 'You never said Old Bill, I hope,' he joked.

'Who is Old Bill, Daddy?' Camila asked innocently.

Bella kicked Michael under the table, before asking Antonio what his answers were.

'I said I would like to be an accountant because I'm good at maths, or a bookmaker. I told Mr Abbot only silly people bet and they always lose their money. I didn't know what else to write, so I put vet and said because I enjoy cutting the dead mice and rabbits up in science.'

When her mobile phone burst into life, Bella excused herself. 'I must call Rupert back, Michael. That's the third time he's rung me today. Bound to be some drama at the office.'

Bella made her way outside before making the call. 'What's happened now? And please do not tell me Melanie failed to turn up for today's shoot? Because if she's let me down again, she is so sacked.'

Rupert chuckled. 'Melanie was absolutely fab today, darling. Blew their socks off. The reason I've called you – and it's probably nothing important – is Michael's brother Vinny is trying to get hold of you. He rang the office at lunchtime and again before I left. He said it's urgent. Probably some surprise Christmas present for Michael, is my guess.'

Experiencing that same horrible feeling in the pit of her stomach she always did when Vinny tried to make contact, Bella replied, 'Yes. Bound to be some surprise for Michael.'

'Dad, I know you've probably got all my presents already, but I've seen one on an advert called "Puppy Surprise" that I want. Get it for me,' Ava demanded brazenly, before putting her arms around her father's neck and hugging him.

Queenie stood up. 'Off to bed now and you'll get what Father Christmas brings you, and I'm sure that'll be far more than most poor children. Get off your dad's lap. Come on, chop-chop.'

Ava leapt off and put her hands on her hips. 'I'm not stupid, Nan. I knew Father Christmas didn't exist when I was five! Come on, Fred, we're going to bed. Oh, and make sure you get him a doggy stocking an' all.'

Queenie slapped her granddaughter lightly on the bottom. 'Please! Have you never heard of the word, please? Out of my sight now, before I ring up Battersea Dogs' Home and get them to pick Fred up.'

As much as he had on his mind, Vinny couldn't help but smile as he heard his daughter giggling all the way up the stairs. Ava truly was a chip off the old block.

Unable to speak freely in front of Ava, Queenie hissed, 'The whore hasn't rung you back yet then?'

'Nah. But she will. Tell me about Antonio, Mum. What's he like?'

'Give me five minutes and I'll find some recent photos. Pour me another Baileys, boy, and get yourself a drink. No Scotch though. You need a clear head right now. Have a lager instead.'

Antonio focused intently on the lobsters swimming around the tank. He pointed towards one. 'I think that's the one we will enjoy eating the most,' he told Michael and the waitress.

Michael winked at the waitress. 'You've had your orders,' he said, before ushering Antonio back to their table.

Bella was deep in thought while stroking her sleeping daughter's hair. Because of the awkwardness surrounding the whole sorry situation, Bella had given Vinny her mobile number ages ago. Rupert, her PA, was incredibly nosy, so Bella had urged the man she loathed so very much to call her personally regarding family events. Bella had even stored Vinny's number as Virginia, so surely if he had something drastic to tell her he would have called her, not the office?

Michael kissed Bella on the forehead, before sitting back down himself. 'You OK, babe?'

Bella smiled broadly. 'I'm fine, Michael. In fact I'm better than fine.'

'So you bloody well should be. You get to wake up with me every morning.'

Vinny Butler studied some more recent photos of the son he had never met. When he'd first seen a photo of Ava whilst in prison, he'd immediately known she was his, and he felt exactly the same about Antonio. 'He looks more like me now than Little Vinny. Gonna be tall an' all. I'm amazed you, being as clued-up as you are, never spotted the likeness before, Mum.'

'How was I to know that slag had enticed you into bed an' all? I often thought Antonio could've been Michael's. I actually remember Michael telling me once that people thought he was his. Strangers and that.'

'So what's he like?' Vinny asked.

'A nice boy. Speaks a bit posh, but has lovely manners. He's a bit serious for his age, that's probably because of that uppity private school the whore sends him to.'

Still staring at his son's image, Vinny asked, 'What interests has he got?'

'I don't know, to be honest, but he's good with Camila. Very protective of his little sister. When you meet him, you can ask him stuff for yourself.'

'That bitch ain't gonna want him spending time with me, is she? And what about Michael? He's virtually raised Antonio, so I can't go steaming in like a bulldozer.'

Thin lips pursed, Queenie announced, 'Oh yes you can! And you will. No father should be denied the right to spend time with his own flesh and blood. Well, apart from yours.'

On the journey home from the restaurant, both Michael and Bella were quiet.

'Have you two had an argument?' Antonio enquired.

Michael chuckled. 'Course we haven't. Hark at your sister, she's snoring,' he said. Camila was sound asleep on his lap.

Bella put an arm around her son's shoulders. 'Well, I thought that was a lovely evening. We must take time to go out for family meals more often, don't you think, Michael?'

'Definitely, babe. We'll have to take your mum and dad

out to a few restaurants over the holiday period. Juanita can have a couple of days off then, eh?'

'Juanita flew back to Spain this morning, Michael. She's spending Christmas with her family. I told you that last week.'

'Did ya?'

'Yes, twice. I'm sure you don't listen to a word I say at times.'

'So who's looking after the kids tomorrow while you're out all day and evening?'

'Their father, Michael. You! I told you that last week as well. Has your brain gone on holiday as well as Juanita?'

'But I've got an important business meeting tomorrow. There's no way I can get out of it,' Michael lied miserably.

'I'm very sorry, but you are going to have to rearrange. Not my fault if you don't listen,' Bella snapped.

Sighing, Michael stared out the window at the bright lights of London. Ever since Bella had made him watch that film *Fatal Attraction*, he'd been even more wary of Katy. She reminded him of a young version of the bird who had boiled the bunny. And Michael actually liked having his bollocks where God had intended them to be.

CHAPTER NINETEEN

Jamie Preston sidled up to the only screw he truly trusted. Black Bob had been on Glen Harper's payroll and was more than happy to risk his job for the right price. 'I need you to get hold of a tool for me. No blades – a sharpened screwdriver. I ain't gonna do anything too silly with it. I want it for self-protection. Glen'll settle up with you on the outside.'

'Leave it with me.'

'As soon as possible, OK?' Jamie muttered, before walking away.

Spotting Richie Woods glaring at him from the other side of the yard, Jamie smirked. If he used the screwdriver to gouge Richie's eyes out, the tosser wouldn't be able to glare at anybody in the future.

'Calum, Regan, if you don't do as your mother asks, neither of you will be going to see Father Christmas, understand?' Little Vinny bellowed.

'Don't care,' replied four-year-old Calum.

When two-year-old Regan giggled, Little Vinny grabbed both his sons by the wrist. 'I'll take you round to Nanny Meg's then. She can look after ya while Ollie and Toby visit Santa.'

Regan threw himself face down on the floor. 'Nooo! I want to see Father Christmas,' he cried, kicking the carpet repeatedly with both feet.

Lip wobbling, Calum announced, 'I want to see him too, Dad.'

'Well, this is your last chance to let Mummy wash and dress you. Five minutes I'll give ya, and if you're not ready, you're not coming.'

When the 'terrible twosome', as Sammi-Lou referred to them, finally did as they were told, Little Vinny picked his eldest up and swung him in the air. 'Who's going to be seven next week? Big boy now, aren't you?'

'Will Father Christmas bring my birthday presents down the chimney with him as well, Dad?'

'I should imagine so. You'll have to ask him.'

Oliver grinned and put his arms around his father's neck. 'I love you, Dad.'

'Not as much as I love you. You're the bestest boy in the whole wide world.'

Michael waved Bella off, then scrolled through his phone. Daniel and Lee hadn't come home last night, which was nothing unusual as they often stayed at the club after working late.

'Aw, Jesus. What time is it?' Daniel mumbled, on hearing his father's voice.

'Nearly eleven. Look, I know this is short notice but I need a massive favour. Bella's out until this evening, and I forgot Juanita's in Spain. I urgently need to be somewhere soon, but I can't take Camila with me. Could you and Lee pop over and keep an eye on her for a few hours? I'll definitely be back before teatime.'

'Sorry, Dad. No can do. Me and Lee have got plans ourselves.'

'Can't you cancel 'em?' Michael asked abruptly.

'No. We can't. We ain't even bought any bastard a Christmas present yet, and we've arranged to meet a couple of fit birds. Don't worry though; we'll be back at the club for the late shift. I take it you won't be showing your face again this evening?'

'I pay you and Lee more than enough so I don't have to show my fucking face and listen to that racket yous youngsters call music these days. Please, Dan, I'm begging you. I've got an important business meeting and I can't let the geezer down.'

Wide awake now, Daniel chuckled. 'You and your mysterious business meetings eh, Dad? Me and Lee reckon you've got a bit on the side. What's her name?'

Yelling, 'Don't talk bollocks and thanks for nothing,' Michael ended the call.

'What-a matter, Daddy?' Camila asked, her big innocent eyes full of concern.

Michael scooped the child up in his arms. 'Nothing, sweetheart. Let's watch some cartoons, shall we?'

Having cancelled going out with the school mums in favour of spending time with Michael, Katy Spencer was busy getting glammed up.

'You look beautiful, Mummy. But your boobies are showing,' Nathan giggled.

Katy smiled. Michael had been a big fan of her breasts when they'd been together, which was why Katy always liked to remind him of what he was missing.

'Can I answer it?' Nathan asked, when the phone rang.

'If it's Daddy, don't forget to tell him you've not been well. You kept being sick yesterday,' Katy reminded her son. She'd actually kept Nathan off school this morning telling him he looked flushed and had a temperature. It was only a half-day anyway and the children were told they were allowed to take in games to play with. Katy was worried Nathan would slip up and tell Michael he had been playing games, hence her white lie.

Smiling as Nathan told Michael exactly what she had said, Katy was handed the phone by her son. 'You on your way yet? Our wounded little soldier is so looking forward to seeing you.'

Michael sighed deeply. It made him feel so guilty when Nathan was ill and he couldn't be at his side. 'I'm sorry, but I can't get there today, Katy. Our housekeeper's on holiday, Bella isn't around and there's nobody else to look after Camila.'

'You are kidding me, right? Our ill son has been staring out of the window for the past hour awaiting your arrival. Bring Camila with you. Nathan would love to meet her.'

'Don't be daft. Cami's bound to say something to Bella. I'll spend some quality time with Nathan either tomorrow or Sunday. I promise you that faithfully.'

'Your promises are totally worthless,' Katy screamed. 'Daddy's not coming to visit you after all, Nathan. He has better things to do.'

Hearing his son sobbing, Michael hissed, 'You bitch. Why couldn't you let him down gently? Put him back on the phone to me.'

'No. He doesn't want to talk to you and neither do I. As for worrying about Camila telling Bella, if I was you I'd start upping your parental game otherwise it'll be me blurting out your dirty little secret. And believe me, I'm not joking. I am seriously on the edge. Get here by five, Michael, or else. I'm warning you.'

As they neared the front of the enormous queue in Harrods, Little Vinny gave his sons a warning. 'Don't forget to say please and thank you to Father Christmas. Once upon a time I wasn't very polite to him and I didn't get any presents that year.'

Smiling when her boys' eyes widened and they began to question their father, Sammi-Lou nudged her best friend as Finn bent down to speak to his son. Toby was three and Finn was no longer with his mother. 'He has a nice bum and you two seemed to be getting on very well earlier,' Sammi whispered.

Charlene playfully slapped her friend's arm. 'Will you stop it! You sound like that Cilla Black on *Blind Date*. Yes, Finn is very easy on the eye, but his ex was a glamour model and that I am not. He's not going to be interested in me, Sam.'

'I think he likes you. I can tell,' Sammi-Lou insisted.

Charlene's face reddened. 'Behave yourself and please don't be saying anything to Little Vinny. I'd feel too embarrassed to be in Finn's company again if you did that.'

'I won't. I swear. I do think you'd make a great couple though.'

'You go first then, Ollie. Don't forget to tell Santa what presents you want,' Little Vinny urged.

What Little Vinny did not realize as he cheerfully ushered his eldest son into the grotto, was that amongst the chaos of the Christmas post, the package containing his taped confession had finally been spotted by an eagle-eyed postman and was now on its way to the address it should've been sent to in the first place.

Mr and Mrs Spencer deemed themselves to be decent, law-abiding people. They went to church regularly and were always donating to different charities to help the less fortunate.

Like all parents, the Spencers had had extremely high hopes for their three children. Firstly Katy had shamed the good family name by falling pregnant out of wedlock to a man they had never met. Then their son Kevin had set up an insurance company and robbed many clients, including lots of their friends, of thousands of pounds. Their eldest, Neil, was the only child to be truly proud of. He was a well-respected solicitor.

'Here we are. I should imagine that sporty number on the drive is our Katy's, so it seems as though she might be home,' Mr Spencer commented.

Katy was lying on the sofa sipping a glass of wine when the doorbell rang. 'I told you Daddy would come, didn't I?' she said, ruffling Nathan's hair. He'd been so upset earlier, had cried himself to sleep.

Checking her appearance in the hallway mirror, Katy flung open the front door and was absolutely deflated on seeing her do-gooding parents standing on the doorstep. 'What the hell do yous two want?' she screamed.

Queenie and Vivian were watching the news.

'Don't she look beautiful in that dress?' Vivian gushed. Both herself and Queenie adored Princess Diana.

'Won't last, that marriage. Look at their body language. I reckon Charles is in love with that Parker-Bowles woman.'

'Royals rarely divorce, Queen, and what about William and Harry? Those boys would be devastated. Anyway, why would Charles even look at another woman when he's got fillet steak at home?'

'Albie had fillet steak at home when I married him. Didn't stop him poking his sausage elsewhere, though, did it? I'll have a tenner bet with you that Charles and Di are divorced in the next five years.'

'I bet they ain't,' Vivian insisted, shaking her sister's hand.

Queenie changed the subject. 'Tara rang me this morning. Asked if it was OK if her and Tommy came for Christmas dinner and stayed overnight. It'll be lovely to see them, but I really could've done without it. I'd hate the shit to hit the fan while they're here.'

Tara was nineteen now, Tommy fourteen, and when Brenda had died, they'd decided to continue living with Dave and his daughter in Dagenham. Neither had wanted to change schools or be parted from their friends, and for all Dave's faults, it had been kind of him to take parental responsibility for two kids that weren't even his. The arrangement had worked out well. Tara was now training to be a hairdresser, and Tommy had a Saturday job on Romford market.

'D'ya know what, Queen, I think you should tell Vinny to hold fire for a while. Christmas is gonna be a bloody shambles otherwise.'

'But Michael and the whore are meant to be bringing the kids over on Sunday. I even said I'd cook for them. No way is she ever darkening my doorstep again. And as for my Michael, I can't lie to him. And what about Antonio? I can't act normal towards him now I know he's my grandson, can I?'

'You'll have to cancel 'em coming, Queen. I'll ring Michael and tell him you're laid up with a flu bug and I'm looking after you.'

'What about the presents? She won't be getting that silk scarf now, that's for sure. I'm gonna get me money back.'

'Dan and Lee can pick the presents up. I'll ring 'em, tell 'em you didn't have a chance to get Bella's because you're ill. Imagine how upset Antonio and Camila will be if their Christmas is ruined? And her parents are visiting from Italy, aren't they?'

'I wonder what Mr and Mrs D'Angelo will think of their slapper of a daughter when they find out the truth? You're right though. I don't want to spoil Antonio and Camila's

Christmas, nor Ava's. Keeping it quiet until afterwards is probably best all round. I'll ring Vinny now. Tell him to hold his horses until after Boxing Day.'

An extremely perceptive PA, Rupert followed Bella and waited outside the ladies.

'What's the matter?' Bella asked.

'I was about to ask you the same thing. You're not yourself today, sweet pea, and don't say there's nothing troubling you as Rupert knows best.'

Bella had actually been in a vibrant mood until Martha, her new young assistant, had informed her a certain Mr Butler had rung the office again this morning. 'I can assure you I'm fine, Rupert. Order me the crab for starters and salmon for main. I need to call Michael, check that Camila's OK.'

Outside the restaurant, Bella took many deep breaths as she scrolled through her phone. What did the evil bastard want? And why did he keep ringing the office and not her? He only had to call Michael first to find out they weren't in one another's company. 'Vinny, it's Bella. My employees inform me you need to speak with me.'

Having already had strict orders from his mother, Vinny walked away from Jay Boy and into his office. 'Yes. I do need to speak with you, but in person. Any chance we can meet briefly on the twenty-seventh? I'm willing to drive over your way.'

'Whatever is this about, Vinny? Can you not tell me now?'

'Nope. I'm afraid not. You'll find out soon enough, when you meet me.'

'But my parents are visiting. I will be spending time with them.'

'Believe me, Bella, it's in your best interests to meet me. Shall we say the Plough, Gallows Corner at twelve, lunchtime? That isn't too far from you and you'll be home within the hour. You can pretend you're popping to the shops or picking up some belated presents. I'll even wrap a few up personally if you want?' Vinny smirked. He was thoroughly enjoying this conversation, would proper get off on it later when he watched one of his more violent films.

Vinny sounded far too calm to have found out about Antonio. And how could he? 'Michael isn't ill, is he, Vinny? Please tell me what this is all about.'

'As I said earlier, I'm only willing to speak to you in person. Twelve p.m. next Friday at the Plough. See you then, Izzy. Sorry, I mean Bella.'

When Vinny cut her off, Bella crouched on her haunches. How the hell was she meant to entertain her parents and act normal now? Her Christmas was ruined. Totally fucking ruined, and she couldn't wait for it to be over.

CHAPTER TWENTY

'What's wrong with you today? Twice you've snapped at Cami this morning for no reason. Time of the month, is it?' Michael asked, voice laden with sarcasm.

'I'm fine. I just didn't sleep too well,' Bella replied, dragging the hoover out of the cupboard. She needed to keep herself busy.

Urging Bella to leave the hoovering and speak to him, Michael noticed tears in her eyes, so took her in his arms. Something was definitely wrong, as Bella crying was a rarity. 'Did something happen while you were out yesterday? You asked me twice when you came in last night if I was ill. I know you'd had a couple of champers too many, but why ask me that? Tell me what's wrong, babe, and I'll sort it.'

'I thought you looked peaky, that's all. Listen, I have decided I'm going to ring my parents, Michael, and tell them to book into a hotel. I'd forgotten I'd given Juanita time off when I OK'd it for them to stay here. We're going to be under one another's feet, and it will be too much hard work. I just want and need a relaxing break. We can still spend lots of time with them, obviously.'

Having listened to the conversation from the landing, Antonio bolted down the stairs. 'You cannot tell Nonna and Nonno to book into a hotel, Mum. That's extremely rude and I'm very much looking forward to them staying with us.'

As much as Michael didn't want Bella's parents staying at his, he also didn't want to upset the father. If Bella told them they couldn't stay, Mr Mafia might think it was down to him. 'Antonio's right, Bella. It's a bit off for you to tell your mum and dad they can't stay here at such short notice. We've got plenty of room, and I'll help out with the cooking and cleaning if need be.'

'Please, Mum,' Antonio begged.

Bella forced a smile. Vinny had completely unnerved her, but she must try to act normal for the sake of her family. 'Of course Nonna and Nonno can stay here, Antonio. Take no notice of Mummy. She's having one of her stressed-out silly days.'

'Nathan, take Jonny upstairs and play with your toys. There's a good boy,' Katy Spencer ordered.

'So, what's happened? You sounded distraught on the phone last night,' Lucy Tompkins asked. Lucy was Katy's lifelong best friend and the only one that knew the true identity of Nathan's father. She'd even been with Katy on the day she'd purchased the pregnancy test.

Katy explained the difficulties she'd been having. 'I was gutted when I thought it was Michael at the door yesterday and it turned out to be my parents. Like I care if my brother Kevin has been put in prison. He was always a crook. But now I feel bad. My mum was sobbing as she left and I was so rude to her and my dad. I blame Michael and the situation I'm in for my mood swings. It's doing my head in. I love him so much and so does Nathan. But he doesn't spend enough time with us. He's very generous, as you know, but that's not enough for me any more. Even if he doesn't want to be with me, I want Nathan to be a bigger part of Michael's life. He's missing out on so much. Brothers, sisters, grandparents, cousins, it just isn't fair.'

Lucy squeezed her pal's hand. 'You're absolutely right. It isn't fair. I think you should ring your mum and dad and apologize, while I pour us a drink. Then we can decide what to do about Michael over a glass of wine or two.'

Katy smiled. Lucy had always been the sensible one. 'OK.'

'Who was that?' Bella asked, when Michael put the phone down.

'Dan. Him and Lee are meeting up with the lads from the club in the Blind Beggar for a pre-Christmas drink. They wanted me to join them, but I won't. I'll help you get the place ready for your parents' arrival.'

'I think you should go, Michael. Will do you good to get out and catch up with the lads. You won't be able to come rolling home drunk with my parents here, so you might as well make the most of it while you can,' Bella joked.

'Nah. The Old Bill are shit-hot on drink-driving these days. It's not worth taking the risk.'

Bella was desperate for some time alone. 'Ring Alan. He'll drop you off and pick you up,' she urged. Alan was her personal driver. 'Honestly, you'll only get under my feet here. I need to change the beds and all sorts. I insist you go out. It will look bad if you don't turn up and buy your staff a drink or two.'

'OK. I'll ring Dan. It's not my staff though, babe. I was referring to Vinny's club. He'll be there as well, and Little Vinny.'

When Michael walked into the lounge to make the call,

Bella cursed herself. Vinny was a loudmouth in drink, she knew that much. Now she would be on tenterhooks all bloody day in case whatever the arsehole planned to say to her, he blurted out to Michael. Why the hell had she opened her big gob?

'Nan, Fred's bored. I think he's missing Mabel. Can we take him to the park?' Ava asked. Mrs Agg had gone to Upminster to spend time with her sister and had taken Fred's girlfriend with her.

'Not on your nelly! I told you before, Ava, I will never take that naughty creature out again after what he did to me last time. If Mrs Agg hadn't caught him with a chicken fillet, the little bastard would still be running around the park now. Why don't you knock for Destiny and have a wander down the market?'

'Because I don't want to leave you.'

'Whyever not?'

Ava put her arms around her nan's waist. ''Cause I sense something's wrong. You seem unhappy.'

Queenie picked the child up and sat her on the kitchen table. 'Nanny's fine. I always get stressed this time of year. You must remember me throwing the date and walnut cake in the garden last Christmas?'

Ava giggled. 'Yes. You burnt the cake.'

'Well, there you go then.' Queenie took a tenner out of her purse and handed it to her granddaughter. 'Treat yourself and Destiny to a Wimpy. Make sure you wrap up warm though. It's taters out there today.'

As brazen as ever, Ava asked, 'Can I spend the change an' all?'

'Yes! Off you trot.'

When Ava left the house, Queenie sat at the kitchen table with her head in her hands. That poor little ha'p'orth was bound to be affected by all the drama beckoning as well. Queenie would break the news that she had an elder brother to Ava as gently as she possibly could. But how the child would react was anybody's guess.

Vinny had closed his club yesterday for the festive period. Most of his clientele were City types who wouldn't be working over the holidays, so it made sense not to bother reopening until the New Year.

Not in the right frame of mind for socializing with any old Tom, Dick or Harry, Vinny had avoided the staff party last night and arranged a smaller gathering today for himself and his main men.

'So, what's the plan?' Jay Boy asked, when Vinny finally got away from his many admirers. Whenever they set foot in an East End boozer, his boss would be treated like a king. Star-gazers, Vinny called the majority. Especially the people he barely knew.

Apart from when he'd taunted Bella on the phone yesterday, Vinny had been as miserable as sin these past couple of days. He might not see much of Michael any more, but he would always love his brother dearly, and dreaded his reaction to the shocking news. As for the son he'd never met, Vinny had no idea what type of relationship he'd have with him, if any. It was all such a fucking mess.

Jay Boy nudged his boss. 'Vin, wake up. I just asked you a question.'

'Sorry, Jay. What did you say?'

When Jay Boy repeated the question, Vinny knocked his Scotch back in one, then grinned. 'I suggest staying 'ere until Little Vinny and Finn turn up, then we go on a massive pub crawl. Later, we'll soak up the booze with a curry in Brick Lane. Whaddya reckon, lads?'

'Sounds good to me,' Carl replied.

'Same 'ere,' Paul added.

Vinny banged the palm of his hands against the table. He had to get pissed to put on a happy act. It was the only way to get through the day. 'Right, you slow-coaches, get those drinks down your 'atches. Pete, your turn to shout 'em up next. Money's behind the bar.'

Over in Kent, Katy and Lucy were still discussing Michael. Their sons had been fed and watered and were now playing happily in the other room.

'What should I do, Luce? I mean, if I blurt out all to Bella, Michael might pull the plug on this place and stop all my money.'

'He won't leave you homeless, Katy. From what you've told me, Michael adores Nathan, and he isn't the type of man to take any issue he has with you out on his son. You're not happy the way things are, you haven't been for years, and you can't stay on those pills the doctor gave you for ever. They will harm you in the long run.'

'I know you're right, but I've been threatening Michael for ages to turn up at his house if he keeps letting Nathan down, yet he doesn't seem to care. He hasn't even rung me today to see how Nathan is, knowing full well he was distraught yesterday. Bella's parents are arriving on Monday, so we won't see him at all then. It will break Nathan's heart if his daddy doesn't show up on Christmas Day.'

When her friend burst into tears again, Lucy hugged her. Katy had been so calm and confident before she'd met Michael; it was tragic she had so many issues now. Lucy wanted Katy to get better and become her old self once again, and if the truth coming out was the only way to force the situation, then so be it.

*

Vinny Butler leapt up, gave his son a manly hug and shook Finn's hand. He liked Finn and was over the moon his son had a decent pal for the first time in his life. Apart from that loser Ben Bloggs, Little Vinny had never had any friends.

'We've just got back from Essex. All is looking fine and dandy for our big New Year rave. We've had that much great feedback, we're charging a score per head now. Gonna make a killing, Dad,' Little Vinny boasted.

Extremely proud of his son for not only standing on his own two feet, but also buying a lovely gaff in Emerson Park, Vinny beamed with pride. 'So how many punters you expecting?'

'We're hoping for approximately three thousand. Nothing the Old Bill can do to stop it as we've privately rented the land. It's going to be advertised on every pirate radio station within a fifty-mile radius,' Finn explained.

'The only thing that can balls it up is the weather, Dad. I looked at the forecast today and they reckon it's gonna snow soon,' Little Vinny added worriedly.

'Don't be taking no notice of weather forecasters, boy. I remember that Michael Fish geezer announcing in '87 that people in the south should not worry as there was no chance of a hurricane. Your nan and aunt's roofs all blew off hours later,' Vinny laughed. It hadn't been funny at the time, mind. Everybody else's roofs in the street had survived the terrible storm and his mum and aunt had had to vacate their homes for a week while repairs were ongoing.

'Can I get everybody a drink, Vinny?' Finn asked politely.

'No. But order what you want, lad. Plenty of money behind the bar. We're gonna leave 'ere in a while anyway. We'll have a swift drink in the Maurice, then shoot down to Stepney. Last time I drank in the Black Boy, I beat some gobshite senseless outside. Let's hope he still don't drink in there, eh?' Vinny chuckled.

'We've gotta wait for Dan and Lee. They're meeting us here,' Little Vinny informed his father.

'Oh right, I didn't know they were coming. You invited Michael an' all?' Vinny enquired.

'Nah. Just Dan and Lee. I thought you would've invited Michael,' Little Vinny replied.

Relief flooded through Vinny's veins. As callous as he could be at times, no way on this earth could he have played happy families with his brother today, knowing the shit was about to hit the fan. His morals wouldn't allow it.

Queenie and Vivian were watching the latest episode of *Minder*. Both thought Terry McCann was very handsome, and Arthur Daley always had them in hysterics.

'That's the one thing these TV shows never get right, Viv. Meant to be a pub full of top villains Terry's walked in. Yet not one is wearing a suit. Ever seen my Vinny and Michael wearing anything but? Roy was the same. Always suited and booted. Clothes and shoes say everything about a man.'

'Your Albie wears suits too, Queen,' Vivian couldn't help but remind her sister.

'Well, apart from that tosser, of course. His suits are cheap old cloth anyway, not like my boys. Bleedin' nuisance!' Queenie huffed when the phone burst into life. 'Pause it, Viv,' she ordered. Video recorders were one of man's finest creations. The number of times her bloody phone rang, she'd never get to watch a programme unless she pre-recorded it.

'Who was it?' Viv asked.

'Vinny. Michael's walked in the pub and he can't stay

there. Wants me to ring in a few minutes to say I'm not well enough to look after Ava. What did Michael say exactly when you told him I had flu and he and the Italian slapper couldn't come for dinner tomorrow?'

Vivian shrugged. 'Not much. Didn't seem too bothered, to be honest.'

'Nice. Stick *Minder* back on, please.'

'You can't sod off, Vin. I've come all the way from bloody Brentwood to have a beer with you. It's been ages since we've had a good night out together,' Michael said.

For the first time ever, Vinny could barely look his brother in the eyes. 'Mum wouldn't have phoned unless she felt proper ill, bruv. And Ava's my responsibility at the end of the day. You enjoy yourself with the lads. I've gotta go.'

'Where's me old man gone?' Little Vinny asked, aware that his father had bolted out of the boozer.

Michael walked back over to the table. 'Home. Your nan's got a flu bug and he's had to pick Ava up.'

Little Vinny was perplexed. 'But he never said Nan was ill earlier. And why didn't he say goodbye to any of us?'

Michael shrugged. 'You know what your father's like. Makes up his own rules.'

Bella had felt edgy all day, but had done her utmost to keep herself busy. Michael had his phone with him and hadn't called her, so surely that was a good sign?

'You OK, Mum? Is Camila asleep?' Antonio asked.

'Yes, darling,' Bella replied. 'Shall we put the film back on now?' She and Antonio had been watching *Home Alone* before she'd gone to check on her daughter.

'In a minute. Can we talk about Christmas first?' insisted Antonio.

'Of course. Are you getting excited?'

'A bit. But can I tell you the present I would like the most?'

Having bought Antonio lots of gifts, Bella hoped it was something she'd already purchased. 'Go on.'

'Thomas, who is in my class, didn't know his real dad either. But his mum got married to her boyfriend Alex, and then Alex officially adopted Thomas, and Thomas now calls him "Daddy".'

Bella stroked her son's thick hair. 'What are you trying to say, sweetheart?'

'That I want you to marry Michael, so he can adopt me and I call him Dad. I love him very much, Mum. And you, of course.'

Unable to stop the tears, Bella planted kisses all over her son's handsome face.

'Why are you crying?'

'Because you are so wonderful and that was such a sweet thing to say.'

'Will you ask Michael, Mum?'

'Yes, darling. One day, but not just yet.'

When Antonio pressed the play button and giggled at the film once more, Bella felt physically sick. If her poor, gentle son ever found out who his real father was, it would totally destroy him.

With their children safely tucked up in bed, Katy and Lucy were sharing their third bottle of wine while finalizing their plan.

'Are you sure we're doing the right thing, turning up at Michael's house tomorrow? Part of me still thinks we should wait until after Christmas,' Katy said anxiously.

Lucy held her friend's hand. 'Now you listen to me. I truly believe you and Nathan have been patient enough already. The truth needs to come out, Katy, and the sooner the better. Michael Butler has a lot to answer for, he really does.'

Katy lifted up her wine glass. 'To the truth coming out.'

Lucy winked. 'The truth, the whole truth and nothing but the bloody truth.'

CHAPTER TWENTY-ONE

Jamie Preston picked up a tray and stood in the breakfast queue. Richie Woods had a job in the kitchen and today was serving up the grub.

Sensing Richie's eyes boring into him, Jamie chose not to make eye contact. Black Bob had come up trumps with the screwdriver, but Glen had visited him yesterday and begged him not to do anything stupid with it. Glen was desperate for him not to jeopardize his chance of parole. Said everything was in place on the outside for them to earn loads of dosh and lead the life of Riley.

Jamie had explained in a hushed tone just how bad things had got, and by the end of the visit even Glen agreed Jamie had to teach Richie Woods a lesson. Woods might be a lot of things, but he was no grass and a dig or two should be more than enough to make him wind his neck in.

It was a damn shame all Glen's cronies had either been released or moved down the system. Two were now in Ford Open Prison, one in Coldingly, and three at home with their families. Jamie would've had plenty of back-up if they were still around, and wouldn't have to rely on a poxy screwdriver for protection.

'Look at me, Preston,' Woods hissed, as Jamie reached the front of the queue.

As Jamie slowly raised his eyes, Woods spat a mouthful of phlegm on his food.

Instead of chucking the plate at Woods's head like he wanted to, Jamie instead took a deep breath and smirked. Little Dave, a screw that hated him, was clocking him. No way was he playing into that tosser's hands.

'Not hungry?' Woods taunted, as Jamie left his tray and walked away.

Mumbling, 'You won't be hungry after I've stuck a screwdriver through your fucking tongue,' Jamie calmly headed back to his cell.

Camila leapt on top of her father. 'Daddy, wake up!' she demanded.

Michael groaned. 'Jump up, darling. Daddy's feeling a bit delicate this morning.'

'Why you sleep on the sofa?' Camila enquired.

'Because Daddy came home late and would've kept Mummy awake with his snoring,' Bella quipped. She'd lain awake until Michael had finally rolled home at three, and had been relieved when she'd greeted him and he'd been totally fine towards her. Bella hadn't been able to get much sense out of him though. He'd been in a melancholy mood, rambling on about how much he missed Adam.

'Get us a glass of water and some strong headache tablets, Bell. My bonce feels like it's been trampled on by a horde of elephants.'

'That'll teach you to overdo it,' Bella laughed, handing Michael his request. 'So, where did you go? I did ask you last night, but you were rather incoherent.'

'Went on an East End pub crawl. Ended up in the Prince Regent, I think. We were all shit-faced, well apart from

Little Vinny and Finn. They were sensible, went on soft drinks. Wish I had now.'

'Was Vinny drunk as well?' Bella asked.

'He didn't come. As soon as I showed up, he left.'

Bella was alarmed. 'Why?'

'My mum's got the flu, apparently. Vinny went round hers to look after Ava.'

'I didn't know your mum had the flu. Are we not visiting her today now?'

'No, babe. Sorry, I forgot to tell ya. Aunt Viv belled me yesterday to tell me Mum weren't well enough. I'll pop round to see her over the next couple of days, take her presents with me.'

'Morning, Mum. Morning, Michael. I'm starving. Can I have some breakfast, please?' Antonio asked, picking up his little sister and hugging her.

Bella walked into the kitchen deep in thought. Perhaps Queenie had a serious illness? Which would explain why Vinny wanted to meet her in person. He would want her to break the news to Michael as gently as possible, surely?

Katy Spencer straightened Nathan's tie. He was wearing a dark suit, white shirt and looked like a miniature version of Michael with his hair parted on the left and a touch of Brylcreem added.

'Where are we going, Mum?'

Katy crouched down. 'We're going to see Daddy, and I need you to do and say as Mummy tells you, OK? I'll explain everything in the car.'

Nathan jumped up and down excitedly. He'd missed his father and could not wait to see him again.

After Glen Harper had been released from prison, Jamie Preston bagged himself a job as a cleaner. His new cellmate was an elderly man called Charlie who'd stabbed his wife for moaning too much, and he didn't stop moaning himself. Usually about his old woman, Doris, and the amount of foreigners now living in the capital. He was also fond of rambling on about the good old days and the war.

The main bonus of being a cleaner was that Jamie was allowed out of his cell mornings and evenings. His job was to clean the association rooms before and after they'd been used.

'All right, Preston. I think you've missed a bit of dust there,' Richie Woods goaded.

Jamie's body stiffened as he reached for the screwdriver in his sock and manoeuvred it inside the sleeve of his sweatshirt. He stood up and turned around. 'I don't want no grief; just fuck off back to your cell, Richie.'

Richie Woods had an agenda. His main concern was his wife and kids being happy, with no more money worries. But he also wanted to impress Vinny Butler. Richie knew that the more he upped his game, the more dosh his family would get, and he'd also have a good chance of Vinny employing him when he finally got out of this dump. 'Scarper, you, and shut the door behind ya. You ain't seen me, and if you snitch, you'll get this sliced across your throat,' Woods said, brandishing a knife.

Petrified, the young prisoner who'd been working alongside Jamie ran from the room.

Jamie edged backwards as Woods approached him. 'Why the fuck are you doing this? I've never done anything to you.'

Vinny Butler had insisted his name be kept out of things. 'Because you're a fucking child killer,' Richie spat, as he wildly aimed the knife at Jamie's face.

When the knife made contact with his neck, Jamie Preston had no choice but to retaliate. 'Have some of that, you mug,' he hissed, aiming the screwdriver into Richie's thigh.

When Richie then stuck the knife in his shoulder, Jamie saw red. Far more red than the blood seeping through his sweatshirt. 'Cunt! You fucking stupid cunt,' he yelled, as he repeatedly stabbed the screwdriver into Woods's stomach.

Seconds later, Woods collapsed on the floor and a prison guard ran into the room. Unfortunately for Jamie, it was Little Dave.

Nathan Spencer was confused. His mother had always told him that his father worked away. She'd also told him he was an only child, but now she was telling him he had a sister called Camila and his dad lived with her mum, Bella.

'How old is Camila, Mum?'

'Younger than you, darling. Camila will be four on Boxing Day. Mummy wanted to wait until you were old enough to understand before she told you the truth, and you're a big boy now, aren't you?'

Nathan grinned. 'Yes. I'm a big boy just like Daddy.'

Pleased with the way her son had reacted to the news, Katy decided to tell him the rest. 'You have two big brothers as well, Daniel and Lee.'

Nathan's eyes opened wide. 'Have I?' he asked. Lots of his friends at school had brothers and he'd always wanted one. Now he had two and could barely believe it.

Katy stroked her son's cheek. 'Yes. You might even meet them today.'

Nathan bounced up and down excitedly, clapping his hands with glee. 'How long until we get to Daddy's house? Does he know we're coming?'

Behind the steering wheel, Lucy Tompkins sighed. She'd urged her friend not to tell Nathan the truth until they knew what the outcome of this visit would be, but Katy being Katy, she'd done the exact opposite. Michael was hardly going to invite them in for cake and tea, and poor little Nathan was bound to be left heartbroken.

Covered in his own blood and Richie's, Jamie Preston was distraught. 'I was only defending myself. He had a knife, what was I meant to do? Wake up Woodsy, you fucking wanker,' he begged, as the four screws dragged him from the room. Little Dave had had no chance of prising Jamie off Richie Woods alone. It had taken three of his colleagues to do so.

'Well, that's your parole up the Swannee, son,' Little Dave taunted Jamie. 'Woods looks brown bread to me.'

'I wouldn't have another wine, Katy, if I were you. The last thing you want is to meet Bella reeking of alcohol. That's if she's even there, of course. For all we know, her and Michael might've gone out for the day,' Lucy warned. When her son, Jonny, had announced he was hungry, Katy had demanded they stop at a child-friendly pub.

'Last one, I promise. I need something to calm my nerves and the boys are still eating. I've only had two and the measures are so small. I'm hardly going to smell like a tramp, am I?' Katy insisted.

Telling the boys she wouldn't be a tick, Lucy followed Katy up to the bar. 'Why did you tell Nathan everything? I thought we'd agreed that we should get today over with and you'd explain things gently to him afterwards. It's bound to go badly, and that poor little mite will be devastated when he doesn't get to spend time with his brothers and sister now you've told him about them.'

Katy shrugged. 'Ever since Nathan was born, my life has been one big lie. I'm sick of it, and I'm also done with lying to my son. I love Michael Butler and want the whole world to know he's the father of my child. One day, hopefully, we'll be together. If not, I'll always own a part of him. Michael loves Nathan and if it wasn't for me that boy would never have been born.'

Unaware that unwanted visitors were heading their way, Bella and Michael were snuggled up on the sofa with Camila on their laps.

'I haven't wrapped my presents up yet. I think I should do that now,' Antonio announced.

Having recovered from his hangover, Michael asked Bella if she fancied going out.

'Let's get a takeaway, shall we? Restaurants will be so busy today; we're bound to struggle to book a table for four at such short notice.'

Michael winked. 'Men like me don't struggle to get tables, babe. Up to you?'

'Do you want to go out, Antonio?' Bella asked.

'I'm not bothered. But if we order a takeaway, can I have crispy duck from that nice shop we ordered from last time, please?'

'You can have whatever you want, boy. Now go and wrap those presents. You better have bought me something nice, or else you'll be getting no more pocket money,' Michael joked.

Antonio poked his tongue out. 'Don't care,' he said, before he ran up the stairs laughing.

'What are you doing, Cami? Come away from that tree,' Bella ordered.

Michael had brought home the biggest real Christmas tree he could find and Camila was currently sitting underneath, sneakily trying to open the presents.

Camila pointed to a box in pink wrapping paper. 'Can I open this one? Please?'

'No! They're not for you. Father Christmas brings your presents, but only if you're a good girl,' Bella replied.

Camila's lip wobbled. 'But I am good.'

Michael leapt up, picked his daughter up and took her into the kitchen. 'Shall we open another door on your calendar? We won't tell Mummy though, eh?'

Camila giggled, then forgot all about the advent calendar when the doorbell rang. She loved visitors.

'I'll get it, Bell,' Michael said. 'I'll kill them boys of mine if they keep leaving that gate open, I swear. How many times have I told 'em?' Michael moaned, as he stomped into the hallway. He hadn't spent a fortune on security gates for nothing.

Camila followed her father and clung on to his leg as he opened the door.

'Hello, Michael. It seems you've forgotten about me and your son. Nathan meet Camila, she's your little sister,' Katy announced loudly. Lucy and Jonny she'd ordered to wait at the bottom of the drive in the car.

The colour drained from Michael's face when Bella marched into the hallway. His time was up and he knew it. 'It's not what you think, babe. I can explain everything,' he grovelled, as Nathan flung himself towards his father, like his mother had ordered him to.

Taking one look at Nathan's features, Bella's first instinct was to cry, but she was far too strong to do so until she was alone. 'What's your name?' she asked his mother.

'Katy Spencer. I was once Michael's housekeeper. I'm so sorry to turn up here like this, but I had no choice,' Katy said, bursting into tears. Even though Bella had little make-up on and was dressed casually, she was far more beautiful in the flesh than Katy could ever have imagined. No wonder Michael didn't want her.

'Yes, you did have a choice, Katy. You're a nutter. You

need medical help. I've never wanted you and you know that. You fucking trapped me when I weren't even with Bella. You're a stalker,' Michael yelled, trying to dig himself out of the biggest hole ever.

When both Camila and Nathan burst into tears, Bella calmly ordered Michael to leave the house.

'No way. She's a loony, Bell. I ain't leaving you 'ere with her. She's like that bunny boiler in *Fatal Attraction*, babe.'

On top of the landing, Antonio put his hands over his ears, and rocked to and fro. He could not believe this was happening.

'And you're a liar, Michael. Now get out of this house. I want to speak with Katy alone.'

'Just let me explain,' Michael begged.

Ordering Antonio to take Camila upstairs, Bella told Katy to take Nathan in the lounge. She shut the door, and turned to Michael, her eyes blazing with fury. 'Get out! And don't fucking come back until I tell you to,' she hissed.

Michael's eyes welled up. 'Please don't do this, Bell. I had a fling with Katy when you fucked off to Italy that time. You weren't even answering my calls. I didn't think you were coming back.'

'You disgust me. That girl looks young enough to be your daughter.'

Not sure what else to do, grabbing his car keys, Michael bolted from the house.

CHAPTER TWENTY-TWO

Katy was comforting Nathan when Bella walked into the room. He'd seen Michael drive off through the window. 'My friend is parked at the bottom of your drive with her son. Is it OK if I let her know what's going on?' Katy asked awkwardly.

'Tell your friend and her son to come inside. I need to see to my children, then I'll put the kettle on,' Bella replied.

Bella went upstairs. She was still in a complete state of shock. 'Don't cry, darling. Everything is going to be OK,' she assured her inconsolable son.

'Is that woman Michael's girlfriend?' Antonio sobbed.

'No. She isn't Michael's girlfriend.'

'But she said her son was Michael's,' Antonio insisted.

Camila didn't understand what was going on, but knew it was something bad because Antonio was so upset.

'I'm going to talk to Katy and find out the truth. Can you stay up here and look after Camila for me, Antonio? As soon as Katy leaves, I'll call you and we'll order our takeaway.'

'I'm not hungry now. Can I go to Edward's house, Mum?'

'No. Mummy doesn't want anybody finding out about this, OK? And I need you to be brave and take care of your sister. I promise you everything will be fine.'

'Where's Daddy gone?' Camila asked.

'I don't know. But he'll be back soon,' Bella reassured her daughter.

'I don't like that Katy, Mum. Tell her to go away,' Antonio said.

'I will. But I need to speak with her first. You two stay up here and I'll call you when she's gone.'

Hearing the front door shut, Bella left her children huddled together on the bed. How could Michael do this to them? She had never in a million years suspected him of cheating on her.

'This is my friend Lucy and her son Jonny,' Katy said.

'Hello. Sit down and make yourselves comfortable. Would you like tea, coffee or something stronger?' Bella asked.

'I'll have a wine please, if you have any? Orange juice, or any soft drink will be fine for Nathan and Jonny. What do you want, Lucy?' Katy asked.

'Coffee, please.'

Bella returned minutes later with a tray and placed it on the coffee table. 'Help yourselves to cake, boys.'

'Where has my dad gone?' Nathan asked, innocently.

Bella studied the child. He looked eerily like Michael, far more so than Daniel and Lee did, and Bella guessed that Katy had dressed and styled his hair in such a way that he resembled his father even more. 'I'm not sure where your dad is. But you're bound to see him again very soon. Would you like to play with some toys in the other room?'

Nathan looked at his mother for approval. 'Go with Bella, love. She'll show you where the toys are. Take your drink and cake with you. And you, Jonny,' Katy smiled. This was all going far better than she could ever have imagined.

Bella led the boys into the play room, then sat opposite

Katy with a steely glint in her eyes. 'I want you to tell me everything from the very beginning. No bullshit. The truth.'

In a complete daze, Michael Butler drove towards Whitechapel. His mother was going to be livid that he'd kept a grandson a secret from her, and Michael wanted to break the news in person before anybody else did.

Hearing Queen's 'Bohemian Rhapsody', Michael turned the volume down. The song was in the charts again, and Michael could remember 1975, the year it was first released, like it was yesterday. Nancy had loved it, and he'd queued up in Downtown Records to buy the single for her.

Feeling melancholy, Michael angrily switched the radio off. Perhaps he wasn't destined to be happy? Nancy had loathed him so much in the end, she'd chosen to take her own life. Now Bella hated his guts as well.

Ava had gone to a friend's birthday party with Destiny, so Queenie was wrapping up some last-minute gifts. Her heart wasn't in it though. Usually, she loved Christmas, but this year she could not wait for it to be over. 'Get off the presents, Fred. I've bought you a doggy stocking. Not that you deserve one,' she mumbled.

When the front door opened and closed, Queenie yelled, 'I'm in 'ere, Viv.'

Michael walked into the lounge. 'It's me. I thought you had the flu.'

'I did. Feel a bit better today though,' Queenie lied. 'You OK, boy?'

'No, Mum. I'm anything but OK. Listen, there's something you need to know. I should've told you years ago and I'm so sorry.'

Queenie stood up. 'Whatever's the matter?'

'I've got a son you've never met. His name is Nathan, and he's five.'

Holding on to the armchair for support, Queenie Butler shook her head in total disbelief.

It didn't take long for Bella to get the measure of Katy. Reasonably pretty. Could've made a living as a topless model, but wasn't that bright, and it was clear she was completely obsessed with Michael.

'So what you are trying to say is that you and Michael have not been in any kind of relationship since I came back from Italy? Is that correct?' Bella questioned.

'Yes, and no. Michael visits me and Nathan regularly, and I can't fault the way he provides for us. He pays the rent and all our bills – and so he should. Nathan is his son, after all,' Katy replied, rather shirtily.

Lucy Tompkins felt embarrassed. All things considered, Bella had been ever so nice. Katy was in danger of showing herself up. She'd drunk far too much wine and was beginning to slur her words.

'What Bella is actually asking,' said Lucy, 'is whether you and Michael have slept together since he found out you were pregnant. The answer's no, isn't it? Be honest with Bella. Michael has always visited and provided for you, but you've never been in any kind of relationship with him, have you?'

Feeling like a stupid schoolgirl, Katy glared at her friend before locking eyes with Bella again. 'No. The relationship myself and Michael have is extremely platonic for the sake of our son.'

Bella forced a smile. 'Would you like another glass of wine, dear? Or are you ready to leave now?'

Queenie was unimpressed at the sight of her youngest son crying. She'd brought her boys up to be tough, and saw tears as a sign of weakness. 'Pull yourself together, boy. Of course I'm upset you kept Nathan a secret from me, but it ain't the end of the bloody world. We can move on from this and I can get to know him now, so that's all that matters. I can't wait to meet him. Does he look like you?'

Nodding his head dismally, Michael buried his face in his hands. He'd already explained to his mother that Katy had turned up at the house earlier with Nathan in tow. 'Bella won't forgive me, Mum. She's always been completely loyal and would never betray me in such a way. I should've come clean as soon as I found out Katy was pregnant. I feel terrible. What am I meant to say to her? That's if she ever speaks to me again. And what about Cami? That little girl's gonna be heartbroken when her mother kicks me out. So is Antonio. I'm such a dickhead, I truly am.'

Queenie's blood was at boiling point. Here was her wonderful son, distraught over that Italian slapper who was harbouring a far worse secret herself. 'Don't be fretting about her. She's hardly Saint Bella herself,' Queenie spat.

Michael looked up, startled. His mother had always adored Bella and vice versa. 'What do you mean by that?'

Queenie sighed. There was no point waiting until after Christmas now, seeing as Michael's Christmas had been ruined already. 'There's no easy way for me to say this, but I need you to promise me you're not going to blame your brother. It isn't his fault. Vinny was as shocked as anybody.'

'Blame him for what?' Michael felt the blood drain from his face.

'I'll tell it to you straight, boy. It turns out Bella had a fling with your brother. It was many years ago when you and Bella weren't together. I only found out a matter of days ago, but it's obvious Antonio is Vinny's son.'

Thunderstruck, Michael stared at his mother as though she were mad. 'This has to be some kind of a sick joke, right? Nah, no fucking way. Antonio's father is a Yank. My Bella would never touch Vinny with a bargepole – and that's a fucking fact. Who told you this shit? Tell me! Who told ya?' Michael bellowed. 'It's insane.'

'Nobody told me anything. I worked it out for myself. Vivvy and I were sorting through old photos recently. We came across some taken at Vinny's fortieth. Viv thought Antonio was Little Vinny until I pointed out where the photo had been taken. The likeness at the same age was uncanny when we put the photo of Antonio next to one of Little Vinny.'

'You're mental! I ain't listening to any more of this crap. Don't you think I've got enough on my plate as it is?' Michael shouted, standing up.

'Sit back down and listen to me. You need to hear all of this,' Queenie ordered. She hated to see the look of confusion in her son's eyes, but he needed to know the truth.

Stomach churning, Michael sat back down as if in a trance.

'I showed the photo to Vinny and, to cut a long story short, he confessed. He was as shocked as you. I'm so sorry, boy.'

Feeling as though his head might actually explode, Michael leapt to his feet and paced up and down the room. 'Nah, nah, nah. This ain't happening. Not Bella and Vinny. Never in a million. So he told you he fucked her, did he? Well, did he?' Michael screamed, picking up his mother's favourite vase.

'Stop that! Stop it,' Queenie yelled, when Michael aimed the vase against her wall. 'Smashing my house up isn't going to change the situation, is it? I know you're upset, and you have every bloody right to be, but it's that whore you need to blame. If anyone should've told you, she should have.'

Michael collapsed to his knees, tears of pure anger streaming down his cheeks. 'If it's true, why didn't Vinny tell me?'

'He should've told you, but he didn't know how to. He recognized Bella on the night of his fortieth, that's why she feigned illness and ran from the party. She recognized him an' all, obviously. He didn't know her as Bella. She'd told Vinny her name was Izzy.'

Michael made a strange gurgling noise. Bella had joked with him in the past that before she'd met him she'd often tell men she had no desire to see again her name was Izzy.

Queenie rubbed her son's back. 'Stay there. I'll pour you a brandy. You're in shock.'

The bottom having dropped out of his world, Michael stared at the big photo of him, Roy and Vinny that took pride of place on his mother's wall. An image of Bella and Vinny writhing naked in bed together flashed through his mind, and Michael retched.

Hearing the sound of glass shattering, Queenie ran into the lounge. Michael was repeatedly smashing her favourite photo against the coffee table. 'Stop it! Roy's in that,' she shrieked.

Michael now had a manic glint in his eyes. 'And so is that cunt who has ruined my life. I'm gonna kill him. In fact, I'll kill the fucking pair of 'em.'

'Michael, no! Come back. Please come back,' Queenie pleaded. When he didn't, Queenie chased her son out to his car and stood in front of it.

As he reversed, Michael smashed into a Ford Sierra. He then performed a three-point turn and drove off like a deranged Stirling Moss.

*

Having missed out on last night's drinking session, Vinny Butler had woken up this morning with an urge to get bladdered. He was spending Christmas at his mother's and, like her, couldn't wait for it to be all over with.

'Sup up, you lightweight,' Vinny ordered. Nobody else had wanted to come out to play, so Vinny had ordered Carl to accompany him. Like him, Carl was footloose and fancy free.

Carl downed his drink in one. 'I'll get 'em in. Why don't you ring Jay Boy again, see if he's up for it now?'

'No point. Under the thumb, since he married Jilly. I did warn him about putting a ring on a bitch's finger,' Vinny chuckled.

'Too right. More grief than they're worth, women.'

When his pal walked up to the bar, Vinny smirked. It was hilarious to think that they'd first met when Ahmed had paid Carl to set him up. Ahmed's plan had failed, and it always tickled Vinny that he and Carl were now such good mates. He really did hope that Turkish bastard was watching them from hell. Carl had turned out to be a decent asset to the business, a real grafter. The only grief Vinny'd had with him was when a couple of geezers he'd conned in the past had turned up at the club, kicking off over some dosh Carl owed them. They'd been sent packing with a stern warning of what their fate would be if they ever troubled Carl or turned up at Vinny's club again.

'What you grinning at?' Carl asked.

'Was thinking about when me and Jay Boy broke those geezers' legs who turned up at the club looking for you that time. Ring your Uncle Frank, get him out for a beer. And don't take no for an answer.'

'OK. It's noisy in 'ere. I'll ring him outside.'

When Carl walked away, Vinny stared at his phone as

it burst into life. It was his mother; much as he loved her, he couldn't be doing with discussing the Michael and Bella situation again. He wanted to forget all his troubles, even if it was only for one day.

Vinny ignored the call, then when it rang again immediately afterwards, made a decision to turn the bastard thing off. Tomorrow, he would tell his mother his battery had died. Surely one stress-free day wasn't too much to ask for, was it?

Bella was savouring a large glass of red wine and trying to act as normally as possible for the sake of her children. Katy and Lucy had left about an hour ago and Bella had cheered up the moment they walked out the front door. Katy had been wearing extremely high-heeled boots and had stacked it, flat on her face, while trying to walk across the gravel.

Once the coast was clear she'd sat her kids down and explained things as best as she could. Antonio was still in an inquisitive mood. 'How old exactly is Nathan then? Because he looks young, and I don't remember you splitting up with Michael.'

Knowing she had an even worse secret, Bella had already decided not to kick Michael out. She was obviously furious with him and certainly wouldn't forgive him overnight, but having met Katy, she knew the airhead was no threat to her. She would also be making some changes. No way was Michael paying for Katy to live a life of luxury in a three-bedroomed house after this. Neither was he spending time with Katy and Nathan. If Michael wanted to spend time with his son in future, he would do so with her and their children present. And if Katy didn't agree to that, Michael would be banned from seeing Nathan until she did. Bella was far from stupid and had guessed that Katy thought by turning up here today it would spell the end of her and Michael's relationship. The thick cow would then have tried to get her claws into him herself.

'Mum, answer my question,' Antonio demanded.

'Do you remember that time we lived in Italy with Nonna and Nonno?'

Antonio nodded.

'Well, Michael and I weren't together then. We'd not been getting on, which is why we went to Italy in the first place,' Bella lied.

'Mummy, I'm hungry,' Camila piped up.

'I'll order us some food and ring Daddy to tell him to come home. Oh, and we don't mention any of this to Nonna and Nonno when they arrive tomorrow. We don't want to spoil their Christmas, do we?' Bella warned, looking directly at her son.

'Of course not, Mum,' Antonio replied.

Autopilot having well and truly kicked in, Bella dashed into the other room, took a deep breath and dialled Michael's mobile. He didn't answer.

Queenie Butler was in an absolute panic. Both her sons' phones were now switched off and she dreaded to think what might be happening. 'Let's get a cab to Vinny's, Viv. He was at home when I spoke to him this morning and he didn't say he was going anywhere.'

Vivian poured her sister a brandy and ordered her to calm down before she gave herself a heart attack. 'Nosy bastards are still out there, all stood round that car, gossiping. Anybody would think Michael had crushed the bastard thing,' she added.

Queenie sighed. It turned out the car that had borne the brunt of her son's anger belonged to a visiting relative of

Mouthy Maureen. She'd already sent Viv out there to tell them any damage would be paid for. 'Sod the neighbours. I can't just sit here. I've never seen my Michael in such a state and I know he's gonna do something stupid. I need to find both my boys before a murder takes place.'

Ava quietly shut the front door and took Fred off his lead. She marched into the lounge. 'Who's getting murdered?'

'Nobody, darlin'. Your nan was talking about something on TV,' Vivian assured the child.

'But the telly ain't even on,' Ava retorted. She wasn't daft, knew what she'd heard.

Queenie stared at Fred in disgust as he positioned his beloved Teddy on her lap and began humping away. 'That's what is wrong with this fucking world. God dropped a massive clanger when he created a John Thomas,' she hissed.

Ava screamed when both Fred and Teddy were unceremoniously dumped on to the floor. 'That's wicked, Nan. You're horrible.'

'Ava, take Fred upstairs, there's a good girl. Your nan isn't very well today,' Vivian whispered, as she ushered the child from the room.

'Is my dad OK? He's not going to be murdered is he?' Ava asked worriedly.

Smiling sarcastically, Vivian reassured Ava as nicely as her hatred of Vinny would allow her to. 'Of course your father is OK. He always is, isn't he? The devil looks after his own and your dad is one of those lucky people he takes extra special care of.'

Bella D'Angelo was becoming more worried by the minute. She'd been phoning Michael for the past hour or so and still his phone was switched off. Even if his battery had died, Bella had fully expected Michael to have called her by now. He should be begging her forgiveness, not bloody blanking her. What the hell was she meant to say to her parents if she still hadn't made contact with him by the time they arrived?

'You've not eaten much, Mum,' Antonio pointed out.

'I'm not that hungry at the moment, love. You and Cami eat as much as you want. I'm going to make some calls, see if I can track Michael down.'

Bella topped up her wine and sat at the kitchen table. It was obvious now why Vinny had asked to meet her in person. He must've got wind of Nathan's existence and wanted to put a spoke in her and Michael's relationship. Vinny'd never met Nathan, Katy had confirmed that to her.

Bella scrolled through her phone, then put it to her ear. 'Hello, Vivian. I hope you're keeping well, and Queenie is on the mend. Would it be possible for me to speak with Queenie briefly, please?'

Vivian put her hand over the mouthpiece. 'It's Bella,' she hissed.

Queenie snatched the phone. 'Got a lot to answer for you have, you fucking whore,' she yelled.

To say Bella was taken aback was an understatement. Did Queenie think it was Katy on the phone? 'It's me, Queenie – Bella.'

'Yes, I know who it fucking is. The Italian slapper. When was you gonna tell my boy the truth, eh?'

'I beg your pardon! Listen here, Queenie, I don't know what twisted lies Michael has told you, but it was his bit of fluff who turned up on our doorstep earlier, not mine,' Bella shrieked.

'Twisted lies! That's some statement coming from you. Michael knows, Bella. We all know.'

'Michael knows what?' Bella whispered, dreading the answer.

'That Antonio is Vinny's son.'

Dropping the phone in shock, Bella let out the most piercing scream imaginable.

Michael Butler neared his family home with a face like thunder. After leaving his mother's, he'd headed straight to Canary Wharf to have it out with his brother, but there'd been no sign of Vinny, so he'd decided to confront Bella instead. He wanted the truth straight from the horse's mouth, she owed him that much at least.

Nearly hitting a vehicle while overtaking, Michael decided to slow down before he killed himself. No woman was worth that, even Bella. And if what his mother had told him turned out to be true, she was the most worthless woman ever to breathe the same air as him.

'Mum, stop it! You're scaring me, and Camila,' Antonio D'Angelo cried. He'd never seen his usually composed mother in such a state before. And now she was demanding he phone his grandparents and tell them they couldn't come to England for Christmas after all.

'Just do as I fucking say, Antonio. Tell Nonna and Nonno I am ill and we will visit them over New Year instead,' Bella screamed at her son.

Leading his sobbing sister into the lounge, Antonio did as his mother asked and was relieved when his grandfather realized something was wrong and told him he would still be flying to England as planned tomorrow, but he wasn't to tell his mother.

Seconds after ending the call, Antonio was even more relieved when he heard a screech of tyres on the gravel outside. He looked out the window and hugged his little sister. 'It's OK, Cami. Michael's home now.'

When his mother yelled at him to take Camila upstairs,

Antonio did no such thing. He opened the front door, ran up to Michael and flung his arms around his waist. 'Mum's acting weird, and it's not because of Katy because she was fine about her after she'd left. I don't know who Mum spoke to when she went into the kitchen, but she told me she was ringing people to track you down. We even ordered Chinese for you, and then whoever she spoke to must have said something bad because Mum started acting like a nutter. She drank lots of wine, was crying and even made me ring Nonna and Nonno to tell them not to come to England,' Antonio sobbed.

Instead of comforting the child, Michael pushed him away. On the journey home, he'd so desperately tried to convince himself his mother had got the wrong end of the stick, but Antonio's words were all the confirmation he needed. Bella had obviously either rang his mother, Vinny, or both?

When Michael stormed towards the house like a raging bull, Antonio chased him, grabbed his arm and asked him what was wrong.

Michael glared at the boy with distaste. He could see both Vinny and Little Vinny in the child's features now. Bella had always lied that Clint, the American boyfriend she'd dreamed up in that sick head of hers, had had black hair and piercing green eyes and Michael felt a fool for believing her. Suddenly he could see things clearly, like staring through a freshly cleaned pane of glass. 'Get upstairs and take your sister with you,' he ordered Antonio.

'Daddy,' Camila cried gleefully as her father walked in the hallway.

Michael stroked his daughter on the head. 'Go upstairs with Antonio, darlin'. Daddy needs to talk to your mother.'

'Come on, Cami,' Antonio mumbled. Michael had been

far kinder towards his sister than he had to him and Antonio had no idea what he'd done wrong.

Michael stared at Bella and for the first time ever loathed what he saw. He grabbed her by the neck and slammed her against the wall. 'How could you do this to me? I loved you so much, you bitch. Was Vinny a good fuck, was he? Better than me? Well, was he?' Michael shrieked.

'Let go of my neck, Michael. Please, you're hurting me,' Bella begged.

Michael spat in Bella's face. 'You repulse me. You're nothing but a lying low-life fucking whore.'

When Michael released his grip on her, Bella slid down the wall. 'Please, Michael, let me explain. Antonio isn't Vinny's. I swear,' she sobbed.

Michael grabbed Bella by the hair. 'Stop fucking lying! You've done enough of that to last you a lifetime. You and Vinny are welcome to each other, sweetheart. You can suck his cock until the cows come home for all I care. You're both dead to me. Cami's all I care about now. And don't you dare even contemplate scarpering back to Italy with your tail between those easily spread legs of yours. Because I swear on Cami's life, if you take my daughter away from me, I will hunt you down and fucking kill you. Understand?'

'Michael, I love you. Please listen to me. I will tell you everything from the very beginning, I swear to you,' Bella wept.

Grabbing his phone charger, Michael ran up the stairs and began packing a case. Bella chased after him, pleading with him to allow her to explain.

'Where are you going, Michael? What's going on?' Antonio asked, bemused.

Michael blanked the child and, remembering where Bella kept the passports, chucked his, hers and Camila's in his case.

When his daughter clung to his legs, Michael picked her up and hugged her. 'Daddy's got to go away for a while, but he'll see you real soon, OK?'

Camila clung to her father's neck as though her life depended on it. 'Don't want you to go away,' she wept.

Bella could never remember feeling so devastated in all her life. Even her brother dying did not compare to the heartache she was currently experiencing. 'I need you and so do the children, Michael. Please don't do this. We can sort things out in time, I know we can,' she pleaded.

Thinking he was helping, Antonio decided to chip in. 'Mum's right, Michael. You're the only dad I've ever had and I need you.'

Michael glared at the child he had once treated as his own. 'Dad! I ain't your fucking dad and never will be. Mummy has mugged us all off, boy. Your real dad is Vinny Butler, my cunting brother.'

Albie Butler loved Sundays. He'd work at the club, tidy up after the strippers had finished their shift, and would get to the Blind Beggar by four at the latest to indulge in a drinking session and game of cards. Since he'd been diagnosed with angina, Albie only allowed himself one heavy day on the sauce per week.

'Your Vinny's just walked in, Albie,' Big Stan said.

Thankful he was sitting with his back towards the door, Albie didn't bother replying. It was common knowledge that he and his eldest son didn't see eye to eye.

After going on a pub crawl, it had been Vinny's idea that he and Carl head back to the Blind Beggar where they'd started out. He knew his old man would be in there and fancied ruining the old bastard's day.

Having receiving his usual hero's welcome, Vinny walked

over to his father and tapped him on the shoulder. 'All right, Daddy Dearest? Losing or winning, are we?'

Albie looked up at his son. Vinny looked drunk and that's when he was at his very worst. 'You OK, lad? Losing at the moment, but I'm hoping my luck'll change soon.'

Vinny smirked. 'I doubt that very much. Once a loser, always a loser.'

Michael Butler drove along the A13 at top speed. He'd rung Jay Boy, acted normal, and had been informed Vinny was in the Blind Beggar. Apparently, his brother had rung Jay Boy in the past half hour, trying to entice him out.

Antonio had been hysterical when he'd left the house, lashing out at his mother. Michael had hated leaving Camila there, but he couldn't take her with him. He had no idea himself where he was going to be staying yet, and his head was in too much of a mess to look after his daughter properly.

On reaching Whitechapel, Michael drove past the Blind Beggar, parked outside his club, leapt out the motor and opened the boot. Antonio had taken up cricket at school last summer and Michael had also bought himself a bat to help the lad practise. Ironic it would now be used to cave in the head of Antonio's father.

'Where you going?' Big Stan asked, when Albie put his coat on.

'I'm gonna get off. I can't be around Vinny in booze. He's bound to start kicking off in a minute,' Albie replied miserably. Vinny and Carl had sat themselves down on a nearby table and Albie felt as uncomfortable as always around his son.

Stan tugged Albie's arm. 'Hold up. Your Michael's just walked in with a cricket bat in his hand.'

Staff and customers looked on in shock and horror as Michael approached his brother from behind. 'You're dead, you cunt,' he said calmly, before repeatedly smashing the bat against Vinny's head.

Vinny fell to the carpet, his natural instinct to try and cover his head with his hands. 'I wanted to tell ya, but I didn't know how to. And I had no idea the kid was mine, I swear, bruv.'

'Not in here, Michael. Take it outside please,' the landlord yelled.

When Carl tried to intervene, Michael clumped him with the bat as well.

'Stop it, boy. You don't wanna get yourself nicked,' Albie shouted, his plea falling on deaf ears. Michael was behaving like a crazed madman and Albie knew something terribly bad must have happened as he'd never seen his youngest son like this before.

'You treacherous piece of shit. Just fucking die, will ya!' Michael shrieked, continuing the brutal attack.

Too drunk to defend himself properly, Vinny's face and head were soon covered in blood.

'Do something. He's gonna kill him otherwise,' Big Stan shouted to the terrified drinkers. Nobody moved an inch. They were far too wary of the Butler brothers to intervene.

Knowing he was the only person who could stop Michael getting a life sentence, Albie tried to grab the bat out of his son's hands. 'Whatever he's done, it ain't worth doing time over. Give me the bat. You've made your point.'

'He's in a bad way. You're gonna fucking kill him,' Carl shrieked, clambering on top of his boss to protect him.

'Bad way! I'll give him bad way. Him and that whore indoors are welcome to one another, the fucking Judases. Antonio's his cunting kid,' Michael yelled, clumping Carl.

'Bella wouldn't do that! Dear Lord, no,' Albie muttered, clutching his chest.

When his father tumbled to the floor, Michael automatically dropped the bat. 'Dad, Dad, Dad!' he shrieked.

CHAPTER TWENTY-THREE

Shirley Preston was beside herself with worry. The prison had phoned her earlier to inform her that an incident had occurred involving Jamie. Shirley'd begged them to explain what had actually happened, but the bastards had refused to do so. Chelmsford police were none too helpful either when she'd phoned them.

At her wits' end, Shirley rang Glen Harper's mum. They'd swapped numbers after their sons had become pals. 'Hello, Dot. It's me, Shirley. I need your help, love. Jamie's been involved in some kind of incident today and nobody will tell me anything. They've cancelled my visit tomorrow and I'm beside myself with worry in case Jamie's done something daft. I dunno if your Glen mentioned it, but after he got released a gang of blokes started picking on Jamie. I was wondering if you'd ring Glen for me, ask him to find out what's happened? I'm sure if anybody can put me out my misery, your Glen can.'

'Try not to worry too much, Shirley. If something really bad had happened, surely they would have to tell you? My Glen'll get to the bottom of it. Only problem is, he's out on a bender today with the lads and hasn't taken his phone with him. Silly bastard's already lost two since he got out.

I'll ring him first thing tomorrow, I promise. I won't get any sense out of him beforehand.'

Thanking Dot, Shirley ended the call. She lived for her grandson, was so disappointed she wasn't able to see him tomorrow, and all she could do was pray he hadn't put the kibosh on his release. If he had, she couldn't cope.

Daniel Butler stared at Sarah the barmaid as she happily sucked away on his penis. His father had ordered him and Lee never to mix work with pleasure, but Daniel couldn't help make an exception when it came to Sarah. She was very pretty, gave extremely good head and what his father didn't know wouldn't hurt him.

'For fuck's sake. Pass me that phone, girl. Whatever nuisance keeps ringing me is stopping me from coming,' Daniel complained.

When Sarah did as he asked, Daniel switched the bloody thing off. There was nothing more off-putting than his nan ringing while he was trying to shoot his load.

Ordering Sarah to turn over, Daniel fucked her doggy style. He enjoyed sex immensely, but had yet to find a girl who tugged at his heartstrings. Katy Spencer had been his first crush, Frankie Mitchell his second and Bobbi the stripper the third. All three had turned out to be wrong 'uns and Daniel wasn't sure true love even existed.

Grunting and groaning, Daniel was about to come when his brother burst into the room. 'Dan, come on, we gotta go. Dad's done Vinny over and Granddad's had a heart attack.'

Erection deflating immediately, Daniel leapt up. 'You've got to be kidding me. Why has Dad done Vinny over?'

'I dunno. But we gotta get our arses down the Beggar, make sure no one grasses.'

*

Nosy Hilda could barely contain her excitement as she scuttled towards Queenie's house. This was major gossip and she couldn't wait to share the news.

Ava answered the door. 'Me nan's busy,' the child said, knowing full well that her grandmother disliked Hilda and wouldn't want to talk to her.

Elated that Queenie obviously didn't have an inkling, Nosy Hilda informed Ava that the matter was very urgent.

Queenie was chopping chicken up in the kitchen. Fred, the fussy little creature, was refusing to eat dog food any more. She marched into the hallway with the knife still in her hand. 'What's bloody urgent?'

'I hate to be the bearer of bad news, but you'd better get yourself up the hospital, Queen. Your Michael's beaten Vinny senseless with a cricket bat. Blood everywhere, by all accounts. And Albie's had a heart attack.'

Ava screamed, Fred barked and an ashen-faced Queenie dropped the knife. It never just rained in her world, always bastard-well poured.

Daniel and Lee Butler cut two mean figures as they stood at the bar in the Blind Beggar. Their father had always insisted if they wanted to be taken seriously in life they should wear suits, especially when working.

It had been Carl who'd rung the club and informed Lee what had happened. Albie having a heart attack and Vinny being out for the count meant he'd had to call an ambulance. The Old Bill were bound to come sniffing around to see who'd beaten Vinny senseless, and before leaving the pub, Carl had told all the regulars to say it was a random attack by a tall dark-haired stranger who they'd never seen before.

Daniel approached the female officer. 'Why do you keep asking people questions about my dad? He arrived at the boozer after the attack on Vinny; I've already told you that. I should know. My old man was at the club with me and Lee beforehand. Ask my brother, if you don't believe me. One of our barmaids was still there, helping us tidy up. She'll also clarify that for you, if need be.'

Frustrated by the lack of cooperation, the officer walked over to her colleagues and bluntly told them they were wasting their time. Word on the street was Michael Butler had charged into the Blind Beggar like a bull in a china shop with a cricket bat in his hand, but proving that was going to be extremely difficult if everybody including the landlord was sticking to the same story. As per usual, with any crime involving the Butlers, the truth was what they wanted it to be.

Queenie Butler was totally beside herself as she waited in the corridor of the hospital. Being back at the Royal London awaiting news of a head injury brought back awful memories of the night her Roy had been shot. He'd never walked again and all Queenie could do was pray Vinny would be OK. All she'd been told was he'd been semi-conscious on arrival and was currently undergoing a scan.

'I wonder how Albie is?' Vivian mumbled.

'Who cares about that old bastard?' Queenie spat, hatred in her voice.

'Whether you like him or loathe him, Albie'll always be the father of your children, Queen. Imagine how poor Michael must be feeling right now? Just found out that Bella's been hawking her mutton with Vinny and he's Antonio's dad, then his own father keels over in front of him. Have a bit of compassion for somebody other than Golden Boy, for Christ's sake.'

Ignoring the direct dig at Vinny, Queenie pursed her lips. 'I wonder where Michael's got to? D'ya reckon he'll come back?' Michael had travelled the tiny distance in the ambulance with his father before shooting off to get changed. His suit had been splashed in Vinny's blood and Carl had warned him to clean himself up at the club in case the police came sniffing around.

'Yeah. He'll be back to see Albie,' Vivian insisted.

Queenie puffed her cheeks out and shook her head dismally. 'This is all my fault. I should never have blurted things out the way I did, and I should've gone to Vinny's flat and warned him. I wanted to, but you stopped me. As for mobile phones – what a waste of time they are. No bastard ever answers 'em.'

'Don't be blaming me or your bleedin' self. Only one person to blame, yet again! And you know who that is as well as I do.'

Queenie was about to give her sister a mouthful when Ava appeared with Stinky Susan and Destiny in tow.

'I'm so sorry, Queen. But I couldn't stop Ava coming here and didn't want her to come alone. She was adamant about seeing her dad,' Susan apologized.

Ava was visibly distressed. 'Where is he? Is Dad gonna be OK?'

'Fingers crossed, darling. The nurses are giving your dad a scan. We'll hopefully be able to see him soon, but you mustn't be upset if his face is a bit of a mess, because it will get better.'

Ava sat on her nan's lap. 'Why did Uncle Michael hit my dad? I don't like him any more. I hate him.'

'None of this is Michael's fault, Ava. So don't be blaming him,' Vivian piped up.

Ava treated Vivian to her finest sulky expression. 'Yes, it is. And I'm not listening to you any more. You told me "Daddy would be OK because the devil looks after his own." Didn't look after my dad, did he?'

Queenie looked at Vivian in horror. 'Well, that's a nice thing to say to a ten-year-old child, I must say!'

Over in Tunbridge Wells, Katy Spencer was staring at her phone, willing it to ring.

'Michael isn't going to contact you today, mate. You've blown his whole family apart. Shall we watch a film or something?' Lucy Tompkins suggested. As much as she loved her friend, Katy's obsession with Michael was beginning to drive her insane, and she couldn't wait to get back home tomorrow.

'It was your idea to go round to Michael's in the first place,' Katy reminded her friend. 'And I can't concentrate on a film. I want to celebrate. I can't wait for me and Nathan to meet Queenie and her sister, Viv. Michael used to chat about them often and I'm sure we'll all get along like a house on fire. They sound like real characters.'

When Katy cracked open a bottle of champagne and dreamily rambled on about Michael yet again, Lucy sighed. She'd felt so guilty earlier when Bella had been kind to them and the kids, she wished she had never suggested knocking on the poor woman's door in the first place. Ripping a family to shreds was hardly cause for celebration.

Twenty-two stitches to his head and face, plus a dose of concussion seemed to be the extent of Vinny's injuries. The scan had revealed there seemed to be no bleeding to the brain, but there was a very slight swelling and Queenie had been informed that Vinny would need another scan, to be on the safe side.

'Five minutes with him, OK? Your son's very tired, and still has a lot of alcohol in his system,' the nurse warned Queenie.

'Dad, are you OK? You look ill,' Ava cried.

Vinny was that drained he could barely keep his eyes open. 'I'm fine, darlin'. Be right as rain tomorrow.'

'Get off the bed,' Queenie ordered Ava, when Vinny picked up the grey sick tray and began vomiting into it.

Having a phobia of sick, Ava ran outside the ward, petrified.

Queenie wiped her son's mouth with some tissue, then stroked the one side of his face that wasn't bruised or cut. 'I'm so sorry for telling Michael earlier, but you don't know what happened. He turned up at mine in bits. You remember that young Katy Spencer who used to work for him?'

'Yeah,' Vinny mumbled.

'Well it turns out what Daniel screamed out at Little Vinny's wedding that time was bloody true. Katy turned up at Michael's house this morning with his son Nathan in tow. Seeing Michael so upset at mine while singing that whore Bella's praises made my blood boil. It seemed the perfect opportunity to tell him, but seeing the state of you now, I wish I'd kept me gob shut.'

'Sly fox, is Michael. Not your fault. He would've taken a bat to me anyway, even if we'd told him together. I was too drunk to defend meself, but I'll live. Couldn't believe the nurses wanted to chop off some of my hair to put the stitches in. I told them where to go. I'd chop their hands off first.'

Feeling relieved, Queenie managed a smile. If Vinny was joking already, she was pretty sure he was going to be OK. Her Roy had never joked again after his injuries, the poor sod.

Seeing Vinny's eyes shut, Queenie was about to leave when her grandson burst into the ward. 'Carl rang me. Whatever's happened? He told me you'd explain all. Is me dad all right?'

'I'm OK, boy. Just need sleep. Come back and see me tomorrow,' Vinny muttered.

Queenie led her grandson into the corridor. 'Your dad's fine, just tired, and a bit battered and bruised. Let's go back to mine and chat there. There are certain things you need to know about.'

After leaving the hospital earlier, Michael Butler had driven straight to his father's home in Barking. He kept an old suit there and his plan had been to get cleaned up, pick up some of his dad's belongings, then drive back to the hospital to wait for news. But when push came to shove, Michael couldn't face going back. His day had been far too traumatic for words and he was now sitting in the dark in a state of shock with a bottle of Scotch for company.

Tears streaming down his cheeks, Michael took in the scent of his old man's favourite armchair. It was as old as the hills, covered in cigarette burns and spilt drops of alcohol, but all he could smell was that wonderful man who was now lying in intensive care, fighting for his life. Life was hard to understand at times. Why couldn't it have been Vinny in intensive care instead?

Michael had rung the hospital a few minutes ago. He'd told the nurse to ring on his father's landline in case of emergency. No way was he switching his mobile on. He never wanted to switch that bastard thing on ever again. A nurse had informed Michael his father's condition was 'serious, but stable'. She'd also told him, in more medical wording, that Vinny was out of the woods. Michael had only asked about his brother in the hope he was dead. The way he felt right now, a life sentence was preferable to ever facing Vinny or Bella again.

The hammering on the front door made Michael jump. 'Dad, Dad! You in there?' Daniel shouted.

Michael didn't reply. He'd purposely moved his car well away from the house so he wouldn't be disturbed. Humiliation was an awful thing and Michael knew he had a bucketload heading his way. Thanks to his treacherous cunt of a brother and lying whore of a bird, he'd be the talk of the East End for many years to come. He, *the* Michael Butler, was destined to be a fucking laughing stock. He'd have to move far away. It was the only answer.

CHAPTER TWENTY-FOUR

DS Terry was handed the brown padded envelope by a young colleague. 'The note inside says it's a murder confession, guv.'

There were so many nutters and hoaxers roaming the streets, DS Terry glanced at the envelope and thought this was a definite wind-up. It had been posted a while back, to the Murder Squad at Whitechapel Police Station, which didn't actually exist, hence it ending up here in Bow.

'Pass me the tape recorder, Hicks. Another fruitcake, I dare say.'

DS Terry pressed the play button and within thirty seconds his hair stood up on end. He'd been a wet-behind-the-ears PC when Molly Butler had been murdered, but remembered the tragedy like it was yesterday. Molly had been the first dead child he'd ever seen and he'd spewed his guts up, to the displeasure of his boss back then.

'D'ya think it's kosher, boss?' young Hicks asked.

Totally stunned, Terry didn't reply until the tape ended. 'Go and get me some blank tapes, and track down the Chief. He needs to hear this ASAP. It's better than kosher. It's fucking gold dust.'

Over in Emerson Park, Little Vinny was explaining to his wife the latest drama to occur in his dysfunctional family. He'd stayed at his nan's last night.

'Oh my God! Bella slept with your dad and Antonio's his son! I truly can't believe that, Vin. How could they do that to poor Michael? It's too awful for words. I could never lie to you like that.'

'Mum, I'm hungry. Make me something to eat,' Calum ordered, kicking the leg of the kitchen table to get his parents' attention.

'Stop kicking that table, boy. I'm trying to talk to your mother. Three times I've told you to go and watch the film with your brothers, so do as you're bloody well told for once.'

Calum Butler glared at his father, kicked the table one last time, then left the room.

Little Vinny put his arms around Sammi-Lou and took comfort in her touch. 'What a bloody nightmare, eh? But it's my granddad I'm most worried about. I belled the hospital this morning and he's still in intensive care. They said he'd had a comfortable night. Is that good or bad news? It can't be brilliant; else he would be out of intensive care. Imagine if he dies, Sam. Christmas will be awful.'

Sammi-Lou rubbed the back of the husband she loved so very much. 'Your granddad's like you: a fighter and a truly lovely man. I'm sure he'll pull through. God will be looking over him to make sure he does, and if he had a comfortable night that's good news, not bad. As for your dad and Bella, I doubt God will ever favour them again.'

'Between me and you, my dad's always been a callous bastard. I used to take after him when I was younger, but not any more. I've tried ringing Michael, but his phone's switched off. Uncle Michael's always looked out for me. I'm not even bothered about my dad right now. If you ask me, he deserves to be lying in a hospital bed, battered and bruised.'

'I couldn't agree more.'

Not realizing that the officers at Bow Police Station were currently listening to him confessing to killing Molly, Little Vinny sighed. 'We reap what we sow in life, eh, babe?'

Daniel Butler was in the temper of all tempers. He had no idea where his old man was, had acquired a half-brother overnight, his grandfather was in intensive care, and celebrating Christmas was a non-fucking-starter. 'Liars, the lot of 'em, bruv. But Bella and Vinny have truly kicked the arse out of it this time. Italian slag! I'll give her what for.'

'I'm worried about Dad. You don't think he'd do anything stupid, do ya?'

'Yeah. He's probably got his cock shoved up Katy, creating us another brother or sister as we speak. I knew it all along. As soon as we bumped into Katy that time and she told us she was up the duff, I instantly knew it was the old man's. That's why I said what I did at Little Vinny's wedding. How could he lie to us all this time, eh?'

'Probably because he didn't want Bella finding out. I wonder what Nathan's like?'

'Bound to be a compulsive liar like the rest of the family. So we've been denied a little brother because Dad was worried about that fucking whore. I always liked her an' all, that's what makes it worse. The thought of her and Vinny at it makes my skin crawl, don't it yours?'

'Yeah. I still can't get me head around Antonio being his kid. Now we know the truth I can see similarities though, can't you? He even looks a bit like Vinny.'

'Both Antonio and Vinny can rot in hell for all I care. Bella an' all. Camila's my only concern now. That bitch better not sod off back to Italy and take our little sister with her, I'm telling ya. 'Cause if she does, I'll track her down and snatch Cami back off her.'

'None of this is Antonio's fault, Dan. We've treated him like a brother for years and it's not fair to take it out on him,' Lee insisted.

'But he ain't our brother, is he? We were always kind to him because he never had brothers, sisters, or a dad. Now he has all fucking three. I've always found him a bit odd, if you want the truth. Not so much when he was a nipper, but as he got older. That school the slag sent him to never did him no favours. Turned him into a posh little cunt. Let Little Vinny and Ava take over as his siblings now. We've done our duty.'

Shirley Preston was tidying up in preparation of her friend arriving for Christmas when she heard a tap on the door. She peeped through the keyhole, and on seeing Dot and Glen standing on her step immediately knew it was bad news.

Fear flooded through Shirley's veins. 'What is it? What's happened? Is Jamie OK?'

'You put the kettle on, Mum, while I explain the situation to Shirley,' Glen ordered.

'I don't want a cuppa. Please tell me what's happened to Jamie,' Shirley shrieked.

Dot took Shirley by the arm. 'Let's sit you down first, lovey.'

'Is Jamie hurt? He ain't dead, is he?' Shirley panicked.

Glen glanced at his mother. Shirley wasn't going to take this well, that was for sure. 'It ain't good news, Shirl. Jamie got involved in an altercation with that geezer who was giving him agg. It all went a bit wonky, but I can promise ya Jamie's gonna be OK. It was self-defence and I'm gonna hire him the best brief going for his trial.'

'Trial! What bloody trial?'

'The other geezer's dead, Shirl. I'm so sorry, love.'

'Dead! Dead!' Shirley spat. Seconds later, she felt a horrific pain down the left-hand side of her body. The whole latter part of her life had been devoted to her grandson, and her one wish had been to see him free and his name cleared of murder before she died.

As Shirley fell to the floor, struggling to breathe, she knew her wish was over. Seconds later, so was her life.

Bella stroked her daughter's long dark hair. She'd been ever so tearful and clingy this morning, even though Bella was trying her best to act as normal as possible. Rupert's arrival had cheered Camila up a bit, but it was obvious the child sensed all was not well.

'Mum, when is Daddy, Daniel and Lee coming home?' Camila asked again.

Having had no joy enticing her son out of his bedroom, Bella was shocked when Antonio marched into the kitchen to confront her with a look of pure evil on his face. 'I hate you. How could you do this to me? I want to see my dad.'

'Go in the lounge with Rupert, darling,' Bella urged Camila.

The child clung to her mother's legs. 'No. Want to stay with you.'

'What's my dad's phone number? Where does he live?' Antonio screamed.

'Your dad isn't a very nice person, Antonio, which is why I lied to you in the first place.'

'I'll be the one to decide that, and if he isn't nice, why did you open your legs to him in the first place? No wonder Michael left you,' Antonio spat.

Furious at her usually polite son's scathing comments, Bella lunged towards him and slapped him hard across the face. 'Don't you dare speak to me like that. I've been a good mother to you – show some respect.'

When Antonio began kicking her mum, Camila screamed.

'Stop it! Stop it now!' Rupert insisted, trying to restrain Antonio. He had always been so mild-mannered in the past; Rupert was stunned by the overnight change in the child.

Bella had tears streaming down her cheeks. 'Get the door, Rupert, and unless it's Michael I don't want to see anyone.'

Rupert did as asked and was horrified to see Bella's parents standing there, suitcases by their side.

Giovanni D'Angelo marched into the hallway. 'Bella, Bella,' he yelled.

It had been Daniel Butler's idea that he and Lee head to Barking and get on the lash early. A few of their old school pals were meeting later for a prearranged Christmas drink.

'Slow down, bruv. You'll be hammered before the boys arrive,' Lee warned Daniel. They'd trailed around earlier, hunting for their father again. They'd also popped to the hospital to see their grandfather, but hadn't been allowed to as he was still in intensive care and the doctor was with him.

'Dunno if I'm in the mood for a night out now. Dad must be at Katy's. I can't think where else he'd be. D'ya reckon he's still boning her? She was a nice-looking bird, weren't she?'

'Yeah. I could never have imagined Dad cheating on Bella, but after what we know now it wouldn't surprise me. Dark horse, ain't he? I wish he'd ring us, Dan, to let us know he's OK. Surely he must be as worried about Granddad as we are? I wish someone knew where Katy lived. We could drive there.'

Daniel didn't reply. His eyes were fixed on a table in the

corner. He nudged Lee. 'Speaking of granddads, look who's over there. He's spotted us. I just caught his eye and he quickly looked away.'

Lee recognized Donald immediately. He hadn't changed at all. The last time he and Daniel had laid eyes on him was about five years ago when they'd kicked off in his and Mary's café. 'Why don't we go over there and offer to buy him a drink? Perhaps it's time to let bygones be bygones. He is your granddad, Dan, and even though I'm not blood related, he and Mary were kind to me when I was little an' all.'

'I dunno. He's going up the bar. You get 'em in round this side and see if he makes eye contact with ya. Get me a chaser as well as a pint. A large one.'

When Lee went up the bar, Daniel thought about his mum. He had loved her in his own way, that's why he'd been so angry when she topped herself. It was easier to see her as selfish and hate her rather than go through the raw emotions of dealing with her death. Knowing what a lying bastard his father was now though made Daniel wonder what she'd had to put up with over the years. She must have been desperately unhappy to chuck herself off Beachy Head, that was for sure. Adam's death had been blamed for sending her literally over the edge, but she'd also found out about Bella around the same time.

'Donald knew I was there, but he wouldn't look at me,' Lee informed his brother.

Daniel necked his chaser in one, then slammed the glass on the table. 'I've been thinking. I know my mum was upset about Adam, but I bet the true reason she killed herself was because Dad was having it off with that Italian whore. Makes me hate Bella even more, that does. Ring the lads and tell 'em we can't make it later. We're going back to Brentwood to confront the slut.'

'Donald's swapped seats with the bloke he's with, Dan.'

Daniel glanced over at the table and immediately felt irate. His grandfather was now sitting with his back towards him. 'Fucking old bastard! Nobody does that to me, especially my own flesh and blood. Who does he think he is?'

When Daniel leapt up, Lee did the same and grabbed his brother's arm. 'Leave it, Dan. Let's get out of here. Donald ain't worth it. Seriously, bruv.'

Daniel Butler was in no mood to be restrained. He stomped over to Donald and prodded him on the shoulder. 'Why d'ya turn your back on me? I'm all you have left of your Nancy. If my mum is looking down, she'd be horrified by what you just did. I'm your fucking grandson.'

The Royal Oak was Donald's local. Not that he was a big drinker, but he'd pop in for the odd pint or two when his son Christopher visited or his friend Derrick Robin. It was Derrick he was with today. 'I don't want any trouble, Daniel. I've come in here for a quiet drink.'

Daniel was amazed to see his grandfather's hands shaking and fear in his eyes. 'Why are you scared of me? I'm your grandson. It's me, Daniel! That same little boy you used to sing fucking nursery rhymes to.'

Donald felt terribly embarrassed. Most of the customers were now looking around and a few of them ate at his café regularly.

'Come on, Dan. He don't wanna know,' Lee urged, trying to drag his brother away.

Daniel Butler was distraught. He had one granddad at death's door and it was clear to see the other was petrified of him. He had to have the last word though. It was in his nature. 'You sad, pathetic old cunt. How you produced my lovely mum I will never know.'

*

Michael Butler was also thinking about Nancy. He'd bought the gaff opposite his old marital home for his father to live in and was currently peeping through the curtains, staring at it.

Watching the family who now lived there unloading bags of shopping from the boot of their car, Michael sighed. He hadn't given Nancy much thought over recent years, had been too content and wrapped up with Bella to bother about his ex. What a mug he'd been. Nancy would never have betrayed him in such a vile manner, and truth be known if Bella hadn't come back on the scene Nancy probably wouldn't have chucked herself off Beachy Head.

Michael walked away from the window and glanced at himself in the mirror. He looked exactly as he felt: like shit. He knew alcohol wasn't the answer to his problems; neither was staying at his old man's house. Barking held far too many memories, not only of Nancy, but also Adam. There were only a few things that could make him feel even remotely better. His dad recovering, getting away from the East End, being around one of his kids and revenge. Katy Spencer could provide three of those.

Antonio D'Angelo was sitting halfway down the stairs, earwigging. He'd politely greeted his grandparents, then excused himself by telling them he'd been given some homework by his teacher that he wanted to finish before Christmas.

'Michael and I have been arguing a lot lately. Not over anything serious, but we mutually decided to take a break from one another,' Antonio heard his mother say.

'I am not stupid, Bella. Something serious must have happened for Michael to walk away from Camila. Has he been cheating on you?' Giovanni asked. He knew his daughter was lying, could see it in her eyes.

'No. Of course not. If you must know the truth, Michael has a son he never told me about. I was very angry with him for not coming clean with me, so I chucked him out. But everything will be fine, Dad. I love Michael and he loves me. The child wasn't conceived while we were together and I needed space to clear my head,' Bella flapped. She knew what her father was capable of, and no way did she want Michael to be in any danger.

Blood boiling at his mother's audacity in blaming Michael, Antonio dashed into the kitchen. 'Tell Nonna and Nonno the truth. Go on! Tell them what you did,' he ordered his mother.

Bella's eyes clouded over, a mixture of fear and anger. 'Go to your room this very minute, young man. I will explain the situation to Nonna and Nonno.'

'She's lying. Mum slept with Michael's brother and I am his son. Vinny Butler is my father,' Antonio screamed.

For once Giovanni D'Angelo was speechless. He'd done his homework on the Butlers, knew Vinny was a piece of work. Surely this could not be true?

Seconds later, Daniel and Lee Butler burst into the house. Their vicious, condescending verbal attack on Bella only confirmed Antonio's allegations and Giovanni's worst fears. To say he was livid and disappointed with his daughter was putting it mildly. He was absolutely disgusted by her.

Queenie Butler squeezed her son's hand. 'How you feeling?' Vinny's face looked worse today. The bruising had come out and it was very swollen on one side.

'Sore, but I'll survive. You heard from Michael?'

'No. I do hope he's OK though, boy. Nobody knows where he is and he ain't visited your father, 'cause I asked the nurses. Out of intensive care already, that old bastard is. They've put him on a normal ward, so looks like he'll live. You seen a doctor again? I hope you're out of here for Christmas. Ava's not been herself. I think it upset her, seeing you like this. I was gonna cancel Tara and Tommy coming tomorrow, but on second thoughts it might cheer Ava up a bit, having them around, take her mind off all the drama.'

'You can't cancel 'em. I doubt the poor little bastards have got anywhere else to go and they must miss their mum this time of year. I'll be out of here soon, don't you worry. The food's shit. I'll discharge meself before Christmas, worst comes to the worst.'

'You can't do that. Not until they're satisfied there's nothing wrong with you. Head injuries need to be treated with caution. Look at poor Roy.'

'He got blasted through the skull with a gun, Mum. It's a bit different. I'm fine, honest. Not been sick any more, and me headache's worn off. Where's Little Vinny? I thought he would've popped back. Did he say if he's gonna visit today?'

'He stayed at mine last night and shot off early this morning. I think he was a bit taken aback by it all, to be honest. I'm sure he'll be fine once he gets his head around it though. You know what a family man he is.'

'So what you trying to say? He sided with Michael, did he?'

Queenie looked sheepish. Her grandson had been both shocked and outraged when she'd explained the situation in detail, but she didn't want to upset Vinny. 'He didn't say too much. It's a lot for him to take in though. As far as he knew, he was your only son. A bit of a bombshell to find out he isn't. And he was worried about Albie. Idolizes that old goat. Perhaps he'll pop in and see you later, eh?'

'I doubt it, Mum. I'm obviously gonna be seen as the Big Bad Wolf in all of this. No wonder I stay single. Women have always caused me nothing but bastard grief. As for that Italian bitch, I rue the day I ever laid eyes on her. I truly do,' Vinny lied. He could hardly admit to his mother he was actually getting off on the fact he finally had a hold over Bella, could he now?

Over at Bow Police Station, the Chief Inspector was listening to the taped confession for the second time. It was transfixing on the ear, to say the very least.

'Shall we bring him in for questioning, guv?' asked DS Terry.

'Not yet. I want a DNA sample from Jamie Preston first; see if we can match it to Molly Butler's prime exhibits. Send somebody over to Charlton to collect the child's clothing and anything else we might have kept. You know how slippery the Butlers are, bound to hire the best brief in town. Little Vinny throttling his own sister, eh? Whoever would've thought it?'

'And if there is no DNA match linking Jamie to Molly?'

'Then we'll have made a massive cock-up that we'll try our damned hardest to put right.'

CHAPTER TWENTY-FIVE

Breakfast hadn't even been served on Christmas Eve when Albie Butler was awoken by the curtains being pulled around his bed. 'Michael!' he exclaimed, immediately wide awake at the sight of his beloved son.

Having sweet-talked the ward sister to be allowed in so early, Michael Butler sat on the edge of his father's bed and spoke in little more than a whisper. 'How you feeling? I had a chat with the nurses and they reckon you're out of the woods and gonna be fine. You have got to take it easy for a while though. No working at the club, and you need to cut down on the booze and fags.'

'Don't be worrying about me. I'm going nowhere yet. It's you I'm concerned about. Where you been staying? Little Vinny popped in to see me last night and said everyone's frantic as nobody can get hold of you. He's on your side that boy, not his father's. He's that disgusted by it all, he didn't even bother visiting Vinny while he was here.'

'I've been stopping at yours, but hid me motor and turned the lights off of a night. Dan and Lee knocked a few times and Little Vinny came round, but I couldn't face anyone. Look, I've decided I need to get out of the East End for a bit to sort me head out. I spoke to Katy late last night and as soon as I leave 'ere I'm going to shoot down to Tunbridge Wells to spend Christmas at hers with Nathan. Seeing as I'm paying for the gaff, it beats a hotel.'

Albie squeezed his son's hand. 'I've learnt over the years it is better to face your problems full-on than run away from 'em, but you do what you feel is right.'

'No way can I stay round 'ere. Must be the talk of the town and the laughing stock of all fucking laughing stocks. I will never live down what those pair of cunts have done to me.'

'You're not and never will be a laughing stock, Michael. Unlike your brother, who people pretend to like through fear, you are genuinely popular and well respected. Of course the gossipmongers will be having a field day, but you'll be the one who comes out of all this smelling of roses. Your brother will lose a lot of kudos. The likes of Eddie Mitchell won't be overly impressed, you mark my words.'

'The way I feel right now, I wish I was pushing up bastard roses. My whole world has been blown apart and I have no idea when I'll get to see Camila again. It's like the worst nightmare ever. I even kept pinching myself the other night to make sure I was actually awake.'

'That's how I felt when my Dorothy passed away, although that is nothing in comparison to what you're going through. I only wish there was something I could say or do to make things right for you. But obviously I can't.'

'Let's look on the bright side. The one good thing to come out of all this shit is you can get to spend some quality time with Nathan now. He's a cracking lad.'

'I will look forward to that very much. A word of warning though, from a none-too-wise old man. Don't let Katy trap you again, boy. We both know you don't love her and you're bound to feel vulnerable at the moment.'

Michael managed a weak smile. 'Truth be known, I don't even like Katy very much, let alone love her. But revenge is sweet and I intend mine to be heavily coated in sugar. Bella who?'

Katy Spencer was in an ecstatic trance. When Michael had called late last night, she'd expected him to have a good old rant at her for turning up at his house before arranging to see their son. But she'd been wrong and was now desperate to share her wonderful news.

Katy dialled Lucy's number yet again, willing her friend to answer. 'There you are! Oh my God! You'll never guess what's happened, Luce. I was dying to tell you last night, but it was too late after I got off the phone, and I've been ringing you all morning.'

'Slow down. I can't understand you properly when you gabble. I take it this is about Michael?' Lucy asked, trying to keep the sarcasm from her tone. She'd heard enough about Michael Butler recently to last her a bloody lifetime.

'He's moving in, Luce. Well, on a temporary basis. Can you believe it? I've been tidying up all morning. Nathan is so excited, bless him. This will be the first time his father has stayed overnight with us since he was born.'

Lucy Tompkins was shocked. 'Really? Michael actually asked to move in with you?'

'Not exactly. But he asked if he could stay over the festive season. He said a lot had happened and he needed a break to clear his head. But he obviously wants to be with me, Luce. He could stay bloody anywhere. I mean, let's be honest, you'd think he'd have the right hump with me after telling Bella, but perhaps he wanted the truth to come out all along? I always said he had feelings for me, didn't I? The sex between us was amazing and I can't believe he'll

311

be sleeping in my bed tonight. It's been so long since I've had sex, but I'm glad I waited for him. I have you to thank for all this. It was your idea we knock on his front door. I'd threatened to do so many a time, but probably would never have had the guts to go through with it without you by my side. I owe you one, mate.'

'I'm amazed Michael wants to stay at yours, but obviously pleased for you at the same time. You must be careful though, Katy. He will be on the rebound and chances are at some point Bella will decide to take him back. I don't want you to get your heart broken any more than it already has been in the past.'

Katy already felt more confident than she had in years. 'Nathan would love a brother or sister, Lucy. I intend to fulfil my son's wish, and believe me, I will.'

It was Christmas Eve tradition that Vivian and Queenie visit the graves of their loved ones. They'd start at Bow with their beloved mother, then move on to Plaistow to pay their respects to Roy, Lenny, Molly, Adam and Brenda. It was always a sad day for both women and it had been Vivian's idea they stop for a stiff drink before hopping back on the train.

The weather being extremely cold, Queenie and Vivian had got more than the bit of warmth they'd hoped to find in the pub. They'd pulled two suited and booted old boys.

'That Ted weren't a bad catch, Queen. I bet he was a right looker back in the day,' Vivian insisted.

'And I bet he's been a right bleedin' womanizer in his time an' all. I married one, so I know the signs. Anyway, his shoes were cheap. You can always tell a man by his shoes. Don't see my Vinny and Michael wearing crap out of Freeman, Hardy and Willis, do you?'

When the train stopped at Whitechapel, Vivian linked arms with her sister for the short walk home. Their one stiff drink had turned into four. 'I feel a bit tiddly. Do you reckon they were buying us doubles?'

'Probably. Men will do anything to get inside your knickers. Won't be meeting them again next week like we promised, that's for sure.'

'Why not? It's only a harmless drink at lunchtime, and we'll be passing the pub on the way home from the cemetery anyway. You can be such an old stick-in-the-mud at times, Queen. That Ted might have the biggest dingle-dangle for miles around, for all you know.'

Queenie chuckled. 'Any man who tried to put his todger near me would get it hacked off immediately. Unless it was Eddie Mitchell, of course! Seriously, we'd better not pop back in that pub. My Vinny and Michael will have a fit if they hear we've been acting like two loose women. I wonder who that car belongs to outside mine? Looks posh, doesn't it?'

When a handsome but severe-looking man stepped out of the passenger side and asked, 'Are you Mrs Butler?' Queenie was rather taken aback.

'Who wants to know?' Vivian asked.

'My name is Giovanni D'Angelo. I am Bella's father. I think we need to have a little chat about our grandchildren, don't you?'

Having asked for the DNA results back as a matter of urgency, DS Terry was like a cat on a hot tin roof. Terry would put his house on it, after hearing that tape, there was no match with Preston, and he was no gambler. It was a damn shame that Ben Bloggs had topped himself because he would have been the weak link without a shadow of a doubt. However, Terry planned to play on Ben's suicide when questioning Vinny Butler Junior. It was a bit too much of a coincidence that the Bloggs lad had chosen to hang himself at the same time as Molly's funeral.

'No news is good news, guv,' young Hicks remarked. He knew his boss was on tenterhooks. In fact there was an air of excitement all around the station today.

Still scrutinizing Little Vinny's statements surrounding Molly's death, Terry got to the part where the lad had told the police he'd fallen into a deep sleep and when he'd awoken his sister had disappeared. 'Asleep my arse, you murdering little fucker,' he hissed.

Giovanni D'Angelo most certainly had an aura about him. Tall, with slicked-back greying hair, he was immaculately turned out. His suit and shoes were of the finest quality and he actually reminded Queenie of an older foreign version of her sons.

Bella had always been rather vague about her parents' lifestyle, had described her father as some kind of businessman. Knowing now what a liar Bella was, one look at Mr D'Angelo told Queenie there was more to him than met the eye. She knew a villain when she saw one, having given birth to three.

'I will need to speak with both of your sons in person, Mrs Butler. This mess we all find ourselves in needs to be sorted out sooner rather than later for Antonio and Camila's sake, wouldn't you agree?'

'Please, call me Queenie. And yes, I totally agree with you. Vinny has been denied a relationship with his son – and me with my grandson – for far too long. Both of us wish to play an active part in Antonio's life from now on,' Queenie replied, in her poshest voice.

Mr D'Angelo was about to reply when a little girl bearing a strong resemblance to Antonio burst into the lounge with a small dog. 'Fred did a big shit on Mrs Agg's carpet, Nan,' the child announced proudly.

Queenie was mortified. 'Take Fred into the garden and help your Auntie Viv in the kitchen, dear. Shut the door behind you, please.'

As soon as her granddaughter departed, Queenie apologized. 'She's at that awkward age, is Ava. I don't allow swearing in this house, but she has picked certain words up at school. Playground talk, I call it. Vinny wanted her to attend a private school like Antonio, but she didn't like it. She'd lost her mum in a car accident and it was too much upheaval for her to be separated from her friends also. Now, where were we?'

'Discussing a meeting with your sons. I have tried calling them, but neither of them seem to have their phones switched on at present. I wondered if you could give me an address where they could be reached?'

'I can't, I'm afraid. My Michael has been on the missing list since the truth came out. And Vinny is recuperating in hospital at present. If you give me your number, I will arrange for them to come here at some point. Not together though. You will need to visit them separately. Tensions are at an all-time high at the moment, as you can well imagine. Your daughter's lies have split my family in two.'

'My daughter's behaviour has disappointed me, to say the least, Queenie. Bella made a mistake, one that has come back to haunt her. But Vinny has been untruthful also, to his own brother of all people. So has Michael. He has a son nobody knew about. Pointing fingers will not do us any favours, don't you agree?'

About to disagree, Queenie took one look at Giovanni's sinister glare and instead found herself agreeing.

*

315

'Daddy!' Nathan Spencer screamed, joyfully throwing himself into his father's arms. He'd been staring out the window for the past hour, could barely believe his father was going to be spending all of Christmas with him.

Michael held his son close to his chest. He already missed Camila dreadfully and if he couldn't spend time with her, being around Nathan was the next best thing.

Thinking how attractive Michael looked in the black Crombie worn over his suit, Katy could not wipe the grin off her face. 'Let Daddy breathe and take his coat off, Nathan. He's been so excited that you're staying with us, Michael. Woke me up at six this morning and has spoken of little else since, have you, son?'

'No, Dad. And Mum has made us shepherd's pie for dinner. She said it's your favourite.'

Quickly butting in before her son informed Michael she had never cooked a shepherd's pie in her life and had spent hours poring over the recipe, Katy joked: 'I know you loved your mum's, and mine's probably rancid in comparison.'

Michael kissed Katy politely on the cheek. 'Thanks. It's the thought that counts. I need to make a few phone calls. You've no objection to me letting my family know I'm staying here, have you? It might mean a few visitors. OK to give your phone number to them as well?'

Feeling like the cat that had finally got the cream, Katy nodded her head repeatedly. If Michael wanted to notify his family and give out her phone number it was obviously over between him and Bella and he planned on staying for longer than she'd anticipated.

Michael stepped out into the garden and rang Daniel. There was no reply, so he tried Lee, who answered immediately. 'So sorry I haven't been in touch, son. I needed time to clear my head after all the drama.'

'We've been worried sick about you, Dad. Dan and I have searched high and low. Dan, Dan! Dad's on the blower.'

Daniel Butler ran down the stairs and snatched at the phone. He and Lee couldn't face being anywhere near Bella, so had decided to stay at the club for the time being. 'You could have fucking rang us, Dad. I know you've had a shock, but so have we. Fancy not telling me and Lee we had a little bro. I'm glad you're OK, but you're still bang out of order. You must've known you could trust us and we'd never have told that slapper.'

'I realize that now and I'm sorry. Why don't you pop over to Katy's on Boxing Day and get to meet your little brother properly? You and Lee'll love him. He's a good kid. Reminds me of Adam.'

'I told you he'd be at Katy's, didn't I?' Daniel said to his brother.

Lee snatched the phone back. 'You'd better ring Nan, she's been worried sick an' all. Oh, and Granddad's perked up a bit. We rang the hospital, and me and Dan are gonna visit him later. He's out of intensive care.'

'I know. I visited your granddad this morning. I need you to do me a favour, boy. Give Bella Katy's number and tell her to contact me here in case of an emergency. And tell her I'll be in touch soon about seeing Camila. You got a pen and paper handy?'

Lee jotted down Katy's phone number and address, and then handed the phone back to Daniel. 'What a fucking wrong 'un Bella turned out to be, eh Dad? And Vinny's no better. I slated her in front of her parents yesterday. The look on her old man's face was a picture. Lee and I want nothing more to do with Bella or Vinny, and we mean that. We wanna see Camila regularly, but not Antonio. He can fuck off an' all.'

'We'll chat properly on Boxing Day when you come over,

but don't say too much in front of Nathan, and do not say anything else in front of Bella's parents. Don't even go back to Brentwood while they're over – promise me that.'

'Why? Me and Lee need to pick some clothes up.'

'Let Lee pick the clothes up. There's more to Bella's old man than you think. Just ring her up, be polite, give her Katy's phone number and tell her I'm staying here, OK?'

'OK.'

Michael ended the call. Imagining Bella's face when she found out where he was, as heartbroken as he felt, he couldn't help but smirk. Bella would surely be devastated and it served her fucking right. What goes around comes around.

After leaving Queenie Butler's, Giovanni D'Angelo drove straight to his daughter's house. His wife was with friends in West London. She would not mention the drama, and Giovanni would deal with this mess alone. That was the way things worked in their marriage.

Bella looked a shadow of her usual glamorous self. Her eyes and whole persona seemed lifeless. 'Lee rung me about half an hour ago with a message from Michael. He's staying with Katy and Nathan in Tunbridge Wells. How could he do this to me and Camila? I know I've hurt him terribly, but how can he move on so quickly? I can't tell the kids where he is. It will break their hearts. I am devastated and so bloody angry. That's it now. This spells the end of me and Michael, and it's entirely my bloody fault. We were so happy. I truly hate myself and Vinny Butler. I rue the day I ever laid eyes on that evil bastard.'

'Swearing does not become you, Bella, so please do not use such language in front of me. Do you have any contact details for where Michael is staying?'

Bella handed her father a telephone number. 'I don't want anything bad to happen to Michael, but Vinny is a different

318

story. Antonio is insistent on meeting him and I can't allow that to happen. Can you make Vinny disappear for me? Please?'

Unbeknown to Bella, Antonio had heard his grandfather arrive and was earwigging behind the door. He burst into the kitchen, a look of hatred on his face. 'Don't you dare make my dad disappear. I will ring the police and tell them if he does, and they will lock you up. I have always wanted a real father like my friends at school have, and you have no right to stop me, Bella. I've decided not to call you Mum any more, by the way. You're a lying, nasty cheat who is not worthy of being my mother.'

'Enough, Antonio! Go to your room and I will speak with you shortly,' Giovanni commanded.

Tears streamed down Bella's face. She had doted on her son from the moment she'd first held him in her arms and it was heartbreaking to see he now despised her with a passion.

Checking that Antonio had complied with his order, Giovanni sat opposite Bella again. 'Guzzling red wine is not the answer to your problems. Neither is letting your appearance go. I raised you to be stronger than that. Your mother and I are shattered by the lies you've told us and obviously Michael feels the same. But he's hurt you too. It must have been a great shock, Katy turning up at your door with Nathan in tow.'

'It was. But I would've forgiven Michael in time. Now he has moved in with her and knows who Antonio's father is, there is no going back. I could never love another man like I loved Michael, so will spend the rest of my life alone, raising my children – who are both bound to hate me.'

'Stop feeling sorry for yourself. Self-pity is an awful trait. I will contact Michael and speak with him. I visited his mother earlier today.'

'You visited Queenie! What did she have to say? I used to get on so well with her before all this happened, and now she hates me too. Perhaps I should just move back to Italy with you and Mum. The children will settle there, given time.'

Giovanni sighed. 'Queenie is a tough woman who holds her family close to her heart. Running away is not an option this time, Bella. You have two children who are desperate for regular contact with their fathers. You must put them first.'

'No way is Antonio spending time with Vinny. He has never even met him,' Bella argued.

There was currently a war going on back in Italy. An awful feud between his men and a rival *famiglia* who were trying to take control. Sons and grandsons had already been targeted and no way was Giovanni going to risk Antonio's life. He had already lost a son, could not suffer such anguish again. 'Every child has a right to meet their papa, Bella. Especially a boy. I will meet Vinny Butler and if he turns out not to be a good father to Antonio, I will deal with it in time. And that is the last word on the matter.'

Back in Whitechapel, Tara and Tommy had just arrived at their grandmother's house.

'Where's your decorations and tree, Nan?' fourteen-year-old Tommy asked. Ever since he could remember, Christmas had meant baubles and tinsel galore in his grandmother's front room.

Vivian gave Tommy a hug. It must be a difficult time of year for him and Tara since their mother had been murdered. 'We were waiting for you two to arrive. Me and your nan are knocking on a bit now. We need help climbing up ladders and getting the tree out the loft,' she lied, not wanting the teenagers to know the ins and outs of the drama.

'Oh, who cares about silly trees and decorations, Tommy. You're fourteen, not four. Have you got any Malibu, Nan?' Tara asked.

'No, I have not. And you won't be drinking alcohol in this house. Don't want to end up with a problem like your mother had, do you?' Queenie snapped.

'But I'm legally old enough to drink alcohol. You let Daniel and Lee drink it and they're the same age as me,' Tara argued.

'They're male and haven't got your mother's genes like you have. Now let's make a start with that tree. Your Uncle Vinny will be home soon. He got into a fight, so his face is a bit battered and bruised. Looks far worse than it is though. Viv, knock at Stinky Susan's and tell Ava we're about to decorate the house and her dad'll be home soon. Destiny can help us too.'

Vivian pursed her lips as she marched a few doors down the road. Queenie'd had no intention of putting the tree or any decorations up this year until Golden Bollocks had called to inform his mother he was being discharged. As bloody always, Queenie's whole world revolved around her number one son.

Daniel Butler was in a foul mood when Lee arrived back at the club with a boot full of their clothes. 'Nan can go and fuck herself an' all, bruv. She always sides with that cunt. We'll take her present back to the shop and get our money back,' Daniel exploded.

'What's happened?'

'She's got him staying there over Christmas. The hospital've discharged the no-good prick. Did she honestly think we were gonna sit round the dinner table playing happy families after what he did to Dad? I told her where to go and she weren't happy at all when I told her Dad was stopping at Katy's. Good! Serves her right.'

Lee slumped on the sofa. Tonight was a sell-out and neither he nor Dan were in the mood for a club full of drunks celebrating what should be a happy time of year. Their nan had only invited them for Christmas dinner yesterday. Fancy her asking Vinny as well. 'Bollocks to the lot of 'em, Dan. We'll get tonight out the way, then go out to a restaurant for our grub tomorrow. Unless we ask Dad if we can go to Katy's?'

'Nah. Let's not bother. He'll be too busy with his new family to want us around for long. Oh well, good job we've got one another 'cause the rest of our family are truly wank.'

Unable to stomach the hero's welcome Vinny was receiving next door but one, Vivian had gone back to her own house for a bit of peace and quiet.

Tears rolling down her cheeks as she sifted through photos of her wonderful son, Viv snatched at the phone as it rang. If it was Queenie asking her to go back, she would most certainly get a mouthful and a reminder of who killed Lenny.

'Oh, it's you, Michael. I thought it was your mother. How are you, love? Silly question, I know, but I hope you're as well as can be expected.'

'I'm up and down like a yo-yo, to be honest. Not sure it's really sunk in yet, but what can you do? No option other than to pick meself up and dust meself down, eh? If I got through losing Adam, this is nothing in comparison and that's what I keep telling myself.'

'You're worth more than those two put together, Michael, and don't you ever forget that. Terrible, what they've done to you. I would never have expected that of Bella, but we live and learn. I feel sorry for the kids an' all. Both innocent in all of this, and I bet they're missing you.'

'I want nothing more to do with Antonio. He's not mine, he's Vinny's problem now. I obviously miss Camila dreadfully, but hopefully I'll get to see her regularly soon. Bella better not try and move back to Italy with her, I'm telling ya.'

'Her father visited your mum earlier. Looked a bit of a villain to us. Is he?'

'Long story, Auntie Viv. I'll tell you another time. Now I need a favour from you, if you don't mind?'

'You name it, boy.'

'Dan and Lee have promised me they'll visit me dad tomorrow morning. I can't get there as I'm staying in Tunbridge Wells with Katy and Nathan. My dad thinks the world of you, Viv, and I swear on my boys' lives that he never grabbed hold of that old slapper at Little Vinny's wedding. If you could visit him later in the day it would really cheer him up and make his Christmas. You'd also be helping me out. I hate to think of him in that hospital all alone.'

Vivian was so choked up she could barely answer. 'Of course I'll visit Albie for ya.'

When Ava had proudly blurted out, 'Antonio is my brother. My dad had sex with Bella,' an embarrassed Queenie told Tara and Tommy in vague detail what had gone on. They were hardly little children any more, and too many people were discussing the love triangle to keep it a secret. Neither seemed bothered. They barely knew Bella or Antonio.

'Look, Dad – Fred's trying to open his stocking,' Ava giggled.

Vinny had bigger things on his mind than Fred. 'Mum,

give me Giovanni's number. I'm gonna ring him now. No time like the present.'

'I'll ring him for you. I want to make sure he comes here,' Queenie insisted.

'No. This is my problem and I'll sort it,' Vinny retorted sharply, before grabbing the piece of paper out of his mother's hand. As much as he loved her, she hadn't stopped fussing over him since he'd arrived and it was beginning to suffocate him.

Vinny went upstairs. He still felt rough and had a headache, although he'd told the doctor otherwise. He punched the number into his phone. 'Giovanni, this is Vinny Butler . . .'

Katy Spencer's mouth was wide open while Michael told her the story of Bella and Vinny. She could barely believe what she was hearing, but was elated at the same time. No way would Michael ever get back with Bella now, which meant he was there for the taking. 'I am so sorry. What an awful shock for you. Let me pour you another drink, Michael. Antonio, Vinny's son? I feel a bit lost for words, to be honest. I don't know what to say to comfort you. There isn't anything.'

'Tell me about it. Gonna have to keep in contact with Bella to see Cami, but I'd prefer it if I never had to lay eyes on her again. What a pair of snides. Their lies make me want to vomit, and to think I raised that bastard's son. Then again, Vinny didn't know Antonio was his until last week. Bella told everybody the lad's father was an American called Clint. She even lied to her own fucking parents, the wrong 'un.'

Katy moved in for a hug. 'I know me and Nathan are no replacement for Bella and Cami, but we both think the world of you and love having you around.'

Prising Katy's arms away before she went for a kiss, Michael forced a smile. 'Thanks. It was lovely reading Nathan a bedtime story earlier. That cheered me up. I'm glad I'm staying here with yous two. Dan and Lee are looking forward to seeing you again and meeting Nathan on Boxing Day an' all.'

Katy beamed from ear to ear. Michael's pain was her gain, and she knew it.

CHAPTER TWENTY-SIX

'Mum, Dad, wake up. Santa's been!' yelled Regan Butler.

'And the reindeer ate his carrot and milk you left out, Dad,' Calum squealed with delight.

'Can we open our presents now? Please?' Oliver pleaded.

Little Vinny and Sammi-Lou exchanged smiles. Christmas was always a special time in their home and they loved nothing more than experiencing their sons' excitement. Last year Regan had been too young to understand the festive activities, bless him.

'You can open half your presents now and the rest when Nan and Granddad arrive. OK?' Little Vinny replied. Sammi-Lou's parents and sister loved watching the boys eagerly opening their gifts too.

'Mummy's going to brush her teeth. No touching any presents until me and your dad come downstairs,' Sammi-Lou shouted after her sons.

Little Vinny chuckled and gave his wife a hug. 'Let the madness commence.'

'I must have the most ungrateful grandchildren ever. Tara and Tommy both asked for money, but when they asked to come over for Christmas I made a real effort to find 'em nice presents they'd like instead. Seemed unthoughtful to give 'em cash and they had sod-all to unwrap. Anybody would've thought I wrapped up Fred's shit by the look on their faces earlier,' Queenie complained.

Vinny shrugged. 'You know what teenagers are like. Tara said yesterday she was saving up to go abroad with her friends next year, and Tommy wanted to treat himself to one of them Nintendo Game Boys. You should've just given 'em dosh.'

'Some Christmas this is gonna be. Ava and Destiny are the only ones without faces like smacked arses. I know it's never gonna be the same without our Molly, Vin, but we must make an effort. Put on a brave face, so to speak.'

'I miss Molly more than words can say, but it ain't only that. I thought Little Vinny would've called me this morning and put the boys on the phone like he usually does. Apart from you, Jay Boy and Carl, no bastard visited me in hospital either. Pete and Paul didn't even bother, although they both belled me this morning, which is more than can be said for any of the family.'

'Daniel and Lee were always going to take their father's side, boy. As for Little Vinny, why don't you ring him?'

'Nah. He knew I was poorly and couldn't be arsed. You can put money on it he's visited that old bastard though. The way people are acting towards me, you'd think I'd been knocking Bella off behind Michael's back for years. I didn't know who she was when we had a fling, did I? And she weren't even with Michael then.'

Queenie sat on the bed and squeezed her son's hands. 'You're not to blame for any of this. It's all Bella's fault. She led you on, got herself pregnant, then denied you your son for years. You keep your chin up. Antonio's gonna need a happy dad, not a sad one.'

*

Gary and Meg Allen watched their grandsons opening the gifts they'd bought them.

'Look, Dad. Mum, look at this! It's James Bond,' Oliver grinned, waving the toy in the air.

'A racing car! Does it go fast, Granddad?' Calum asked gleefully.

'Yeah. But we need to put some batteries in it first. Give us it here,' Gary replied.

'I want that,' Regan grumbled, snatching at the toy.

Calum held on to the car for dear life. 'No. It's mine.'

When Regan punched his brother, Little Vinny lifted the child up by his arm and slapped him firmly on his backside.

Gary glanced at his wife. He'd been insistent for the past six months or so that both Calum and Regan had some kind of behavioural problems, but Meg wouldn't hear of it. Boys were naturally more boisterous than girls, she insisted.

'Stop that now or you'll go to your bedroom and the rest of your presents will go to the poor children in the orphanage,' Sammi-Lou threatened. Regan was now having one of his infamous tantrums.

Fourteen-year-old Millie kneeled on the floor and handed her nephew the toy she'd bought him. 'Don't cry, Regan. Open this one,' she urged.

'Don't wannit,' Regan screamed, throwing the gift at Millie's head.

'That's it, Sam. Get him out my sight before I do him some permanent damage. He can come out of his room when he's calmed down and is ready to apologize to everyone,' Little Vinny bellowed.

'He'll be fine in a minute. They get over-excited at Christmas, kids, don't they?' Meg said awkwardly. She knew exactly what her husband was thinking, and as much as she hated to admit it, was beginning to think he might be right.

Giovanni D'Angelo liked to catch his prey unaware. When Vinny had called him yesterday, Giovanni had told him he'd be in touch very soon. And it had been an easy task to find out Katy's address, once he knew her phone number.

Plans to stay with their daughter scuppered, the D'Angelos were now staying with Italian friends in West London. 'Where are you going?' Mrs D'Angelo asked her husband, surprised that he had his coat on.

'I am taking Antonio and Camila to visit their fathers. I will be back before dinner is served.'

'Does Bella know?'

'I haven't asked our daughter's permission, if that is what you mean. The world doesn't revolve around Bella and it was her choice to spend Christmas alone, wallowing in self-pity, rather than with us and her children. Antonio and Camila are extremely unhappy and I intend to put a smile back on their faces.'

'Bella will be furious with you.'

'Our daughter made her own bed, now she must learn to lie in it, my dear. End of subject.'

'How's business?' Gary Allen asked his son-in-law. Regan had now calmed down and been forced to apologize for his behaviour, and all three boys were finally playing nicely with their presents.

'Not bad. Finn's coming round later. We cancelled that big outdoor New Year's Eve gig and are now holding a smaller one in a warehouse. Gonna hold the original one when it warms up a bit. Was a silly idea to try to hold it this time of year anyway, to be honest, but God loves a trier,' Little Vinny chuckled.

'Vin, can you start laying the table? The turkey's nearly cooked,' Sammi-Lou shouted out.

'Can I have some dark meat please, Dad?' Oliver asked.

'I don't want no turkey. I'm a vegetarian now,' Millie proudly announced.

'She watched a programme on TV showing animals being slaughtered. Refused to eat meat or poultry since,' Gary explained, following his son-in-law into the dining room.

Little Vinny raised his eyebrows. 'Kids, eh? Sammi keeps on about wanting a daughter, but I've told her we've got enough on our plate with the boys for now. The thing is, we can't even guarantee a girl, can we? As much as I love the little 'uns, they're hard work. I think being close together in age they wind one another up. I certainly couldn't handle another boy, and I know Sammi would be gutted if it weren't a girl. Ollie's no trouble, mind, never has been. The perfect son, him.'

'He sure is, and I think you're right to bide your time. If you want to try for a girl you'd be wise to wait until the boys at least start school. You're only young. Got many happy years ahead of you,' Gary advised.

'We're not expecting anyone, are we?' Sammi-Lou yelled when the doorbell rang.

'It might be Finn. Perhaps his ex didn't want him to stay for dinner after all?' Little Vinny replied.

'I'll answer it,' Oliver said. 'Dad, it's some policemen here to see you,' he shouted, seconds later.

Little Vinny dashed into the hallway, closely followed by his wife and in-laws. Apart from the illegal raves, which certainly didn't warrant the Old Bill knocking on his door on Christmas Day, he'd done sod-all else wrong. Surely another member of his family hadn't suddenly died an awful death? 'What's occurring?' he asked.

DS Terry stared the cocksure young man in the eyes.

'Vinny Butler, I am arresting you on suspicion of the murder of Molly Butler. You are not obliged to say anything, but what you do say will be written down and may be given in evidence. Understand that, do ya?'

'Is this some kind of joke? Molly was his sister and you already have the boy that killed her locked up,' Sammi-Lou stammered, grabbing her father's arm for support.

'New evidence has come to light and we now have every reason to believe that it was actually your old man who throttled his sister,' Terry replied bluntly.

His face a greyish colour, Little Vinny tried desperately to stop his hands from shaking. 'It's a mistake. Don't worry. I'll go to the station, answer their questions and be home before you know it. Ring my dad, Sam. Tell him what's happened and to get me a brief.'

As the love of her life was led handcuffed down the driveway in full view of her children and the neighbours, Sammi-Lou burst into uncontrollable tears.

Knowing he would be the talk of the town, Vinny Butler was determined to revisit the pub he'd been beaten up in sooner rather than later. He'd learned over the years it was better to act blasé over such a scene than shy away from it.

The electric atmosphere fell silent as Vinny sauntered into the Blind Beggar. Expecting the nudges and whispers, Vinny strolled up to the bar as though he didn't have a care in the world. Tara and Tommy had been bored at his mother's so he'd brought them with him as a bit of moral support.

'You OK, Vin? We've all been worried about you. You didn't look too healthy when they carted you out of here,' Big Stan said.

'It'll take more than Michael waving a cricket bat to

finish me off,' Vinny joked. 'Merry Christmas, everybody. This round's on me.'

Relieved that Vinny was in a jovial mood, the bubbly festive spirit returned to the pub in seconds. Handshakes, well-wishes and pats on the back soon followed. Vinny Butler was far better to have as a friend than an enemy.

'Get that ratpig and its disgusting toy away from me, Ava. I mean it. Otherwise I will dropkick both,' Vivian ordered.

'Don't be so nasty. Fred's only playing with Teddy and he's not harming you. Tell her, Nan,' Ava grumbled.

'Her! I think you mean Auntie Viv, don't you? Why don't you and Destiny take Fred over Mrs Agg's so he can spend some time with Mabel, Ava? Then you can try out those roller skates Dad bought ya both. Don't go far and I'll give you a shout when dinner's nearly ready,' Queenie said.

'Can I put my new denim outfit on?'

'No. Mrs Agg's house is none too wholesome, you know that. Wear your dungarees when you go somewhere special.'

'But I don't go anywhere special,' Ava argued.

'If they play that Johnny Cash record once more, I'll give 'em ring of fucking fire. I'll knock next door and set light to the bastard record in front of the pair of notrights,' Vivian complained, referring to Roger and his mother Doll who lived in the house that separated hers and Queenie's.

'God, everybody is so miserable today. Come on, Fred, we're going out,' Ava announced, grabbing the dog's lead.

When the front door slammed, Queenie sat opposite her sister. 'She does have a point. What's the matter, Viv?'

'Missing my Lenny. Plus I've got one of me bad headaches. Mixed me drinks yesterday, didn't I? I reckon them two blokes bought us trebles, I dunno about doubles,' Vivian lied. There was sod-all wrong with her head, but she was determined to escape after dinner and visit Albie as she'd promised Michael. She was actually looking forward to it. Anything was better than spending the day with the man who'd killed her son. Albie had a good sense of humour and she'd missed their friendship, truth be known. He was the only one who truly understood how she felt about Vinny.

'Answer that, Viv. Vinny's left his phone 'ere so unless it's Michael, tell 'em I'm busy cooking. I'm in no mood for silly talk today.'

Vivian's blood ran cold as she listened to what the caller had to say. 'Try and calm down, love. There must be some mistake. Vinny's only popped down to the local. I'll get a message to him immediately, OK?'

'Whatever's wrong? You look as white as a ghost. And who wants to tell Vinny what?' Queenie demanded. If it was Daniel kicking off again, there would be hell to pay after the way he'd spoken to her yesterday. That boy had no respect whatsoever.

Tears in her eyes as it brought back memories of the actual event, Vivian squeezed her sister's hands. 'The police turned up at Little Vinny's. They've arrested him on suspicion of murdering Molly. My blood's gone cold, Queen.'

Queenie snatched her hands away. 'Don't talk so fucking daft. Jamie Preston's been locked up for years. Who was it on the phone?'

'Sammi-Lou. Beside herself, she was. You stop 'ere, pour yourself a brandy. I'll shoot round the Beggar and find Vinny, tell him what's happened.'

Queenie put her hand over her mouth and shook her head repeatedly. She was gobsmacked, literally.

'How long until we get to Nanny Queenie, Granddad?' Camila asked innocently. She was extremely confused by everything that had happened recently, but was happy that she was going to visit her nan, then her father today. Her mum was very sad, kept crying all the time and even though this was the first Christmas Day Camila had spent away from her mother, she wasn't that bothered. Her mum worked lots of hours anyway and she was more used to Juanita's company. Cami missed Juanita and couldn't wait until she got back from holiday. They played lots of games together and had fun days out. Whereas her mum usually took her to restaurants, which Camila found tedious.

'We'll be there soon. The traffic has been far worse than I anticipated. Are you looking forward to calling Queenie "Nan" for the first time, Antonio? Don't call her Nonna, for goodness' sake, she won't understand that,' Giovanni joked. Antonio had been very quiet on the journey, which was understandable. He was bound to be nervous at meeting his real father for the first time. What child wouldn't be?

Giovanni's own father had abandoned him before he was even born, disappearing into thin air the day after his mother had disclosed she was pregnant. Giovanni had tracked him down many years later, only to be shunned for a second time. By that time his father had another family and had not wanted the past dredged up.

The experience had left a bitter taste in Giovanni's mouth. That was why he was so determined his grandchildren would both have a steady relationship with their fathers. Vinny Butler might not be perfect, but he'd done well in life and had seemed keen to build a father-and-son bond with Antonio when they'd spoken on the phone. As for Michael, he adored the ground Camila walked on and would surely be devastated if he didn't see the child regularly.

'Do you think my dad will be pleased to see me even though we haven't told him we're coming?' Antonio asked his grandfather.

'Of course he will. I'm sure everybody will give you a huge welcome. Family is extremely important. Never forget that, Antonio.'

Vinny Butler looked at his aunt as though she were stark raving mad. As stunned as he was, he still had the foresight to lead her outside the pub away from prying eyes. 'They've actually arrested him? You positive? When? Where is he?'

'I don't bloody know, do I? Sammi-Lou could barely string two words together she was so upset. Today, I should imagine, else the girl would've rung earlier. All she said was the police had arrested Little Vinny for murdering Molly and he needed a brief. Your mother's in shock, as you can well imagine. What the hell is going on, eh?'

'The tape,' Vinny mumbled, as initial shock wore off and the penny dropped. 'Don't worry. I'll sort it.'

'Tape! What tape?'

Instead of replying, Vinny left his aunt standing in the Whitechapel Road and sprinted towards his mother's house.

Queenie Butler felt as sick as a dog. Not knowing what else to do, she'd rung Sammi-Lou back. Gary Allen had answered and said the police reckoned they'd unearthed some new evidence.

Molly's murder had without a doubt been the most upsetting experience of Queenie's life. Losing Roy, Lenny, Adam, Brenda and her beloved mother came close, but Molly being taken the way she had topped the lot. At first they'd thought she'd been abducted and it had broken Queenie's heart when her body was finally found. Molly had been all on her own in a shallow grave for days, the poor little mite. She'd even been lying there dead while they filmed a TV appeal for her safe return.

'Vinny! You heard the news? It can't be true. Look at

what a good dad he is to his own kids. No way would he be capable of killing Molly. Never in a million years,' Queenie cried.

Vinny held his distraught mother in his arms. 'It's gonna be OK. I know what this new evidence is. Little Vinny told me about it ages ago. That bastard Ahmed tried to set him up. I'm gonna sort a brief now. Colin's on a cruise, but his sidekick'll get Little Vin out the nick. Jamie Preston killed Molly. A jury found him guilty. The Old Bill ain't got a leg to stand on.'

Vivian arrived back at Queenie's at the same time as Giovanni pulled up. 'Give your aunt a kiss and wish her Happy Christmas,' Giovanni ordered Antonio and Camila.

'Does Queenie know you're visiting?' Vivian asked, ignoring both children.

'No. Antonio wanted to surprise his father,' Giovanni said, following Vivian inside the house. He locked eyes with Vinny. The resemblance between father and son was clear to see. 'Say hello to your dad,' he urged his grandson.

When Antonio walked towards him with his hand outstretched, Vinny knew he had to get out the house. He'd had enough surprises for one day. 'Look, I'm sorry, but now isn't a good time. I've got to go out, but I'll be in touch soon,' he mumbled.

Giovanni could've cried for his grandson as Vinny grabbed his mobile phone and dashed from the house without as much as a backward glance. He knew exactly how Antonio must be feeling: abandoned.

DS Terry pushed the piece of paper towards Little Vinny. 'We know you killed your sister, so you might as well sign the confession now. A judge will be more lenient on you if you've cooperated with us, and he or she will take into account your age at the time. Go on, sign it. It'll wipe a few years off your sentence,' DS Terry urged.

Having always been instructed by his father to give an answer of 'No comment' if arrested, for once Little Vinny ignored that advice. It was awful, reliving the horrid mistake he'd once made, but he had his wife and kids to think about. They were his priority now and as much as he wished Molly was still alive, she wasn't. 'I ain't signing nothing. I know what all this is about, and I'm innocent. I loved my little sister, would never harm a hair on her head.'

DS Terry leaned forward, elbows on table, and locked eyes with Little Vinny. 'Tell me about Ben Bloggs. So you got him to help you, eh? That's why he killed himself, wasn't it? Unlike you, Ben couldn't live with the guilt of killing an innocent child. It was you that throttled Molly though, wasn't it?'

Little Vinny shook his head vehemently. 'You're talking shit. Ben killed himself because of his terrible home life. His mother was a whore and a druggie. Ben loved kids, virtually raised his brothers and sisters on his own. He also loved Molly. Ben wouldn't hurt a fly, let alone a nipper.'

DS Terry smirked. 'I get what you're saying, which makes me even more positive something terrible must've happened for Ben to take his own life. He wouldn't have wanted to leave his brothers and sisters to fend for themselves, would he now? My guess is you told Ben you were only taking Molly for a little adventure somewhere. I bet he was as shocked as anybody when you put your hands around that poor child's throat and throttled the life out of her. Am I right?'

'Wrong,' Little Vinny hissed.

'Well, I must be getting warm as all of a sudden you're looking decidedly clammy yourself, Vinny lad.'

'No I ain't. And I know what the evidence is. My dad knows all about it too because I told him as soon as I was set up. He'll tell my brief, then you'll know I am telling the truth, and you'll have to let me go. If I had anything to hide, I certainly wouldn't be talking to you until my brief arrived.'

'I know you killed Molly, son. And I'm determined to lock you up for a very long time, unless you play ball.'

'Jamie Preston killed Molly. You know that as well as I do. He even rang the Old Bill at the time to say he'd abducted her, and he kept all the newspaper cuttings. Your mob've always hated my family. That's why you're picking on me. You know I never touched Molly. You wanna lock me up 'cause my old man has always been one step ahead of ya.'

'DNA testing has come a long way in the last eleven years. Back when Molly was found, we had no way of knowing that Jamie Preston hadn't come into contact with your little sister.'

'I dunno what you're on about.'

Terry grinned. 'We were savvy enough to keep hold of her clothes, you see. One of the officers had their suspicions about your story at the time. I should imagine you must remember what Molly was wearing? Things like that tend to stick in your mind, so most child killers tell me. There's no match for Jamie Preston's DNA on any of the prime exhibits from your sister's case. But I'd put my house on it that your DNA's all over 'em. If I was you, I'd start talking before your brief arrives. Telling us the truth will go in your favour in the long run. Was it a moment of madness? Or was it an accident? Accidents do happen, I know that. Did you not mean to kill Molly?'

Knowing that it was probably time to shut his big mouth, Little Vinny kept talking. What was the alternative? He would rather focus on how he was going to word his answers than let his mind dwell on the sight of his petrified sister's eyes bulging out of her head as he'd strangled her.

Giovanni D'Angelo was annoyed. Vinny had talked the fatherly talk on the phone the previous day, but he certainly hadn't walked the fatherly walk.

After her son had bolted, Queenie had vaguely explained that something terrible had happened and Vinny needed to go to the police station to help his other son, who'd been arrested by mistake.

'Will we see Daddy soon? I need a wee-wee,' Camila said.

Giovanni sighed. He'd thought the element of surprise would work in his grandchildren's favour and could only hope that turning up at Katy's house unannounced wouldn't turn out to be another disaster. 'You OK, Antonio? Things will be different next time you meet your father, I promise.'

'I don't want to meet him again. I didn't like him.'

Giovanni ruffled his grandson's hair. 'But you have not had a chance to speak with him properly yet. I am sure once you do, you will like him.'

'No I won't. He didn't even shake my hand. I hated him. I want Michael to still be my dad.'

Katy Spencer had lived a daydream for years. She'd always convinced herself that one day Michael would be hers, which was why she'd taken cookery lessons with the mother of Nathan's best friend.

'This is nice, Katy. The parsnips are lovely and crispy, like my mum cooks 'em,' Michael lied. They were actually burnt and the dinner wasn't a patch on what he was used to, but he knew Katy had made a real effort today.

Katy beamed from ear to ear. Michael had slept in

Nathan's bed last night, but things were going so well between them she hoped tonight he would sleep in hers. She longed for his touch again. He was more than just an amazing man; Michael Butler was also an incredible lover.

'Someone's at the door!' Nathan grinned. This was his best Christmas ever, spending the whole day with his father.

'I'm not expecting anyone. Perhaps it's the boys arriving early?' Katy said happily. Seeing as she'd helped raise Dan and Lee as kids, she was looking forward to playing a surrogate mum to them again.

'Daddy!' Camila screamed, excitedly throwing herself at her father.

'Hello, Michael. I know the situation and am not here to cause trouble. The children were desperate to see you. They are missing you greatly.'

Katy stood behind Michael, smiling. 'Do come in. I will put the kettle on. Say hello to your little sister, Nathan. Go on, don't be shy,' she urged her son.

Antonio felt like a spare part. Michael hugged and kissed Cami, yet blanked him just like his real dad had. This was all his mother's fault and he hated her for it.

Gary and Meg Allen didn't know what to do for the best. Gary had rung a few local police stations to try and find out what was going on, but Little Vinny wasn't being held at any of them. 'I dunno where else to ring. Some Christmas this is turning out to be. You don't think he could've done it, do you?' Gary whispered to his wife.

'Don't be so stupid. You know how he loves children. Don't you dare let Sammi hear you say that. She'll never forgive you. Is she still in tears?'

'Yeah. So is Ollie. Millie's consoling both, bless her. She's been an angel today. The little 'uns don't seem to have clocked on, which is good. They're playing. I'm not being funny, Meg, but the police must have something concrete-ish to have carted our son-in-law off like they did. Don't jump down my throat – I'm not saying he's guilty. But he would've only been young around the time Molly died. Many a time, he's admitted he was a bad boy in his youth and meeting Sammi changed his life.'

'Being a bad boy does not equal murdering your own sister, Gal. We know he was a bloody tearaway. Remember the time he turned up at ours drunk that Christmas? That's the type of behaviour Little Vinny probably means when he talks about being a tearaway. He took a swipe at you an' all, if I remember rightly?'

'Yeah, he did. Oh well, what will be will be. But I'm telling you now, Meg, if they charge him, our lives are over round 'ere. Mud sticks, sweetheart, especially when a kiddie has been topped.'

DS Terry could've quite happily smashed the truth out of Little Vinny. Back in the old days, he'd probably have got away with it too, if all the tales he'd heard were true.

Terry had fully expected the cocky little bastard to have gone down the 'No comment' road and had been delighted when he hadn't. But he'd yet to slip up, which was annoying Terry immensely. Did he have no remorse whatsoever?

'Why don't we listen to the evidence then? Or shall we wait until my solicitor arrives?' Little Vinny asked brazenly. He kept forcing himself to think of his sons' innocent faces rather than Molly's. Every single time the police asked him a question, he pictured Ollie, Calum or Regan. It was the only way he could get through this. Those boys needed him and so did Sammi-Lou. As for his father and grand-mother, he could never allow them to know the truth. It would kill both, if they didn't kill him first.

'Listen to the evidence? How do you know there is

evidence to listen to? We could have anything on you. Even a witness,' Terry taunted.

Little Vinny wasn't stupid. If a witness had spotted him and Ben with Molly they would've come forward ages ago. As for his DNA, of course it would be all over Molly's clothing. Not only did he live with her at the time, he'd also supposedly been looking after her that day. 'As I've already told ya, I know what evidence you think you have. But you haven't got jack-shit as I was set up to say stuff. My dad and brief will explain all.'

About to interrogate the lad further, Terry was called outside the interview room. 'The cocky little bastard's father and brief are here. They know about the tape,' he was informed.

'Have you eaten, Antonio? Would you like me to make you a turkey sandwich?' Katy asked. Michael and Giovanni were chatting in another room, Nathan and Camila were playing nicely, and Katy could tell Antonio felt awkward.

'No thanks. I'm not hungry. Is it OK if I use the bathroom?' Antonio asked.

'Of course. It's the door in front of you at the end of the hallway.'

Antonio shut the lounge door. He could hear voices in another room and wanted to listen to what was going on.

'I know this is an awful situation, but Antonio is very fond of you. You're the only father he has ever known and none of this is his fault. He is a good boy, who you've raised for many years as your own,' Giovanni reminded Michael. 'Please, don't punish him.'

'I'm very sorry, Giovanni, but my decision is final. I need to move on with my own life, and Antonio being part of that will be a constant reminder of how your daughter has ruined me and ripped my family to shreds. Cami, I want to see as often as possible, but not Antonio. He's Vinny's baggage now, not mine.'

Antonio burst into the room, tears of pure hurt in his eyes. He threw his arms around Michael's waist. 'I don't want Vinny to be my dad. I want you to. I love you, Michael.'

Tears welling up in his own eyes, Michael gave the child one final hug. All he could feel were Vinny's son's arms around him, so quickly shrugged him off. 'I'm so sorry, Antonio, but this has to be goodbye. You're not my son, and never will be. You're my brother's, end of.'

Queenie could not remember a more terrible Christmas. Even when there had been a death in the family, the rest of her brood usually pulled together to make the most of it. But this year there truly was little else that could go wrong. Even Tara and Tommy had cadged a lift and sodded off back to Dagenham.

'Can I have some more potatoes, Nan? Destiny needs more turkey an' all. So does Fred,' Ava added.

'You've got hands, haven't you? Everything's in the kitchen. Help your bleedin' selves. No other bastard is going to eat it,' Queenie replied. She had been unable to swallow a morsel all day. Her stomach was in knots.

Vivian put her knife and fork down. 'I can't eat no more, Queen. Gonna go back to mine and have a lie down, see if I can get rid of this headache. I'll pop back later, see if there's any more news.'

Queenie looked at her sister in disbelief. 'You can't leave me, not with all this going on. Take some tablets, eh? You'll be OK.'

Vivian sighed. She'd been going to tell her sister that Michael had asked her to pop in to see Albie after the visit. Somebody was bound to recognize her and she didn't want another fall-out. She could hardly leave Queenie now though, could she? The visit would have to be put on hold until tomorrow.

DS Terry sat opposite Vinny Butler and the brief. Darren Fitzgerald was the protégé of Vinny Senior's solicitor and both were insistent on Vinny making a statement before the solicitor was allowed contact with his son.

'Fire away then,' Terry ordered.

'I take it you've got your hands on a taped confession where my son admits to killing his sister?' Vinny asked. He knew it couldn't be anything else. It was madness to even think his son was capable of killing Molly, let alone arrest him on Christmas Day.

'You wanted to make a statement, so make one. I'll answer your questions afterwards,' Terry ordered.

'OK. I know you are in possession of a tape where my son admits to killing his sister. Little Vinny was set up by somebody I thought was my friend. He actually had a gun held to his head while recording what you think is evidence. He told me straight away afterwards and I went looking for the bastard who had put him through such an ordeal. My so-called friend must have realized I was on to him though and had disappeared. My guess is he returned to Turkey with a false passport. Ahmed Zane is the man you're looking for. Find him and I guarantee he'll admit the truth. He won't want me knowing where he is, that's for sure. I'll kill him if I ever get my hands on him,' Vinny bluffed. He knew Ahmed and Burak had been properly disposed of as Eddie Mitchell had sorted that side of things. However, he still didn't want to open another can of worms.

Terry stared defiantly at Vinny Butler. 'Let's listen to the tape then, shall we? Only in my humble opinion, if your son was being held under duress while it was recorded, then I'm Inspector Clouseau.'

With Nathan tucked up in bed, Katy poured herself and Michael another drink, then sat next to her man on the sofa. He'd been a bit quiet since Giovanni had visited, but it had still been the best Christmas ever. 'Shall we watch a film? If there's nothing watchable on TV, I have lots of videos,' Katy suggested.

Michael yawned. 'I'm wiped, to be honest. That stressed me out, Giovanni turning up with the kids earlier. Cami cried as she left and I shouldn't have said what I did to Antonio, but I can't help the way I feel. Every time I look at him now I picture Bella and Vinny having sex.'

The mention of the word 'sex' made Katy's clitoris tingle like never before. It had been so long, but she was glad she'd waited for Michael. 'Let's go to bed,' she whispered, before leaning in for a kiss.

Michael pulled away the moment Katy's tongue connected with his. Nevertheless, he still allowed her to lead him up the stairs and into her bed. There was no kissing, foreplay or warmth in the cold-blooded shag that followed. All Michael could think about was Bella as he lifelessly pumped away. Katy was all about revenge for him, not love.

CHAPTER TWENTY-SEVEN

Queenie Butler was awoken early Boxing Day morning by the sound of the front door opening then closing. She put on her dressing gown and ran down the stairs. 'Well? Have they let him go?'

Vinny Butler shook his head in despair. 'He's still being held, but they can't question him for that much longer, not without a court order. I wish Colin wasn't on fucking holiday. He would've sorted this crap by now.'

'Bloody scandalous. Poor little sod must be terrified. What evidence have they supposedly got?'

Explaining that Ahmed had forced his son to record a confession which Little Vinny had then told him all about, Vinny put his head in his hands. 'I couldn't listen to it all, Mum. Made a right mug of meself when I ran out the room, crying. It was like reliving Molly's death all over again. I couldn't handle it.'

'That's natural, boy. I'd have done the same. So how comes the filth have suddenly got their dirty paws all over this? You sure Ahmed's definitely dead?'

'Of course I am. Dead as a dodo. The Old Bill wouldn't say how they came across it, but it's obvious the bastard kept a copy and some undesirable got their hands on it.'

'I told you never to trust that Turk from day one, didn't I? It's all in the eyes, and his were more than shifty. What I can't understand is why he would make Little Vinny do something like that? Was it solely to get at you?'

'Ahmed planned to play me the confession on my deathbed. He told me that much before I ended his sorry existence. You were right, I was wrong, but I can do without the "I told you, son"s right now, Mother, thanks very much.'

'Sorry. So I take it you told the Old Bill you knew about the confession and it was forced?'

Vinny put his head in his hands. 'That's the fucking problem; it doesn't exactly sound like a forced confession. If I didn't know my own son better, I'd say it was real. Well, the bit I listened to sounded genuine anyway. Obviously it isn't, but Darren listened to the whole lot and said the same. That's why they're still holding him. They reckon it will stand up in court.'

'That's the most ridiculous thing I've ever heard. Have they forgotten they locked Jamie Preston up?'

'That's another problem. They kept Molly's clothing and there was no DNA match to Preston.'

'Bastard must've worn gloves.'

'Yeah, and Little Vinny was pissed when Ahmed forced him to confess. I only listened to about twenty seconds, but he sounded out of his nut. I know Ahmed had plied him with drink and drugs 'cause he told me. I forgot to tell the Old Bill that bit though. My head was all over the place, to be honest. I can't believe this is happening.'

Queenie lifted Vinny's chin. 'Keep your head up, boy. Little Vinny is gonna be fine, I can feel it in my bones. It's absurd to even suggest he was capable of killing his own sister, and the filth know that. They've only dragged him in to get at you. He'll be released later today without charge, I'd put my house on that.'

'I fucking hope so, Mum. I really do. Be the end of me if they charge him. Be the end of us all.'

Daniel Butler opened his eyes and groaned. Lauren might be old enough to be his mother, but she gave a damn good blow-job. He'd never been with a bird that solely wanted to concentrate on his cock before. She'd even snorted her cocaine off of it.

Orgasm done and dusted, Daniel sat up. His head felt heavy, as though it wouldn't rest on his shoulders alone. Yesterday had been a mad one to say the very least. He and Lee were still half-pissed from Christmas Eve when they'd gone on a lunchtime pub crawl and met Lauren and her sister. The women had spent the morning visiting their dying mother in a care home and it had been Lauren's idea to get totally obliterated. She'd had the cocaine on her. 'Whereabouts are we?' Daniel mumbled. He remembered getting in a cab back to Lauren's, but didn't have a clue what area it had taken them to.

'Epping, and your brother's fine, before you ask. My sister is taking good care of him,' Lauren smiled, fondling Daniel's penis once again. She and her sister liked a toy boy. Why wake up with some beer-bellied middle-aged man when you could pull a young stallion?

'Me stomach feels like me throat's been cut,' Daniel muttered. Dinner had gone out the window once Lauren produced her big bag of gear yesterday and he hadn't eaten properly since Christmas Eve.

Lauren leapt out of bed. 'Zoe and I will cook you and Lee a nice fry-up. You're not in a rush to go anywhere, are you? There's plenty more champagne in the fridge and cocaine in my closet,' she chuckled.

Daniel grinned. Usually when he woke up after a heavy night with a stranger he couldn't wait to get away, but

Lauren was pretty for her age and had a very fit body and big tits. She was obviously also loaded. He remembered being extremely impressed by the cars on the drive and the gaff when he'd arrived. 'Nah. Me and Lee ain't gotta rush off, babe.'

As soon as Lauren vacated her bedroom, Lee entered and reminded his brother that they were meant to be going to Kent to meet Nathan and see their father.

'Look at the state of the pair of us. We can't go anywhere like this. Was Zoe a good shag, bruv?' Daniel enquired.

'Her sis was. Probably the best I've had,' he bragged.

Lee grinned. 'Same 'ere. Zoe couldn't get enough of me.'

'Snap. Which is why today we're staying put. Never look a gift horse in the mouth, Lee. They've got plenty more gear and bubbly, so Lauren reckons. Fuck Dad. He didn't even bother ringing us yesterday. As for Nathan, we can meet him some other time.'

Lee shrugged. 'It's your call.'

As far as Vinny Butler was aware, nobody but those closest to him and the Old Bill knew his son had been arrested, so he was shocked when he answered his phone to a number he did not recognize and Eddie Mitchell was on the line calling from prison.

'How you doing, pal? Long time no hear from. I thought you'd forgotten I existed,' Vinny quipped, trying his hardest to sound jovial.

'I'm OK. Went out clubbing last night. You got a pen handy?' Eddie joked back.

Vinny grabbed one. 'Yeah. Why? What's up?'

'I know about Little Vinny. Do yourself a favour and use my brief. His name's Larry Peters and this is his number,' Eddie said, reciting it. 'Sack that Darren, he ain't no good. My man'll have your boy out the nick in no time.'

349

Startled, Vinny replied, 'How d'ya know? He's innocent, of course.'

'I know that, you muppet. I wouldn't be offering to help if I thought any different. I've already spoken to Lal. It'll cost you, but he seriously is different gravy and he's expecting your call.'

'But who told ya?' Vinny asked again.

'I'm Eddie Mitchell, Vin. Not a lot passes me by, even in this dump. Get on the blower to Lal now, eh? I'll bell you again tomorrow. Laters,' Eddie said, hanging up the phone.

Vinny's hands shook as he dialled Larry Peters' number. If a banged-up Eddie knew of his son's arrest, who the hell else knew?

Bella D'Angelo was fuming. Her father had no right to have taken her kids to see Vinny and Michael without her permission. But it was Michael's reaction to Antonio that had upset her the most. She'd thought more of him as a man than to take his bitterness out on a ten-year-old child. 'You are seriously out of order, Papa. They are my children and I will decide if and when they see their father or Vinny,' Bella screamed. She found it extremely difficult to refer to Vinny as Antonio's father, always would.

'I am sorry you feel that way, but I was only trying to help. You chose not to spend the day with your children and they were very sad.'

'I needed to be alone. Was taking your advice and working out how I was going to sort my life out. That's going to be even more difficult now though, thanks to your meddling,' Bella replied sourly. Antonio hadn't even looked at her on arrival. He'd blanked her and gone straight to his room.

'Why don't I take us all out for lunch?' Giovanni

suggested. He did feel guilty, and sorry for Antonio. The child had barely uttered a word all morning, apart from demanding to be driven back home.

Bella opened the front door. 'This is my mess, Papa, so I will be the one to mop it up. Ciao.'

Vinny Butler was on the phone doing his best to reassure Sammi-Lou that all was going to be fine when his daughter yelled, 'Dad, there's a woman outside who wants to speak to you.'

'Sammi, I've gotta go. But please don't make your way to the police station. It'll only complicate matters. He'll be home later today, honest,' Vinny promised, before ending the phone conversation. Gary Allen had insisted on knowing the ins and outs of a maggot's arse and Vinny had needed a chat with him today as much as he needed a leg chopped off.

'Who're you? And what d'ya want?' Vinny asked. The woman was visibly upset. 'Only it's Boxing Day if you hadn't realized,' he added sarcastically.

'I'm Richie's wife. My mum's looking after the kids,' the woman wept.

'Richie who?'

'Woods. Look, I know he was doing a job for you on the inside, Vinny, and you must've heard what happened to him. Can we talk somewhere more private?'

'Wait by my car. I'll get the keys,' Vinny hissed. 'You been earwigging?' he yelled at his daughter, as the door opened and hit her.

'No. I was straightening Nan's mat,' Ava lied. She'd actually heard every word and wondered who Richie Woods was. Her dad was a legend round this neck of the woods, she knew that much. Even the older kids at school treated her with the utmost respect, and Ava had decided long ago that being Vinny Butler's daughter was a good thing, not bad. 'Where you going?' she asked nosily.

'Out. Tell Nan I'll ring her later.'

Vinny gestured for Richie's wife to get in the passenger seat. He then drove the car in silence. It was hardly his fault her useless husband had allowed Preston to get the better of him, was it? Word had it, Preston had now left hospital and been shipped out to Long Lartin, a category-A prison in the West Midlands. He'd also heard a rumour that Shirley Preston had croaked it, but that was yet to be confirmed.

'Where you taking me?' Kaz asked, a hint of anxiousness in her voice.

Vinny didn't reply until he'd stopped the car behind a building. The area was desolate today, as he'd known it would be. 'What is it you want? Money? Only it ain't my fault if your old man couldn't hold his own, is it?'

'Apart from the money your blokes brought round, which I've already spent on bills and presents for the kids, I don't have a bean,' Kaz sobbed. 'My Richie died helping you. Surely you owe me and the kids something?' she added bravely.

Vinny turned to face Kaz and treated her to one of his most penetrating glares. 'Your Richie actually died trying to help you, sweetheart, not me. He felt guilty knowing you were struggling and begged me for a bit of work to take the onus off you. Perhaps you shouldn't have kept nagging and telling him how tough you were having it, eh? How did you expect him to earn dosh in a prison? However, I ain't a total ogre. So I'll get one of the lads to drop by in the next day or two with a couple of grand condolence dosh. That's the end of any debt you think I owe, and in return for my generosity I expect you to keep your trap shut about my involvement in all of this. OK?'

Kaz nodded. She'd been hoping for at least five grand, but a couple was better than nothing.

'Oh, and another thing: you ever betray me or turn up at my mother's gaff like that again, I will set your house on fire with you inside it. Now, do we understand one another?'

'Yes. I can walk home from here. Thanks,' Kaz mumbled, scrambling to open the car door. She'd never had any personal dealings with Vinny Butler in the past and seriously could not get away from him quick enough. The rumours about him were definitely right. The man was a psychopath.

DS Terry was in a foul mood. Darren Fitzgerald had supposedly gone down with a sickness bug (which the whole station knew was a load of old codswallop) and Larry Peters had been drafted in as a replacement.

There wasn't a copper in the country who didn't dread the news that Larry Peters was getting involved in an arrest. He'd always been a mastermind at getting clients off on technicalities, and his reputation had risen sky-high when he got Eddie Mitchell off both murder and manslaughter for killing his wife. Terry guessed Mitchell was the one who'd instigated the swap in briefs, even from his cell. It was common knowledge among the authorities that Vinny Butler and Eddie Mitchell were pals, although Butler was yet to visit Mitchell in prison by all accounts.

After another fruitless couple of hours questioning Little Vinny, who now had Peters sitting next to him and would only reply 'No comment', Terry was called out of the room and told his boss needed to speak to him.

Knowing that Little Vinny was lying through his teeth, Terry entered his boss's office full of optimism. 'He hasn't folded yet, but he will if we keep him here.'

'He's not going to fold and you know that as well as I do, Terry. The lad's a Butler, for fuck's sake. The tape will be deemed inadmissible, especially with his father having known about it and given a statement.'

'But he's guilty. I know he is,' Terry argued.

'And Jamie Preston has now killed a man inside. How do you think that's going to look in a court of law?'

'Not great. But I intend to get Little Vinny to spill his guts anyway.'

'Listen to me carefully, Terry. I've had a long, hard think about the evidence we have and the position we're in and I've come to the conclusion that some stones are best left unturned. The press would have a field day if they even got a sniff we've made a cock-up and locked up the wrong bloke. Both you and I worked on Molly's case originally. Do you want to be demoted and end up with egg all over your fucking face? Because I sure don't. There'd be a lot of heads on the chopping block if this got out, you get my drift?'

'I know what you're saying, boss, but Preston never killed Molly Butler. I'd put my house on that.'

'And if you lose your job you won't have a fucking house. Whether Preston is guilty or not, he's no good. If he hadn't stabbed a bloke to death a few days ago, you can guarantee he'd have been out soon, terrorizing Essex and flogging drugs with his old cellmate, Glen Harper. Do you seriously think a man like that is worth risking all you've worked for, Terry?'

Digesting the underlying threat, DS Terry defeatedly shook his head. 'No, boss.'

Bella D'Angelo tapped on her son's bedroom door. Cami thankfully seemed happier now, and was downstairs watching *Home Alone* for the tenth time. 'Can I come in, please?' Bella asked, her tone gentle.

'Whatever.'

Bella entered the bedroom. Antonio was lying under his duvet with his back towards the door. She sat on the edge of his bed and put the tray on the floor. 'I made you some sandwiches and a chocolate milkshake.'

'I'm not hungry.'

Bella stroked her son's hair. 'You have to eat, otherwise you will become ill. Look at me, please. We need to talk.'

Antonio propped himself against a pillow, arms folded and a sullen expression on his face.

'I know you hate me at the moment, but I want you to know that I love you very much and will do anything I can to make you happy again. Tell me what will cheer you up and Mummy will sort it.'

Antonio shrugged.

'How about we invite Edward for a sleepover?'

'I don't think Edward wants to be my friend any more.'

'Why do you say that?'

'Because I told him Michael left us. Then I rang him again earlier and his mum said he is busy for the rest of the holiday. It's because of you, I know it is. I'm not going back to that school because everybody will know what you did.'

'You don't have to go back there. We can choose another school and you can start afresh. Would you like me to call Vinny and make some kind of arrangement for you to meet him properly?'

'No.'

'Why not?'

'Because I don't like him.'

'Why don't you come downstairs and watch *Home Alone* with me and Cami? You love that film, don't you?'

'I don't want to watch it again.'

Bella stroked her son's cheek. 'You tell me what I can do to make you happy then.'

Pushing his mother's hand away, Antonio yelled, 'Go away and leave me alone. That will make me happy.'

Michael Butler was in an agitated mood. He couldn't get hold of Daniel or Lee, and Katy's lovesick behaviour and constant fussing over his every need was beginning to drive him insane.

'I fancy a bit of fresh air. I'm gonna take a wander down the pub. I won't be long,' he told her.

After waiting so many years to finally get him in her clutches, Katy wasn't going to let Michael out of her sight that easily. 'Nathan and I will come with you. The pub on the green is child-friendly.'

'Nah, you stay put, babe. I spotted a bookies as I drove 'ere the other day, so I'm going in there first.'

'I didn't know you gambled,' Katy questioned.

'I don't as a rule. But I fancy putting a bet on the football today. I'll only be a couple of hours tops, and if the boys turn up in the meantime, bell me and I'll come straight home. Got a feeling they ain't coming now though. Probably out on the lash somewhere.'

Last night's lovemaking hadn't been a patch on what Katy recalled in the past. But Michael's penis had been back inside her where it belonged and that's all that mattered. 'You've not changed your mind about Bella, have you? Only I'd rather you be straight with me than sneak about to phone or visit her.'

'Give me a break will ya, Katy? I won't be getting back with Bella, ever. I just need a bit of space, OK?'

'What time are my brothers coming, Dad?' Nathan shouted out.

'I dunno, boy. They might not be able to make it today after all, but you will meet 'em real soon, I promise.'

As soon as Michael left the house, Katy told her son the

exciting news. 'Mummy and Daddy are back together and we're all going to live happily ever after now.'

'Are you getting married?' Nathan asked innocently.

Katy chuckled. 'Not yet, but perhaps one day. When your dad comes back I want you to tell him how happy you are we're back together and that you love having him living here. You mustn't let him know I told you to say it though. Shall we have a practice? You say it in your own words. Pretend I'm your dad.'

Nathan nodded. 'Dad, I am so happy you and Mummy are back together and I love you living here with me.'

Katy grinned and hugged her son. 'You're such a clever boy. That's perfect.'

Vinny Butler stuffed five grand in the envelope, rather than the two he'd promised Kaz. Richie Woods might have been a bit of a dick, but he was trustworthy and Vinny felt a tad guilty for scaring his old woman. He'd needed to ensure her silence though. If Glen Harper found out that he was behind Preston's torment, Vinny could foresee trouble ahead and another gangland war was the last thing he needed at present.

He was about to drop the money off with Carl when Larry Peters phoned him.

Vinny Butler felt relief flow through his veins as he was told the good news. 'Thanks so much, Lal. I'm on my way there now.'

Queenie Butler turned to her sister. 'That was Vinny. Little Vinny's being released without charge. I should bastard-well think so too. Must have been to hell and back, stuck in that nick having to go over his sister's death again. I need to make some calls. We don't want nobody knowing about this. You know what they're like round 'ere with their "No smoke without fire" comments. I'll ring Sammi-Lou first, then I need to get hold of Tara and Tommy, make sure they keep their traps firmly shut.'

'I'm gonna pop back to mine for a bit, Queen. Something I need to do. Great news they're letting him go. I'll be back in an hour or two.'

'What you gotta bleedin' do?'

Vivian put her coat on. 'A favour I promised. You make your calls and I'll explain all later.'

Sammi-Lou knelt on the carpet and hugged her boys. 'Daddy's coming home soon,' she informed them, tears of relief in her eyes.

'Will he play my mouse game with me, Mum?' Regan asked.

'Of course he will.'

'Will Dad be home in time to read me a bedtime story?' Calum enquired.

'Yes, he will, darling,' Sammi grinned. It had been an awful Christmas, but they'd make up for that over the next few days.

Understanding the situation a bit more than his brothers, Oliver looked worried. 'Will the police come back and take Dad away again?'

Gary Allen picked his eldest grandson up. 'Of course they won't. Your dad's done nothing wrong.'

Meg Allen smiled. 'You'd better ring Finn, Sammi, let him know.' Little Vinny's business partner had been sick of sitting around doing nothing and had left about half an hour ago to drive up to Bow Police Station.

Gary poured himself a large rum and took it into the kitchen. Meg followed him out there. 'What a relief. I never doubted he was innocent, mind.'

Pulling his wife into his arms, Gary rested her head on

his shoulder. 'Been a terrible Christmas, eh? We'll wait until Little Vinny gets home, then make a move. He must be shattered and I doubt he'll be in the mood for company. I'm gonna pray tonight that's the end of the matter for all our fucking sakes. Smoke, fire – I'll say no more.'

Little Vinny was rocking to and fro in his cell when it was finally unlocked. He'd had no sleep last night. Every time he'd shut his eyes Molly had haunted his thoughts, so he'd forced himself to stay awake.

'You're free to go,' an officer said.

Little Vinny felt like crying, but instead replied boldly, 'I should think so too. Where's Terry? Hiding?'

'No. I'm here. Wanna sign for your belongings, mouth almighty? Daddy is waiting for you in reception.'

Little Vinny glared at Terry. 'Don't be taking the piss out of me. You should be apologizing, you prick.'

Gesturing for the other officer to walk away, Terry grabbed Little Vinny by the throat and pushed him against the wall. He tightened his grip, but was careful not to mark the lad. 'This is how your sister must've felt when you put your hands around her throat, you evil piece of shit. I was on duty the day she was found, you know, and I will never forget the sight of her lifeless little body being dug out that shallow grave. One day you will pay for your sins, because I'm making it my mission in life to get justice for Molly and send you down. Watch your back, child killer.'

Now fully on the road to recovery, Albie Butler was propped up against his pillow watching the black-and-white portable TV Big Stan had kindly lent him.

'Hello, Albie. How are you?'

Albie's eyes lit up. 'Hello, Vivvy. What you doing up 'ere, love? You visiting someone?'

'Yes. You, you silly old sod. Now I thought you might be peckish, so I've made you some sandwiches. You've got beef and horseradish – which I know is your favourite – cheese and pickle, and ham. I wrapped up some cherry tomatoes in foil for you an' all, plus a couple of pork pies if you're allowed 'em.'

Albie grinned from ear to ear. 'Me mouth's watering already. Food in 'ere ain't much cop, but they do try their best. The nurses are nice. They gave us party hats, crackers and all sorts yesterday. Irish Mary's a right case. Always on a wind-up she is, but she ain't working today. Sneaked me home-made mince pies in last night, bless her.'

'You had many visitors?' Vivian asked.

'Big Stan's been to see me. He brought that telly in this morning. Daniel and Lee popped in yesterday, but only stayed about quarter of an hour. Hungover, the pair of 'em were. I told 'em to go and get hair of the dog. Oh to be young again, eh, Viv?'

Vivian squeezed Albie's hand. 'You'll never be old, you, Albie Butler. Always been able to charm the birds out the trees, and now the bleedin' nurses. I dunno what we're gonna do with you,' she tutted.

Albie winked. 'It's so good to see you, Viv. I've missed our little chats. Does Queenie know you're here?'

'No. But I shall tell her when I get back. It'll cause World War Three if I don't and some other bastard does. I've missed our chats too, and I'm sorry I didn't believe you over that turnout at Little Vinny's wedding. I suppose I felt it was my duty to side with Queenie. You know what she's like when she gets a bee in her bonnet.'

'Don't I just! Never mind, we're friends again now and that's all that matters.'

*

Tainted Love

Vinny Butler thanked Larry Peters and shook hands with him, then ruffled the back of his son's hair. 'It's all over now. You OK?'

Little Vinny's eyes welled up. He had no idea how he'd got through the ordeal, and Terry's parting words had sent shivers down his spine. He definitely knew the truth and somebody else knowing his terrible secret was enough to put the fear of God inside Little Vinny. The fact he was a copper made it even worse.

'We'll shoot round your nan's before I drop you home. You'll feel better once you get a bit of grub inside ya. A brandy or two won't do you any harm either,' Vinny said.

'I don't wanna go to Nan's. Take me straight home, Dad.'

'We won't stay long. Your nan's been ever so worried about ya, so I promised we'd pop our heads in.'

Unable to keep up an act any longer, Little Vinny broke down in tears. 'Best you fucking unpromise her then. Did you not hear what I said? I want to go home,' he screamed.

Back at the hospital, Albie and Viv hadn't stopped laughing. Old Jack in the bed opposite had got involved in a heated immigration discussion with Derrick, the elderly black man in the next bed, and the nurses had been forced to intervene to calm the situation down.

'Like watching *Love Thy Neighbour* that was, Albie. I ain't laughed so much in ages. I thought Jack was gonna have a heart attack when Derrick called him a "white pussy".'

'In all fairness to Derrick, Jack had referred to him as a "spear thrower".'

Vivian laughed. 'They both gave as good as they got and there was no real harm meant. Remember what we used to sing as kids? "Sticks and stones may break my bones, but names will never hurt me." So bleedin' true that, Albie.

361

Country's gone downhill since the do-gooders made us mind our P's and Q's. I mean, what a load of old shit on TV these days. They deem anything decent as racist or sexist. I used to love me *Wheeltappers and Shunters*. Poor old Bernard Manning wouldn't even be allowed to crack a decent joke in this day and age.'

'The BBC needs a bit of Jimmy Jones to liven it up,' Albie said, referring to the X-rated comedian. 'As for me, a swig of brandy would do,' he joked.

Vivian delved inside her handbag and tucked a miniature bottle under Albie's bed covers. 'I knew you would be gasping for a brandy, so I came fully prepared.'

Albie couldn't wipe the smile off his face. 'You're a legend, Vivian Harris. Anyone ever tell you that?'

'Only you, you daft old so-and-so. Now drink that quickly before the nurses catch ya with it. I'll take the empty bottle away with me.'

Bella was loading the dishwasher when the phone rang. 'Answer that for me, Cami,' she yelled.

Her daughter skipped into the kitchen. 'A man wants to speak to you, Mum.'

'Hello,' Bella answered.

'Hi, Bella. It's Vinny. How are you?'

'What a stupid question. How the hell do you think I am?'

'Look, I haven't rung to cause trouble. You aren't the only one who has lost Michael's love and respect. He hates me too, if it makes you feel any better. I just spoke to your father and he said Antonio was now at home. I want to apologize to him for my behaviour yesterday. I couldn't talk to him because Little Vinny had been arrested and I needed to get to the police station. That's all sorted now, and I was wondering, if it's OK with you, could I spend some time with Antonio in the next few days? Obviously, he barely knows me so I thought perhaps I could take him for lunch to start with? You and Camila are welcome to join us if you wish.'

'I would rather starve than be seen out in public with you,' Bella spat, as she ran up the stairs. She tapped on Antonio's bedroom door. 'Vinny is on the phone. He wishes to speak with you.'

'I don't want to talk to him.'

Bella barged into the room and handed her son the phone. 'Then tell him that yourself. Only he will keep ringing back otherwise and I don't want to talk to him either.'

'You'll never guess what,' Queenie said, when her sister let herself in.

'What?' Vivian asked. Queenie sounded happy, which was a good thing, seeing as she'd been expecting a rollicking for disappearing for three hours.

'The rumours about Shirley Preston only turned out to be bloody true. Nosy Hilda knocked earlier. She knows somebody who lives opposite Shirley. Turns out someone went round to tell her Jamie stabbed that bloke to death in prison and Shirley croaked it on the spot. Talk about God pays debts without money. Must've been the shock of finding out her evil grandson was actually a killer after all that finished her off. Serves her right for insulting Molly's memory by insisting he was innocent all these years. He'll never get out now. Be locked up for life.'

Vivian didn't like Shirley Preston, but admired her unwavering loyalty. Queenie would've done exactly the same thing had Little Vinny committed a murder. She would've proclaimed his innocence until the cows came home, like she always had with his father.

'Aren't you pleased? She can rot in hell as far as I'm concerned.'

'Yeah, course. Listen, I've been to visit Albie – and before you go into one, I did it for your Michael. That was the favour I mentioned earlier. Michael was extremely worried that his father wouldn't have any visitors over Christmas and pleaded with me to pop in and see him.'

Queenie looked at the clock. 'You've been gone over three hours. You didn't spend all that time with the old goat, did ya?'

'Of course not. I had a lie down to get rid of me head-ache first. It's gone now, thankfully,' Vivian lied.

'So how is the womanizing old wanker? Still breathing, obviously.'

'Seems to be doing OK. I didn't stay long. Took him a couple of sandwiches in and had a quick chat, that was it. I rang Michael to let him know and he was ever so pleased. That's the main thing, eh? Got enough on his plate, that boy. I said I'd pop up there again if he needed me to. I think it put his mind at rest.'

'They'll be calling you Saint Viv next. Oh well, let's hope Albie chokes to death on his sandwiches,' Queenie cackled.

'Fancy a sherry?' Vivian asked, conveniently changing the subject.

'I should coco. We can toast the witch's death.'

Vivian smiled as she turned her back on her sister. She'd got away with visiting Albie. Which was just as well, as she'd promised to go and see him again tomorrow.

Little Vinny managed to hold it together in front of Gary, Meg and Millie, but once the front door shut behind them he could barely look Sammi and Finn in the eye, let alone speak about his arrest.

'Leave your dad alone now, boys. Go upstairs and play in your bedrooms,' Sammi ordered. She'd never seen Little

Vinny look so ill. His skin was a deathly white colour and he had the shakes.

'Don't wanna play upstairs. Wanna play with Daddy,' Calum sulked.

Regan lay on the floor having a tantrum. 'Play with me, Daddy,' he screamed.

'Shall I go?' Finn asked awkwardly.

Feeling a watery sensation reach the back of his throat, Little Vinny ran from the room.

Michael Butler turned the lamp out. He'd been reading Nathan a bedtime story until his eyes drooped. 'Na-night, boy,' he whispered, kissing his son on the forehead.

With a heavy heart, Michael made his way down the stairs. This was the part of the day he dreaded the most, him and Katy all alone. No way was he sleeping with her again tonight. Last night had been a sympathy/revenge fuck. Nothing more, nothing less.

'I've opened us a bottle of wine, Michael, and put some nibbles out. Turn the lights out. I've lit the candles for us. Much more romantic.'

'We need to talk,' Michael said bluntly.

Katy felt her heart lurch. Surely he wasn't going to leave her and Nathan already? 'About what?'

Michael sat on the armchair opposite Katy. 'Us. This is all a bit too much too soon for me. You gotta remember I was with Bella a lot of years and what has happened has mashed my head up.'

Katy's eyes welled up. She knew what was coming next. 'You're going back to London or Essex, aren't you?'

'No. I'm happy to chill here for a while with you and Nathan, but I don't wanna rush into another relationship. When I came back from the boozer earlier, Nath said how happy he was we were back together. He obviously heard us at it last night and I don't wanna confuse him in case me and you don't work out.'

'Nathan couldn't have heard. We barely did anything,' Katy reminded Michael.

'Well he must have clocked I stayed in your room then, to say what he did. I just want to take things slowly, Katy. Who knows what the future might hold, but right now I'm not ready to be with anyone.'

'But you are going to stay here?'

'If you don't mind? I thought we'd go shopping tomorrow. I'll treat you and Nath to some goodies, and while we're out I'll buy a bed for the spare room. It ain't that I don't fancy you, Katy. You're a beautiful-looking bird. It's just, after everything that's happened, I don't feel ready to be intimate and I don't wanna be a roll-on roll-off merchant like I was last night. You deserve better than that.'

Katy forced a smile. She craved Michael's touch more than life itself at times, but she'd just have to continue wearing the batteries out on her vibrator until he was ready. At least he wanted to stay with her and Nathan, that was the main thing. 'I understand and I'm sorry if I've come across as a bit needy. I've never told you this before, but since you dumped me all those years ago, I've never been with another man. Perhaps that's why I seem like such a desperate saddo?'

'You're no desperate saddo, babe. Unlike that slag of an ex of mine, you're a decent girl who has put our son first. You've got good morals and I truly admire you for that.'

Katy grinned broadly. 'Come and sit next to me and drink your wine. I won't leap on you, honest. Let's watch a film together.'

Michael winked. 'Only if you let me choose the film. None of that slushy shit. Gangsters and guns all day long for me, girl.'

*

Bella D'Angelo picked her phone up and punched in the number her father had given her. She had to have it out with him, tell him his fortune. There was no going back now, not after the way he'd treated Antonio.

'Katy, it's Bella. Could I speak with Michael briefly, please?'

'Erm, hang on while I ask him if he wants to speak to you,' Katy replied coldly, mouthing the word 'Bella' to Michael.

'Pause the film, babe,' Michael said loudly. He was glad she'd phoned. It gave him an opportunity to hurt her like she'd hurt him. His heart was beating wildly as he took the phone out of Katy's hands. 'Pour us both another drink an' all, girl,' he added, knowing full well Bella could hear every word.

Michael walked into the kitchen and casually said, 'All right? Whaddya want? Only if it's about seeing Cami, I was gonna bell you tomorrow to make some arrangement.'

'Pause the film, babe. Pour us another drink, girl,' Bella repeated in a mocking tone. 'Couldn't you have demanded your orders to Katy in a softer tone? No, of course you couldn't, and the reason being because I was meant to hear them. What a sad, childish man you've turned out to be, Michael Butler. To take your hatred of me out on a ten-year-old boy who has idolized you all his life is something I thought you of all people would never be capable of. It's despicable, and you have scarred Antonio for life, so I do hope you're fucking proud of yourself. You make me sick to the stomach – Katy is more than welcome to you.'

Michael was shell-shocked. He'd fully expected Bella to be remorseful at the very least. 'What was I meant to say to him? The boy ain't my son, is he?'

'No. And do you know what, I am glad he isn't. I never thought I would hear myself say this, but I truly thank

God now that Antonio is Vinny's because he is twice the man you will ever be. In more ways than one.'

Bella's cruel words, especially regarding Vinny, felt like a dagger being prodded deep inside his heart. 'You cunt,' he yelled.

Katy ran into the kitchen. 'Whatever's wrong?'

Michael did not reply. He was far too busy smashing the phone into tiny pieces.

Vinny Butler took a deep breath before plucking up the courage to answer. Michael had been continuously phoning him for the past ten minutes and Vinny had needed to work out what to say for the best first.

'Before you say anything, bruv, I want you to know I ain't angry with you for what you did. I should've told ya, and I fully understand how—'

Michael's loud, sarcastic laughter stopped Vinny from continuing his pre-planned apology. 'You're a fucking nutjob, you. Need sectioning, you cunt. Now you listen to me and listen very carefully. If you ever come within a mile radius of me or any of my kids, I swear I will gouge your eyes out and ram 'em straight down the back of your throat. As for you and Bella, you can fuck one another senseless until the cows come home for all I care, but you never have contact with Camila, understand? If you defy me, I swear I will kill you.'

'Michael, calm down. I'm sorry, OK? Please let's try and sort this – we're brothers, for fuck's sake. I don't want Bella, never did,' Vinny lied.

'We were brothers, Vinny, but we ain't any more. This is the end of us and the end of the Butlers. It's over. Finito.'

PART THREE

What greater punishment is there than life
When you've lost everything that made it worthwhile?
                                                    Anon

CHAPTER TWENTY-EIGHT

Winter 2001

Michael and Lee Butler were in high spirits as they made the journey to Wandsworth Prison. Daniel was being released today after serving eighteen months for GBH and they'd laid a surprise party on for him later.

'You don't reckon that Raj's mates would have the front to turn up later, d'ya?' Michael asked Lee. Raj was the reason for his son's imprisonment. A local drug dealer/gang leader, the boys had told him many a time if they caught him dealing at the club he'd be barred. One evening it had all kicked off and Daniel had done Raj with a baseball bat. His sentence could've been longer had the jury believed Raj's brief, who insisted the attack was racially motivated.

'Nah. They've kept well away since Raj got banged up himself. Older and wiser now, I should imagine. Some of 'em have probably been marched up the aisle like me,' Lee laughed.

'How is the lovely Beth?' Michael asked fondly. His son had got married in June '99 and it had been a fabulous day. The weather was glorious, the venue perfect and, unusually for an event involving the Butlers, the day was drama free. Beth was only five feet tall and Lee towered above her. What she lacked in height, she made up for in personality though. The girl was a cracker and Michael couldn't have chosen a better wife for his son had he hand-picked one personally.

'Beth's good, thanks. She's doing far too many hours at the hospital though, and we're still not having much luck on the baby front,' Lee admitted.

'These things take time, boy, and the more the pair of you worry about it, the less it's likely to happen. Beth's only young, you've got years ahead of you to have kids.'

'She gets so disappointed every month when, you know. I hate seeing her upset,' Lee replied. At twenty-four Beth was four years his junior, and she'd been adamant lately that there was some underlying reason why she couldn't conceive.

'Can't she have a word with one of the doctors where she works?' Michael suggested. Beth was a recently qualified nurse and loved her job at Oldchurch Hospital. She and Lee had bought a nice house in Romford, not far from the dog track.

'I think she feels embarrassed. Anyway, let's not talk about it no more, let's talk about Dan. What's the betting when we ask him what he wants to do first, he'll want to get his leg over.'

Michael chuckled. Daniel did like a bird or three on the go, and Michael had been the same in his youth. Daniel and Lee had been born seven months apart by two different mothers, and were at different stages in their lives. Both were twenty-eight now, but Dan had never had a serious relationship. He was happy to just love 'em and leave 'em.

'How's things with Katy, Dad? And Bella? And Sophie?' Lee smirked.

Michael raised his eyebrows. At fifty-one, his love life

was far more complicated than that of a poxy teenager. When the truth had come out about Bella having a fling with Vinny back in '91, Michael had been easy pickings for Katy. She'd been kind and incredibly patient with him and he'd been vulnerable and desperate for revenge. In November 1992 their daughter Ellie had been born, and from that moment onwards Michael had felt trapped. He didn't dislike Katy. She was a good mother and she clearly adored him, but as much as Michael had tried, he couldn't love her. Their relationship now consisted of him sleeping at his so-called home two nights a week. The rest of the time he stayed in London to help run the casino he'd invested heavily in. Michael wished Katy would call it a day, but she was like a leech that would not let go of him. As long as he fucked her once a week and she could pretend to her friends all was fine and dandy, Katy seemed happy enough to put up with the situation. She liked to keep up appearances and Michael didn't have the heart or balls to tell her it was over. He would've walked away years ago though if it wasn't for their children. Nathan was fourteen now; a bright lad, who was popular and doing well at school. Ellie was eight and was into horses and showjumping. She was far too spoilt for Michael's liking, but he wasn't at home enough to stop Katy giving in to her every whim.

Time was a healer to a certain extent and even though Michael could never forgive or forget, he and Bella were now on speaking terms again. They had to be for the sake of their daughter. Camila had blossomed into a stunning teenager who was destined to follow in her mother's footsteps and carve out a successful career. She attended a drama school and already had a healthy bank account from shows and TV adverts she'd appeared in, but Michael worried about her constantly. Camila looked far older than her thirteen years and he knew better than anyone how young lads' minds ticked. He'd only been around Camila's age when he'd lost his virginity to his babysitter, but his daughter seemed to have a sensible head on her shoulders, thankfully. Michael of course put that down to his genes, not Bella's.

As for Sophie, she was just the latest in a long line of affairs he'd had over the years. An attractive thirty-three-year-old businesswoman, Michael had chatted her up in a restaurant up town and like all the others she'd been unable to say no to his irresistible looks and charm.

'You awake, Dad? You haven't answered my question,' Lee said.

'Sorry, boy. I was daydreaming. Katy's OK. Still putting up with me. Bella I spoke to last night. Cami's appearing in some West End musical soon, so I said I'd go. Sophie's starting to grate on me to be honest. That's her been texting every five minutes today. Will have to let her down gently soon, unless she eases off a bit.'

Lee laughed. 'You do make me smile, Dad. No wonder Daniel won't settle down. He's a chip off the old block. Like father, like son.'

Queenie and Vivian were on their soapboxes throughout the programme and felt incredibly sad once it had finished. Sky TV had opened up a whole new world to them. No longer did they have to watch the politically correct shit the BBC shoved down their throats. They now had a choice of channels and could watch anything from nature and sport to re-runs of old soaps, or programmes about the history of the East End like the one they were viewing. Sky had so many channels to choose from, it was unbelievable, and to think Queenie had initially refused Vinny's offer of having it installed and paid for at his expense. Viv had been that impressed with it, as much as she hated

Vinny, she'd allowed him to pay for and install it at hers as well.

'Those were the days, Viv,' Queenie said wistfully.

'They sure were. I'd go back in heartbeat if I could. We might not have had much back then, but we were happy with our little lot.'

'Have a look out the window, Viv. Is it that motley crew pulling up again? Me legs are killing me today and I want to save 'em for later,' Queenie moaned. She was seventy-four now and thanks to arthritis hobbled rather than walked some days. She was still young in her mind, kept herself looking good, but her body seemed to have given up on her lately, especially her legs. Full of aches and pains.

'Yeah. It's them. Another two going in there I've never seen before. Then again, they all look alike, don't they?'

Nosy Hilda had died a few months ago and Queenie and Viv rued the day she'd croaked it. The council had moved a foreign mob in her house and it seemed the world and its mother were living there. They were always coming and going, especially at night. They also collected scrap and owned a tipper truck, like gypsies.

'I wonder where they're from. Mouthy Maureen said they're Romanian. But how would she know? She could hardly've asked 'em. They don't speak a word of bastard English,' Queenie said.

'Fat Brenda reckons they're Polish,' Vivian informed her sister.

Queenie shook her head in despair. Her beloved Whitechapel certainly wasn't what it once was. As much as she'd hated a lot of her old neighbours, now that many had passed away or moved, Queenie and Viv missed them. The notrights who'd lived in the house between them were long gone. Doll had died five years ago and her son Roger had gone to live with his uncle in Clacton. Indians lived there now. They were quiet neighbours and pleasant enough, but the cooking smells that wafted from the house made Queenie and Viv feel ill. They'd never liked the smell of spicy food, and most of their pension was now spent on air fresheners.

The only old neighbours still left were Mouthy Maureen, Stinky Susan and Big Stan and his wife. Even Mrs Agg had left the area. She'd moved to Collier Row with Mabel and Fred. Ava had been fourteen by then and Fred had pined for Mabel that much, Ava had allowed him to live out his latter years with the Jack Russell bitch he'd fallen in love with. She didn't have as much time for Fred at that stage anyway, as she was out gallivanting with her mates all the time.

'Shall we watch that royal family programme we recorded?' Vivian asked Queenie.

'No. I think we've depressed ourselves enough for one day, don't you?'

'I'm gonna make a move then. I shall pop over the cemetery and tidy up Lenny's grave before I start getting ready.'

'You sure you ain't got a secret boyfriend on the go? You only tidied Lenny's grave up on Monday. It's bleedin' freezing today.'

'Don't be so bloody daft,' Vivian replied, hoping she wasn't blushing. 'I like a bit of fresh air and it comforts me, visiting my Lenny. When I'm on me own over there I talk to him like he's still here with me.'

'Aww, bless ya. What you wearing tonight, by the way?'

'That mauve dress I bought in Wallis when we last went to Lakeside. You?'

'I'm wearing me peach frock with the silver round the neck. I can't wait to see Daniel, bless him. I hope he enjoys the surprise. Blokes can be funny when they come out of nick. My Vinny certainly wasn't normal.'

Tempted to reply Vinny had never been normal, Vivian instead bit her tongue and smiled. 'Daniel will be fine. He's a Butler through and through.'

Daniel Butler grinned as he sauntered towards his father and brother. 'Oi, Oi. What's occurring?'

Lee gave Daniel a hug. 'Free as a bird again, and not before bloody time – it's your turn to start putting in some shifts at the club,' he joked.

Michael put an arm around his son's shoulders as they made the way back to the car. Daniel had sailed through his sentence and looked as fit as a fiddle, thanks to his new obsession with the gym. 'What shall we do first then, boy? I was thinking a nice T-bone steak and a couple of bottles of bubbly.'

'Sounds good to me. Can we shoot over to Charlton first though? I'm on a promise with that Janine bird. You can wait outside. I'll only be ten minutes.'

Michael looked at Lee and both burst out laughing.

Queenie sobbed into a handkerchief. Bored, she'd decided to watch the programme about the royals after all, and as always it had upset her immensely.

There'd been some awful tragedies in the nineties, the Dunblane massacre being one of them. But there were two events that had affected Queenie incredibly on a personal level.

The sight of poor little Jamie Bulger being led out of that shopping centre by those two evil bastards that killed him would haunt Queenie for ever. So would the sight of his poor parents being interviewed on TV. Both Queenie and Viv had cried floods of tears for that sweet innocent child. But what made it worse for Queenie was it brought back terrible memories of Molly's death. Queenie continued to hope and pray the animals responsible would one day be tortured to death themselves, but knowing the do-gooders in this country they were probably leading the life of Riley on the inside. The more wrong you did in this day and age, the better the authorities treated you, and it wouldn't even surprise Queenie if the boys responsible were let out sooner rather than later with new identities, paid for by the taxpayer of course.

Another day that would live in Queenie's thoughts until the day she died was 31 August 1997. Viv had gone round to Mr Patel's to get the Sunday papers and there'd been a shocking headline on the front page of the *News of the World* stating Dodi Fayed was dead and Princess Diana had been badly injured in a car crash in Paris.

Queenie had immediately switched the TV on and was horrified to learn Diana had also died. All usual radio and TV programmes were cancelled and Queenie and Viv'd sat glued to the TV for hours, sobbing their hearts out. They'd been thrilled that Diana had finally found some happiness, and how ever would poor Prince William and Harry cope without their beloved mother?

Diana's funeral had been a sombre affair. Queenie and Viv had recorded the service while joining thousands of other mourners lining the streets of London to say a final goodbye to their favourite royal. They'd even bought Diana a beautiful bouquet and put a personal message on the card. Princes William and Harry had never replied to their kind offer of joining them for tea, though.

Her granddaughter's arrival spelled the end to Queenie's reminiscing. 'Me and Destiny are getting ready and staying here tonight, Nan,' Ava announced.

'Erm, I think you mean is it OK for me and Destiny to get ready and stay 'ere tonight please, don't you?'

'Yeah. Is it OK?'

'Only if you come straight home after the party. There'll

be no more rolling home the following day in this house again, because next time I will tell your father,' Queenie threatened.

'Of course, Nan. I'm only nineteen and wouldn't dream of going out clubbing again,' Ava laughed, before heading up the stairs with her outfit for the evening.

Queenie puffed her cheeks out in exasperation. Ava would be the bloody death of her. She wasn't all bad, but Queenie felt too old for the responsibility now. Vinny still owned his club in Holborn and lived in Canary Wharf, and Ava flitted between the two abodes. She would stay with her father and act like a demure princess to ponce money, then she would stay at hers and play up while she spent it.

Queenie blamed the local school and Vinny for Ava's unemployment. Her granddaughter had been very bright in infant and junior school, but by the time she reached the seniors, Whitechapel was that multicultural the teachers spent far more time teaching kids English than they did concentrating on the likes of Ava. She was one of only four English-speaking kids in her class, so never stood a chance.

Vinny was even worse than the school in Queenie's eyes. She'd suggested many a time that Ava get a job, but Vinny did not want his daughter taking some minimum-wage position and she wasn't qualified for much else. He wouldn't let her sign on, so bunged her money regularly. Queenie found that morally wrong. She'd always taught her boys, even as youngsters, that they needed to earn a bob or two if they wanted nice things in life. She'd done many a crap job herself before her sons had been old enough to support her, and even Stinky Susan's Destiny had a bloody job. She'd turned out a lovely girl and done well for herself, considering who her mother was. Queenie obviously put that down to the influence her own family had in Destiny's upbringing. And she chose to forget that Destiny had attended the same senior school as Ava, yet had left there with far more exam passes.

Ava swanned into the lounge again. 'I'm starving. What you got nice to eat?'

'There's some lamb stew in the fridge that I made yesterday.'

Ava turned her nose up. 'That's fattening and boring. Haven't you got anything else? Can't you make me something nice?'

Queenie stood up and glared at her granddaughter. At five feet seven, Ava was head and shoulders above her small frame. She was also incredibly cheeky, pretty and knew it, but in Queenie's eyes no Butler kid was ever too old for a slap. She raised her hand as a gesture. 'Make your bloody self something – and while you're at it, you can make me a cuppa. It's about time you started earning your keep, young lady.'

Ava grinned as she strolled into the kitchen. Little did her nan know she was actually earning her keep. Her father was training her up to be manageress at his club.

'Cooey. Where are you, Albie?'

'Up here, love. I'm debating what suit to wear tonight. Need to look smart if I'm gonna serenade my favourite lady, eh?'

Grinning like a teenager, Vivian chose Albie's outfit for him. 'Needs a proper iron, that shirt. I'll do it while you eat your lamb stew and dumplings that Queenie made.'

Albie chuckled. It was a standing joke between them that whenever Queenie's back was turned, Vivian would steal some of whatever stew she'd cooked and put it in a plastic container to warm up for him when she next visited. Either that or she'd cook him a nice meal herself. A true diamond was Vivian, and Albie couldn't imagine her not being part of his life now.

Queenie would have a fit if she ever found out about their secret liaisons. Vivian would visit him at least twice a week, sometimes more if Queenie's arthritis was playing up. Their friendship was purely platonic. As Albie often joked, it had been a long time since he'd been able to play a tune on his fiddle. But he knew Viv thought the world of him, and the feeling was mutual. It was hard to believe they'd once been at each other's throats. Sad as it was, it'd been Lenny's death that had strengthened their bond. They both loathed Vinny with a passion and were so glad he wasn't invited to Daniel's homecoming party. Vinny and Michael had had nothing to do with each other for years now.

'That's your shirt ironed. Fancy a game of dominoes?' Vivian asked. It was a shame, but her and Albie couldn't risk going out in public together. If they did, Queenie would be bound to hear about it, and then all hell would break loose.

'Go on then. But today I'm gonna beat you, Vivian Harris. I'm sure you cheated last Wednesday.'

'Sod off, Albie Butler. Won that fair and square, I did. You've just met your bleedin' match in life.'

Albie grinned. 'I sure have, sweetheart.'

'That was absolutely blinding,' Daniel Butler said, patting his bloated stomach.

'I bet that Janine bird never said that about you, seeing as you were in and out of hers in eleven minutes flat,' Michael guffawed. He and Lee had had a tenner bet on how long Daniel's ejaculation skills would last and he'd won. Lee had guessed eighteen minutes, Michael thirteen.

'Shut up, you pair of pricks. I don't even like the bird, what did you expect?' Daniel grinned. 'Right, what we doing when we leave 'ere? Fancy a bit of table dancing meself. Not me personally, of course.'

'You've already "dipped your wick", as your nan says. Me and Lee have got the whole day planned, so chill out,' Michael urged.

'How's Cami? I can't wait to see her,' Daniel grinned. His little sister had written to him regularly in prison and Daniel had loved receiving her bubbly letters. She'd also visited him on his birthday and at Christmas with his father.

'Cami's fine. Landed herself another decent part in a show. We'll have to arrange something so you get to see her soon,' Michael replied, slyly winking at Lee. Daniel would actually be seeing his little sister this evening as Bella had surprisingly agreed to her attending his homecoming party. Cami was bringing a friend, and they were being dropped off and picked up a couple of hours later by Bella's usual driver.

'How's Beth, Lee? You got her up the spout yet?'

'Beth's fine and, nah, no pitter-patter of tiny feet any time soon. I've been busy at the club and Beth at the hospital, so we're like ships that pass in the night at the moment,' Lee replied, giving his father a warning look to keep his mouth shut. Daniel could be a real piss-taker at times and this was a delicate subject.

Daniel started laughing.

'What's so funny?' Lee asked.

'I was thinking of the faces on Beth's family when I did me best man speech. The story about them two old birds we pulled that Christmas was a classic.'

Lee raised his eyebrows and shook his head in mock disbelief. The story was a classic, all right. The two rich old tarts they'd spent one Christmas shagging hadn't informed them until Boxing Day evening that their husbands were in the nick for murder. Dan and Lee had never bolted from a house so fast in their lives, and Beth's family hadn't looked too impressed when Daniel told the story at the wedding. Thankfully, he'd left out the drug-taking part.

'One day you'll get married, bruv, and I swear I'll pay you back for that.'

Daniel chuckled. 'Not a cat in hell's chance.'

'Antonio, Antonio! I've been calling you for the past five minutes. Has that music finally made you go deaf?' an exasperated Bella asked, tapping on her son's bedroom door. He kept the door locked, so entering without permission was a no-go.

Antonio turned his music down. He was obsessed with the grunge scene, Nirvana in particular. Kurt Cobain was his all-time hero and even though his death was extremely sad, Antonio thought it was ultra-cool the way Kurt had chosen to end things. Not many men had the guts to blast their own brains out. 'What's up?' he asked casually.

'Your sister wants your opinion on her new outfit, and Vinny has been on the phone again asking why you haven't rung him back yet.'

Antonio opened the door, looking as bleary-eyed as Bella had known he would. He was permanently stoned and, as much as Bella had tried, she could not stop Antonio smoking whatever crap he smoked.

'I'll call Vinny back tomorrow. Where's Cami?' Antonio asked.

'In the lounge. And while you speak with her, I demand to change your bedclothes. Juanita says you haven't allowed her to change them for three whole weeks!'

When Antonio staggered down the stairs, Bella entered his dope-stinking room. Her son was nineteen now and a total disappointment to her in more ways than one. Such a bright boy as a child, he had thrown his education away by pressing the self-destruct button. After he'd got himself expelled from two private schools for fighting and smoking weed, Bella had managed to get him into a third. Antonio had then deliberately flunked his exams because he had no wish to go to college or university, and had refused to do sod-all ever since.

Bella blamed herself for the way her son had turned out, of course. For all Vinny's faults, he had tried to be part of Antonio's life. But Antonio had little time for either of them, apart from when he was after money. He was still close to her parents, especially her father, who he spoke to regularly on the phone. And he was a decent enough brother to Camila, although it did worry Bella that Cami was old enough now to know what he got up to in that bedroom of his. As for Michael, Antonio refused to be in the same room as him, let alone speak to the man who had once raised him.

Bella sighed as she spotted a mound of dirty clothes under her son's bed. He lived and died in washed-out-looking T-shirts and faded jeans. She could've understood him turning out to be a bum if she had taken up with other men, but after Michael's departure all she had done was concentrate on her modelling agency and children. There had been the odd date, but Bella had never felt an attraction towards another man. They bored her, and as much as she hated to admit it, her heart would always belong to her ex. There was only one Michael Butler.

Vinny Butler wasn't in the best of moods. He knew all about Daniel's homecoming bash and the thought of his mother getting glammed up to spend the evening at the club he and Roy had worked their balls off to buy in the first place grated on Vinny enormously. Even Ava and Little Vinny were going, the bloody traitors.

'Penny for 'em,' Carl said, helping himself to a Scotch before topping his boss's glass up.

'What?'

'Penny for your thoughts.'

Vinny forced a smile. Unlike Jay Boy, who'd sodded off back to Liverpool, Carl had stayed loyal to him over the years and was now his right-hand man at the club. 'Family shit. You know how it is.'

Carl tried not to laugh as a familiar face walked up behind Vinny and put his hands over his eyes. 'Guess who or I'll kill ya.'

'Ed!' Vinny exclaimed, leaping out his chair to give his pal a man-hug. 'What you doing 'ere, mate?'

Eddie winked at Carl. He'd rung the club earlier to check Vinny would be around and had told Carl not to mention he was on his way. 'My good lady has taken the little 'uns to visit her friend, so I thought I might as well make the most of it. Been ages since we had a proper session. You up for it, or what?'

Thinking how very apt the 'You can choose your friends but not your family' saying was, Vinny grinned. 'You bet I am.'

CHAPTER TWENTY-NINE

Roxanne huddled up to her friend Alex at the bus stop. It was bitterly cold, but both girls were excited about the evening ahead and knew how uncool it would be to turn up at the club in winter clothing. They would rather freeze to death than look undesirable, and seeing as they came from the north of England, the winter in London was mild in comparison.

'There'd better be some fit lads there. Tracy said there isn't many as a rule, but she reckons tonight will be different because it's a private party to do with the owners,' Alex said.

'I'm not dating any more lads after Marty. I want a man and he has to be rich. No way can I stomach working for Stavros much longer and living in that dump,' Roxanne stated boldly.

The future had seemed so bright when Roxanne had left her parents' home to run away with Marty Burns. Marty was the nineteen-year-old lead singer of Roxanne's favourite local indie band, The Sharks. He'd certainly lived up to his band's name when she'd surprised him by turning up after a gig and caught him in a comprising position with some slag of a groupie.

Marty had grovelled and begged for her forgiveness. He'd insisted that the groupie was not in fact giving him a blow-job but had merely been rubbing his stomach because he had a belly ache, but Roxanne wasn't stupid. She'd nicked Marty's wallet before disappearing from his life, for good.

London itself was full of sharks and Roxanne had been approached by pimps, perverts and all sorts of undesirables before she'd thankfully met Alex in a café in Camden Town. Alex had a job working in a hotel for a guy called Stavros, and Roxanne had jumped at the offer of cash-in-hand employment which also included a roof over her head.

Neither the job or the accommodation turned out to be what Roxanne had hoped they would be. Stavros was a slave driver who obviously took advantage of runaways and young girls who'd come to London to seek their fortune. The hotel was dingy and seedy and Roxanne and Alex were made to graft continuously from six in the morning until six in the evening. Their duties included helping out in the kitchens, cleaning and being general dogsbodies all for a measly seventy-five quid a week, plus their awful accommodation.

The daughter of wealthy parents, Roxanne had never seen anything quite so squalid as the living conditions she and Alex were forced to share. There was barely enough room to swing one of the many cockroaches they'd found, let alone a cat. The bathroom was shared, and out on the landing. It was always dirty and the girls would have to scrub furiously at the tidemarks before having a soak. They also chose to wee in a bucket of a night and empty it the next morning rather than use the scummy toilet and bump into any weirdos.

'Perhaps they might need staff at this club? If we like the look of it, we could always ask. Tracy said both the lads that run it will be there tonight. That's what the party's for, the brother who has been released from prison,' Alex informed her pal.

Roxanne had never met Alex's friend. Tracy had worked for Stavros and shared a room with Alex before she'd arrived in London. 'Are the brothers single? How old are they?' Roxanne enquired.

Alex shrugged. She'd only received the letter from Tracy yesterday with a phone number where she could be contacted. 'All Tracy said on the phone was that I could come to the party and it would be OK to bring a mate. I've got a feeling the owners might be villains. Tracy said everybody knows and respects them.'

Roxanne grinned. She had no idea why, but she'd always had an obsession with the underworld and the East End of London. Back when her school friends were reading Charles Dickens, she'd had her head stuck in a book about the Krays or Jack the Ripper.

'What you grinning at?' Alex asked.

'Not only is our bus coming, I've got a feeling tonight is going to be a good night. Don't forget the golden rule, will you, pet.'

Alex chuckled. Roxanne could be quite immature in some ways, yet had a very adult head on her in others. 'Play hard to get.'

Linking arms and laughing, the girls got on the bus.

Daniel Butler feigned surprise when he was greeted by family, friends and the DJ playing 'Tie a Yellow Ribbon Round the Old Oak Tree'. He'd guessed the moment his father and Lee had said they had to stop off at the club to pick something up that they'd organized a party for him.

'Look at you! All muscle, ain't he, Viv? Give your nan a hug then, boy,' Queenie ordered.

Daniel obliged then did the rounds, accepting all hugs, pats on the back and handshakes. Half a dozen of his and Lee's old school pals from Barking were there, which was nice. There were lots of birds as well, some of whom Daniel didn't recognize.

It had been years since Queenie and Vivian had set foot inside the club. The trade there was at an all-time low, which was why Michael had invested in another business. Tonight, however, apart from the awful décor, was like old times. Michael had insisted on a singer as well as a DJ and it brought back plenty of memories, good ones and bad.

'Oooh, I've gone cold, Queen. I just had a vision of my Lenny DJing on that stage and how he might look now,' Vivian said.

'That's a sign. He's here with us in spirit. I bet my Roy is an' all. His pride and joy this club was. How time flies. Doesn't seem all them years ago we came to the opening night, does it? We both had furs on and felt like royalty, remember?'

'Course I do. I remember Kenny Jackson being the first ejected an' all. Roy threw him out for being a drunken pest.'

Queenie's face clouded over. It was Kenny's grandson Jake that had stabbed her Brenda to death. The police had never caught him, and even though Vinny had put a bounty on his head, nobody had a clue where he was.

Knowing she'd hit a raw nerve, Vivian changed the subject. 'Not heard you mention Tara and Tommy for a while. You heard from either of 'em?'

'Nope. Not since their Christmas card,' Queenie replied. Brenda's kids thankfully hadn't turned out to be alcoholics like their mother. Tara had met a lad on holiday in Spain a few years ago and had moved to Leeds to be with him; Tommy had followed her up there a few months later. Now

Tara had become a mum, with a little girl Queenie had yet to set eyes on.

'Don't Camila look a picture, Queen? Look, over by the door with her mate. Such a beautiful child.'

'Takes after her gran,' Queenie chuckled. 'I see that old bastard's over there making himself busy. Shouldn't be allowed round young girls, him.'

Vivian looked at her sister in disbelief. 'I know you hate Albie, but you can't go around saying things like that, Queen. He might be a lot of things but he ain't no kiddie-fiddler. You'll cause a riot, people hear you say stuff like that.'

'What people? I'm only bleedin' talking to you. Always on the defensive these days when it comes to that old goat, you are. Don't think I haven't noticed it, because I have.'

'You're talking out your arsehole as usual,' Vivian retaliated.

Ava plonked herself on a chair. 'What's up with yous two? Not arguing, are you?'

'Your nan's having one of her senile moments, dear,' Vivian replied.

'And your aunt has had a sense-of-humour bypass,' Queenie responded.

'For goodness' sake. You're meant to be enjoying yourselves. It's a bloody party,' Ava reminded her warring relations.

Queenie and Viv glared at one another one last time before laughing.

'Tracy, meet Roxanne. Roxy meet Tracy,' Alex said.

Roxanne held out her right hand. 'Lovely to meet you, Tracy. I've heard lots about you.'

'Wow! You two even sound alike. You a Geordie as well?' Tracy asked.

'Whey-aye, pet,' Roxanne laughed.

'Roxy has taken your place at Stavros's wonderful establishment, and your luxury room, Trace. I do hope you aren't too jealous,' Alex joked.

'Poor you. Awful, isn't it? Has Stavros tried to touch you up yet? He did me.'

'If he touches me, I'll stick this in him,' Roxanne boasted, waving the flick-knife she carried in her bag.

'Oooh, put that away. You don't want to be flashing it about inside the club. The Butlers won't be happy,' Tracy warned, glancing at Alex in the hope she was going to keep her new friend under control.

'Where's the bar?' Alex asked.

'I'll show you. Drinks are free, but don't get too bladdered, will you? I really like my job here and I'd hate Lee to think I was taking liberties. It was Lee who told me to invite a couple of pals.'

Thinking how boring Tracy was, Roxanne touched her hair and lipstick up before marching into the club area. 'What's this crap music? It's not this singer all night, is it?' she complained.

'No. There's a disco as well. Why did you have to bring her with you?' Tracy hissed to Alex when Roxanne went to get the drinks.

'Roxy's OK, pet. She's just showing off a bit, that's all. I'll make sure she behaves herself, I promise.'

'You'd better,' Tracy replied. Lee had given her the night off to enjoy herself and she rather wished she was back behind the bar now.

Roxanne tapped a bloke in a suit on the back. 'Excuse me. Can you pass me three drinks off that tray?'

Daniel turned around and was immediately bowled over by the girl's beauty. Back in the day, he'd had a thing for Pamela Anderson. The sight of her strutting about in swimwear was worth watching *Baywatch* for, and this bird reminded him of a young, dark-haired version of Pamela.

'Cat got your tongue?' Roxanne grinned. She had no idea who the bloke gawping at her was, but he was gorgeous.

'You're a cheeky one, you are. What's your name?'

Roxanne could feel her heart beating faster than usual. His piercing eyes and boyish grin were having an unusual effect on her. 'Who wants to know?' she managed to reply.

'The owner of the club you're stood in.'

Roxanne put her hands on her hips. 'I'm not underage, if that's what you're thinking. I am old enough to drink alcohol.'

'Never said you wasn't, did I? Got some attitude you have, ain't ya?'

'I prefer to call it personality. So, are you going to pass me those drinks, or not?'

Daniel's eyes twinkled. Her style suited her and that included the pierced tongue. She was wearing a tight red dress that matched her bright lipstick, lots of dark eye make-up, black stilettos and a short leather jacket. Definitely a rock-chick, Daniel thought, deciding to wind her up some more. 'You gotta say please and tell me your name before I even consider passing you those drinks.'

'Don't bother. I can reach them myself now.'

Laughing at his brother's astounded face, Lee slapped him on the back. 'Finally, I think you've met a bird to silence you. Now that's a fucking first.'

A short distance from the club, Vinny Butler and Eddie Mitchell were on a pub crawl. It had been Vinny's idea to have a drink in the Grave Maurice and the Blind Beggar, knowing word would get back to his family and hopefully spoil their evening.

'Michael's probably staring at the door as we speak,

afraid we're gonna bowl in,' Vinny said bitterly. He'd tried to make things right with his brother over the years, but Michael had made it extremely clear that Vinny was no longer part of his life. Vinny truly couldn't understand why his brother was still holding a grudge all these years later. It was such old news now.

'It's Michael's loss, mate. Forget about him and move on,' Eddie advised.

'I have. But it still pisses me off that he now talks to Bella again and not me. Why am I the bad bastard in all this? Twenty years ago I had a one-night stand with a bird who was a complete stranger. Like I'd have gone anywhere near her, had I known who she was. I could understand him despising me if I'd knocked her off behind his back, but you know me, Ed, I'd never pull a stunt like that. Why can't Michael let bygones be bygones?'

'I dunno, Vin, but let's not talk about brothers, eh? Reminds me of Paulie and Ronny.'

'Sorry, mate. How's Gina and the kids doing?'

After spending years behind bars, Eddie Mitchell had found love again and remarried. Gina was the private detective he'd once hired to spy on his twins, and they now had two young children together, Rosie and Aaron. 'Yeah, Gina's good as gold and so are the little 'uns. I had another lead on Georgie and Harry last week, but it was a false alarm again. Breaks my heart every time I have to tell Frankie it isn't them. I think in future I'll tell her nothing until I actually have 'em in my grasp. That's if they're ever found,' Eddie said miserably.

'You'll find 'em one day, Ed. Men like you and me never give up until we've achieved what we set out to achieve. Kids don't just disappear into thin air.' Georgie and Harry were Ed's grandchildren. They'd been snatched by their gypsy relatives back in '93 and hadn't been seen since.

Eddie knocked back his Scotch. 'It's depressing in 'ere. Fancy a curry?'

Vinny smiled. 'Lead the way, Mr Mitchell.'

Back at the party, Vivian felt a warm glow as Albie belted out 'Spanish Eyes' for her. She daren't look at him though, in case Queenie clocked her and had another hissy fit.

'You all right?' Queenie asked, when Little Vinny stormed over to the table, his face like thunder.

'No I ain't! Them two little bastards have only gone and smashed a shop window in the High Road. Sammi's doing her nut and the Old Bill might be on the way for all I know. We're gonna have to go, but Ollie wants to stay at yours tonight with Ava. That OK? I don't see why his evening should be spoilt.'

'Of course Ollie can stay at mine. And try not to worry too much about Calum and Regan. I know they're sods, but you and Ben Bloggs were no bleedin' different at their age. I remember catching yous pair up to all sorts.'

Little Vinny shuddered at the mention of his dead mate. It had taken him a long while to get over being questioned about Molly, and he would never forget Terry's parting words. He'd suffered from panic attacks afterwards, and still had them now whenever Calum or Regan brought the Old Bill to his front door. 'I gotta go, Nan. I'll ring you tomorrow.'

Aware that Daniel's eyes were firmly focused on her, Roxanne swayed her body in an extremely seductive manner to the rhythm of the music.

Tracy felt embarrassed and annoyed. 'Tell her to calm it down a bit, for Christ's sake, Alex. She looks like a bloody stripper.'

'Whatever's wrong with you tonight, Trace? I really

appreciate your invite, but you haven't stopped moaning. Roxy isn't harming anyone and your new boss certainly isn't complaining. He's fascinated by her. Look,' Alex urged.

Tracy already knew that Daniel could not take his eyes off Roxanne. That's why she felt so annoyed. She'd been hoping she might be in with a chance herself and couldn't understand what a classy bloke like Daniel could see in that immature, trappy slapper.

Roxy lit up a cigarette. 'I'm going outside for some fresh air. Bet you any money you like he follows me,' she stated confidently.

Alex laughed. 'Just make sure you put a good word in for us about a job if he does. We're far more suited to working for him than Stavros.'

Tracy's expression was suddenly that of a bulldog chewing a wasp. 'There are no jobs going here,' she hissed.

'You need to chill out more, you do, pet,' Roxanne smirked, before flicking back her hair and flouncing off.

Over the other side of the club, Michael Butler was chatting to his father and pal about Vinny. Of course he'd heard his brother was in the vicinity with Eddie Mitchell. But was he bothered? No chance.

'What a childish fucktard that man is. Obviously thought it would ruin our evening to know he was lurking nearby. Like he'd have the guts to stroll in here anyway. He'd get lynched by the doormen, let alone me,' Michael laughed. 'As for Mitchell, I'm surprised at him for allowing Vinny to use him to play silly buggers. I thought Eddie had a bit more class than that, but obviously not.'

'Forget about the pair of 'em and enjoy the party, mate. Plenty of people've got your back if he turns up here. Me and your boys included,' Kev said, jokingly holding his fists up while repeating the famous Muhammad Ali 'Float like a butterfly' line.

'This is what he wants, us all talking about him. So let's not give him another bleedin' mention,' Albie said, before asking Michael where Nathan was.

'At home. If I'd have mentioned the party, Katy would've insisted she and Ellie come too, so I didn't bother. Nath can catch up with Daniel another time.' Michael leaned forward. 'Your bird keeps looking over 'ere. I think she's trying to catch your eye, so me and Kev'll leave you to it,' he whispered in his father's ear. He was the only other person who knew Vivian visited his father, and he found it highly amusing.

'Shush. You'll get me shot. And don't you ever let on to Viv I've told you. She'll have me guts for garters,' Albie warned.

Michael chuckled. 'Don't worry. Your sordid little secret is safe with me. Mind you, don't get her pregnant though. Our family tree is fucked up enough as it is.'

Roxanne knew it was him who had walked up behind her even before he opened his mouth. She could smell his aftershave, had caught a whiff of it earlier inside the club. 'Roxanne my name is, Mr Club Owner,' she said, before turning around and grinning at him.

Daniel chuckled. 'You psychic, or what? How did ya know it was me?'

'Because I saw you staring at me inside and knew you'd follow me out here.'

Daniel watched Roxanne seductively blow smoke rings and felt a stirring in his groin. He'd met some birds in his time, but none like this one. 'Tell me about yourself.'

'What d'ya want to know?'

'Everything. How old are you, for starters?'

Guessing that Daniel was about twenty-six, Roxanne replied, 'Twenty-one. What about you?'

Daniel smirked. He knew she was lying. 'I'm twenty-eight, and no way are you twenty-one. You're younger than that.'

'No I'm not,' Roxanne replied defiantly.

'Yes you are. How old are ya really?'

Hands on hips, Roxanne glared at him. 'I've already told you once, and I won't tell you again. No point us chatting, is there, if you're not going to believe what I say.'

Daniel grabbed Roxanne's wrist with one hand and put the other on the lower part of her back. He stared deep into her blue eyes. They were mesmerizing, just like she was.

The kiss blew them both away, especially Daniel, who was by far the more experienced. He wondered fleetingly if he was feeling this way because he'd been incarcerated for the past eighteen months. But he knew even at this early stage it was far more than that.

The unthinkable had finally happened to Daniel Butler. He'd met a bird he actually wanted to get to know rather than just sleep with, and that was a novelty for him. Perhaps that old saying 'Love at first sight' wasn't such a load of claptrap after all?

CHAPTER THIRTY

Within four weeks of meeting Roxanne, Daniel Butler was ready to take their relationship a step further. 'I know it's early days, but I'm gonna ask Roxy to move in with me,' he informed his father and brother.

In a café in Mile End, Michael nearly choked on his mouthful of baked beans. 'Bloody hell. You don't beat around the bush, do ya? You sure you're ready to make such a commitment? It's a big leap, living together, and Roxy's a lot younger than you,' Michael warned. He'd only met the girl briefly on a couple of occasions and could see why his son was besotted with her. She reminded him a bit of Nancy when they'd first got together. Had those same big lips and doleful eyes. She also had a bit of Bella about her. A wild streak, with clever answers and a carefree nature. Beauty and brains was a fatal combination, Michael knew that much.

'Dad's right, bruv. You've only known her a month, therefore you don't properly know her yet at all, if you know what I mean?' Lee added. He didn't dislike Roxanne, but found her a bit of a closed book. She was reluctant to talk about her past and, as far as Lee was concerned, Daniel knew sod-all about her.

'I know this makes me sound like a right soppy prick, but she hates her job and I want her to be happy. I can't stop thinking about her, and when I'm with her she makes me go all funny inside.'

Michael smiled. 'Well, you've caught the love bug, that's for sure. I felt the same when I first got together with your mum, and Bella. No other female has ever made me feel that way, so grab it with both hands and enjoy it. True love is hard to find.'

'What about you, Lee? Surely you felt the same way about Beth when you first got together? I remember you talking about her non-stop,' Daniel reminded his brother.

'Yeah, I did. But your feelings tone down a bit once you've been together for a while. What will Roxy do for work? Her job comes with her accommodation, don't it? We can't be taking no more staff on at the club with the way things are, Dan.'

Takings at the club had hit an all-time low and Daniel was thankful his brother had hidden that from him whilst inside. Muslims were no longer the minority in the area, they were by far the majority and, unfortunately for Daniel and Lee, most didn't drink alcohol and neither did they seem to like clubbing.

'I've had an idea how to buck trade up a bit. We'll do away with the grab-a-granny night and have a student disco on a Monday instead. We can charge a pound a drink, alcoholic or soft. There's thousands of Muslim students round our neck of the woods and hopefully we can start enticing 'em in. Whaddya reckon?' Daniel asked, grinning broadly.

'I dunno. Might be worth a try, I suppose. The way things are going, I'm gonna be struggling to pay my mortgage soon. So what exactly is Roxanne gonna do for work?' Lee asked again.

Sick of his brother's downbeat attitude towards his love life and the club, Daniel decided to have a pop at him. 'Nothing. She's my girl, so I'll be looking after her. And that, Lee, is what real men do.'

Over at Stavros's seedy establishment, Roxanne and Alex were having a well-earned tea and fag break.

'No news on the job front yet, I take it? Why don't you take the plunge and ask him outright? He's obviously in love with you to want to see you every night and I'm getting sick of sitting in that shitty room on my own. There has to be more to life than this,' Alex complained.

'Be patient. Daniel isn't going to want me working, he's already said as much. It won't be long now before he asks me to move in, and when he does I will make sure you get that bitch Tracy's job, I promise.'

Alex smiled. She had to admire Roxanne. Her friend was totally smitten with Daniel Butler, and who could blame her? Yet she was still holding out in the bedroom department and always returned to their digs rather than stay at the club. Roxy was clued up and reckoned it was the only way to ensure that Daniel asked her to live with him sooner rather than later. 'So what did you do last night? Did you wank him off again?' Alex laughed.

Roxanne smiled. 'I actually put it in my mouth for the first time and had a little suck. I stopped after about thirty seconds though because he started getting too excited. I'm so into him, Alex. I never thought I'd love any bloke more than I did Marty, but I do. Daniel is a man not a boy, and he treats me like I'm fragile and precious. I'm going to marry him one day.'

'Whey-aye! Best I get meself a hat then, pet.'

*

400

Unlike most of the males in the Butler clan, Vinny had never been what you would call a 'ladies' man'. As a teenager, he'd got his heart broken by his first love, Yvonne Summers, and from that moment on, apart from female members of his family, Vinny had despised anything born with a fanny. Even Little Vinny and Ava's mothers he'd felt nothing for. Which, with hindsight, was probably why he'd had them both bumped off.

Bella D'Angelo had been the one woman who'd always had a strange kind of hold over Vinny. She'd made it very clear from the start of his relationship with Antonio that she loathed him, but that didn't stop Vinny fantasizing about her. Many a time he'd played out scenes in his mind where he'd take her by force and strangle her while raping her. Which was probably why he'd recently become obsessed with his new member of staff.

Felicity Carter-Price was a twenty-six-year-old upper-class bit of totty. Carl had hired her and when Vinny had first seen her dance, he'd been gobsmacked at how much she reminded him of Bella in her prime. Dark skin and hair, the same tall slender body and, most importantly, her face bore a striking resemblance to Bella's.

Clocking Felicity staring at him again, Vinny darted towards the safety of his office. She'd been showing out to him big time, especially this past week, and he didn't know what to do about it. He'd been celibate for years now; his own choice, to stop him potentially committing murder and spending another stint behind bars. But despite his best efforts, Felicity was having an effect on him and he could feel all those old urges returning.

Vinny poured himself a Scotch and downed it in one. At fifty-five, the last thing he wanted was more female-related drama in his life. He'd kept himself looking good.

Still had his thick dark hair slicked back with Brylcreem, worked out regularly in the gym, and strutted around in the finest suits. His penis was still in good working order as well. Vinny regularly tested that when watching his hardcore porn and snuff films. Twenty-six was fucking young though. But she so reminded him of Bella back in the day, and her posh accent alone was enough to get him off. What the hell was a man to do?

Katy Spencer smiled as she studied her reflection in the mirror. The gold number that had set Michael back five hundred quid was worth every penny. It clung to her toned figure and showed every curve to perfection, including her recently acquired DD silicone breasts, her Christmas present from her man.

Katy wasn't dumb. She knew Michael didn't love her, not in the way she loved him anyway. But she and her children lived a life of luxury and were the envy of all of her friends.

When Ellie was born, Katy had insisted that they needed a bigger property. After much persuasion, Michael reluctantly bought the lovely four-bedroomed detached house with the big garden, driveway and electric gates that Katy'd had her eye on. She'd also demanded that Ellie attend a private school rather than the local primary. Nathan was settled and doing well, therefore didn't want to move schools. But what was good enough for Bella's daughter was most certainly good enough for hers, so under duress yet again, Michael paid for and was still paying for Ellie's private education.

'Mum, Dad's home,' Ellie shouted.

Katy touched up her lipstick and hair. She had stopped snooping through Michael's belongings and credit card statements. What was the point in trying to work out who his latest floozy was or how many times he'd seen her that month? There was no sense in torturing herself when she knew Michael would never actually leave her. He might only spend two nights a week at home, but he always made love to her and it was *she* and their children that enjoyed a two-week summer holiday with him in an exotic destination every year – not one of his floozies.

Of course, things could always be better. But overall, Katy was content with her life. She'd never had to work and happily spent her days enjoying her exclusive gym membership, sunbed sessions, massages and general pampering. And if she was bored, she would take her unlimited credit card out and spend, spend, spend. Michael Butler might not be perfect, but he was the nearest to perfection she was going to get – and Katy knew it.

There wasn't much in his world that Vinny Butler didn't hear about, therefore he was well aware what a success his brother and Leo McCann had been having in the gambling game.

To say Vinny had been pissed off when he'd found out Michael had gone into business with Leo was putting it mildly. He'd been absolutely livid that his brother could even consider going into business with a geezer whose brother had once opened up a nightclub on the Butlers' doorstep and lured away all their customers. Well, if Michael wanted to play silly games, let him. Vinny had bigger fish to fry and knew his brother would feel far more pissed off than he had when he and Eddie Mitchell opened up their gambling club. They were currently struggling to find suitable premises though, which was very annoying.

'Shame that gaff was so small eh, Vin? Not a bad location,' Eddie said.

'Perhaps we could extend it somehow, build an upstairs?' Vinny suggested.

Eddie Mitchell shook his head. He knew Vinny had been desperate for them to set up a business together for a long time and it was only because he fancied being part owner of a casino that he'd finally agreed. He was, however, an astute businessman and if they couldn't find the right venue, then the joint venture wouldn't go ahead. 'You're talking big bucks, you start doing all that. Plus some of these councils in Essex are bastards when it comes to planning permission. They don't tend to take a bung as easily as they did on our old manor,' Eddie laughed. Like many of the old school, Eddie now lived out in Essex. Rettendon wasn't the liveliest place on earth, but he and Gina were happy there and it was a decent area to raise their young children.

'Maybe we should broaden our search? I bet I could find us a decent joint in London if I put the feelers out.'

Eddie shook his head again. 'I told you at the beginning that this has to be right for me, Vin. If I'm investing heavily in a new venture, then I aim to be part of it. I don't wanna be schlepping up to the smoke regularly, thanks very much. Got Gina and the kids to consider, so it has to be on my doorstep, so to speak.'

Vinny took a sip of Scotch. 'I get where you're coming from. We'll carry on looking in Essex. Just rein me in if I come out with any more cuntish ideas. Can't help meself at times. My muvver used to say "Impatience" was my middle name.'

'I've gotta take this call, Vin. It's Frankie,' Eddie said.

Having stopped off at a quiet boozer in a country lane, Vinny watched with amusement as all heads turned towards his pal as he sauntered from one side of the pub to the other with the phone glued to his ear. Of all the geezers he knew, Mitchell was by far the coolest. He was incredibly handsome, oozed charm and looked at least ten years younger than his age. Ed's magnetism could only be good for their joint business venture, Vinny thought proudly. It had been a personal dream for many years for himself and Eddie to go into business together, and Vinny knew that when it finally happened, he and his pal would be the talk of the town, and so they should be. Two legends of their time, him and Ed.

'Daughters – who'd have 'em, eh?' Eddie sighed, as he sat back down.

'Everything OK?' Vinny asked.

'So-so. Frankie was meant to be going out with Stuart today, but she blew the poor sod out, yet again. He's not exactly admitted it to me, but I know the lad's in love with her. Unlike that fucking toe-rag Jed, Stuart would only bring my Frankie happiness, if she'd give the poor bastard a chance,' Eddie sighed. Stuart was the lad Eddie had shared a cell with in nick and, just as Vinny had with Jay Boy, Ed had given Stuart a job on the outside.

'I've got all this to come with Ava,' said Vinny. 'As far as I know, there's been no serious boyfriends – yet! I dread the day she brings one home. Give 'em the third degree, I will.'

'Boys are far less of a worry. Well, unless they turn out gay, like mine,' Eddie retorted. It was now common knowledge that Frankie's twin Joey batted for the other side.

Knowing that Eddie was still struggling to get his head around Joey's sexuality, Vinny deftly changed the subject. 'I've got a bit of a dilemma meself at the mo. There's a young bird working at the club who is proper showing out to me. She's a real posh 'un, and I'm truly tempted.'

'Nothing wrong with having a young bird on your arm, mate. You're only as young as the woman you feel. Look at me and my Gina.'

'But Felicity's only twenty-six,' Vinny said seriously.

Eddie Mitchell spat his Scotch back in his glass before laughing. 'Fuck me! That is a bit young. But at least she's legal – well, only just.' Seeing Vinny's expression, he toned down the humour. 'Nah, I'm only pulling your leg, mate. If you like her, go for it. You're a long time dead, pal.'

Daniel Butler groaned with ecstasy as Roxanne's mouth made contact with his penis, but his ecstasy was short-lived as she quickly stopped again.

'For fuck's sake, Rox. You've gotta stop doing this. I want you badly and I'm beginning to think you're a prick tease,' a frustrated Daniel mumbled. If his father and Lee knew that he had yet to get his leg over with Roxanne, they would roll on the floor laughing. That's why he'd pretended they'd done the deed early on in the relationship. It was also another reason why he was desperate for Roxanne to move in with him.

'I've told you before, Dan, I need to know you're serious about me before we take things further. You know I've only slept with Marty, and look what he did to me. No way will I ever give myself to another man, including you, unless I know it's for real this time.'

Daniel propped himself up on his elbow and stared at the girl who had hit him for six. Her hairstyle kind of suited her personality. It was big and untamed, same as she was. Kissing the colourful rose tattoo on the top of Roxanne's left arm, Daniel stopped and looked her in the eyes. 'Will it prove I'm serious about you if I ask you to move in with me?'

Feeling a glow of happiness inside, Roxanne desperately tried not to show it. 'It might. Depends if you're actually going to ask me properly, or not?'

For a laugh, Daniel got down on one knee. 'Roxanne Smith, will you please do me the honour of giving up that crappy job and accommodation of yours and allowing me to take good care of ya? The reason being, I think I might be in love.'

Roxanne burst out laughing. 'You're a proper Bobby Dazzler, you are. When shall I move in?'

Daniel leapt on top of Roxanne. 'How about tomorrow? And you do know we'll be sharing the same bed, don't you?'

Stroking Daniel's rock-hard penis, Roxanne said, 'Do you think you can handle me?'

'You bet I can. It's you that needs to worry if you can handle me,' Daniel groaned, pushing Roxy's hand away before he ejaculated all over her clothes.

Roxy grinned. She knew how badly Daniel wanted her and rather enjoyed teasing him. The feeling was mutual though. She could not wait to feel him deep inside her. 'We'll see who can handle who the best tomorrow then, shall we?'

CHAPTER THIRTY-ONE

Roxanne crammed all her belongings inside two large sports bags. She'd had wardrobes full of clothes and shoes back home, but had left virtually all of them behind.

Alex barged in the room, out of breath. 'Stavros is on the warpath, looking for you. He thinks I've gone to find you. Oh, mate, I really am going to miss you. I dread to think who I'll be sharing with next. I hope he don't put a Pole or Litho in here. I cannae bloody understand 'em.'

'I've left the club number in your drawer. Ring me whenever, and keep your chin up, pet. I'll get you that barmaid's job, I promise.'

'I doubt it will pay enough for me to rent accommodation though,' Alex said worriedly.

Roxy was about to reply when an angry Stavros appeared. 'There you are, you lazy girl. Get back to work this very minute or I will dock your wages,' he yelled, his ugly fat face even redder than usual.

Roxanne glared at the man, then picked up her bags. 'You can stick your shitty job and room right up your big fat arse.'

When Stavros lunged towards Roxanne, Alex intervened. 'Leave her alone. Go, Roxy, now,' she screamed.

Feeling a tad guilty at leaving her friend behind, Roxanne ran from the room, out of the hotel and straight into Daniel Butler's arms.

Little Vinny led a quiet life these days. His brush with the law had scared the shit out of him, and he was determined never to give them a reason to question him again. Since that torrid interrogation, Little Vinny hadn't come face to face with Terry and had no wish to. But he'd heard through the grapevine that Terry had been promoted to chief inspector of the bloody murder squad, and all Little Vinny could hope was that the bastard had forgotten all about him. Surely there was no more evidence to come to light after all this time?

Little Vinny still worked with Finn, but all events they organized were now above board. Illegal raves were a thing of the past, and their official job title was 'Club and Rave Promoters'. The only stroke they pulled these days was to rob the taxman of a good few quid, but they had their arses well covered by their dodgy accountant. Last year had been an extremely prosperous one. Ibiza and Ayia Napa were where they had earned the bulk of their dosh and this summer they planned to branch out to Magaluf as well. Sammi-Lou didn't like it when he had to spend time abroad, but Little Vinny had never cheated on her and never would.

'Do I look OK in this dress, Vin? I feel ever so fat. Charlene's been going to Slimming World and she's lost over half a stone in a month. I might give it a try.'

Little Vinny put his arms around his wife and squeezed her backside. Sammi-Lou was thirty-four now, a year younger than his good self and he still saw her as beautiful. She was only a size bloody twelve and he liked her curves. 'You look gorgeous as you are. A man doesn't wanna grab hold of skin and bones,' he reassured her.

When the sound of the buzzer made her jump, Sammi-Lou peered out the window. They had electric gates, but the drive wasn't enormous like her parents'. 'Oh my God! I think it's the police, Vin. That's definitely a cop car. Have a look.'

Little Vinny stood rooted to the new wooden floor they'd recently had laid, fear flooding through his veins. He could feel a panic attack coming on. His mouth was dry and his hands were shaking. He'd only heard last week that Terry had been promoted. Surely he hadn't unearthed some new evidence to bang him up like he'd once vowed to? 'I ain't 'ere, if they ask. Tell 'em I'm at work,' he said, opening the back door.

'What you done, Vin?' Sammi-Lou asked, when the buzzer sounded for a second time.

'Nothing, I swear. Just come and get me when they've gone. I'll be in the shed.'

The ten minutes Little Vinny waited for his wife to return were truly awful. He felt physically sick and could not stop trembling. Was this God paying him back for the one awful mistake he'd made? If so, he was doing a damn good job of it.

Sammi-Lou yanked open the shed door, her complexion a deathly white. 'We've got to go to the police station. Regan's stabbed a teacher with a pair of scissors.'

'You what!'

Sammi-Lou burst into tears. 'They can't take him away from us, Vin. Say they put him away?'

Snapping out of his own dark thoughts, Little Vinny stood up and held his wife. 'We'll get him a good brief. He'll be fine, I promise. Did they say if the teacher's OK?'

'No. I forgot to ask. What we done so wrong? We've been good parents, haven't we?'

Remembering one of his nan's sayings, 'What's bred in

the bone comes out in the flesh', Little Vinny shuddered. He couldn't help but wonder if it was true.

When Daniel had come out of prison, the first thing he'd noticed about the club was how tatty and dirty the décor had become in his absence. So this week he had hired decorators, and now wished he hadn't because it meant he would have to wait until tonight to make love to his stunning girlfriend.

Roxanne already knew the layout of the upstairs like the back of her hand, as she'd spent virtually every evening there since they'd met. She wasn't as high maintenance as Daniel thought she might be, was quite happy to chill indoors with a film and takeaway rather than be wined and dined. 'Is that all your clothes and stuff?' Daniel asked, putting his arms around her waist.

Roxanne nodded. 'I left home in a bit of a rush and couldn't be bothered going back for the rest. My mum and dad would've only kicked off and tried to handcuff me so I couldn't leave,' she explained.

'Have you told 'em we're moving in together?'

'Not yet, but I will ring me mam soon,' Roxanne lied. She didn't miss her overbearing parents at all and had no intention of contacting them any time soon.

Feeling his cock stiffen, Daniel pulled away. 'While that mob are banging and crashing about, I thought we'd go out for a bit. Let's go shopping and I'll treat you to some new clothes. Afterwards, we can grab a meal and a few drinks somewhere. I'd like you to meet my nan properly an' all. She rang me earlier and seemed thrilled you're moving in. "About time you settled down with a nice girl, Daniel,"' he laughed, mimicking Queenie's voice. 'Then by the time we get back, we'll have the club all to ourselves,' Daniel added, his voice full of longing.

Roxanne smiled. This was so much better than scrubbing floors and having that letch Stavros gawp at her breasts. 'OK. We'll do whatever you want.'

Little Vinny sat opposite his son in the custody suite. Instead of looking scared or upset as you would if you'd been nicked for stabbing your teacher, twelve-year-old Regan had a sulky expression on his face, bolshie attitude, and kept insisting the incident wasn't his fault.

Little Vinny was furious, but they had a bloody copper supervising the pair of them so he had to watch what he said.

'Hallsy has been winding me up ever since I started at that school, Dad. And he's a nonce. Gavin Joseph reckons he touched his bum in the changing rooms once,' Regan explained, arms folded and lips pouting.

Little Vinny leaned forward. He'd been warned he mustn't say anything to influence the course of the interview. 'Sit up and stop slouching. You might think you're clever, but you're not. You're an idiot. You'll have a reality check if you get sent away, that's for sure. There'll be none of your home comforts then, so if I was you I'd drop the attitude and be very sorry for what you did.'

'That's it. Your time's up. You cannot be telling him what to say. You were warned,' the officer said.

Little Vinny tipped his son a wink before being marched out of the suite. Now all he could do was hope the brazen little bastard had cottoned on and would take heed of his warning.

'What's up? Don't you like the look of the grub in 'ere?' Daniel Butler asked. He'd taken Roxanne to a nice French restaurant he'd been to a few times with his dad and could tell she wasn't that comfortable.

Roxanne handed Daniel her menu. Her parents were home birds and she'd rarely eaten in restaurants, especially poncy ones like this. 'Choose something chicken-based for me.'

Daniel ordered the food, then sipped his wine. He could tell Roxanne wasn't a wine drinker by her look of distaste, so asked if she wanted something else.

'Cider please,' Roxanne smiled.

Daniel called the waiter over again, then held his girl-friend's hand. 'Now we're living together, I wanna know everything about you. You've told me all about Marty, but little about your life back home and your family. I know you don't get on with your parents, but why?'

Roxanne shrugged. 'It's hard to explain.'

'Well, try at least. My family are by no means normal, so you won't shock me,' Daniel chuckled.

'My parents are too normal. Really dull and boring, like. They'd never let me out of their sight as a child and I was never allowed to play out like all the other kids. My mam especially suffocated me, but things got a bit easier when my brother and sister were born. They started suffocating them instead.'

'I didn't even know you had a brother and sister. You've never mentioned them before. How old are they?'

'Seven. They're twins. My mam couldn't fall pregnant again naturally, so had IVF treatment.'

'You must miss the twins, surely?' Daniel asked. Time was a healer, but he still thought about Adam. He and Lee would always visit their brother's grave once a month and on special occasions.

'Yeah. But, I had to get away, and the twins are a small price to pay. They've got each other and my parents have managed to mould them into the dream children they always craved,' Roxanne replied sarcastically. 'I was always the "rebel without a cause", me,' Roxanne admitted, quoting the title of one of her favourite films. She was addicted to old movies, especially black-and-white ones.

Daniel smiled. 'I can imagine you being a handful. I was the same.'

'I bet you didn't nick your father's brand-new Mercedes at the age of fourteen and after getting off your head on cider, write it off by accidentally crashing it into the churchyard wall,' Roxanne bragged.

Daniel laughed out loud. 'No, I didn't do that, but I did pull some strokes. I once stabbed me nan's next-door neighbour – but don't tell her that when we visit later, 'cos I never actually confessed my sins.'

Roxanne felt a warm glow inside. Daniel truly was her very own James Dean.

'What you smiling at?'

'Thinking how alike we are.'

Daniel winked. 'Bonnie and Clyde ain't got nothing on us, babe.'

Sammi-Lou Butler was on tenterhooks. Her husband had rung her a couple of hours ago to reassure her the teacher was fine, but there was still no sign of him or her unpredictable son. She wouldn't be able to cope if they carted Regan off to one of those awful places they sent bad boys to, and she doubted he would either.

'Sit down, for Christ's sake, Mum. You're wearing the carpet out,' Calum said.

'Mum's worried, Cal, and so am I. You would be too if you had a brain,' Oliver sniped.

'Got more of a brain than you'll ever have – and so has Regan, which is why he'll be fine. You ain't ever been nicked, so what do you know about the Old Bill?' Calum argued.

'That's enough silly gangster talk. You've got some growing up to do, Calum Butler, that's for sure. Good job your grandfather isn't here, listening to you spout such drivel. Getting into trouble with the police isn't clever. It's downright stupid,' Meg Allen bellowed. Gary hadn't been at home when Sammi-Lou had rung up in tears explaining the latest drama surrounding their grandsons and Meg was dreading telling her husband later. Gary would go apeshit to learn Regan had stabbed his teacher, and there was no way Meg could tone the crime down as she usually tried to whenever Regan or Calum got into trouble. Why couldn't they be more like Oliver? He'd never caused any of them a moment's worry in his life.

'Dad's pulling up. Regan's with him,' Oliver announced.

Sammi-Lou darted to the front door and yanked it open. 'What happened? Why did you do it, Regan?' she cried.

'Get up to your room, now,' Little Vinny ordered his delinquent child.

'No. I want to hear what he has to bloody say for himself first,' Sammi insisted.

Regan Butler wasn't stupid. He'd understood his father's warning and been full of remorse in the interview. He'd wanted to laugh when the Old Bill had asked him 'Do you know what you did was wrong?' but had instead kept a straight face and replied, 'Yes, officer. It was very wrong and I'm truly sorry from the bottom of my heart.'

Deciding to play the same sorrowful act to get his mother off his back, Regan told her exactly what she wanted to hear.

Meg Allen was almost ready to believe the child until she caught him and Calum sharing a triumphant glance and smirk. The realization that Regan was a wicked liar as well as a violent little toe-rag made Meg feel terribly ill.

Queenie waved goodbye to Daniel and Roxanne while at the same time asking Vivian, 'What did you make of her?'

'Pretty, but a bit punky-looking. She isn't what I'd expected.'

Queenie marched into the lounge. 'If she's twenty-one, then I'm Doris Day. And as for that stud in her tongue and awful bloody ink on her arm, whatever does Daniel see in that? Could have any girl he wanted, good-looking lad like him. Must want his head tested.'

'She was pleasant enough, Queen, but I thought she was younger an' all. Didn't like all that thick eye make-up either. Took the beauty away from her face.'

'I couldn't understand a word she bleedin' well said. Whyever didn't he settle for a nice London girl? There's plenty out there to choose from.'

Vivian burst out laughing. 'I think she thought you were deaf. You kept saying "Ay" then she kept saying "Aye". I thought to meself, "Ay-aye, what's going on here then?"'

Queenie couldn't help but chuckle. 'Anyone ever tell you you're a funny fucker, Vivian Harris? You should've been on stage.'

'Dad, are you going to show me those orders on the computer, or are you going to stare at that tramp all evening? Put your tongue back in, for goodness' sake. It's embarrassing. She isn't much older than me.'

Feeling like a fool, Vinny led his daughter into the office. For some reason, Ava was the only person he knew who had the ability to make him feel like a silly old bastard. When he'd arrived home yesterday with Scotch in his veins after being out with Ed, Vinny had invited Felicity Carter-Price to share a drink with him after work. The drink had turned into two bottles of champagne, but nothing unto-ward had occurred. Vinny had kissed her politely on the cheek when she'd left, even though he'd been sorely tempted to fuck her brains out. Surprisingly for him, he'd rather enjoyed her company. Birds usually bored him rigid, but Felicity was intelligent, especially about world affairs and politics, and he loved that posh accent of hers. It was a massive turn on and he could listen to her for hours.

Deciding to take his daughter down a peg or two, Vinny ordered her to sit down. Ava had a decent head on her shoulders and would be an asset to the club in the long run, which was why he'd decided to teach her the ropes. Especially if he was going to be spending less time here once he and Eddie had the casino up and running. Ava and Carl could run the joint between them in his absence.

'What?' Ava asked, her bright green eyes blazing with anger, just like his own.

'Let's get some things straight, Ava. I will not be spoken down to in the club I worked my nuts off to buy. Neither will I have you call our dancers "tramps". I actually thought you was ready for this when I took you on, but perhaps I was wrong? You're obviously still a child at heart and if you can't act professionally, how the hell can I ever leave you in charge?'

'Oh, come on, Dad. I'm not stupid, which is why you offered me the bloody job in the first place. You know what an asset I can be to you, and you also wanted to stop me from going out clubbing and having a steady boyfriend. You don't want me making mistakes in life and I fully understand that. Have I not got the right to stop you from doing the same? Because I am telling you now, if you start sleeping with that stupid posh tart, you will be a laughing stock. Imagine Nan finding out. And you think she'll have a fit if she finds out I'm working here,' Ava laughed. 'She will literally have a cardiac if she claps eyes on your new fancy piece, I'm telling ya.'

Knowing Ava's words were true, but not wanting to admit it to himself, Vinny's anger increased. 'There is sod-all going on between me and Felicity. And even if there was, it would be none of your fucking business – or anybody else's, for that matter.'

Aside from being disgusted that her father clearly fancied a tart not much older than her, Ava was jealous. She'd never known her dad to be interested in women and hated the thought of having to share him, especially now they were so close. She waved her hands in the air and grinned. She knew she was thoroughly annoying him, but was determined to nip this tart in the bud. 'Oooh, Felicity and Vinny. What a lovely ring that has to it,' she mocked. 'You'll soon be the new Hugh Hefner.'

Absolutely livid, Vinny was about to give Ava a short sharp slap when Carl burst into the office without warning. 'Eddie Mitchell's on the phone. Says it's urgent. He's been trying to get hold of your other mobile. He said to call him on this number,' Carl said, handing Vinny a piece of paper.

'Get out of my sight,' Vinny hissed at his daughter. He then composed himself before switching on the dodgy mobile that wasn't registered in his name. 'What's up, mate?'

'We're gonna have to put that viewing on hold tomorrow. I've gotta shoot up north. Frankie's had a visit from some pikey bird who reckons Jed is still alive and is living in Scotland with Georgie and Harry.'

'Jesus wept! Do you reckon it's kosher?' Vinny asked. Everyone thought Jed O'Hara had been killed and the kids snatched by his gypsy family. The code of silence in the gypsy community couldn't be cracked even by a man with Eddie Mitchell's legendary connections and determination.

'Frankie is ninety-nine per cent sure it's kosher, so that's good enough for me. I'll be in touch, but only from payphones. Don't ring, just in case.'

'I won't, and if you need me, say the word. Good luck,

Ed.' Vinny ended the call, poured himself a Scotch and spun around in his office chair until he felt dizzy. It reminded him of playing with his brothers on the park roundabout when they were kids, so he stopped. He had no brothers left now. Roy was long gone, and he and Michael were dead to one another. There was no point in torturing yourself, was there? Sometimes you had no choice but to move on in life, and even though his daughter clearly hated her, Vinny's pulsating penis told him that Felicity Carter-Price might play a small part in that moving on process.

'What's bothering you, Daniel? You've been acting weird since I went to the netty. Has somebody upset you?' Roxanne asked. It had been her idea they pop in the Blind Beggar. She'd read about the pub in books and wanted to see it in the flesh. Daniel had got a massive welcome when they'd walked in and Roxanne was so proud to be introduced as his girlfriend.

Daniel Butler was worried. He'd rung his nan while Roxanne was in the bog to see what she'd thought of her and his nan was insistent she was younger than the twenty-one years she claimed to be. He'd always been wary that Roxanne had lied about her age. Even his dad and brother said she looked younger. 'You got your passport at the club?' Daniel asked her.

'No. Why?'

'You must have some sort of ID. Where's your passport?'

'I haven't got any ID. I left home in a hurry and forgot to pack it. What's this all about, Daniel?'

'Not here. Let's talk back at the club.'

Roxanne's heart beat wildly as she followed her boyfriend out of the pub and along the High Road. It had to be about her age. She'd clocked his grandmother and aunt studying her closely. Both women had been incredibly inquisitive, firing question after question at her and she'd felt extremely uncomfortable. It had been more like an interrogation than a bloody visit.

Daniel's silence was unnerving. Roxanne had never seen him like this and couldn't bear the thought of losing him. 'What have I done wrong?' she asked fearfully.

Blanking her question, Daniel unlocked the door and ordered Roxanne to sit down. He poured himself a drink and sat opposite her. 'No more lies, OK? It's never gonna work if we can't be honest with one another, and if you lie to me now, it's over. How old are you, Roxanne? And please do not insult my intelligence by insisting you're twenty-one again.'

When Roxanne burst into tears, Daniel immediately felt guilty. He crouched in front of her and held her hands. 'Just be honest with me, eh? Then we can move on. I don't care if you're younger – we ain't gotta tell anyone else. I can understand why you lied, because I'm a lot older.'

'I'm only eighteen and I'm so sorry I lied to you. I thought you'd see me as some silly kid and not want me.'

Daniel smiled. 'Age is only a number. It's lies that I can't stand. We love each other and that's all that matters. So let's go christen that bed, shall we?'

CHAPTER THIRTY-TWO

Summer 2001

Daniel Butler grinned as he stepped out of the changing room. It was strange what life threw at you at times. A year ago he'd been whiling away the hours in a prison cell and would never have believed just twelve months later he would have a baby on the way and be planning his own wedding. 'Well? How do I look?' he asked his father and brother.

'Very dapper,' Michael replied.

'Apart from that dodgy tie. She'll run a mile if you walk up the aisle with that on,' Lee joked.

'Cheeky bastard,' Daniel laughed. 'Make yourself useful and grab a table in that boozer over the road. Ravenous, I am. Order me fish and chips.'

'You OK, boy?' Michael asked, putting an arm around Lee's shoulders as they crossed over the road. Lee and Beth were still having no luck on the baby front and he knew how tough it must be for him that Daniel and Roxanne would soon become parents.

'I'm all right, Dad, but Beth's struggling a bit at the mo. Her eyes fill up with tears every time I mention Dan's baby or one of her friends gets up the spout. Don't say nothing to anyone, but I've agreed to go for tests now. Dreading it, I am, in case the problem lies with me. I dunno if I can deal with being told I'm a Jaffa. I'd feel a right mug – and where's that gonna leave me and Beth? She's that desperate for kids, it's become an obsession with her.'

'I doubt it's your fault, son. Us Butler males are anything but seedless. I bet the problem lies with Beth, but you can cross that bridge when you come to it. There's plenty the medical profession can do these days – IVF and stuff. You and Beth'll get through this.'

'But we can't afford it. IVF costs a fortune and the way the club's been we've had to dip regularly into our savings.'

'Son, anything you need, you come to me, OK?'

'Thanks, Dad. That'll cheer Beth right up when I tell her.'

'That's what fathers are for, boy. So, what's your feelings now on Dan and Roxy? I seriously had me doubts at first, especially when it turned out she was only eighteen. But I've grown to like her, and she and Dan seem like a match made in heaven. He's seriously calmed down since he met her. I've never known him so happy.'

Neither Lee nor Beth were overly impressed with Daniel's wife-to-be, but Lee kept his thoughts to himself. As long as his brother was happy, that's all that mattered. 'Yeah, they're good together. Dan's gonna have to find 'em a new place to live when the baby arrives though. The club ain't no place to raise a nipper. Not sure how he's gonna be able to afford that. The student night's turned out to be a disaster. We only had about forty punters in last Monday.'

'You should never have got rid of the strippers. Sunday lunchtimes was always a good little earner back in the day, and the strippers were part of the furniture.'

'Back in the day everything was a good little earner. But we ain't back in the fucking day, Dad. We're in the present, stuck with a club in freefall in a shithole of an area where no one drinks. It ain't never gonna get any better, only worse.'

Michael picked up a menu and said nothing. When he'd first invested in the casino, he'd still been taking a 20 per cent cut out of the club, but had since stopped doing so when he realized how tough the lads were having it. The gaff still solely belonged to him though, so maybe it was time to sell up? A property developer would snap it up, and he'd see his boys more than all right so they could set up another business elsewhere.

'What's up?' Lee asked.

'Nothing. Whaddya want to eat? Let's order.' Michael wasn't ready to disclose his thoughts just yet. Daniel had a lot on his plate, and Lee had his own problems. This was something he had to think long and hard about, and only he could make the gut-wrenching decision to sell a property that had proudly displayed his family's name since the early sixties.

Bella D'Angelo spent ages choosing her outfit. Camila was appearing in a show at the Queen's Theatre in Hornchurch this evening and Michael had offered to pick Bella up so they could arrive together.

'You aren't ever going to win him back, Mother. Making a fool of yourself at your age isn't a good look, you know. I told Granddad earlier that you've been acting like a lovesick teenager lately and even he thinks you've lost the plot,' Antonio said casually.

Bella glared at the son she'd once doted on. He was munching on a bowl of cornflakes, milk dribbling down his chin while trying to wind her up. 'You're a fine one to give out advice. What would you know about relationships? The only girlfriend I've ever known you to have lasted all of a week. Why don't you go back to your room and play computer games while getting stoned? Because that and music is your whole life, Antonio. If anybody is a fool in this house, it's you. You're an embarrassment to me and your sister.'

'Slag,' Antonio spat, before walking away. He'd actually upped his abuse at his mother recently. The reason being she and Michael were getting along far too well for his liking. Michael often popped round the house now, and he'd even had the cheek to stay for dinner a few times. No way was his mother getting back with that vermin if he had anything to do with it. Over his dead body.

Feeling slightly guilty over the way she'd spoken to her son, Bella pushed it to the back of her mind. She rarely bothered answering Antonio back, but his constant sniping was beginning to wear thin. She knew why he was doing it. Relations had improved dramatically between herself and Michael, and her son could not handle that.

Bella sighed. It was such a shame Michael had cut out Antonio and said such cruel things when her awful secret had first come to light. She could fully understand why he'd lashed out and knew he truly regretted the way he'd treated Antonio. Michael had tried to make things right with her son lately. But Antonio it seemed did not have a forgiving bone in his body.

'Whey-aye! The bairn's started showing. You still look amazing though, you bitch,' Alex laughed. She would forever be grateful to Roxanne for her new happy life. Her pal had kept her promise and got Tracy the sack from her barmaid job very soon after moving in with Daniel. It was there Alex had met Stevie. His father owned a mini-cab office in Bethnal Green and her and Stevie both worked there now and lived in the flat above.

'You're looking well, too. How times change. We've most certainly moved on from our days with that perv Stavros, haven't we?' Roxanne laughed.

'Sure have, pet. So have you booked the big day yet? You don't want to be waddling down the aisle.'

When Roxanne had found out she was pregnant, she'd been anything but overjoyed. Being a mum wasn't something she'd planned at her age, and the thought of giving birth and the responsibility that came afterwards filled her with fear. She'd actually been hoping Daniel would want to pay for a termination. He'd been stunned when she'd told him, but once he'd got over the initial shock he'd insisted they keep the baby and get married before it was born. 'September the twelfth. We booked it yesterday, and I want you to be a bridesmaid – I'm only having two, and Daniel wants his sister as the other. We're getting married in the East End, a registry office. No way am I walking into a church and facing a vicar, not when I'm pregnant.'

'I'd be honoured to be your bridesmaid. Who'd have thought when that miserable cow Tracy invited us to the club that night, you'd end up marrying the boss? She was so jealous. I think the ugly cow fancied Daniel herself,' Alex laughed.

'I know. It's mental, isn't it? We're holding the reception at the club. I've told Daniel I don't want a load of people there. I don't want a big fuss.'

'He's got a big family though, hasn't he?'

'Yeah, and obviously they will come. Apart from his Uncle Vinny. Daniel's dad and him don't get on.'

'Vinny Butler is a real face around here. Stevie's told me all about him. Apparently, years ago, he used to knock about with some Turkish bloke and one night they had a massive fight with a gang of men outside the cab firm. Vinny pulled out a blade and cut one of the men's faces real bad. He dropped a wad of money in the cab firm the next day and told Stevie's dad, "You say nothing."'

Roxanne grinned. She had never met Vinny, but had him to thank for sorting out the fake passport which had enabled her to register with a doctor, open a bank account and get married. She'd had to come clean with Daniel in the end, had told him she was positive her father had a dodgy past which he and her mother had hidden. She'd also told him she thought her father was on the run from the police, which was true. The only thing she had lied about was why she thought he was on the run, and her own little secret. She couldn't tell anybody that – not even Alex.

Lee Butler was on his fifth pint. Unlike his father and Daniel, he wasn't a wine or spirit drinker, but today he was drinking faster than them. Beth had been in a terrible state yesterday, hadn't even gone to work last night. Truth be known, he was dreading going home later. Babies, babies, bloody babies, he was sick of hearing the word. And even though he tried not to be, he could not help being jealous of Daniel's ability to knock Roxanne up so quickly, which was why he was in the mood to stir the pot. Both he and Beth were sure Roxanne was hiding something about her past. There was definitely something dodgy about her.

'You wanna slow down a bit, bruv. You're starting to go boss-eyed,' Daniel joked. Since marrying Beth, his brother wasn't the biggest drinker in the world.

'He's got a point, Lee. You do look a bit like Norman Wisdom,' Michael laughed.

Not in the mood for jokes, Lee changed the subject. 'So,

I take it the mysterious Roxanne has invited her even more mysterious family to the wedding?'

'Nah. Roxy don't get on with her family. You know that because I've told ya, and so has she. Her mate Alex is gonna be a bridesmaid alongside our Cami.'

'Not being funny, Dan, but I want Dad's opinion on this. Don't you think it's weird that we know fuck-all about Roxanne and her family? Something ain't right; I can feel it in my bones. You sure she ain't undercover Old Bill?' Lee laughed.

Daniel glanced at his father. He was the only one he'd disclosed the truth to about Roxanne's past. He'd known his dad was worried when he'd admitted she'd lied about her age, so he'd come clean. He would never tell anybody else though, including his brother. She was ashamed of what her father had done and he didn't blame her.

Queenie Butler was a suspicious person by nature, but rarely of her own kin. Family meant everything to her and if you could not trust them, who could you bloody well trust? However, something about Vivian's regular visits to talk to her Lenny at the grave, which had recently become more frequent, did not ring true to Queenie. She was spending hours on end over there, which was why Queenie had decided to surprise her sister by turning up today.

Feeling guilty about using her deceased son as an excuse to spend time with Albie, Vivian actually did pop to the cemetery some days. She only stayed briefly and would then hop back on the train to visit Albie in nearby Barking. Today was one of those days, and Viv was just about to leave when she spotted her sister. She was horrified. She had her big shopping bag and it had a container full of stew for Albie inside. 'What you doing 'ere?' she asked, trying to keep the disappointment out of her voice.

'The pains in me leg wore off after you left, so I thought I'd surprise ya. You don't look very happy to see me. What you got in your bag?' Queenie asked.

'Shopping. Not that it's any of your bloody business. You're checking up on me, aren't you? How dare you!'

'No, I'm not! I do have family at this cemetery an' all, in case you had forgotten. Why you being so narky? I only wanted to surprise you. I thought we'd have a bit of lunch out together – my treat. Been ages since we've done that.'

Saddened that she wouldn't be able to spend the afternoon with Albie, or even let him know that she couldn't make it, Vivian had no option but to force a smile and hope that Queenie didn't get a whiff of her own homemade stew.

'You all right, babe? How did it go with Alex?' Daniel asked, flopping on the sofa. Lee had spoilt his day by getting drunk and acting like a prick, and Daniel planned to have a serious chat with him tomorrow. No way was he going to have his best man showing him up on his wedding day.

'Alex can't wait to be bridesmaid,' Roxanne grinned. 'And I saw a wicked outfit that I put a deposit on. The woman said she can get it altered for me if I get too massive. I'm not telling you any more about it though. So don't pry, canny lad,' she chuckled. She was actually looking forward to getting married now. The connection between herself and Daniel was awesome. She even knew what he was thinking at times, and he seemed to be able to read her mind too. They were soul-mates and their age difference wasn't a problem at all.

'Lee made a right tit of himself today. I felt like knocking him out at one point, but me dad calmed it down.'

'What did he do?' Roxanne asked. She was very fond of

Daniel's father, but not overly struck on Lee or his wife. She could sense they were jealous of her and Daniel's happiness and had told her boyfriend as much.

'Turns out you were right, but we mustn't say anything. Me dad had a quiet word in me shell-like after we'd dropped Lee off. Him and Beth are having tests to see why she can't get pregnant. Lee don't dislike you, but keeps having little digs about your past. Obviously jealous that I have good sperm that are actual swimmers,' Daniel chuckled.

'You didn't tell him anything, did you?' Roxanne asked, alarmed. She'd had to tell Daniel something when he'd kept on about her applying for new identification, so had told him her parents were on the run because her dad had once mown down and killed a child in his car whilst drunk. Roxanne explained how they'd moved home the very next day and her surname had been changed.

'Nah. I told him jack-shit, so don't worry. Vinny's the only one who knows everything and he can be trusted,' Daniel reassured her. Unbeknown to his father or Lee, Daniel actually got on well with Vinny these days. His uncle had written to him a lot in prison and had certainly come up trumps with Roxanne's fake ID. Vinny dealt with a geezer who could actually provide a National Insurance number as well, and even though Roxanne had been worried, she'd had no problems registering with a quack. Daniel had no idea where the ID came from, as Vinny'd been reluctant to tell him. All he'd said was it was kosher, had cost a lot of money, and to accept it as a wedding gift from him.

Roxanne smiled and cuddled up to her fiancé. She was a good liar, but what she'd told Daniel wasn't all lies. It was fact, mixed with fiction for her own benefit.

*

Michael Butler nudged and grinned at Bella as his daughter strutted across the stage singing 'Oom-Pah-Pah'. Camila had actually had a part in the 1994 West End revival of *Oliver*, but she'd only played one of the orphans back then. Tonight's adaptation was much smaller and had been put on by the drama school his daughter attended. She was playing Nancy, one of the biggest parts, and Michael felt as proud as a peacock.

'Wow! Our little girl is officially amazing,' Bella whispered in Michael's ear.

'Gets it from me, especially that Cockney accent,' Michael chuckled.

'I'll allow you the credit for her accent, but her beauty and talent are definitely my input,' Bella retorted.

Overcome by the moment, Michael squeezed Bella's hand. 'Shall we take Cami out to celebrate afterwards? I know a nice restaurant not far from 'ere.'

Bella returned the squeeze. 'Cami would love that, and so would I.'

Roxanne smiled as she stared at Daniel sleeping peacefully. He always had a habit of falling asleep quickly after one of their marathon love-making sessions, but it didn't bother Roxanne. She saw it as a sign of contentment.

Not feeling tired herself, Roxanne got out of bed and crept into the kitchen. She made herself a brew, took her purse out of her handbag and stared at the photo of her brother and sister. There'd been twins of around the same age in the café she and Alex had met in today, and it had momentarily reminded Roxanne of how much she missed them.

She stared at the photo for a couple of minutes, kissed it and put it back in her purse. One day she would come clean to Daniel about her big whopper of a lie, but only when the time was right. The twins could come and visit them then, be part of her life again. Unfortunately though, that wouldn't be any time soon. If the truth reared its ugly head now, it would definitely blow her happiness to pieces without a shadow of a doubt.

CHAPTER THIRTY-THREE

The morning before his son's wedding, Michael Butler was awoken by Katy's hand around his cock. He leapt out of bed at rapid speed. 'I ain't got time today, girl. Got shitloads to do, as you can imagine, and I can't let me own son down on his stag piss-up. I'm gonna jump in the shower.'

'You certainly know how to make a woman feel good, you do, Michael. Last night you were tired and this morning you're in a rush. I don't ask for much from you. There aren't many women who would put up with you spending the bulk of the week in London getting up to Christ knows what. Don't take me for a fool, because I will make sure you regret it.'

Not wanting a bad atmosphere at the wedding tomorrow, Michael reluctantly got back into bed and gave Katy what she craved.

Daniel Butler checked his appearance in the mirror. Lee had suggested they go away and have a proper stag do, but Daniel didn't fancy a mad one. An East End pub crawl suited him fine and even though he wasn't getting married until tomorrow afternoon, he was determined to be home by about midnight at the latest.

Roxanne chuckled as she watched her fiancé admiring himself. He was wearing a black suit and looked a proper gangster with his dark sunglasses on.

Daniel turned around and took Roxanne in his arms. 'How lucky are you to be marrying me tomorrow, babe?'

Roxanne playfully punched him. 'You're the bloody lucky one and don't you ever forget it. You still meeting Vinny first?'

'Yeah. Gonna have a few bevvies with him over Canary Wharf before I meet the others. He's got some young bird on the go, so I'll suggest the four of us get together after the wedding. He's looking forward to meeting you and I can't wait to see this bird of his. He's a funny one, my uncle. Never been a player. I've not known him to have a bird since Jo.'

'Is Jo the mother of his kids?' Roxanne asked. Daniel had a very big family and Jo was a name she'd never heard mentioned before.

'Was. She's dead now. Jo was Ava and Molly's mum. Got killed in a car crash, she did. Changing the subject, I wonder what my nan's got in store for you? I hope you like Chas and bleedin' Dave,' Daniel smirked. When Roxy had first met his nan it had been awkward, to say the least, and it amused Daniel greatly they were now good buddies. So much so, Queenie had insisted on organizing a small hen party at hers. Roxanne was planning to stay over and get ready there tomorrow. He was getting ready at the club with his dad and Lee.

'Who the hell are Chas and Dave?' Roxanne asked innocently.

Daniel laughed. 'You'll find out later, and for Christ's sake don't tell me nan and aunt you've never heard of 'em. They'll hate you.'

'Stop winding me up, and make sure you behave yourself today. I love you, Daniel Butler.'

Kissing his wife-to-be, Daniel pulled away and grinned. 'Crazy, ain't it, to think we're gonna be husband and wife tomorrow? We didn't even know one another this time last year. But when something feels right, it feels right. I love you too, babe. Bundles.'

'Cooey, Albie. Got away quite easily today, love. Queenie's too busy preparing for the hen party to be worrying about me going out. Gone a bit overboard, if you ask me. Had banners and all sorts made. I wouldn't mind, but she didn't even like the poor little bride until a few weeks ago. Said she was nowhere good enough for Daniel.'

Chuckling, Albie stood up and gave Viv a peck on the lips. 'That's our Queenie for you, dear. As two-faced as they come. Sit yourself down and I'll make you a cuppa.'

'No. You sit down, Albie, and I'll put the kettle on. I've got some crusty rolls in me bag and a nice bit of boiled bacon for lunch. Bought us some big Spanish tomatoes an' all, but I'll rinse them under the tap for ten minutes first. If they've come all the way from Spain you don't know what diseases they're bleedin' carrying,' she said in earnest.

'You're a tonic, you are, Vivian Harris. Anyone ever tell ya that?'

'Yes. My old man on a regular basis. Until he ran off with that young barmaid. So whaddya reckon about tomorrow, Albie? You looking forward to it? Daniel seems very settled now, doesn't he? Nice enough girl, but I still can't bleedin' well understand her. Queenie apparently does though. She's taken it upon herself to translate between us.'

'I can't understand her very well either, but I do like her. She's very bubbly. Only time will tell if they rushed into things. As for the actual wedding, bound to be a bloody drama of some kind, Vivvy. There always is with our mob.'

*

'You're looking very suave and well, lad. Excited or crapping yourself?' Vinny Butler chortled, slapping his nephew on the back. He was genuinely fond of Daniel, thought he'd turned out well. But it did also bring a wry smile to Vinny's face that the boy had come to him for help regarding his bird's fake ID, rather than his father. He also got off on Daniel meeting him behind Michael's back.

'You ain't looking too bad yourself. Whoever this young bird is, she's obviously taking good care of you,' Daniel grinned, returning the slap on the back.

'She sure is. But keep it between me and you, OK?' Vinny winked, tapping the side of his nose. 'If Ava finds out, I'll be skinned alive. And if your nan finds out, she'll chop me nuts off and feed 'em to the birds as fat balls.'

Daniel laughed. 'What's her name and where did ya meet her?'

Vinny explained the score with Felicity. Carl and Eddie Mitchell were the only two that knew, and it felt good to finally tell a family member. 'It's early days though, boy, and Felicity's a lot younger than me. I'm just enjoying it for what it is. Can't see meself ever living with a bird again, if I'm honest. Too long in the tooth and set in me ways. She's a fucking wild one in the sack though. Keeps me fit, put it that way,' Vinny smirked.

Daniel chuckled. 'I never thought I'd settle down, but as soon as I met Roxy that all changed. Big age gap an' all, but who cares? You gotta do what makes you happy in life. I'm proper excited about being a dad an' all. I feel ready for it now.'

Vinny clicked his fingers. 'Bring us over a bottle of your finest bubbly, mate,' he told the barman. He turned back to Daniel. 'Do you ever think of your mum, boy? The reason I'm asking is, Ava's started giving me the third degree about Jo recently. Wants to know what she was like as a person and stuff. I wondered if that was normal after all this time? Or is it because she's got a whiff that I'm knocking off Felicity, d'ya reckon?'

'Funny you should say that, me and Lee were only talking about me mum the other day. Lee suggested we pop in and see Mary and Donald, tell 'em about the wedding and see if we could build some bridges. But they ain't got the café no more. They retired and moved away. Other than that, I've barely given my mum a thought for years, if I'm honest. I reckon Ava must've got wind you're at it, Vin.'

'Yeah, probably. She had her suspicions I had the hots for Felicity before I even went there. Donald and Mary, now that's a blast from the past. She weren't too bad, her. But he was a proper poker-faced do-gooder. So was their son. I bribed him, as a kid. Joined the police force as an adult, he did,' Vinny grinned. 'Would you have invited 'em to your wedding? I doubt your dad or nan would've been too happy.'

'Well, I have, sort of. The couple who run the café now have a forwarding address. They wouldn't give it to us, but promised to pass on a letter to Donald and Mary, so I stuck an invitation in an envelope. We'd been on the piss in Barking, me and Lee, and it seemed like a good idea at the time.'

Vinny spat his champagne back in the glass. He was the only family member not to be invited to the wedding, for obvious reasons. 'I'd love to be a fly on the wall if they turn up. Talk about throw a spanner in the works!'

'They won't show up. They fucking hate me.'

'You hope,' Vinny quipped.

Daniel laughed. 'The wonders of alcohol, eh?'

'All right, lads. Where's the main man?' Little Vinny asked.

'Gone on the missing list. Well, he ain't answering his phone, put it that way,' Lee replied solemnly. He and his father had fancied lining their stomachs properly before the heavy session ahead, so had popped down to Kelly's in Roman Road for pie and mash. The Hand and Flower was around the corner, so they'd decided to have a couple in there before meeting Daniel and the rest of the lads back in Whitechapel.

Little Vinny had rung them while in Kelly's and it had been Michael's idea to wind him up when he arrived. 'We think Dan's got cold feet, Vin. Nobody could get hold of him yesterday and Roxanne's in pieces,' he gloomily explained.

'You're kidding me!' Little Vinny exclaimed, his mouth wide open.

A serious look on his face, Lee shook his head. 'Nah, he ain't, and I blame myself. It was my idea we have a stag drink with our old school pals in Barking last Saturday, and Dan met this stunning bird. A model, with the biggest pair of knockers I've ever seen. He went home with her after the pub, and I covered for him with Roxy. But now he's disappeared again.'

'Fucking hell! Why does nothing ever go smoothly at weddings for our mob? I thought Dan and Roxanne were happy. And what about the baby? Does Nan know yet? She'll go ballistic if he stands her up at the altar.'

It was at that point Michael burst out laughing. 'We're winding you up, you numpty. Dan belled me earlier. He ain't meeting us until half two. Now get that down your neck,' he ordered, handing his nephew a drink.

'You bastards,' Little Vinny chuckled. He'd so needed to get out today and let his hair down for once. As much as he loved his wife, all she went on about lately was bloody Regan. The judge had ordered that his youngest son be sent to a secure unit in Hackney as punishment for stabbing his school teacher, and ever since Sammi-Lou had droned on about his welfare non-stop.

'How's the family, Vin? Regan coping OK?' Michael asked.

'Yeah, all good. Me and Sammi were allowed to take him out last Saturday. Let's talk about something else today, though, eh? I've come out to get away from the pressures of family life.'

'Me and you both, cuz. Now Vin's 'ere, Dad, tell us about this big surprise you have in store for Dan. I've been wracking me brains for days and I still haven't got a clue what it is,' Lee said. He and his brother were now firmly back on track. Lee had apologized for his stupid outburst in the pub, and had made more of an effort with Roxanne since.

Michael grinned. 'It's more of a surprise for the whole family, not only Dan. I pulled off a masterstroke. We've got two special guests attending the reception.'

'Who?' said Little Vinny.

'Jesus – is it Donald and Mary?' Lee asked, wondering if they'd received the invitation and somehow got hold of his father.

Michael laughed. 'Donald and Mary! As if! Let me tell Dan myself, but I've only gone and booked the real Chas and Dave to sing at the reception. We're still having the DJ and singer, but can you imagine your nan and aunt's faces? Their crew are setting their stuff up on stage early tomorrow morning. I remember seeing 'em in a few boozers round the East End before they were famous. But your nan and aunt won't have.'

'Brilliant! I'll put money on it Nan and Auntie Viv get up on the stage with 'em,' Little Vinny said.

'That is so fucking funny. And I bet Roxanne has never even heard of 'em,' Lee added.

Michael grinned broadly. 'Gonna be a wedding people talk about for years to come, lads. A true Butler occasion.'

*

'Cooey, Queen. Christ it's quiet in 'ere. Where's the music? Haven't the girls turned up yet?' Vivian asked, hanging up her jacket in the hallway.

'Oh, Viv. Something terrible has happened. You not heard? Come and have a look. Been bawling me eyes out, I have.'

Wondering what the hell was wrong, Vivian dashed into the front room. Her sister, Ava, Roxanne, Alex and two girls Viv did not recognize were all staring solemnly at Sky News. 'Whatsa matter?'

'Look! The Twin Towers in New York have been hit by planes. Flew straight into 'em they did, Viv. The poor people who work there have been jumping out of windows and all sorts. There must be loads dead. I reckon it's got to be a terrorist attack of some kind. One plane could've been an accident, but not two. It's truly sickening. I can't believe what I'm seeing.'

Taking in the horrific scenes on TV, Vivian put her hand over her mouth. 'Oh, dear Lord! Those poor souls.'

Along with the rest of the nation, Daniel, Michael, Lee and Little Vinny watched the horrendous scenes unfold with an expression of shock on their faces.

'One's smashed into the fucking Pentagon now!' Little Vinny exclaimed, spotting the breaking news at the bottom of the screen.

'London's being evacuated – well, the City is anyway. They reckon the bastards that did it might strike here next,' a stranger shouted out.

Daniel Butler looked at his family and friends in dismay. The boozer had an eerie atmosphere and there was no way they could go on a rowdy pub crawl with this atrocity occurring. It wasn't appropriate at all.

*

At Queenie's the mood remained extremely sombre and Roxanne was beginning to get restless. She had never heard of the Twin Towers before today, or the Pentagon, and she didn't want to spend the whole of her hen party watching distressing scenes on the television.

Alex nudged her friend. 'You OK, pet?'

Roxanne nodded, then took off the silver crown with a veil attached that Queenie had handed her on arrival. The room was decorated with banners and balloons, but it felt more like a funeral than a celebration. Why did such an awful thing have to happen today? She only hoped it wasn't a bad omen for tomorrow.

CHAPTER THIRTY-FOUR

'Wakey-wakey, boy. Rise and shine. You're getting married today, remember?' Michael announced, as he yanked open the heavy curtains.

Feeling like crap, Daniel sat up and put his hungover head in his hands. 'Get me some water, Dad. I'm dying of thirst.'

'Serves you right. I did warn you and Lee that having a shot-drinking competition wasn't the wisest idea in the world, but you two were on a mission. Your brother's ill an' all. Been chucking his guts up since six,' Michael smirked.

Daniel managed a smile. There was only so much horror and tragedy one could watch, so yesterday had turned into a bit of a stag party after all. And the last memory of it Daniel had was of him and Lee belting out Wham's 'Bad Boys'. 'I dunno whose idea it was to get the karaoke machine out, but it certainly wasn't mine.'

'It was Kev's. You know he always turns into a Rasta and thinks he's Bob Marley after a few,' Michael chuckled.

'I still can't believe Chas and Dave are performing 'ere tonight. Gonna be a belter of a reception. Cheers, Dad.'

Michael sat on the bed and fondly ruffled his son's hair

as he had when he was a nipper. Daniel had been a bastard as a child, but Michael had always known he'd turn out OK. 'I'm not getting all soppy, but just want you to know how proud of you I am. Roxanne's a lovely girl, and you two were made for each other. I'm not gonna show you up later by talking a load of sentimental old bollocks, so have kept my actual speech light-hearted. I felt it only right to give your mum a decent mention though. You OK with that?'

'Yeah. Course. Mad, ain't it, Dad? I can't believe I'm about to get hitched. Never thought I'd meet a bird to tempt me down the aisle.'

An image of Bella flashed through Michael's mind. 'Enjoy every minute. True love only comes around once in a lifetime.'

'Wow! You look wicked. Better than any bride I've ever seen before,' Ava Butler said in awe. She and Roxanne had only met one another for the first time a few weeks ago, but had immediately clicked and swapped phone numbers.

'Do you think Daniel will like it?' Roxanne asked, her blue eyes shining with excitement. Her outfit wasn't your traditional wedding get-up. She'd chosen a square-necked scarlet satin number with big puffy sleeves; the front of the dress was knee-length, and the back was long and trailed along the floor. She'd teamed it with clunky high-heeled silver sandals and studded earrings, necklace and bracelet. Roxanne felt a million dollars. She'd always had her own unique style ever since she could remember and had once been described by her art teacher as 'a young Paula Yates in the making'. That had pleased Roxanne no end as she'd loved Paula. It had been awful when she'd been found dead last year. Roxanne had cried her eyes out, but took comfort that she'd finally be reunited with Michael Hutchence.

They'd had a Romeo and Juliet type thing going on, just like her and her Daniel.

'Daniel will love it! He's a very lucky man. I'm so happy for the pair of you, I really am. I hope one day I get to meet the man of my dreams. Not going to be easy with my father, though. He wants me to be a spinster. Even Noel and Liam he'd find fault with,' Ava laughed. She was an Oasis fan and had snuck off with a pal to see the Gallagher brothers perform at Knebworth back in '96. Her dad had gone apeshit when he'd found out. He'd had to drive all the way to Knebworth to pick her up the following day, and had promptly grounded her for a month.

Alex barged into the room with a bottle of champagne. 'Whey-aye, pet! You look incredible! Do I look OK? I had to get away from that youngest bridesmaid. No disrespect, Ava, I know she's family. Camila's lovely, but that Ellie is a spoilt little diva if ever I did meet one. She's driving that poor lady doing our hair up the wall. Her whinging voice has gone right through me head – so much so, I need a bevvy.'

Ava laughed. 'Don't be worrying about upsetting me. I barely know the child and feel exactly the same way about her.'

Roxanne sighed. When Katy had found out Camila was going to be a bridesmaid, she'd kicked up that much of a stink with Michael that he'd asked Daniel if it was OK for Ellie to be a bridesmaid too. Roxanne felt she had no choice but to agree. Michael was paying for the wedding after all.

'Don't look so glum. I'll keep me eye on the brat,' Ava said.

'What a shame we never met earlier. I would have insisted you be a bridesmaid. I want this day to be perfect.'

'Well, if past family weddings are anything to go by, you're in for a rough ride, Roxy. So tighten your seatbelt, girlie,' Ava joked. 'Bound to be something that goes Pete Tong. There always is with us Butlers.'

Michael Butler pinned his carnation on to his lapel. His son had opted for a coat-and-tail look in the end. All the Butler males would be turned out in black suits, white shirts, black shoes and bow ties.

'You're quiet, Dad. What's up?' Lee asked. After chucking his guts up earlier, he was now raring to go again. The 'hair of the dog' had worked its magic this morning.

'I'm OK. But I wish Katy wasn't coming. She's done us no favours, not allowing Ellie and Cami to build a relationship without her being present. When I picked Ellie up earlier she was fine, then as soon as Cami got in the car the atmosphere was dreadful. They're like strangers, not sisters. Makes it so awkward on occasions such as this.' Michael would actually have preferred neither Katy nor Ellie attend his son's wedding. But Daniel wanted Nathan to be part of it, so he'd had no choice other than to invite both and ask if Ellie could be bridesmaid.

'The limo's 'ere, lads,' Albie shouted out.

Lee put an arm around Daniel's shoulders. 'I know we haven't always seen eye to eye this past year, but I want you to know I am truly happy for you and Roxy, bruv. You make a great couple and you'll make blinding parents.'

Daniel gave Lee a hug. Everyone had predicted the nerves would kick in today, but he felt no anxiety whatsoever. Only a strong desire to marry the girl who had stolen his heart. He clapped his hands. 'Get those drinks down ya, boys. I will not keep my beautiful bride waiting.'

Dressed in smart skirt-suits – Queenie's being pale blue and Vivian's emerald green – the two sisters were again glued to Sky News. What had happened in New York yesterday would stay with them forever more. Hundreds had been confirmed dead and there were Christ knows how many more still unaccounted for. 'I reckon the death toll will hit two or three thousand, ya know. The sight of those poor souls jumping out those windows will haunt me for the rest of my days, Viv. What a choice to make: jump or burn. God bless 'em and their heartbroken families,' Queenie said, shaking her head in despair.

'They'll be lucky to find any more alive now. Bastard terrorists want stringing up,' Vivian spat.

'Can we turn that off, please? This is meant to be a happy occasion and the bride-to-be is ready to show you how amazing she looks,' Ava announced, switching the TV off before her nan and aunt had a chance to reply.

Alex and Ava hummed 'Here Comes the Bride' as Roxanne swanned into the room. The hairdresser had suggested she tone her wild hair down a touch, but Roxanne was having none of that. With the massive scarlet flower she'd bought to match her unusual outfit, Roxanne knew she'd stumbled across perfection.

'Gawd stone the crows! You can't get married looking like that,' Vivian exclaimed.

Ava laughed. 'Don't be so old-fashioned, Auntie Viv. I think Roxy looks incredible and if I ever get married I want her to come dress-shopping with me.'

'Aren't brides meant to get married in white?' Ellie asked.

'Not when they're already up the duff,' Vivian mumbled.

'I love your outfit. It's so different,' Camila sighed.

Queenie hated it, but wasn't about to admit that. She absolutely adored the ground Roxanne walked on, had taken the girl to heart. 'I think you look beautiful, dear. Different, but dynamic.'

Vivian looked at her sister in absolute amazement. She'd never heard the silly old cow use the word 'dynamic' in their lifetime. Wait until later when she'd had a few sherries. She would absolutely cane her. What an arse-licker!

Daniel Butler felt the first stab of nerves as he stood at the front of the Registry Office. He'd just remembered he'd sent an invite to Mary and Donald, but could see no sign of them, thankfully. He and Roxanne had opted to ask only close family and friends – all of whom were his – apart from Alex and a couple of the barmaids Roxy had got friendly with. They'd also attended her hen party round at his nan's yesterday.

Stamping their own personal touch on their big day was something both Daniel and Roxanne had agreed on. As well as old films, Roxanne loved old-time songs and she wanted to walk down the aisle to the Al Jolson version of 'For Me and My Gal' rather than the traditional 'Here Comes the Bride'. She reckoned the song was perfect for them. They'd also written a few words of their own to say at the altar.

Michael was sitting next to Katy, who was chewing his ear off as usual. 'I do not understand why I had to make my own bloody way here. Felt a right idiot, turning up all by myself. I should've arrived with the bride, your family and our daughter. I do hope Ellie's OK. She doesn't know your family that well.'

'And whose bastard fault is that?' Michael hissed. 'I've already told you the reason why I wanted Ellie to get ready at my mother's without you smothering her. So she could get to know the rest of the bridesmaids before the wedding kicked off. Cami hasn't got her mother here, has she?'

'I shouldn't think so, seeing as Bella slept with Ava's father,' Katy hissed back.

'Shut it and be glad you're invited at all. Today's about Daniel, not you or Ellie.'

Aware of the unrest, Albie tapped his son on the shoulder. 'Fancy a quick smoke outside, boy?' Both he and Michael had given up cigarettes a long time ago, but still enjoyed the odd cigar on special occasions.

Glaring at Katy, Michael followed his father. Sophie, his latest fancy-piece, he'd finally binned a few weeks ago, but she was having none of it and had been stalking him ever since. Why did he always seem to attract nutty women?

Once out in the fresh air, Albie gave his son a cigar and some words of wisdom. 'Anybody can see how unhappy you are with Katy, son. Why don't you cut your losses and move on? If I was you, I would swallow my pride and live my days out with the woman I truly love. I know she hurt you badly, but life's too short to hold grudges and it's obvious she still loves you too. A very pretty woman like Bella would've moved on years ago if she didn't.'

Michael took a long pull on his cigar and leaned his head against the wall. 'I dunno, Dad. If only it was that easy to forgive and forget. I still love her though and that's what hurts the most.'

Thanks to Queenie spilling a cup of tea all over her outfit and having to get changed, the bride's limo was running behind schedule.

'I hope Daniel isn't worried. He knows how much I love him and would never let him down. You don't think it's crossed his mind I'm having second thoughts, do you?' Roxanne asked Viv.

'Nah. Got nerves of steel has Danny Boy. We'll be there soon and his eyes will light up big time when "Here Comes the Bride" plays and he sees you walking towards him in that gorgeous outfit.'

'We're not having "Here Comes the Bride". I chose a different song.'

'Different song! Whaddya mean, different song?' Vivian asked, perplexed.

'I'm walking down the aisle to "For Me and My Gal,"' Roxanne announced proudly.

'Aw, my gawd!' Queenie mumbled. She'd had an eerie feeling yesterday when the terrorists had struck that this wedding was doomed. Now, her grandson was going to greet his wife to the very same song as she and Albie had chosen for their first dance as a married couple.

Aware that her sister was remembering her own wedding, Vivian could not help but smirk. She'd had designs on the handsome Albie Butler herself back then, but unlike Queenie, she was too young for him. It might have taken many years, but now Albie was her man, nobody else's.

Vinny Butler breathed a sigh of pure relief as he and Eddie Mitchell shook hands with the owner. They'd searched high and low across certain parts of Essex to find the right location to pursue their joint venture, but such was Eddie's natural caution, Vinny had begun to think it would never happen. But it finally had. And to happen today of all days could not be a better tonic for Vinny.

Already gutted that he was the only family member not attending his favourite nephew's wedding, Vinny had been well pissed off earlier when his son had rung to inform him Michael had booked Chas and Dave to play at the reception. Vinny knew how much his mum and aunt adored them, and even though his aunt no longer loved him, he still loved her, and would kill to see the look on both of their faces. He was also pissed off with Michael. He and Roy had built that club up from nothing when Michael was no more than a wet-behind-the-ears kid. Was this yet another form of his brother paying him back for his fling with Bella? Or was it a genuine gesture of his love for the family?

Eddie Mitchell slapped his pal on the back as they walked away from the premises. He knew Vinny was having a tough time of it today, and he'd been through hell himself this year. Eddie had never disclosed to anybody – Vinny included – what exactly had happened that fateful day when his feud with the O'Haras had come to a messy end. But he'd lost a son in the battle and gained two grandchildren who were as untamed as the wildest of wolves. 'I think a celebratory drink is in order, don't you, Vin?'

Vinny grinned. 'Not arf. This is the start of something truly special, mate. The Butlers and the Mitchells – what a fucking force to be reckoned with.'

With Al Jolson belting out the words to 'For Me and My Gal' Daniel Butler had tears in his eyes when Roxanne walked towards him holding Alex's arm. She'd wanted her pal to give her away, said if it wasn't for Alex bringing her to his club that night, they'd probably never have met.

'You look so beautiful, babe. I love you,' Daniel whispered, squeezing Roxanne's hand reassuringly.

'She isn't what I expected at all. Looks ever so young,' Sammi-Lou whispered in her husband's ear.

'Shush,' Little Vinny ordered. 'And tell Calum to put that game away and sit up straight,' he added. He liked Roxanne and knew, once Sammi was introduced to her properly, she would too.

'Can I please use the toilet? You won't start without me, will you?' Ellie Butler asked politely.

Jenny, the registrar, glanced at her watch. The bride had already turned up forty minutes late and she had another wedding at two. However, being a local woman herself, she was aware this was a Butler wedding and wasn't about to say no to any request. The other couple would just have to wait. 'Go on, lovey. Be quick,' Jenny said.

Roxanne smiled at Daniel. He looked so handsome in his smart suit, and she could not believe he was about to become her husband. 'Ask them to play our song again,' she whispered in his ear.

'Oh, for crying out loud,' Queenie moaned, when Al Jolson came bashing out the speaker once more.

'What's the matter? Something *dynamic* occurring?' Vivian asked, tongue in cheek at her sister's earlier turn of phrase.

Albie was sitting in the row opposite, next to Michael, and Queenie couldn't help but glare at the side of his head. 'Don't want to keep being reminded of past mistakes, that's all,' she spat.

When Albie glanced across and treated her to a cheeky wink, Vivian smiled. If only she'd been the older sister and got her claws into him before Queenie. Life would have turned out so very differently.

'Cheers, business partner,' Eddie Mitchell said, holding his glass aloft. He wasn't dumb, knew how long Vinny had craved this particular partnership. But Eddie was very cautious and savvy. And as much as he got on with Vinny, some of Mr Butler's past shenanigans left a lot to be desired. That was why Eddie had not wanted to leap into a joint venture of any kind, until he was totally sure his pal had mended his once violent ways. Killing men who had wronged you was one thing, but strangling brasses was another and Eddie could not have tangled himself up with that type of shit. Apart from accidentally blasting his beloved wife to pieces, Eddie was a gentleman when it came to women, whatever their profession.

'How's it going with Georgie and Harry?' Vinny enquired.

'Don't even go there. My heart bleeds for what could've been and how they've actually turned out. Had to move

Frankie into what can only be described as a safe house near me now. They keep trying to run back to their pikey loved ones, and the only way to stop 'em bolting is to keep 'em under lock and key and watch the pair like hawks. Let's change the subject, eh? Depresses me, and after the deal we've just done I'd rather celebrate.'

'Family, eh? Can't live with 'em, can't live without 'em. Thank fuck we can choose our friends in life.'

Eddie raised his glass and clinked it against Vinny's. 'To us and our casino. Onwards and upwards, me ole mucker.'

Daniel Butler felt choked up as he and Roxanne exchanged the vows they had made up themselves. 'I knew you were *the one* the moment I first laid eyes on you, Roxanne, and I promise to look after you and treat you as a princess until my dying day.'

'And I knew you were *the one* for me too, Daniel. My knight in shining armour, and I promise to be a faithful, loving wife to you for the rest of my life. You are my everything and my best friend.'

'How moving. Bless 'em,' Queenie mumbled, dabbing her eyes with a tissue.

'I don't remember that arsehole I married looking into my eyes like that. Bill couldn't wait for the service to be over with, so he could drink himself senseless at the pub,' Vivian whispered, wistfully glancing across at Albie.

The registrar smiled at the clearly besotted couple, before continuing, 'This place in which we are now met has been duly sanctioned, according to law, for the celebration of marriages. We are gathered here today, as you know, to witness the joining in matrimony of Daniel Butler and Roxanne Smith. If any person here present knows of any lawful impediment to this marriage, he or she should declare it now.'

As the door burst open and a voice screamed, 'Stop the wedding!' heads turned in shock.

'It's Mary Walker! What's she doing 'ere? And who's that with her?' Queenie nudged Viv, her mouth wide open.

Michael stood up. Was it a ghost or was it her? His legs buckled. Her hair was now brunette, the large dark glasses hid her eyes, but there was no mistaking who it was. 'Nancy!' he said, in no more than a stunned whisper.

'Gawd stone the crows! I've gone cold,' Vivian shivered.

Trembling like a leaf, Nancy blurted out the torrid truth: 'You can't marry him. It's against the law,' she sobbed. 'He's your brother.'

CHAPTER THIRTY-FIVE

'Brother! You're lying! You just don't want me to be happy. You never have,' Roxanne screamed, tears mixed with black mascara running down her face.

'Annie, let's wait outside, love. Come on,' Mary urged.

Daniel stared at his bride in utter disbelief. 'Annie! Who the fuck is Annie?'

Finding her voice, Queenie leapt out of her seat. The rest of the family were dumbstruck, far whiter than the so-called ghost Queenie approached, forefinger wagging wildly. 'What a wicked liar you are! First you leave your son and pretend to be dead. Then you have the cheek to turn up 'ere saying Roxanne is your child. She's eighteen, for Christ's sake! You were still with my Michael back then, you despicable woman.'

'Her name's Annie, not Roxanne. And she isn't eighteen, she's fifteen. That's why I disappeared, to protect her. I didn't want her growing up as a Butler, especially after what happened to Adam.'

'You what!' hissed Michael.

Nancy burst into tears. Everybody was staring at her in horror and she truly could not blame them. 'I'm so sorry, but she's yours, Michael. Annie is your daughter.'

Recoiling as Roxanne tried to grab his hand, Daniel Butler emptied the contents of his stomach all over the registrar's feet. Running from the building was his next move.

Vivian found Albie leaning against the wall outside. For once, there were no words of comfort she could offer. What had just happened was one of the most sickening scenes she'd ever witnessed. Brother and sister. It was just too awful for words.

'Oh, Vivvy. That poor lad. We need to find him,' Albie gasped.

'There's a bench over there. Let's sit you down for a minute. Your skin looks grey. You got chest pains?'

Knowing Viv would demand he go straight to the hospital, Albie lied. 'No. I'm just in shock. How is Daniel ever going to live this down? She's fifteen, his own sister, and bloody pregnant.'

Vivian led Albie over to the bench, sat next to him and clasped her hand over his. 'I know, lovey. I know.'

Inside the registry office, Lee Butler was going ballistic and being held back by his wife. Little Vinny grabbed Lee's arm to stop him from following and personally confronting Nancy and Roxanne. 'Pair of lying cunts! I knew she was a wrong 'un and hiding something. I fucking knew it!' he screamed, punching the wall in frustration.

Calum Butler marched over to his father. 'Mum wants to take us home, but I wanna stay here. It's well weird, getting your own sister pregnant, ain't it, Dad? Ollie reckons the kid will be born a div. You know, have something wrong with it.'

Little Vinny clipped his son around the ear. 'Shut it, mouth almighty. Sammi, take the boys home. Now!' he bellowed. Like the rest of his family, he was stunned and distraught over the situation, but somebody had to keep a calm head. In the midst of this debacle was a heartbroken groom, who needed to be found, quickly.

Queenie marched over to her grandsons. 'Where's Viv? And Michael? You'd better ring your father, Vin, let him know before he hears it from the gossipmongers. Be in their element, they will. How the hell we ever meant to live this one down, eh? That bastard who runs heaven must hate us, I'm telling ya.'

Lee immediately switched his anger towards his grandmother. 'That all you're worried about, is it, Nan? The gossipmongers? Only if it is, fuck you and them.'

Little Vinny shoved his cousin against the wall. 'Don't speak to Nan like that. It's not her fault, is it? Apologize to her, now.'

Michael Butler roughly grabbed hold of the woman's arm who – in the eyes of the law – he was probably still bloody married to. 'Ain't trying to sneak away and disappear off the face of the earth again, are you? 'Cause let me tell ya, you're going fucking nowhere this time, Nance. Have you any idea what you've caused? What harm you've done to *our* kids? You do know she's pregnant, don't you?'

'Pregnant! Who is? Annie?' Nancy gasped.

Michael glared at the woman he had once walked up the aisle himself. 'Yes, you stupid cow. Thanks to you and your evil fucking lies, I can proudly announce our fifteen-year-old daughter, who you conveniently forgot to tell me existed, has a bun in the oven by our twenty-eight-year-old son, who just happened to think you were dead. Happy now, are ya?'

Unable to take any more shocking news, Nancy collapsed on the spot.

*

'Where's Michael, Queenie? Nathan can't find him and Ellie's distraught. Look at her,' Katy urged.

Queenie glanced at her least favourite grandchild. Ellie was lying face down across two chairs. 'He's not her daddy, he's mine,' she sobbed, referring to the bride.

'Michael's busy. Get yourself and the kids home, Katy. We've got a lot of important family stuff to sort out.'

'But we're family too, and Michael's booked us a hotel in London tonight,' Katy protested.

Queenie was not a fan of Katy. She knew Katy had trapped her son when he was at his most vulnerable, and she knew Michael did not love the gold-digging tart. 'You're not a Butler. Your surname's Spencer. Now do as I say and get the kids out of 'ere. Michael will ring you later, OK?'

Roxanne Smith was confused, hysterical and totally devastated. When Daniel had run from the registry office, her instinct had been to chase after him. But Daniel had ignored her desperate cries, kept on running, and now Alex and her nan had caught up with her. 'I'm not going back. I need to see Daniel. You can't stop me from seeing him. I love him and he isn't my brother. There must be some mistake.'

Aware that passers-by were gawping at her distressed friend, Alex put her arms around her. 'You're in shock and you have every right to be. Let's get you back to mine, shall we? We can't stay here.'

'Annie's coming with me and her mother. The car's parked at the registry office,' Mary mumbled. It had been the biggest bombshell ever, receiving a wedding invitation from Daniel with a photo of himself and his bride-to-be on the front. Annie had been missing since earlier this year, had run away from home while nobody was in, and the family had been worried sick about her ever since. They would have involved the police in her disappearance, had circumstances been different. But Nancy's brother, Christopher, had forbidden them to. He said they'd all be locked up and he would do all he could to find Annie on the quiet. Christopher was a DI in the police force, so knew what he was talking about.

'Stop calling me Annie! I hate that name. It's boring, just like you and Mam, or so I thought. Nancy, that's Mam's old name, is it? And if me dad ain't me dad, who the fuck is that bloke who brought me up?' Roxanne screamed at her grandmother.

Tears rolled down Mary's cheeks. 'Let's go and find your mum and she will explain everything to you, sweetheart.'

Roxanne pushed Mary away and walked backwards with fear in her eyes. 'I'm not coming with you. I don't even know who you are any more. Help me find Daniel, Alex. Come on,' she begged.

When the two girls ran off down the road, Mary had no chance of catching them. She struggled to walk these days, let alone run. 'Annie – I mean, Roxanne, don't do this to me. Come back,' she shrieked.

'My nan and aunt only live locally, but drive slowly, eh? Make sure you get 'em home safely and you can keep the change. Nan, I'll ring you as soon as we have any news. We'll find Dan, don't worry,' Little Vinny said.

'I wanna know why your father ain't answering his bleedin' phone and where Michael's gone. Ring me as soon as you get in touch with either of 'em. They'll know what to do,' Queenie ordered.

Vivian took her hat off, placed it on her lap, and glanced at her watch. The chaos had continued for what seemed like hours, but was in fact only fifty minutes. The registrar had to be led away, in an unfit state to perform the next wedding ceremony. Nancy had collapsed. Nobody knew where Roxanne or Daniel were, but the worst thing for Viv had been seeing Albie carted off in that ambulance. He hadn't exactly keeled over, but looked so grey, and when he'd admitted to having slight chest pains, Vivian had asked Little Vinny to dial 999. She had wanted to accompany him, but couldn't leave Queenie with all the other drama going on around them. She had promised Albie that she would get to the hospital as soon as she could though, bless him.

As if reading her sister's mind, Queenie said, 'I saw you fussing over that old tosspot earlier. What was wrong with him?'

'Chest pains. And I wasn't bloody fussing; I was only making sure the man was OK. Don't you think Michael and Daniel have got enough on their plates without something happening to Albie?'

Queenie looked contrite. 'I'm sorry, you're right. Oh, Viv, what a day. No way could I face the shame of arriving home in that limo. We're never gonna live this one down, ya know. Laughing stocks, we'll be – and them poor kids. How the hell can they ever be normal again?'

Clocking that the obese, sweaty cabbie was glancing at them in his mirror and listening to every word, Vivian nudged her sister. 'We'll talk indoors, and get the change back. Nosy bastard,' she hissed.

Nancy hadn't set foot in Whitechapel since 1985. That was the last time she'd laid eyes on what was then Michael's club. That was when her whole world had collapsed around her. Firstly, her beloved son Adam had been hit by a train and killed. Then, she'd learned of Michael's relationship with Bella.

Having just found out she was pregnant with her and

Michael's third child, Nancy had felt like a rabbit in the headlights. Being a Butler meant you were constantly surrounded by death and drama, and no way did Nancy want to bring another child up in that environment. At the time, Daniel was a nightmare of a son, and Nancy could not help but blame him for Adam's untimely death. He and Lee were meant to be looking after their younger sibling, not encouraging him to bunk train fares and run across tracks.

It was Nancy's brother Christopher who had come up with the idea of leaving her car on top of Beachy Head with a suicide note for Michael. Desperate to start a new life as far away from the Butlers as possible, Nancy had made contact with Dean Smart – Brenda's ex-husband – and he had been instrumental in her escape. Having disappeared into thin air himself many years beforehand in order to escape the Butlers, Dean understood better than anyone. The pair of them had since lived a quiet life together. Initially they'd passed themselves off as Sue and David Smith, but Dean had been recognized by an old school pal in Glasgow so they'd been forced to up sticks and move to the North East. They were now formally known as Sue and David Jones.

Annie had always been the one bugbear in their wish to live a quiet, uneventful life. She was a difficult child – a true Butler – and Nancy had put it down to her genes. You can take the girl away from the Butlers, but you can't take the Butler out of the girl, so to speak. However, nothing could have prepared Nancy for the shock of her mother receiving that wedding invitation. She'd had a feeling all along that Annie had run away to London, as the East End was an area that her daughter had always been obsessed with. But to find out she was in a relationship and about to marry her own brother was the most sickening feeling

459

in the whole wide world. Nancy and Dean had never told their children they had any links to London. They had explained away their accents to their kids and others by saying they'd been brought up in a small Essex village. How could fate be so cruel? Nancy could not help but wonder if God was paying her back for her own awful deceit.

Michael Butler poured three brandies and pushed two glasses across the table towards Nancy and Mary. Daniel and Roxanne were still on the missing list and with the boys out searching for them, Michael had insisted that somebody should wait at the club in the hope that one if not both of their kids would return to where they'd been living, even if it was only to collect some belongings. 'Right, start talking and I wanna know everything. If you lie to me, I swear I will involve the Old Bill. What you've done to this family is fucking despicable,' he said, a menacing edge to his voice.

'I want to talk to Michael alone, Mum. I owe him that much at least,' Nancy wept.

'I'll go for a walk, see if I can find her. I've got my mobile with me. Ring me if you hear anything,' Mary said.

Michael let Mary out and stormed back to the table where Nancy was sitting, a stony expression on his face. 'Take a look around, Nance. Go on! Look at the destruction you've caused,' he yelled, pointing at the massive banner on the opposite wall that read *CONGRATULATIONS ON YOUR WEDDING DAY, DANIEL AND ROXANNE.*

Nancy took off her dark glasses, put her head in her hands and sobbed. 'I'm so very sorry.'

'Sorry don't cut it this time. Tell me what was going through that sick, fucked-up head of yours the day you decided to fake your own death and leave your kid.' Michael slammed his fist against the table. 'Do you realize what you've done? Now cut the crocodile tears and start cunting-well talking.'

'Oh, it's you, Alex. Any sign of 'em, love? I'm so worried,' Queenie said, glancing out the front door before she shut it. Judging by the number of neighbours hanging around outside, gossiping, the rumour mill was already in full swing. Big Stan had walked past the window looking in at least four times, and even that awful family of foreign gypsy types opposite seemed to be having a good old laugh over something when she and Viv had pulled up in the cab earlier. One of the men had shouted something in his own language, to which Queenie had replied 'Fuck off' before slamming the front door.

'No news yet, but I'm sure I'll find Roxy,' Alex lied. 'I've come to pick my bag up. My phone's in there and I need to start making some calls. Roxanne might've been in touch with some of our old friends we used to work with. OK to go upstairs, Queenie?'

'Of course, love. Did Roxanne leave her phone here too? There might be some clues to her whereabouts on that.'

'I don't think she did. Probably back at the club,' Alex lied again.

Darting up the stairs, Alex grabbed her belongings and checked Roxanne's purse and phone were still in her bag. 'I'll be off now, Queenie. As soon as I have any news, I'll pop round and let you know, pet.'

Having nipped back to her own house to change out of her wedding outfit, Vivian asked, 'What did she want?' as Alex ran down the road.

'Left her bag 'ere. Is there people out there? Did anyone say anything?'

'No. Calm down and stop being so paranoid, Queen.

Today's news is tomorrow's chip wrapper, whichever way you look at it.'

'Not in this case, Viv! My granddaughter – the one I never knew existed – is up the spout by my fucking grandson. Makes me sick to the stomach to even consider the pair of 'em, you know, cavorting and stuff. Can you imagine what people are saying about us? It's incest – and Roxanne's only a bloody child. We'll never live it down, I'm telling ya. Never! The good name of this family will be tarnished forever.'

About to remind her sister that Vinny had trashed the good name of the family many times over the years, Vivian decided this probably wasn't the moment.

Hearing music accompanied by laughter, Queenie glanced out the window. 'Look at 'em. Sitting on a mattress swilling beer down their necks now. Where do they think they are, eh? Fucking Butlins. Vinny's right you know, Viv. We should move to Essex. It's had it round 'ere. All the good 'uns are gone. There's nothing left for us. Foreigner-infested shithole, I hate it.'

Vivian was horrified. 'But we can't move, Queen. We wouldn't be able to settle anywhere else. Whitechapel is our home.'

Back at the club, Michael had just had another almighty shock. 'Dean Smart! So you're telling me you faked your own death and left our son to grieve for you so you could shack up with my sister's ex? Perhaps incest runs in the family, eh?'

'Please, Michael, stop,' Nancy sobbed. 'No, that isn't what I'm trying to tell you. Hear me out, will you?'

Downing his brandy, Michael slammed the glass against the table. 'Jesus wept! You could not sink any lower if you tried. Go on then, fire away. I'm all ears.'

'Dean and I were never an item before I left, you have to believe me when I say that. But we did have a bond. I felt at times he was the only person in the world that could truly understand what I was going through. My head was all over the place after Adam's death and when I found out about you and Bella, I couldn't take any more upset. I know you must see things differently, but I always loved you, Michael, and I had known in my heart for a while that you no longer loved me. I'd only just found out I was pregnant when my mum told me about Bella. Telling you then would've only complicated matters, and you would never have let me leave if I was carrying your child. All I wanted was the chance to start afresh and be happy myself again.'

'No surprise you and him bonded. He left two kids behind. Ever talk about Tara and Tommy, does he? Oh, and by the way, Brenda's dead,' Michael announced, his voice laden with sarcasm.

'Dean and I were told about Brenda's death by my mum and were genuinely shocked and saddened by it. And of course Dean has never forgotten his children. We've cried many a tear when we're alone together over what we left behind, but believe me, Dean had his reasons for leaving as well, Michael. When he was working at the club, he overheard a conversation between Vinny and Ahmed. They were having a good old laugh about murdering Dean's father, and what they'd put him through. Is it any wonder Dean left rapidly?'

'Still no excuse for leaving your kids, Nance. Not in my world, anyway.'

'Your world is a place of violence and betrayal, Michael, which normal people like Dean and I don't belong to. Running away was our only option to be free. You know as well as I do Dean knew too much and Vinny would've hunted him down. He'd have murdered him, like he did his father. Look, I'm trying to be straight with you here. I am to blame for the awful situation we are currently in, but your family aren't exactly blameless. Have you any idea how hard it was, being your wife? Yes, you chucked money at me and the kids, we wanted for nothing in that respect. But what I and the boys truly craved wasn't money and gifts; it was you being part of our lives. You were never at home and we rarely did anything that normal families do. You were always too busy at the club or out securing some dodgy business deal. You never wanted to spend quality time with us. I felt like a drudge, stuck at home day after day, bringing up three young sons, one whom wasn't even mine, may I add.'

Knowing that Nancy had a valid point, Michael wasn't in the mood to listen to it. 'Don't be trying to blame this situation on my family. It was you who faked your own death and allowed your own son to sit through some fucking warped memorial service that your notright family put on. How could you allow that to happen, Nance? There's low, but that's scraping the bottom of the barrel. No wonder Daniel had issues with you as his mother. And who helped you and lover boy set up new identities, eh? Let me guess. Was it that cocktard do-gooding, law-abiding policeman brother of yours? Do you think I'm stupid? I saw the look of horror on both your face and your mother's when I threatened to call the Old Bill earlier. A DI now, ain't he? For how much longer, though, I wonder?'

Nancy stared at the man she had once married. He was still so bloody handsome, and part of her would always love him. Dean was steady and reliable, and she wouldn't swap him for all the tea in China, but he'd never made her heart race in the same way Michael had once been capable of. 'Yes, Christopher was involved. But that isn't the only reason I'm asking you not to involve the police. This isn't about me or you, Michael. It's about our children and what we can do to sort this awful mess. Can you imagine how Annie and Daniel must be feeling right now? Involving the police is not the answer. That will only make matters worse for them.'

'Stop calling her fucking Annie, will ya! To me she's Roxanne. Jesus wept; she must've picked her skills of deceit up from you, that's for sure. If Daniel had known she was only fifteen he'd never have touched her with a bargepole. This is madness, Nance. I can't believe we're sitting 'ere having this conversation. What the fuck are we gonna do?'

'How are ya, love? I take it they're keeping you in?' Vivian asked. Albie looked a far better colour than he had earlier, thankfully. And he was sitting up, which was also a good sign.

'I'm not bad, Vivvy. They don't think it was a heart attack, just a funny turn. I'm waiting for a spare bed. They're going to keep me in tonight and see how I am tomorrow. Told 'em I'd had a bad shock, but I couldn't say what, obviously. Poor Daniel, I can't stop thinking about the lad. Has he been found yet?'

Vivian filled Albie in on the latest, then handed him a carrier bag. 'Couple of chicken breasts in there, tomatoes and a buttered French stick. I didn't know if you'd be allowed to eat or not, but guessed you might be starving later. Popped into the club on the way here. All the food laid out and the gaff draped in white. Must've cost Michael an arm and a leg, poor sod. He was there with Nancy, so I didn't stop, just asked if Daniel had been in touch. I can't believe Nancy's still alive, can you? Must have been terribly unhappy to do what she did. Then again, she was never quite right in the head, was she? I could never have left my Lenny, ya know. Would've walked over hot coals for that boy.'

Albie squeezed Vivian's hand. 'I know you would. Unlike Queenie, you were always a bloody good mother. She only ever wanted sons, her. Never had a lot of time for our Bren. And she's to blame for how them boys turned out. Even when they were toddlers, she was determined to mould their futures. I remember she'd tell Vinny and Roy this story about how they were little lion cubs and one day they'd grow up into massive lions who would gobble everybody up around 'em and maul them with their big teeth. Not exactly *Jackanory*, eh? Trust me: Queenie had those boys' futures mapped out before they were bleedin' well walking.'

'And I weren't much help, was I? Being around all the time and getting in the way of your and Queenie's relationship. I'm sorry, Albie. I was never nice to you, back in the day.'

Albie Butler was not a man to hold grudges. 'Forget all that now. It's in the past. I do reckon I married the wrong sister though,' he winked.

Even though today had been totally awful, Vivian could not help but grin. She had always longed to hear those words.

Vinny Butler comforted his distraught mother as best as he could. He was genuinely worried about both Daniel and Michael. As for Nancy still being alive, Vinny was stunned and angry. But not as angry as he'd been earlier when Eddie Mitchell had informed him he had a pal in Ford Open Prison and word was Jamie Preston was up for parole soon. Just the thought of that scumbag being back on the streets after what he had done to his beautiful daughter made Vinny want to vomit. Preston would most definitely get his comeuppance at some point. But now was not the right time to be informing his mother of such news. She had enough on her plate as it was.

'I'm gonna give Carl, Pete and Paul a ring. They'll help with the search for Daniel. He can't have gone far, Mum. We will find him, I promise. Best you prepare yourself for the gossipmongers though. Incest ain't something people are liable to forget in a hurry. Keep your chin up and anybody says anything untoward, you tell me and I'll deal with 'em, got that?'

Queenie nodded. 'Roxanne needs to be found an' all, Vin. She's only a kid herself and needs to get rid of that baby sharpish. I still can't believe she's my granddaughter. It's beyond belief, all this. Too much to take in. My heart breaks for poor Daniel. So in love with a bright future ahead, and thanks to his lying, scheming whore of a mother it turns out that love was tainted all along. Why is life so fucking wicked at times?'

'Look who it is! Auntie of da noncy boy,' a male voice shouted out.

Vivian glanced to her left. There were five of them and she couldn't see them properly as they were all wearing tracksuits, had their hoods up and it was dark.

'Daniel ever stick his pinkie up your batty? Bad boy is dat Daniel,' one joked, much to the amusement of the others, who fell about like laughing clowns.

'Fuck off,' Vivian hissed, before crossing over the road. She'd stayed at the hospital far longer than she'd intended to. A bad accident involving a coach on the A13 had meant Albie had a long wait to be wheeled off to a ward and she hadn't wanted to leave him all on his own.

'You like a bit of ma cock in your mouth, old lady?' a voice taunted from behind her.

Silly little gang members with their fake Jamaican accents did not bother Vivian as a rule, but as she turned around again and stared into many pairs of cold eyes, she suddenly felt out of her depth. They all had their mouths covered now, with what looked like cotton scarves or handkerchiefs.

One lad grabbed hold of his crotch. 'Wanna suck on dis?'

As another made a grab for her handbag, Vivian screamed, 'Help! Somebody help me!' She was terrified.

Seconds later Vivian was punched so hard in the temple, she went down like a ton of bricks. As her head connected with the kerb, she lost consciousness immediately.

Queenie Butler breathed a sigh of relief when the front door opened and closed. 'There you are. Where you been? I was about to ring the police to send out a search party.'

'I am the search party. Been out looking for Daniel and Roxanne,' Ava replied.

'Oh, it's you. I thought it was Vivvy. How did it go, love?'

After an exhausting day, Ava flopped on the sofa. 'No sign of either of 'em. Me, Destiny, Lee and Little Vinny have driven everywhere. He's in a proper state, Lee. We're gonna go out searching again tomorrow.'

'Oh, dear Lord. I wonder where they are? Worried about Viv an' all now. I can't find her either.'

'Whaddya mean, you can't find her?'

'She left here earlier when your dad rang and said he was on his way over. I had a feeling she might pop up the hospital to see how the old goat was, but she's not come back. No way would she still be there now, Ava. This was this afternoon. She ain't indoors though. I've just checked again.'

Ava's complexion whitened. 'Oh, Nan. As we were driving home there was a commotion round the corner.

Little Vinny stopped the car so we could make sure it was nothing to do with Dan and Roxy, and when I asked the crowd stood there they said some elderly lady had been attacked. You don't reckon—'

The doorbell sounding ended any more speculation. It was the police. Seconds later, Queenie's screams of pure anguish woke up the entire street.

CHAPTER THIRTY-SIX

One Week Later

Michael Butler gently prised Bella's arms from around him, then quickly leapt out of bed. Making love to her seemed the most natural thing in the world when inebriated. But in the sober cold light of day, thoughts of her writhing naked with Vinny tainted his mind once again.

Bella put her dressing gown on. 'I'll make you some breakfast, Michael.'

'Nah. Don't bother, not today. I don't feel hungry. Just want it to be over with. A coffee would go down well though, thanks.'

When Bella left the room, Michael sat on the edge of the bed, head in hands. To say this past week had been traumatic was the understatement of the fucking century, but it had also built some bridges. Nancy had finally travelled back up north after learning that Roxanne had been in touch with Alex to say she'd moved up that way and was staying with a pal. She'd given no indication where she was actually staying or who the pal was, but Alex had assured them that Roxanne sounded OK on the phone and had promised to contact her mother as soon as she'd had the abortion.

Daniel had also been in touch, but only with Lee. He had told his brother he was stopping with a pal he'd met in prison and wanted to clear his head before he contacted anybody else. He had made it clear though that he would never return to London, which was why there was now a big 'FOR SALE' sign above the club.

Saying goodbye to Nancy yesterday had felt weird. They'd spent many hours this past week in one another's company, liaising over their missing children, and even though Michael could never forgive her for what she'd done, he had a slightly better understanding of why she'd done it. He had promised to keep Dean Smart's involvement a secret, for now at least. Roxanne had only ever known Dean as David, so there was no need to complicate matters. They were complicated enough as it was. Nancy's brother Christopher was another person Michael had sworn to keep out the equation, and Nancy seemed eternally grateful for that. They had even shared an awkward hug as she'd left, and would obviously keep in touch. With two messed-up children who needed all the support they could get, they had no choice but to cooperate.

Sighing at the thought of the day ahead, Michael got in the shower, hoping the hot water immersing his body would make him feel better. For once it didn't, and no wonder. Ever since he could remember, his Auntie Viv had been an enormous part of his life. She was like a piece of treasured furniture who'd always belonged in his mother's house, such was the little time she'd spent in her own. Her presence there was sorely missed, as was her getting on her soapbox, yelling at the TV, the waft of her Estée Lauder perfume and every other trait she had possessed. The woman was a legend and Michael dreaded saying goodbye to her.

*

Ramming his rock-hard penis up Felicity Carter-Price's arsehole was the only way Vinny Butler could cope with the day ahead. Luckily for him, Felicity liked a bit of rough, which was why they'd gelled so well.

The horrid little bastards who'd been responsible for his Auntie Viv's plight had been caught within forty-eight hours. A couple of witnesses had come forward, and they were now banged up awaiting trial. A local gang of mixed race, the leader of them being Raj's brother, the lad Daniel had spent time inside over. All were under eighteen and Vinny knew only too well how the system worked. His grandson Regan was having the time of his life where he was paying the price for stabbing his teacher. The do-gooders involved in punishing the young nowadays allowed them every bastard privilege going.

Vinny shot his load, rolled on his back and stared at the fly walking across the ceiling. He'd swat it in a minute, splatter the life out of it, just like he would to the scum who had ruined his mother and aunt's lives once they'd served their cushy little sentences. Poor Viv hadn't stood a chance once her head connected with the edge of that kerb. Fractured skull, swelling and bleeding on the brain, and all because some bastard punched her in a road she'd happily walked along thousands of times before. It beggared belief, it really did.

Michael turned his phone on. He knew before he even listened to his messages that most would be from Katy. He was right, of course. She had left six, all ranting at him in that deranged voice. She'd obviously been on the wine again last night, and so had Sophie, by the sounds of it. His last fling had turned out to be another stalker who wouldn't stop ringing him. No doubt the pair of them would go ballistic if he took the plunge and properly got back with Bella.

The last message was from Vinny, so Michael dropped him a text to say he'd be in Whitechapel within the hour. The attack on Vivian had kind of built a bridge between him and his brother. They were now on speaking terms for the first time in years, and it wasn't just to appease their mother. Both were distraught over their beloved aunt's fate and it was natural, stuck up that hospital day after day, they'd end up grieving together.

'Good morning, Dad. That's five nights you've stayed here on the trot now. Does this mean you and Mum are officially back together?' Camila asked cheekily. She so wanted her parents to reunite and her mother was being very cagey about the situation. She doubted her brother would be impressed though. Antonio was currently in Italy, visiting their grandparents, and Camila knew how much he hated her dad. He wouldn't even speak to him.

'I told you earlier, Cami. Stop asking awkward questions. Your father's going through a tough time at present, as you well know.'

Michael downed his coffee. 'I'd better get off now. I'm not sure whether I'll be back tonight. It's gonna be a tough one, so I'll probably end up crashing at my mum's or the club. I'll bell ya later though.'

Bella D'Angelo wasn't stupid, especially when it came to reading people, and she could currently read Michael like a book. She followed him to the front door, Madam Lydia's advice firmly in her mind: *Do not chase him – he will come to you. You are soul-mates.*

'Laters then,' Michael said, pecking Bella on the cheek.

'Goodbye, Michael. I will be thinking of you today. You know where I am if you need me, my love.'

Katy Spencer was in a foul mood. She knew Michael was going through a difficult time, but since calling to tell her about his aunt being attacked, the only contact she'd had from him was the odd text. Was he turning to Nancy for comfort? Or Bella? Because something untoward was occurring and Katy knew it. Even at the wedding, she and their two children she shared with Michael had been packed off back to the hotel room as though they were mere guests, not family.

As though reading her mother's thoughts, Ellie asked, 'Why doesn't Daddy come home any more? Has he left us?'

Screaming at her cleaner to mop the kitchen floor again, Katy marched her daughter upstairs. 'We never talk about Daddy in front of strangers, Ellie. And you must never say he hasn't been home recently to your friends, their parents, or anybody else, for that matter. People have a lot of respect for us in this area and that's because your father is an extremely important man. I was so very proud of you and Nathan for keeping that whole wedding fiasco quiet. You don't think the Harrisons would've invited you to go to Lapland with Sara-Jayne this week had you blurted that out, do you? People have lots of respect for us because of Daddy, darling, and that's the way it shall stay. I promise you faithfully, as soon as Auntie Viv is buried, your father will be coming home again on his regular days. Mummy will make damn sure of it.'

Dressed from head to toe in black, Queenie Butler stared dismally out of the window. When the doctor had explained yesterday that even if Vivian did wake up – which was doubtful – it would be highly unlikely she would ever be the same person again, it had been Queenie's decision to today turn off the equipment that was the only thing keeping her once-vibrant sister alive. Seeing Vivian in a coma, tubes stuck in her arms and mouth, was heartbreaking. Having cried enough tears to fill a river, Queenie could cry no more. Her grief had now been replaced with bitterness and anger at what her beloved Whitechapel and London in general had become.

Memories of her Roy had been in the forefront of Queenie's thoughts all week. Her son had been a completely different person when he had come out of his coma, and Queenie knew for a fact that Vivvy would not want to live out the rest of her days being unable to walk, communicate properly and sipping through bastard straws. They had discussed the subject many a time and had always promised to do the right thing for one another if such a dreadful situation were to occur. Done up to the nines, strutting up and down Roman Road market on a Saturday afternoon was how they wished to be remembered. Not gawped at with people feeling sorry for them because they no longer had all their marbles intact.

Watching the horrid kids opposite jumping up and down on the filthy mattress that was now a permanent fixture in their disgusting shithole of a front garden, Queenie decided to busy herself until her sons arrived by packing up some more personal belongings. Vinny had taken her to view a bungalow in Hornchurch yesterday, not far from where Little Vinny lived, and Queenie could not wait to move there next week. Everything about Whitechapel reminded her of Vivian, and no way could Queenie live there any more. What had happened to the good old days when you could leave your front door open without fear of being attacked? Or burgled, for that matter. And even more scarily, what had happened to the respect her family's name had once commanded in this neck of the woods? Nobody would've dared say a bad word, let alone lay a finger on herself or Vivian once upon a time; such was the fear of her sons' reprisals. She hadn't just been referred to as 'Queen' by the locals; she had been fucking treated like one too. Well, her reign was over now and for all she cared Whitechapel could rot in hell.

Tears pouring down his cheeks, Albie Butler squeezed Vivian's lifeless hand. Michael was the only one who knew she was on her way home from the hospital when she had been attacked. An unopened packet of cigarettes had been found amongst the scattered contents of her handbag and Michael had told him to keep schtum about her whereabouts: 'It will only make Mum and Vinny hate you more, Dad, and it changes nothing. Best to let them think she popped out for fags.'

'Do you want to say your goodbyes to Auntie Viv on your own, Granddad? I've already said mine,' Ava said.

'Yes please, lovey.'

Ava gave her aunt one final kiss and then hugged her grandfather. 'Do you think Lee was all right earlier? I thought he was acting oddly, so did Little Vinny.'

'Probably just missing his brother, love. Been a tough week for all of us, hasn't it?'

'I suppose so. I'm going to meet Destiny now. Will you wait with Auntie Viv until the others arrive? It doesn't seem right, leaving her all alone.'

Queenie had insisted that only she, Michael and Vinny would remain in the room with Vivian when the ventilator aiding her breathing was switched off, which hadn't surprised Albie in the slightest. That's the way the witch had always wanted it: just her and her precious boys around her. Saying a private goodbye suited Albie better anyway. He had personal things he wanted to say to the woman he had grown so fond of. And he wanted to sing her favourite song to her one last time. 'You get off, love. I won't leave Vivvy's side,' Albie promised.

When Ava left the room, Albie stroked Vivian's deathly

white cheek. His tears dripped on to her face as he joked, 'I'm sorry I'm not dressed a bit better, my darlin'. Would've worn your favourite suit if I could.' Albie was still in the same hospital himself. Such was the shock of learning what had happened to Viv, he'd had a minor heart attack, which was why he was kitted out in pyjamas and a dressing gown.

'Dunno what I'm gonna do without you, Viv. If I could swap places with you, I would, my angel. Why didn't I marry you instead, eh? We could've been so happy together, and we'd have had lovely sons. They'd have been like your Lenny, not my Vinny. We wasted our lives, me and you.'

Receiving no response, Albie clasped Vivian's hand, shut his eyes and broke into the opening chords of 'Spanish Eyes'. She loved him singing that, did Vivvy. Said he sang it just like Al Martino did.

Seconds later, the machine started bleeping strangely. 'Nurse, nurse! Come quickly.'

Michael Butler handed his brother a Scotch. 'Did you have a word with Mum this morning about Auntie Viv?'

Vinny sighed. Both he and Michael wanted to give their aunt more time to heal, but since hearing the news from the doctor, his mother was having none of it. 'She's adamant we let her go peacefully in her sleep, bruv. Says no way would Viv want to spend the rest of her life sitting in her own piss and shit, and if anything similar ever happens to her we're to make the same decision. Threatened to come back and haunt us if we don't.'

'Oh well, that's that then. I'm dreading watching her take her final breath. I know the quack said she'd never be the same if she woke up, but we don't know that for sure, do we?'

'Roy was never the same though, was he? I should

imagine that's one of the reasons why Mum is insistent we end things this way. She reckons Champ'll be waiting with open arms and will take care of his mum.' Champ was Vinny and Michael's nickname for their deceased cousin Lenny.

'I'm worried about Lee an' all now. Been acting proper strange, by all accounts. Had his old woman on the phone this morning in bits. She's worried he might be planning on killing himself,' Michael informed his brother.

'Nah. Lee's too strong mentally to do that. He's obviously missing Dan. Been a fucked-up week for all of us, eh?'

'You can say that again. I've spent the last five nights in Bella's bed,' Michael announced, clocking his brother's reaction closely.

'About bloody time. That woman loves you so much, Michael, it's untrue. I don't like going over old ground, but me and her meant nothing. Two strangers who did not know one another from Adam, and it's so long ago now it feels like a different lifetime. You've got to forget about it and move on. You and Bella are still young enough to spend many happy years together. Life's too short for regrets.'

'It's not that easy though. Your son despises me, for a start.'

'It's about time Antonio was made to stand on his own two fucking feet. He ain't a kid any more, needs to grow a pair of balls and be a man. Don't let him get in the way of your happiness. I'll set him up in a flat if need be. I want you and Bella to make a go of it, bruv, and I mean that from the bottom of my heart. Seeing Auntie Viv lying there with all those tubes coming out of her brings it all home to ya. None of us know how long we're on this earth for, do we?'

'We sure don't. Speaking of which, let's go and pick Mum

up, get this over with. Poor Auntie Viv. Who would ever have thought it would end this way for her?'

Flanked by her handsome sons, also dressed in black suits, Queenie Butler marched into the hospital with a look of twisted hatred on her face. She could not believe this was happening, it all seemed so surreal, and she just hoped the evil little fuckers responsible for her anguish would die in the slowest and most painful way possible. Vinny had promised her one day they would, but nothing could make Queenie feel better right now. The second that machine was switched off, half of Queenie would die with her sister. In fact, the way she felt right now, she could never imagine laughing or even smiling again.

As they turned into the corridor where Vivian was, Queenie was horrified when a nurse informed her, 'I'm so sorry, my love, but your Vivvy's already slipped away.'

'But I wanted to be with her, say a proper goodbye. Oh dear Lord, the thought of her dying all alone.'

The nurse squeezed Queenie's hand. 'Viv wasn't alone. Your Albie was with her.'

Daniel Butler leaned against the barrier at the Arrivals gate at Palma airport. When he had run away from that registry office he hadn't a clue where he was going, but instinct had told him to pop home, grab his passport and get as far away as possible.

Jonjo Hopkins was a bloke Daniel had palled up with in nick. His old man owned a bar out in Magaluf, and when Daniel had phoned and said he needed to get away from England ASAP, Jonjo had suggested he get on the next flight. Not only would he put him up, there was a job waiting for him if he wanted it.

Having spent the past week on the lash and shagging

birds to try and forget what he couldn't even bring himself to tell Jonjo, Daniel grinned as his true soul-mate strutted through Arrivals, sports bag in hand. 'You came! I was worried you'd bottle out. Didn't tell anyone where you was going, did ya?'

Lee Butler gave his brother the biggest hug ever. They'd only been apart a week, but it had felt like a whole bloody year. For as long as Lee could remember, he had looked up to Daniel and without him he was nothing. 'Course not. Did as you said and popped the letters in the post before I left London. Got a message from Granddad before I binned the phone. Auntie Viv died today. So sad, ain't it? Can't believe we will never see her again.'

'It is, but Auntie Viv wouldn't want to live like Roy did. Neither would she want us to be miserable. She'd want us to go out and celebrate her life tonight, and that's what we shall do. You wait until you see it out 'ere. It's a wicked life: birds, booze and cocaine on tap. You ready to have the party of a lifetime?'

Lee Butler grinned. When he had married Beth he had truly loved her, but her banging on about the baby stuff and the pressures that came with trying to pay a mortgage every month was not for him. It had got even worse when the test results had come back. Beth had been told it was unlikely she would ever be a mother; the problems conceiving lay totally with her. Her whinging and crying had done Lee's head in since. That was why he had decided to end his marriage by letter and move on with Daniel by his side. 'I'm ready, all right. Let's party.'

Many miles away in Essex, Alex and Roxanne were sitting in a private abortion clinic. Roxanne had been in a terrible state since her doomed wedding and Alex had been staying with her and comforting her ever since.

'I can't do it. I'm not doing it!' Roxanne announced, standing up.

Alex sighed. Her boyfriend Stevie was getting sick of the Roxanne drama. He was extremely concerned because she was only fifteen – and a Butler. And also worried because they were currently staying in the empty flat above his sister's shop in Colchester. Stevie's text yesterday had read:

Once she gets rid of that kid tomorrow, Alex, she's no longer your problem. I don't need nor fucking want no agg with the Butlers and she's Michael's daughter. Get the baby out of her belly and your arse back here. I'm missing ya x

When Roxanne ran out of the building, Alex chased after her. 'Roxy, don't be silly now. You're fifteen years old and you cannot be giving birth to your brother's child. I know it's difficult, pet, but in years to come you will move on and meet a lovely lad and have lots of babies with him.'

True Butler fire in her eyes, Roxanne turned around and glared at her friend. 'I never knew Daniel as a brother, did I? Therefore he isn't my bloody brother. We never grew up together and I still don't believe all that rubbish that was said at the wedding. My mam's a liar and would say anything to split us up. To me, Daniel is my soul-mate. I love him so much; I cannot get rid of our child. If I do, I lose part of him. And if I don't, part of him will always belong to me.'

Mouth wide open, Alex wondered for the first time if her friend was actually mad. 'You're not thinking straight, Roxy. I know you loved Daniel but you can't keep his baby, pet. It isn't right. It's sick. This isn't love, it's tainted love.'

The phrase 'Tainted Love' brought a smile to Roxanne's face. Daniel had loved that song, had taught her all the words. She hugged her friend. 'Thanks for everything, Alex, but this is my baby, my decision and my life.'

'Roxy, Roxy, come back!' Alex screamed.

Ignoring her friend's desperate cries, Roxanne carried on running.

EPILOGUE

Queenie Butler stared sadly at her beloved birds pecking away happily at their seed. Who would feed them after today? Shame she couldn't catch them and take them with her, but there was bound to be plenty of other birds who would need feeding in Hornchurch.

'That's all your clobber in the lorry, Mum. You sure there's nothing else you wanna take out of Auntie Viv's?'

'No. Anything valuable or sentimental I packed in those boxes. The rest of Viv's stuff can be binned, or given to charity. A dog one preferably, or bird.'

It was six days now since Vivian had died, and not only was Queenie guilt-ridden that she hadn't been at her sister's side, she was also extremely fucking bitter Albie had been there. One of the nurses had let slip Albie was singing to Viv when she'd croaked it, and in Queenie's eyes, after having that old bastard crooning in your ear, death must have been a relief.

'You OK, Mum?' Michael asked worriedly. He knew how much of a wrench it must be for her to leave the house she had treasured and the area she had lived in all her life.

'I'm all right, love.'

483

'You ready to go? Or shall I wait outside with Vin, and give you five minutes alone?'

'Nah. I'm ready.' Taking one last look around, Queenie picked up her bag and shut her front door for the very last time.

A handful of people had gathered outside.

'I know we've had our moments, Queen, but I am truly gonna miss ya,' Mouthy Maureen said.

'Bye, Queen. We're gonna miss ya too, love,' Big Stan added.

'Good luck in your new home, Queen. I hope you'll be very happy,' Stinky Susan shouted out.

Ordering Pete and Paul to head off in the lorry, Vinny put an arm around his mother's shoulders. 'Wanna say a proper goodbye to anyone? Or pop in the club one last time? I think Michael's still got a spare key,' Vinny suggested. The club was soon to be knocked down and turned into flats. A beady-eyed property developer had snapped it up within days of it going on the market.

Queenie glanced at the women walking past dressed from head to toe in black burkas, the gang of hoodies over the road looking menacing, the filthy disgusting pavements that were once kept tidy but were now littered with rubbish, and the vulgar family opposite who were sitting on that stinking mattress in their front garden scoffing chips like animals. 'No stop-offs needed. Take me straight to Hornchurch, boy.'

When Vinny pulled away from the kerb, Queenie shut her eyes. She thought back to the street parties they had once held to celebrate the Queen's Silver Jubilee and Charles and Diana's wedding. What a wonderful street it had been to live in then. Everybody watched one another's backs and respect was in the air wherever you walked. That's how she wanted to remember it, not see it as the shithole it was today.

Queenie opened her eyes just in time to see the BUTLERS sign above the club for the very last time. She could remember the opening night there like it were yesterday. Her and Vivvy sipping their sherry, done up to the nines in their furs, diamante necklaces and earrings. Vinny and Roy as fresh-faced teenagers looking mint in their smart suits. Albie pissed as per usual. The proudest mother on earth she had been that evening, watching her strapping lads greet their guests.

'End of an era, eh, Mum?' Vinny said wistfully.

'Sure is, boy. The Butlers' reign over Whitechapel is officially over. But it will never be the end of the Butlers.'